TINKER TAILOR SOLDIER CHEF

PHILIP BRADY

About the Author

Phil lives in west London with his wife, two children and some animals, which also like to call the house home.

He is somewhat obsessed and bemused with the public and media's fixation with celebrities. This forms the backdrop of his books, which also tend to feature spies, gangsters, hitmen and TV chefs.

His main rule in life is never to let tomato ketchup touch any food that is green. This may not have any deep meaning, nor may it be the soundest of principles to live by – but it's better than many he's come across down the years. Best not to go there though.

Copyright

First published in 2021 by 5W Press.

ISBN (Paperback): 978-1-9168769-1-0

Cover design by Kostis Pavlou.

Also by Philip Brady

The Meal of Fortune Series

The Meal of Fortune

Language Warning

Firstly, kudos to *That Peter Crouch Podcast* for making a thing out of the language warning. Glad I can do my own small bit to pass to pod.

Some readers (including my mum) were surprised about the amount of swearing in my first book, *The Meal of Fortune*. I've cut it back quite a bit for this one but there are still a few choice words. So best to give everyone a heads up. Here goes.

This book contains adult themes and a bit of fruity language; typically words like gobshite, bellend and arsehole.

Sorry about that.

These words aren't really that offensive and can be funny in the right circumstances. But if they aren't for you, other comedy thrillers are available. Just not that many involving TV cookery.

As always, for Megan, Dylan and Annabel. Nothing else is really important.

Prologue

'Jesus, will you slow it down a bit?'

Henwell lengthened his stride instead, forcing the smaller man beside him to break into an undignified little trot to keep up. On most days he was mindful to moderate his walking speed when he had company.

Not today.

It was hard to be bothered about little things like that when they were going to take it all away from you.

'Just listen to what he has to say, OK?' His companion was puffing hard, beads of sweat threatening to break out across his forehead.

Henwell increased his pace again.

'Mark!'

And then some more.

'DCI Henwell!'

'What!' He slowed and turned, allowing Chief Superintendent Russell McDonald to catch up.

'You won't do anything stupid in there, will you?' McDonald ran a hand through his untidy grey hair.

'Like using my initiative to smash some of the country's biggest drugs gangs? That kind of stupid? Why would I think of doing anything like that?'

Henwell had succeeded where so many others had failed, actually starting to stem the tide of drugs flowing onto London's streets. But now they were about to kick him out.

McDonald sighed. 'What you did was illegal.'

'What they were doing was illegal. Let's just get this over with, shall we?' Henwell turned and set off again.

'All I'm asking is that you keep your cool. This could mean your job.'

'It will mean my job. But I'll find something else.'

'Come on. You're a bit young for the private-security game.'

Henwell slowed once more, this time with a deep sigh. McDonald did have a point.

'So you'll just hear him out then?' The chief super caught up again.

'Yes.'

'And you'll be respectful to a senior officer?'

'Yes.'

'Yes, what?'

'Yes, sir.'

'That's better.'

'Piss off, Russell.'

*

The secretary replaced the phone and stood up, making a show of slowly smoothing down her skirt as she moved around the desk. 'Deputy Assistant Commissioner Connor will see you now.'

Deputy Assistant Commissioner Connor could have bloody well seen them forty-five minutes ago when the meeting had actually been scheduled to start.

Henwell felt McDonald's hand on his arm as they stood.

The message was clear. Keep calm!

The secretary knocked lightly, and then pushed the door open, beckoning them to enter.

'Come in.' The man behind the desk looked up but didn't stand. 'Sit down, gentlemen.' No hint of a welcoming smile or any offer of tea of coffee. But then it probably wasn't going to be that kind of meeting.

'Sir.' Henwell nodded then waited for McDonald to take his pick of the chairs, holding the Deputy Assistant Commissioner's eyes for a second or so before he sat.

It was the first time that Henwell and Connor had met. DCIs at the operational sharp end didn't tend to mix with DACs. Connor sat ramrod straight in his chair, uniform creaseless. Even sitting down, it was clear he was tall, probably as tall as Henwell's six foot five. He looked to be in his mid to late fifties, but he'd managed to retain a full head of dark hair, which was only now greying at the temples. He looked fit, lean too, with a light tan.

Henwell suspected the lines around his eyes came from time spent outside in wholesome pursuits rather than the cares of the job. Everything he'd heard about Connor suggested the man was a self-interested career administrator with little time or stomach for real police work. A political animal concerned only with steepening the trajectory of his own rise. Just what the Met needed in its senior ranks right now.

Connor waited for them to settle then turned his attention to McDonald. 'How's the golf coming along, Russell? Haven't had you along for a four-ball for a while. Let's get something in the diary.'

The reminder was less than subtle; McDonald was on the fringes of the elite. And you didn't tend to make it into the inner circle by backing your man against a DAC.

Not that Henwell expected or wanted his boss to damage his own career. This was on him and him alone, even if Russell had basked in the reflected glory of the arrests at the time.

Connor sat back and let out a long slow breath. 'Your file makes impressive reading, Detective Chief Inspector.' His eyes flicked back to Henwell before he looked down at the papers on his desk. 'Graduate fast-track. CID at twenty-three, sergeant at twenty-six. Good stint in homicide, then drugs. DCI by the age of thirty-four. Very impressive.' Connor paused. He didn't look impressed.

'He's always done well wherever he's been,' McDonald weighed in. 'Worked hard.'

Henwell felt a little stab of guilt for doubting his boss's loyalty.

'Worked hard or cut corners?' Connor looked up, his eyes boring into Henwell.

'We did what we had to do to get results.' He held the DAC's gaze.

'But it was phone hacking.'

OK, technically, but…

'It's still a toxic issue,' Connor went on. 'The media got crucified. Remember the Leveson Inquiry? What do you think would happen if they knew we'd been up to it as well? They've got long memories.'

'With respect, it's hardly the same thing, sir.'

'With respect, Detective Chief Inspector, it's exactly the same thing.'

Henwell breathed deeply and tried to keep his cool. Was Connor really suggesting a little eavesdropping on criminals was no better than the press's tawdry snooping on the royals and a bunch of celebs?

It had all been down to luck, at least at the start. An informant had given Henwell the number of a burner, an unregistered pay-as-you-go mobile used by the gang bringing the drugs into the country. Imagine his surprise when he found out that the silly criminal had only gone and forgotten to reset the factory password on the voicemail. From then on it had been a simple matter of listening to the messages to find out where and when the next deal was going to take place. They'd picked up the first drug dealer on the way back from the rendezvous with all the evidence they needed spilling out of a holdall in the back of his van. Henwell had decided not to arrest the importers on the off chance that they would use the same phone to arrange another deal.

Never in his wildest dreams had he imagined the burner would be used to set up five more deals. Each time, they'd taken the dealer on his way home and let the distributors go free – until deal number six, when they'd crashed in and arrested the lot of them.

'And your superiors never asked how you came about this information?' The DAC turned his gaze towards McDonald.

'I said it was from an informant.' Henwell wasn't letting Connor drag his boss into all this. 'The convictions are rock solid and I had to protect my original source.'

'And you never thought about the consequences?'

'Drugs off the street, criminals in jail. Those sorts of consequences?' He stole a glance at McDonald, who just shook his head.

When he looked back at Connor, the DAC's eyes were cold

and hard. 'Started a right little war, didn't you?'

Yes, there was that too.

None of the criminals had been quite smart enough to work out how the police kept crashing the party and gang member had swiftly turned on gang member. It meant a few more lowlifes were off the streets and the Met had got a couple of easy murder convictions to boot. Henwell could live with that.

'And just how long did you propose to carry on this little operation?'

'As long as we kept getting results, sir.' Henwell's team had already got hold of another couple of burner numbers. But then a stray comment by one of his sergeants had reached the ears of another DCI, one whose results were nowhere near as impressive. The police jungle drums had done their thing, and Henwell had received a visit from everybody's favourite boys and girls in Anti-Corruption. Things had all gone a bit *Line of Duty* on him after that, the investigation swift, thorough and utterly ruthless.

And it had found him guilty of misconduct in public office.

A three-month suspension had followed, the decision on further disciplinary action pending. Those three months ran out tomorrow.

'Jesus, what a mess.' The DAC sat back with a sigh. 'It was unauthorised surveillance.'

'They were using illegal burner phones.'

'It doesn't matter. Any decent lawyer would have a field day.'

Claiming the poor little criminals' human rights had been violated no doubt.

'Sir –' McDonald tried to cut in.

But Connor raised a hand. 'We could have kicked you out already.'

And that was the funny thing; normally they would have.

No pay-off.

No pension.

But so far, just the suspension. And now this meeting with Connor to decide what happened next. Not Russell or even Russell's boss but a fully-fledged DAC.

Well, if they expected him to go down without a fight… 'You really think it was just me?'

Connor made to speak, then paused, his eyes flicking towards McDonald and then back down to the safety of his desk.

Well, well, well. It seemed like Henwell's shot in the dark had hit the bullseye.

'It's not just me, is it?' Henwell kept his expression neutral, despite the temptation to smile. Other units had been phone hacking too.

Connor looked up slowly, the expression on his face saying it all.

So that was what this was all about. Damage limitation.

If the story got out, it would spiral out of control. The press had tried to play the 'one bad apple' card over their phone-hacking scandal. And look where that had got them. Editors in jail, multi-million-pound compensation funds and the country's best-selling Sunday newspaper consigned to history. The last thing the Met needed was a disgruntled former officer spilling it all on social media.

Connor held Henwell's eye for a few more seconds, then shook his head again and sat forward. 'We just think it's best if we keep this quiet.'

Of course they did. Henwell's position in the game might not be quite as weak as he'd first imagined.

'So I am going to recommend a return to active duty. We can't leave you in drugs. If this ever does come out, we need to be able to show that we acted.'

Needed to cover their arses, more like. Henwell nodded, again forcing back a smile.

'You'll be demoted to DI and moved to another division.'

Harsh, but he'd take that if it meant staying on the force.

'And you'll have your own team. You'll just be going somewhere where you can't make so much trouble.' Connor closed the file in front of him and reached for another. 'We've seen a steady rise in threats and crimes against celebrities over the past few years, people who are prominent in the media and public eye.

The entertainment business brings in quite a lot of money and prestige for the country, and it's been decided that the people who work in it need more protection.'

He couldn't be serious…? Henwell tried to catch McDonald's eye, but his boss seemed very interested in his own feet all of a sudden. Jesus, the bastard had been in on it from the start.

'We're setting up a new unit. Crimes Against People in the Public Eye. We want you to lead it.'

Henwell worked through the words in his head. 'But that's CRAPPIE?'

'I beg your pardon?' Connor reddened with anger.

'The name, it spells out CRAPPIE. Sir.'

'CAPPE, actually.'

'Yeah, but that's not what people will call it. Least of all the media.'

'The other option is Crimes Against Prominent People.'

'That's still CRAP, Sir.'

Connor reddened further, his mouth opening and shutting a few times without any words coming out.

'I think he means it *spells out* CRAP, sir.' McDonald raised a hand as he leaned forward.

'Yes, Russell, I do understand that.' Connor flicked the chief superintendent an evil look before turning back to Henwell. 'We're going with CAPPE, OK? If you don't like it, we can always find you something else. Fraud maybe?'

So that was his choice. Become a laughing stock babysitting D-list celebs or spend his time going after accountants with sticky fingers?

'Liaison with the celebrity community will be an important part of the role.' Connor was smiling again. 'They're high profile and have a strong voice. We have the Met's reputation to think of.'

So it was a PR job, plain and simple. Well, they could stick it… But then Henwell thought again about fraud.

'I'll take it.' If there was ever a moment to swallow his pride, this was it.

'Well, that's great news.' Connor stood and reached out a

hand. ‘Welcome to CRAPPIE, Detective Inspector Henwell.’ A wide smile spread across his face, as he rolled his tongue around the letter ‘r’.

Part One

Dead Famous

Three months and several murders later…

Chapter 1

Anna looked up at the apartment block and thought again about turning around and walking away. It was just that, well… Something about the whole set-up felt off.

Three times she'd met Olivier before, all in the same city-centre café 500 yards from Lille's opera house. The last time, she'd got the distinct impression that he was dicking her about, avoiding showing his hand as he flirted a little more and tried to extract a higher price for his 'information'. Anna had left convinced they wouldn't be meeting again. Part of her had even suspected he just wanted to sleep with her. Although pretending to have a secret to sell to MI5 seemed a pretty elaborate ruse to get a girl into bed. And Frenchmen, she thought, tended to be more a little more direct. But at least the coffee was good, the stroll to and from the station pleasant and the journey back to London by Eurostar was fast and reliable.

But when Olivier had called again, the conversation had been different. A little less flirting this time and more readiness on his part to do a deal.

So Anna had agreed to another meeting, making it clear that she'd walk away if they couldn't come to an arrangement this time. It had felt like the right call, like so many of the calls she'd made since her return to active fieldwork eighteen months ago.

Headstrong and impulsive. Those were the words that had condemned her to the desk job in the research section. Anna was sure a few of her colleagues still used them now, just not quite as loudly.

She preferred to think of it as decisiveness – a decisiveness that had served her well last May when she'd stopped a rogue Russian arms dealer from selling a Soviet nuclear weapon to the highest bidder. There'd been some help from a highly unusual source as well as a large slice of luck involved. And some of her actions that night would always remain a secret from her MI5 bosses. But it was the result that mattered.

She looked up at the apartment block once more. It was clean and smart, a prime example of the stylish urban regeneration that had swept through France's former textile capital in recent years. It was exactly the sort of place you'd expect a suave young tech entrepreneur to call home.

Olivier's business had grown fast, securing lucrative IT security services contracts with many of the big data warehousing operations that had set up shop in Lille and nearby Roubaix. Among all those terabytes of data he was supposed to be keeping safe Olivier believed he'd spotted something: intelligence he claimed related to a specific terrorist threat against Britain. MI5 had been the obvious people for him to contact, right? Well, maybe after the French security services? But Anna suspected the idea of trying to sell info to his own country's spooks might have felt a little unpatriotic. Or perhaps he just thought the Brits would pay more. His business, though healthy, still had quite a lot of debt. Nothing like selling a few secrets to get you back into the black.

The information Olivier had to trade was likely to be low-grade. But then that was the way with most intelligence. It was only when you collected all these seemingly insignificant scraps and painstakingly pieced them together that a clear picture sometimes emerged.

Anna took a last look up and down the quiet street as she stepped towards the door. It was time to stop dithering and get on with it. She reached out for the buzzer to Olivier's apartment but paused again. Why had he insisted on the change of venue? He'd claimed he needed a little privacy, if he was going to share a sample of his information. It made sense she supposed.

'Red Two, copy.' She spoke into her lapel radio.

'Copy, Red One.'

'Are you in position?'

'Affirmative.'

Couldn't the girl just say *'Yes'*? Anna tried her best to control her irritation at the sound of the voice on the radio. Maybe it was the 'help' she'd brought along that lay behind her anxiety?

Anna had worked hard over the past months to build a tight little team. But it was a team whose dynamic had been forever changed by the arrival of Felicity Diamond. Little Miss Prada Trousers had strolled straight in from the graduate programme, put her designer boots up on the furniture and proceeded to wreak her own subtle form of havoc.

Chris and Adrian, Anna's two intelligence officers, had been quick to trip over their dicks in their haste to impress the new arrival. And the team's two female support staff now seemed to favour cooing about Felicity's extensive range of handbags over actually doing any work.

And Felicity Diamond? It even sounded like a spy's name, or at least one made up by a trashy novelist (male of course) who'd never grown out of a boyhood fetish for leather trousers and posh accents. Either way, Felicity would have been better off plying her trade over the river with MI6.

And yes, OK, maybe Anna was the teeniest, tiniest bit jealous. She was big enough to admit that. Not because someone younger (although not necessarily prettier) had joined the team. What got Anna's goat, what really got her goat, was how easy everyone seemed to be making things for Felicity. Anna had been forced to do it the hard way, working every day to prove herself. Then doing it all again, just to confirm she hadn't got there because of her father, David Preston, the all-round MI5 legend. And then a third time because half the wankers still hadn't believed in her.

And here was little Felicity having it all handed to her on some handcrafted silver platter.

Exactly how many cheery little calls had Anna received from her superiors about the girl? They always started out with queries about some spurious piece of intel, before slyly getting to the point.

'And how is young Felicity getting on?'

'You are looking after her?'

'… stretching her enough?'

ARRRRGHHHH!

She'd been against bringing Felicity to Lille from the beginning. The new girl just didn't have the experience for a live op yet. But with the pressure to blood Felicity mounting, Anna had relented, figuring the risk was low.

'OK. I'm going in.' She reached for the buzzer again. 'Stay in position.'

Position for Felicity was a doorway fifty yards up the street on the opposite side, well back and well out of harm's way.

And out of Anna's way too.

'Copy that.' The girl's tone was half bored, half patronising. As if, on her very first operation, she didn't need anyone telling her what to do.

'Come on up.' Olivier answered after a couple of seconds, sounding serious as he buzzed her in. No jokes, no flirting. Hopefully, they could get down to business and finally get the deal done.

Anna pushed her way into the lobby, eyes scanning around for threats. But it was empty. Olivier's apartment was on the fourth floor, but she moved quickly past the lift and headed for the stairs.

Through the door, another pause. Looking and listening.

All clear.

She took the steps two at a time, keeping up a steady jog all the way. Her role as section leader had left Anna with less time for the gym, and she had to take her exercise where she could get it. She felt a little flush of pride as she reached Olivier's floor barely out of breath and with only a hint of burning in her thighs. Couldn't see Everyone's Perfect Little Spook making it up four flights that easily.

She pushed open the door from the stairwell and stopped to listen.

Again nothing, so she headed on into the corridor. The apartment was the second on the left and she reached it in a few strides. Her hand hovered over the buzzer then stopped; a different kind of bell ringing in her head as she saw the door was already ajar. But she brushed the concern away. Olivier had clearly left it open, knowing she was on her way up. He'd be in the kitchen now, probably putting the kettle on. *'A nice cup of tea for my English friend?'* She remembered how he'd laughed with astonishment the first time in the café when she'd opted for coffee instead.

'Hello.' She pushed the door open and stepped into the apartment. 'Olivier?'

No reply. But maybe he had a noisy kettle?

She took another couple of steps, about to call again. Then she stopped herself, as the alarm bells jangled once more.

The entrance hall was bigger than she'd expected from the floor plan, more of a lobby in fact. There were two doors straight ahead of her, with two more on the right and one on the left. But there was certainly no noisy kettle, her footsteps echoing on the polished parquet floor was the only sound.

She could still abort, or at the very least call for back-up. But then Anna reminded herself who that back-up was. Three quick steps took her to the door to the living room, the first on the right. She stopped again, holding her breath as she listened.

All quiet.

She stepped through the doorway. Chic minimalist furniture, white walls, large modern prints on canvas. Nothing out of place, but she knew from the floor plan the room was L-shaped, at least half of it out of sight around the corner.

It was still not too late to get the hell out. But Anna forced herself to move forward, scanning the rest of the room as it came into view. Her eyes arrived first on the little black cap that usually sat at a jaunty angle on Olivier's head. Right now it was lying a little dejectedly in the middle of the floor. And without the hat, his head looked quite different. But that might have been more to do with the highly unusual angle of his neck. The rest of him was slumped down in an armchair in front of the supersized TV, which was silently playing a football match.

Anna had only encountered one dead body during active service. And that one had turned out not to be dead at all. But she knew enough about necks and angles to know Olivier's story wouldn't end so well.

Every last bit of her good sense was telling her to turn and run. Instead, she started towards the body, only realising her mistake as she caught a blur of movement off to the left and heard footsteps coming for her across the wooden floor.

Chapter 2

'Detective Inspector, how are you?' DAC Connor stood and came round the desk, hand outstretched. It was a far warmer welcome than last time Henwell had been here, three months before.

'Fine, sir, and you?' He took the DAC's hand, searching Connor's eyes for any clue to what this might be about. 'You wanted to see me.'

'Tea, coffee?'

And drinks this time too…

'No thanks.' He shook his head.

'So how goes it with celebrity crime?'

'Good, sir.' Henwell narrowly avoided the face he wanted to pull and came up with a smile instead. Surely he hadn't been asked here for a simple status report?

'Keeping you busy?' Connor headed back to his chair, beckoning Henwell to sit.

Busy wasn't the word for it. The DAC had wasted no time in going public with the story of the new celebrity squad. A press conference, the works. Henwell's phone hadn't stopped ringing since. And with just one detective sergeant and a single detective constable on his team, the three of them had been flat out.

He'd learned swiftly that his celebrity callers fell into two broad categories. First were the regular crimes, suffered by people who happened to be famous. Like the newsreader who'd been burgled, the former darts player who'd been punched in a road-rage incident or the TV gardener who claimed to be a victim of card fraud. All were crimes that could and should have been reported to the local police station. But why would you bother with that when you had a dedicated celebrity crime squad to help you jump the queue? Fame, however minor, seemed to come with its own vast sense of entitlement.

'I'm hearing good things.' Connor's smile stayed in place as he sat.

'Thank you, sir.'

Henwell's second category of callers was entirely different. The profile hunters – minor celebs of every stripe, all reporting supposed crimes to grab a few tawdry column inches and tweets of outrage and or sympathy. Every last offence had been dreamed up by their publicists, of course. Having a crime investigated by CAPPE seemed to have become the latest celeb accessory, like boycotting social media, having a prominent tattoo of some meaningless Eastern symbol or adopting a baby from one of the more fashionable African crises.

And as soon as the news had hit the celeb gossip sites…?

'Police are investigating reports that [INSERT NAME OF VACUOUS CELEBRITY HERE] has fallen victim to online abuse/stalking/an attack by killer llamas…'

Well, the complaints would be dropped, wouldn't they?

Funny that. Best not to let the police actually ask any tricky questions.

It was hard not to see the celebrity crime squad as one humungous own goal. But Henwell's orders were clear. Each and every complaint had to be taken seriously and followed up. So he'd had no option but to keep his head down, play the game and hope he'd eventually find a way out.

'You're doing a great job. The Met needs to be seen to be protecting our celebrity community.' Connor nodded; his face was stern. Then he paused, suddenly uncomfortable. 'Which brings me to these murders.'

The celebrity slayings, as the more lurid tabloids had dubbed them. They rather holed the idea of the Met protecting celebrities beneath the water line. The first killing had been little more than three months ago, with six more since. Each murder had been carried out in a manner that both reflected and mocked the victim's career.

'Yes. I emailed you about them, sir.' Maybe Henwell's way out was closer at hand than he'd thought. 'Several times if I remember.'

And each time Connor had ignored him.

Each of the murders had been followed up with a video posted online, claiming the deaths were punishment for the victims' pursuit of empty fame.

Someone out there really didn't like celebrities, and they had the whole of the showbiz community running scared.

The DAC opened a file on his desk. 'Your first email was after Charlie McGee, then Jane Holland and then Matt Street. You're persistent, I'll give you that.'

'Well, I do run the celebrity crime squad, sir. We should be involved.'

'That's not really why we set it up.' It was the closest Connor had come to admitting CAPPE was little more than a PR exercise. 'But, quite frankly, we're struggling. Someone's been going around bumping off celebrities and we haven't got the first clue. You'll have noticed we're getting crucified by the press.'

With good reason. If celebs kept dying at this rate, there'd be nobody left for the noble boys and girls of the Fourth Estate to make things up about. They might have to start reporting some proper news.

'So…' Connor sighed again, looking uncomfortable once more. 'We need your help.'

'You're giving me the investigation?' Henwell couldn't quite believe what he was hearing.

'Good God man, don't be ridiculous. We've got a whole major investigation team on it. Sixty officers, unlimited overtime.'

And yet they needed him. Henwell kept quiet. There was an almighty 'but' heading down the tracks.

'You know DCI Simpson, I assume? He's heading up the MIT.'

'We trained together, sir.'

'So you'll know he's a fine officer. Always does it by the book.' Connor nodded approvingly.

For 'fine officer' read 'oily little arsewipe.' And, in Henwell's view, the 'book' Simpson followed only ever got you results in open-and-shut cases.

'He's under great scrutiny, can't be seen to cut any corners.'

'Whereas I…?' Henwell could see exactly where this was going now.

'Can't be seen to cut any corners either. But you've always operated with a bit more, how shall I put it kindly? Latitude?'

In other words, he knew how to get results.

'Officially, your remit will be to dig more deeply into the lives of the victims. Use the contacts you've been cultivating in the celebrity community.'

Henwell waited again, knowing there was more.

'Unofficially, we need you to shake things up a bit. Look through the files again to see if they've missed anything. Sweat the witnesses and find us some suspects. We're not after evidence we can use directly. Just intel to point us in the right direction. Simpson's team can build the case from there.'

If Connor was at all troubled by asking Henwell to use the same tactics that had seen him booted off the drug squad, he wasn't showing it. It was the sort of moral flexibility that had almost certainly aided the DAC's rise through the ranks.

'And Simpson gets all the credit?'

'Of course. He's a rising star, future leadership material.'

'And if I overstep the mark?'

'If you're *seen* to overstep the mark.' Connor held his eye.

Henwell nodded, acknowledging the distinction. More rope with which to hang himself.

The DAC gave a brief smile. 'Then we'll really throw the book at you.'

Presumably not the same one DCI Simpson lived his life by. The poor man wouldn't have the first clue what to do without it.

'What's in it for me?' It was a dangerous question to ask a man like Connor.

The DAC's smile was back. 'How else are you going to get out of CRAPPIE?'

Well, when he put it like that.

Connor picked up a sheet of paper from his desk and offered it to Henwell. 'This is the letter I've sent to DCI Simpson seconding your team to his investigation.'

Henwell was more interested in the yellow Post-it note that was stuck to the top corner. He read the words, an address in Balham scrawled in blue pen. Then he looked back up at Connor, already knowing the answer.

'Reported this morning.' The DAC sighed. 'It's eight murders now, not seven. What are you waiting for, Detective Inspector?'

*

The drive from Scotland Yard to south London took less than twenty-five minutes with the afternoon traffic unusually light. Henwell fought back his growing sense of elation with every turn of the wheel. Ironic, wasn't it? If he solved the celeb murders he'd be out of CAPPE for good.

Go figure…

Although it was still a big 'if'. Simpson's team had been going hard at it for months and didn't have a sniff. But then, as Connor had said, Henwell had the licence to get a little creative.

By 2.30 p.m. he was pulling up outside the house of Mickey Morris, former sitcom actor.

Former house too, he supposed.

Just another ordinary semi on another ordinary street. Smart enough, with new-looking paintwork and a tidy front garden. Still, the home seemed a pretty paltry return for the best part of two decades on TV. But then hadn't there been rumours of drink and drug binges? Gambling debts too? Or maybe it was just a reflection on Balham house prices.

He parked behind the scene-of-crime van and hurried across the road, flashing his warrant card at the uniform on the gate. 'Is DCI Simpson here?'

The PC nodded.

'He's expecting me.' This wasn't entirely true but Henwell ducked under the police tape and headed up the pathway before the constable could object. Had it been Henwell's crime scene, he'd have roasted the officer for letting anyone wander in like that.

The SOCOs had set up a tent outside the front door, and he flashed his card again before grabbing a crime-scene suit, gloves and shoe covers. He was about to head for the front door when it opened and three similarly dressed figures emerged. The one in the lead stopped abruptly and removed his hood – Simpson himself.

'DI Henwell.' The voice was as cold as the man's eyes.

'Sir.' He nodded back. It had been close to ten years since they'd last met, and Henwell was surprised to see how grey the man had gone. And just how many new lines had etched themselves on Simpson's hard little face.

'Care to explain what you're doing at my crime scene?' He fixed Henwell with a frosty stare.

Simpson might have had the rank and reputation, but at five foot six, he barely came up to Henwell's shoulder. So Henwell gave the DCI his special 'little man' look, the one that avoided the eyes altogether, focusing on a point a couple of inches above Simpson's head. 'You've seen the letter from DAC Connor attaching me to your inquiry, sir?'

'A letter which makes it amply clear that CRAPPIE, sorry, my mistake, CAPPE, is to focus on a deep dive into the backgrounds of the celebs. Crime scenes and forensics are outwith your ambit.'

Who even used words like ambit? And as for outwith? Was that how they told you to speak on management courses? But Henwell resisted a smile, knowing he had to play nicely.

'A little background would help. Sir. Just a quick look.'

'Sorry, the forensics teams haven't finished. We'll send you the report.'

If it was meant as a dismissal, it didn't work. Henwell stood his ground.

Simpson sighed as he started to unzip his crime-scene overall, revealing an immaculate grey suit underneath. 'The killer took his head clean off. Is that enough background for you? Some sort of medieval battleaxe. It was left on the floor next to the body. No attempt at concealment.'

'It was a halberd, actually, sir.' The figure next to Simpson took down her hood, revealing a sharp-featured woman with a severe blonde bob. 'Blade for chopping and a hook for pulling riders from their horses.'

'Thank you, Detective Sergeant.' Simpson sounded like he was in no mood for a lecture on the finer points of medieval weaponry. And since it was unlikely Mickey Morris had been riding a horse around his living room, the detail seemed spurious at best.

'DS Madeleine Prim.' The woman reddened at the rebuke from her boss, then stepped up to Henwell and extended a hand.

Definitely a Madeleine, not a Maddie. And Prim just about said it all. Another one who liked to play it by the book, Henwell suspected. Simpson's Mini-Me, riding his coat tails all the way up the ladder.

'Madeleine will be your point of contact.' Simpson still hadn't bothered with a handshake of his own. 'You'll report anything you find to her.'

A lowly DS as his liaison – it was another put-down. But as Henwell didn't plan on doing too much reporting back, he let it pass. 'Why the axe?' All the other killings had been related to the victim's careers. 'Mickey Morris was an actor.'

Prim pulled out her phone, tapping the screen a couple of times before turning it to Henwell. 'Thought you of all people would be keeping up with the celebrity gossip.' The screen showed a picture of Mickey Morris, dressed in some kind of medieval doublet. '*A Hard Day's Knight.* It's a new reality show due to start next week. Twelve celebrities living in a fourteenth-century castle.'

It certainly explained the choice of murder weapon.

'So, any leads on this halberd?' Henwell would probably be told this was 'outwith his ambit' again, but it was worth a try.

Prim slipped her phone away, looking to Simpson for permission to continue.

He gave her a sour little nod.

'Apparently, there are more of them about than you'd think. Museums, enactment societies. Very common weapon back in the day apparently.'

'But you'd notice if one had gone missing.'

'You'd hope.' Simpson cut in. 'But that's another thing you don't really need to concern yourself with. Just focus on the backgrounds. I need to know if there is a link between the celebrities. I've already asked for copies of all the case files to be sent to your team.'

The one good thing about these 'by-the-bookers' was they tended to be quite strong on the admin. Henwell would be able to get cracking right away. 'Any video from the killer yet?'

'Not yet.' Simpson shook his head. 'Now I should introduce Dr Neil White.' He nodded towards the third member of the little party. 'Our criminal psychologist.'

The man had stayed quiet until now, busying himself with extracting his considerable bulk from the scene-of-crime suit. Under it, the psychologist wore a blazer, tie, chinos and an unmistakable air of superiority.

Pretty much like every profiler Henwell had ever met.

'Dr White's already given us invaluable insights into our killer. You'll do well to listen to him.'

Hmm, yes… Invaluable. That was exactly the word Henwell would have used. He was tempted to ask how many leads the psychologist had given them.

It was fair to say that police opinion on profilers was divided. And at the risk of being labelled a dinosaur, Henwell was more than happy to admit he fell into the camp that viewed their output as a load of utter bollocks.

'Our killer's an interesting one.' White took a little step back as he started to speak, inviting his audience to gather round and benefit from his knowledge and wisdom.

Henwell didn't gather.

'He's most likely to be white, well educated, in his twenties or thirties, but stuck in a low-level job. That will just fuel his frustration. Probably a loner, subjected to violence or at least images of it from a young age. A strained relationship with his mother and a high chance of an absent father.'

Really? Wasn't that the identikit profile of pretty much every serial killer there'd ever been? Henwell wasn't aware of a single case where profiling had led directly to the apprehension of a serious criminal.

'Why celebrities?' He kept his eyes on Dr White. It was another question White's cod psychology had come nowhere near to answering.

'Ah well, you see. That's the easy part. Deep down, most serial killers crave attention. What better way to get it than to kill people who are already famous?'

It made sense, but none of this told them anything about who the celeb killer was and where he might strike next. Just that he was pretty screwed-up. Something they'd already worked out for themselves. Simpson would have been better getting it from a textbook and putting White's fee towards the overtime budget.

But the DCI looked pretty sold on the whole thing. 'I've sent you Dr White's profile along with the case files.'

Oh good.

'Mind you read it carefully.' White gave a pompous little nod. 'It could save you a lot of time going down blind alleys.'

'I'll make sure I do.' Henwell turned away, keen to make a quick exit before the psychologist embarked on another lecture.

He stopped and turned back as he felt a hand on his arm.

'This is my case. Remember that.' Simpson's grip on his elbow was surprisingly firm. 'Anything you find, report to DS Prim. Immediately.'

'Of course, sir.' Henwell turned away again quickly and headed for the car, hoping Simpson hadn't spotted the lie in his voice or in his eyes.

Chapter 3

Anna swivelled on her heels and crouched, throwing up an arm to block as the man charged at her. The attack still drove her backwards, but nowhere near as far as he would have expected.

He was small and wiry, no more than five foot seven or eight, and probably weighed little more than she did.

Small yes, but he was fast with it.

A punch snaked out towards her head, but Anna blocked again and tried to get a grip on his jacket. Her black belt in judo had come long before she'd joined MI5. If she could get a good hold, it would be easy enough to throw him and the fight would be all but over. But he wasn't falling for that one and skipped away backwards, pulling a flick knife from his pocket and springing it open as he went. If he was feeling at all unchivalrous at fighting a woman, he was hiding it pretty well.

It was Anna's turn to back away, but only so she could cover the door. He was going to need more than an itsy-bitsy little knife to scare her. Her eye caught Olivier's body again, noticing for the first time the blood staining the cushions of the chair. It was probably the broken neck that had killed him, but the long gash up his thigh might have played its part.

'Red Two. Subject down, armed intruder.' She kept her eyes on the knifeman as she spoke into her lapel radio. 'Get up here fast, copy.'

'Copy, Red One, on my way.' Excitement had replaced the Felicity's tone of bored superiority. Her first op and a real live 'situation' to boot.

Not that Anna would need her junior's help. MI5's training had helped her build on her martial-arts skills, adding moves from disciplines like Krav Maga and Brazilian jiu-jitsu, which would have got her thrown straight off her university judo team. She kept herself between the man and the door, watching as his dark eyes flicked around the room, scanning for other escape routes. Then she jumped back as he thrust with the knife. He'd already lost much of the advantage it gave him. With a gun, it was OK to take your time, back away, assess the options and shoot anytime you liked. With a knife, you had to get up close. And if you didn't do it quickly, your opponent had time to adjust.

Anna took a step forward, eyes alternating between the knife and the killer's face, reading the next move in his eyes and posture almost before he even knew it himself. As he lunged forward, she dodged around the blade and delivered a sharp kick to his thigh, which sent him sprawling. He swore in French as he hit the floor.

She closed in fast, keen to pin him down, but he was quick enough to roll away before springing back to his feet. His eyes darted around the room again, still on the hunt for another way out. Then he leaped forward, grabbing Olivier's fallen hat as he came, flinging it in Anna's face. Her sight obscured for a second, instinct kicked in and she ducked, feeling the knife slice the air as it passed close to her right ear. She spun round, bringing her right arm up to block the predictable return thrust. But instead, he kicked her hard in the stomach. And now it was Anna's turn to go down, the wind knocked out of her. The pain took a second to gather itself like a ball in the guts before tearing outwards in all directions. But she knew she had to move. Gambling, she rolled to the right, away from the knife strike that…

… never came.

She heard the sound of running feet heading out of the apartment and off down the stairs.

Coward. Anna would have had the sneaky little bastard if he'd stayed to fight.

But if Felicity met the knifeman on the stairs, she might be in trouble. The girl had topped her self-defence classes in training, but Olivier's killer was quick and skilled. She tried to speak into her radio but with no air in her lungs, the words wouldn't come. So she grabbed the arm of a sofa, using it to pull herself upright, finally managing to catch some breath as she headed for the door. Bad enough having to explain how such a routine operation had gone so far south. The very last thing she needed was any harm coming to the golden child as well. Anna was halfway to the front door when Felicity came striding in. Walking fast but certainly not troubling herself with running.

'What happened? Where's…?' Four flights of steps and the girl wasn't even out of breath.

'You didn't see him on the stairs?' Anna managed to get the words out this time.

'No. I took the lift. It was already on the ground floor.'

'If the lift was down there, he had to use the stairs.' Anna fought to keep her anger inside. 'Didn't you think?' Felicity had probably touched up her make-up on the way up too. But at least she wasn't hurt.

'I'm sorry. I thought it would be quicker.' The girl's cheeks reddened, but she sounded more angry than contrite. 'It sounded like you needed me.'

As if…

All the colour drained back out of Felicity's face as she looked past Anna towards the body. 'Is that Olivier?'

'Yes. And yes, he is dead.'

'We've got to get out of here.' Felicity backed towards the door.

She was right of course, but Anna raised a hand. 'Not until we've searched the place.' She tried to keep her voice calm. The last thing she needed was Felicity bottling it. 'He must have been after the same information we are.' The chances of the knifeman being a common burglar caught in the act were hovering somewhere around zero.

Felicity nodded and took a breath, looking calmer now.

'He wouldn't have had time to search the place properly before I got here.' Anna's eyes were already darting around the room. 'So we're looking for laptops, tablets, phones, memory sticks, notepads even. You do the bedrooms. I'll do the sitting room and kitchen.' She fished in her pocket for a couple of pairs of plastic gloves and handed one to Felicity.

'Someone might have called the police.' The girl slipped the gloves on, still not looking 100 per cent convinced.

True, the neighbours might have heard a struggle and reported it, but it wasn't the police Anna was worried about, right now. If the killer hadn't found what he was looking for, there was every chance he'd return with back up. Someone had known Anna was coming and made sure Olivier didn't talk. They'd want to be equally certain they'd secured any information he'd planned to share.

'Let's get moving. Three minutes tops then we're out of here.' Best not to share her worries about the hostiles coming back mob-handed. Anna held Felicity's gaze and gave an encouraging nod, reminding herself it was the girl's first op.

Felicity headed for the first bedroom as Anna began to search the sitting room. She started carefully, putting everything back in place. But what was the point? With a dead man in the armchair, it didn't really matter how much mess they left. And if the police saw it as a burglary gone wrong, it would help cover their tracks. She moved from drawer to drawer, tipping them out and quickly going through the contents.

Nothing.

'Two minutes,' Anna called out to Felicity as she moved on to the kitchen. Then she went to work again, drawers and cupboards open, contents thrown out.

Again nothing, although she did help herself to a small kitchen knife, before making for the door.

'Nothing here.' Felicity emerged from the second bedroom.

'OK, let's go then.' Short of sending in a full search team and giving them several hours, there was nothing else they could achieve. Anna strode past Olivier's body and led the way across the foyer. She knew it would hit her hard later – the dead man, the knife fight. But right now her focus had to be on getting them out of there. She opened the apartment door and stopped dead, staring at the little orange arrow that indicated that the lift was coming. Then she heard the sound of running footsteps on the stairs. Two of them or maybe three, plus whoever was in the lift.

That was too many.

'Come on.' Anna started for the stairs to the fifth floor. They'd have to go up, get onto the roof and see if they could cross to another building.

'No.' Felicity pointed back towards Olivier's apartment. 'There's a fire escape outside the bedroom window.'

Smart cookie, maybe it had been the right call to bring her along after all. Anna followed Felicity back into the flat, passing the first bedroom and heading for the second. Then she stopped, her brain nagging away at her. What had she just seen?

'Come on.' Felicity already had the window open and was starting to climb out onto the fire escape.

'Just wait.' Anna's brain finally clicked and she ducked back towards the other bedroom as she heard voices outside and then the ping of the lift arriving.

'They're coming.' There was a hint of panic in Felicity's tone now.

A quick glance into the room confirmed what Anna thought she'd spotted on the way past. She darted in, pulled the object from under a small pile of books, and then bolted back for the fire escape.

The voices were closer now, but Felicity was still there holding the window. Anna hopped through and slid it shut behind her. Then they hurried down the fire escape to the alleyway below.

So far, so good. But they weren't out of this yet. Anna took the lead, jogging down the alley until they reached the entrance to the street. A quick check confirmed that the men hadn't left a lookout. Not very professional, although it didn't mean they weren't still dangerous.

'Gloves off.' Anna slipped off her own pair and took Felicity's, dropping them into a bin before wiping the knife for fingerprints and throwing that too.

Another check. All clear. She led the way across the street, eyes scanning for any hint of trouble as they headed into a small park and out the other side. They walked on calmly, side-by-side. Just two friends out for an afternoon stroll. Nothing to see here.

An archway between two buildings brought them out into the next street, a boulangerie and a tabac on one side. Everything normal and quiet, no hint of what they'd left behind.

Anna raised her hand, gesturing for Felicity to stop as she found the number for Arnaud Duroc, her contact at the DGSI, the French internal security service. He answered on the first ring. She gave him the address and the basic facts, promising a full report, then cut the call and walked on. If the French police got a shift on, maybe they'd arrive in time to arrest the men in the flat.

Not that Anna was about to wait around to find out. You were never out until you were fully out. She led the way down the street, took a right turn then headed on for another couple of blocks. Both she and Felicity walked in silence, each focused on their counter-surveillance checks. But there was nobody following. Eventually, they hit a main road and flagged down a passing taxi to take them back to the station.

'Oh my God, we made it.' Felicity collapsed into the back seat, shaking.

Hardly surprising after what they'd just seen. Anna knew that her younger colleague had done well to hold it together and would almost certainly need some time to come to terms with what she'd been through. Maybe counselling too.

Felicity bent forward continuing to shake, more violently now.

This was far, far worse than Anna had thought. She needed her junior to hold it together until they were safely away. It took her another second or two to work out that Felicity Diamond was laughing.

Actually laughing.

Anna felt the touchpaper of her anger start to burn. A man, not to mention a valuable source, was lying dead up there. But she breathed deeply, letting it settle. People handled stress in different ways. And Felicity's lack of experience meant she deserved some slack.

And a little credit too.

If it had been left to Anna, they might well have been trapped on the roof right now.

Maybe not that much credit though.

Anna had given her one job to do – search the bedrooms.

One job…

If Felicity was that good, she would surely have spotted the slim laptop Anna now had tucked safely away under her jacket.

Chapter 4

'Dermot. How the devil are you, my friend?' Anton Du Beurre threw himself down into the chair on the other side of the desk with a flash of his twinkly-eyed smile.

Dermot spoke to the chef most days, often more than once. But Anton always greeted him as if they'd met by chance in the street, perhaps on a fine spring morning after a separation counted in months or even years.

'And all is good with the contract, yes?' Anton leaned forward eagerly, a dash of concern dampening the smile now.

'Of course.' Dermot nodded. All was very good. 'Emilie's just bringing it in. We can sign today.'

The twinkly smile was back, full-on Hercule Poirot. Soon after they'd first met, Anton had revealed that he'd modelled his whole appearance on the fictional detective. His reasoning was that Poirot was just about the only Belgian most people in Britain had heard of. So it was what they'd expect a Belgian to look like, right? Anton hadn't stopped at the twinkly-eyed smile, going all in with the moustache and habitually dressing in a natty three-piece suit and bow tie. That's where the resemblance ended. As far as Dermot remembered, Agatha Christie's detective had been a bit of a short-arse. Anton, on the other hand, was six foot three and at thirty-nine-years-old had the look of a former rugby player who'd put on a bit of timber since hanging up his boots.

'And it will be good for my profile?'

Dermot nodded again, even though the answer was a big fat no, this time. It was a frying-pan endorsement deal, more about the dollar than the fame. But you had to milk it when you were hot. And Anton Du Beurre was the very definition of hot right now. A year on from bagging the role of host on popular cookery show *The Meal of Fortune*, the Belgian was the brightest star in the daytime TV firmament. He'd come a long way since launching his snappily titled YouTube channel *Brussels from Brussels*. The concept had been simple enough: smartly edited videos of Anton talking about his life in the Belgian capital as he cooked up a selection of tasty and convenient sprout-based recipes. The show had gained a cult following, opening the door to an increasing number of opportunities on mainstream TV, first in Belgium and then the UK.

'And the money is good?' Anton was all seriousness now, as he always was when the subject turned to finances.

Dermot nodded. The money was very good, especially with the lucrative option to extend the deal from frying pans to the full range of cookware. As the Belgian's agent, it was Dermot's role to advise him on such things and then bank his 10 per cent on the chef's growing earnings.

Anton relaxed back into his chair once more. 'Who'd have thought it? Just a humble boy from Brussels –'

A smart little knock on the door cut the chef off.

Thank God for that. Many were the hours Dermot had spent listening to Anton bang on about the obstacles that littered the path to fame if you happened to be Belgian.

The door swung open and Emilie Pieters strode in with a smile that illuminated the whole room.

'My dear. Radiant as ever.' Anton leaped out of his chair and embraced the girl with an extravagant triple-cheek kiss, despite the fact he'd seen her when he'd arrived ten minutes earlier.

Emilie stepped back with a smile. 'Thank you, Uncle Anton.'

Dermot had never been sure that 'uncle' was strictly accurate. Emilie had explained that she was the niece of one of Anton's cousins. There may even have been a further level of separation in there that he'd forgotten about. But family was important to Anton Du Beurre apparently.

Emilie turned from Anton and walked slowly around the desk towards Dermot, those huge brown eyes smiling at him with every sway of her hips. He held her gaze, immune now to the temptation to let his eyes slide down, however fleetingly, to her tight yellow T-shirt and the jeans hugging those almost impossibly long legs. At twenty-five, Emilie was little more than halfway between his daughter's nine years and Dermot's own thirty-five. That alone would have put him dangerously deep into dirty-old-man territory. More importantly, 'Uncle' Anton was Dermot's most lucrative client right now. He was certain the Belgian chef would sack him out of hand if he suspected anything was going on.

Which it most definitely wasn't.

The only snag was that Emilie showed every sign of having a weapons-grade crush on Dermot.

'I have the contract.' She completed her slow journey around the desk and rested a hand lightly on his shoulder.

Did she have to do that?

Then she leaned in close as she placed the contract on the desk. Was that her arm brushing his shoulder now or…?

The office suddenly felt very hot.

Dermot shifted in his chair, pushing it backwards and a fraction to the right. But Emilie just moved in that little bit closer.

It definitely wasn't her arm.

Jesus, how could Anton fail to notice…?

Dermot did his best to keep his eyes on the Belgian as Emilie's subtle perfume played with his nostrils.

Thankfully, Anton only had eyes for the contract, reaching across the desk to grab it before flopping back into his chair and starting to scan the text.

Emilie finally straightened and took a step back, leaving the warmth of her touch and the lingering scent of perfume. She looked down at him with a smile that reached from her lips to her big brown eyes and back again. 'Will that be all, Dermot?'

'Yes, thank you.' He wanted her out of the office before Anton jumped to the wrong conclusion.

She gave him one last smile before heading for the door. But then she stopped and turned again, her face serious. 'I just wanted to say again how grateful I am for the opportunity you gave me. And I wanted Anton to hear it.'

'Well, it's really him you need to thank.' Did she have to do this now?

Eyes still on the contract, Anton just grunted.

'Yes, but you've been so kind.' She smiled that smile again as she turned once more and slowly made her way to the door.

Too kind perhaps? Maybe that was the problem. He'd probably been more attentive than he would have been with other assistants because of her relationship to Anton. That was all. And she'd gone and got the wrong end of the completely wrong stick.

'No, wait.' The chef looked up from the contract, eyes first on Emilie before moving to Dermot.

Was that a hint of suspicion in his gaze? But then the Belgian broke into his trademark smile again. 'I'll just finish reading and sign. Then we can all go for champagne, to celebrate.' His eyes returned to the paper in his hand.

Champagne… That wasn't good. Emilie was obvious enough about her crush at the best of times. Who knew what she'd be like if she got a bit tipsy? Her smile widened as she came back across the office and perched on the edge of Dermot's desk, again just that little bit too close for comfort.

'Wow.' Anton spoke without looking up. 'Fifteen per cent commission on sales, I thought they were only going to offer twelve.' Then his eyes flicked up to Dermot. 'Everyone says how lucky I am to have you as my agent.'

That was kind of them, because, well… Actually, it was the other way around. Little more than two years ago Dermot had been pretty much skint; his dwindling client list and paltry earnings forcing him to give up his office and work out of his front room.

The spiral of decline that had got him there had been as long and hard as it had been predictable. Lost clients, mounting debts, drinking, more debts, more drinking, etc.

It was Molly who'd got him through. The twin pictures of his daughter now stood like sentinels on his desk, guarding against a return to the bad old days. On the left, five years old and in a pink anorak, smiling in Kew Gardens. And on the right, seven and all grown up, wearing a black Puffa jacket for a ride on the London Eye.

Dermot's darkest times had coincided with his ex-wife's decision to take Molly to live in Scotland with her new boyfriend, a tech entrepreneur turned organic cheese maker. Thankfully, romance in the glen had swiftly curdled, and mother and daughter had returned to London. These days, his ex could actually stand to be in the same room as Dermot for more than twenty seconds and hadn't called him a prick for at least three months.

Anton grunted again with appreciation at another clause in the contract. The chef's call had come a couple of months after Molly and Sarah's return. Anton had just been approached about hosting the *Meal of Fortune* job and was on the hunt for an agent to help him negotiate the best deal. Dermot's years of representing the show's previous host Marcus Diesel made him the perfect candidate in the Belgian's eyes. They'd shaken hands over lunch the very next day. The one condition was that Dermot offered Anton's niece Emilie a job.

Having such a rising star as Anton on his books had led to requests for representation from all sorts of other celebs. First, an ageing breakfast-show presenter, then three low-ranking TV chefs hoping to catch a bit of daytime TV action. Two quiz-show hosts and a stand-up comic had quickly followed. Dermot's latest signing, former world snooker quarter-finalist Eddie Dee, was already attracting a range of offers on the back of his creditable third-place finish on reality train-driving show *Celebrity 'Mind the Gap'*. And with cash flow looking more positive, a proper office had quickly followed. It might only have been a couple of rooms above a chicken shop in Holborn, but the rent was reasonable, and it was handily placed for meetings from Soho to Shoreditch.

'Perfect.' Anton finally reached the end. He whipped out a Montblanc pen and signed the contract with a flourish. 'There. Now, how about that champagne?'

Maybe Dermot could cry off, claiming another meeting? But Emilie managed his diary and would know the rest of the day was clear.

But then Anton's face fell. 'Mon Dieu. Sorry, how silly of me. I forgot I am meeting an old friend for drinks. Let's do tomorrow night instead. I'll take you both to dinner.'

'There's really no need.' This was escalating out of control now. A glass of champagne Dermot could have managed. But a whole evening? Anton was sure to notice Emilie's behaviour.

'Nonsense.' The chef smiled again. 'I insist. Emilie, ring The Ivy and say Anton Du Beurre wants a table, 8 p.m. sharp.'

The chef was so hot right now he'd almost certainly get it too, despite the restaurant having a waiting list of several months. He jumped up out of his chair, heading for the door before stopping and turning back, a look of concern on his face. 'I meant to ask. These murders. Should I be worried?'

Dermot held Anton's gaze, hoping the chef hadn't spotted the flash of panic in his eyes. 'No. There's nothing to worry about. But we can arrange more security if that would make you feel comfortable.'

The Belgian shook his head slowly. 'I'll be OK with Serge.'

Dermot thought so too. The former member of Belgium's Special Operations Regiment had acted as Anton's driver cum bodyguard for more than a year now. He looked like he could handle himself.

'OK, got to fly.' The concern was gone from Anton's face as he turned once more and headed for the door, stopping only to kiss Emilie. And then he was gone.

She hopped off the desk and turned to Dermot, a question in those huge brown eyes.

'Better do as he says.' He managed a weak smile, hoping he'd got it all wrong with her. He'd hardly be the first older man to misread the signs with an attractive younger woman. All he needed to do was be a bit more stand-offish, and maybe a little less friendly. Perhaps he'd have a word about office etiquette and personal-space issues too.

'I'll do it right now.' Emilie smiled her biggest smile yet, eyes lingering on his before she turned away.

And Dermot was left in no doubt that the crush was 100 per cent genuine.

Oh God.

Chapter 5

With the traffic building towards rush hour, it was almost five by the time Henwell got back to the base Connor had secured for him at Charing Cross Police Station. On the plus side, it was central and the local coppers seemed happy enough to share their spare office space. Aside from the predictable CRAPPIE jokes at the start, Henwell and his team had been largely left to themselves. Of course, the coffee from the machine in the station was undrinkable, but being on the fringes of Covent Garden meant there were plenty of decent cafés where Henwell could indulge his weakness for bucket-sized lattes. And he could pick up the odd treat for his team if they behaved themselves and didn't make too much of a mess.

He headed through the front door, stopping to exchange a word or two with the desk sergeant, before taking the stairs to the second floor two at a time. He opened the door to the CAPPE offices and walked straight into a maelstrom of sound and frenzied motion.

Henwell had decided that if he ever moved to the country, he'd get himself a dog. A big one too, not one of those rubbish little efforts you saw around town, struggling even to keep up with their wheezing overweight owners. No, his would be a big shambling beast that didn't know its own strength, or how to control itself when it got excited. And he already knew what he was going to call it.

Lidstone.

After his big, clumsy and over-enthusiastic detective constable.

The young DC was up and out of his chair before Henwell was even through the door. 'Sir, sir. We've got a lead on the kidnap.'

'What kidnap?' Had something significant actually happened in the world of CAPPE while Henwell had been out?

'Johnnie Devale's cat.'

Oh that. The TV interior designer had reported his cat missing, convinced that it had been snatched by an embittered rival. Henwell's view was that the man was such an overbearing bully, the poor moggy had probably just padded off to live elsewhere.

'Don't worry about that now, Danny.' Henwell held up a hand, slowing Lidstone to a halt before he could do any damage. 'We've got the murders.'

'*The* murders? You're joking?' This was Sam Roberts. The fat detective sergeant levered himself slowly out of his chair and came puffing around his desk, getting dangerously far from the life-sustaining pack of biscuits he kept beside his computer. It had to be the most enthusiasm the man shown since joining the team.

'But the cat?' Lidstone didn't seem quite so keen, a look of concern spreading across his face.

'You can follow it up when you get a minute.' Henwell didn't want to sound heartless. There was no evidence of catnapping and the creature would either show up or it wouldn't. But it wasn't their priority now.

The DC nodded, seemingly reassured that they weren't abandoning the cat completely.

'And there's been another one.' Henwell paused to let it sink in. 'Either of you remember Mickey Morris?'

'He's dead?' Roberts was turning to reach for his biscuits but stopped short. 'The wife used to love him.'

'Well someone didn't. Took his head off with some sort of battleaxe. There's real pressure to get a result. That's why we're involved.' Henwell scanned around the room, his eyes finally resting on the three large boxes on the table by the door.

'Dropped off about an hour ago.' Roberts was already retreating to his chair. 'Some stuck-up DS rang. Said you'd know what they were.'

That would have been Prim no doubt.

'Case files for all the murders. Our first job is to go through them, see if there's anything the MIT have missed.' Henwell picked up the first box, read the label and ferried it over to Roberts' desk. 'You get the two most recent ones, Sam. Danny, you do numbers three, four and five and I'll take the first ones.'

The selection was deliberate. In Henwell's experience, if something had been missed, it would be right at the start, before the investigation had found its rhythm. So the earliest ones for him and then Lidstone, who he trusted more than Roberts. The DC might have been clumsy and green, but he had a good-enough brain on him, and the way he organised his desk suggested an element of OCD that could be useful when it came to detective work. Henwell had already decided that he was going to do his best to turn the lad into a half-decent policeman.

Sadly, that ship had sailed long ago for Sam Roberts. Sailed, hit an iceberg and sunk with all hands on deck. If there was a good copper lurking somewhere inside Roberts, the detective sergeant was doing a great job of hiding it behind a large gut, sour attitude and poorly suppressed authority issues. It was a miracle that he'd managed to negotiate his sergeant's exam. But at fifty-one it seemed unlikely he'd be troubling the promotions board again. Disliked on his previous team and a written warning away from a suspension, Roberts probably saw CAPPE as the path of least possible resistance to his thirty years and retirement.

But then beggars really couldn't be choosers. Connor had generously promised Henwell his pick of all the officers who volunteered to join the new celebrity crime squad. Lidstone and Roberts had been the only applicants to date. There was budget for two more detective constables, but so far there'd been no takers. Until there were, Lidstone was going to have to make up for Roberts' laziness and fetch more biscuits whenever the sergeant ran out.

'Let's give it a couple more hours tonight then regroup at seven.' He didn't feel at all guilty at asking them to work late or come in early. This was a multiple murder inquiry, and Connor had approved the overtime.

Lidstone's eager nod was more than offset by Roberts' long slow sigh.

'And no calls, please, unless they're urgent.' Henwell didn't wait around to hear more, grabbing his box of files and retreating into his little office, before pushing the door shut behind him with his foot.

He put the box down on his desk and looked around the tiny office from which he was supposed to assist the hunt for the celebrity serial killer. Just enough room for a desk and stuffy as hell, even in mid-November. He'd given up trying to open the window weeks ago. Probably for the best, as it looked out onto an alleyway full of bins that had seemingly never been emptied.

Sixteen years with the Met, and it had come to this. But it was the choices he'd made that had brought him here.

Choices he didn't regret.

And now, far sooner than he could have hoped, he had the chance to put things right. He moved around the desk, nearly tripping over another box on the floor. It was the current home to the few meagre possessions that he'd brought from his old office. A couple of times he'd thought about emptying it out. But what was the point? There were no snaps of a wife and kids to set proudly on his desk. Other officers routinely complained of relationships and families broken on the wheels of their police careers. But Henwell had always been a little too busy turning that same wheel to meet the right woman, or even the wrong one. He kicked the box further under his desk and sat down, opening the top file in front of him.

Dr White's profile.

'Mind you read it carefully.'

He dropped it straight into the bin and reached for the next folder.

Murder number one.

The lifeless face of Charlie McGee stared up at him from the first page. Henwell had actually quite liked the Geordie comic in the early days as he'd started to make a name for himself on the stand-up circuit. TV panel shows had followed, and eventually Charlie had carved quite the niche for himself, presenting a series of motoring programmes. He'd been killed on his way home from a TV awards bash, where he'd been nominated for, but failed to win, the award for best host. Despite this cruel blow to his ego, Charlie had apparently left the event in high spirits. His abrupt meeting with a car bonnet had put an end to all that.

Henwell read his way through all the witness statements, double-checking for any inconsistencies and omissions, but everything seemed to be in order. It looked like Simpson's team had done a thorough job.

With no other killings on the books at that point, the police had initially put McGee's death down to a hit and run. At least until the video had gone live.

He grabbed the memory stick that had come with the files and plugged it into his computer. No doubt he could have found the video easily enough online. Despite the best efforts of the Met's tech team to take it and the other videos down, versions kept popping up and being shared. As ever, there was the suspicion that the likes of Google and Facebook could have pulled their fingers out a bit faster.

The video opened up on McGee's face. A slowed down shot through a car windscreen, it captured the exact moment when the comedian realised the vehicle was going to hit him. Then it cut away to an edited highlights package of Charlie's TV career, all set to a jaunty little tune. Then back to an even closer shot of his face. The fear spreading in slow-mo, a different tune now, dark and threatening.

More highlights and jingle, then more face and sombre dirge and back to the highlights once more. Finally, a wider-angle shot of the car ploughing into Charlie McGee, his ragdoll body spilling over the bonnet, then into the windscreen before flying into the air and landing limply on the tarmac. Then silence before a burst of cartoon-baddie laughter, 'Mwah hah hah hah,' as a wash of red flowed down the screen like blood. Then the words appeared, white out of red.

'Dying to be famous?'

The question mark blinking like a cursor.

Not the highest production values Henwell had ever seen but it made its shocking point all the same. He clicked the video shut. There was nothing to be learned from another viewing, and although the things he'd seen over his years of policing had cauterised certain parts of his brain, footage of a man being killed was never going to be an easy watch. Henwell reached into the box for the next file. Second up had been Jane Holland. She'd built on a modest start, presenting the TV weather in East Anglia, to become one of those general all-purpose celebrities that popped up everywhere. This has been achieved without an overt display of any specific talents, other than being chatty and pleasant enough on the eye. A selection of panel shows, the odd bit of guest presenting and regular reality-show appearances had helped her maintain a screen presence for the best part of a decade.

Cause of death, strangulation with a pair of tights. Initially, the smart money had been on a sex game gone badly wrong.

Until the video appeared.

Henwell decided to give this one a miss. Again there'd be nothing to learn, and viewing a woman's murder was even less palatable than watching a man's. If that was an example of the type of gender bias he kept getting memos about, then Henwell was more than happy to fess up to it.

Simpson's team had really got going after that one, especially when their investigation established that the victim had worn the fatal hosiery for her appearance in the final of a celebrity dancing show. The dancer strangled by her tights, motoring presenter McGee run down, easy enough to see what was going on here.

Henwell checked his watch – quarter past six. Perhaps it was time to contact some of his old informants, offer to spread around a bit of cash, see what they could find out? A couple of them were well connected within London's underworld and could adopt the sort of techniques the Met couldn't. And Connor had told him to use a bit of licence. He was searching up the first number when he heard a quiet knock on the door. It opened slowly to reveal Lidstone, nervously hopping from one foot to another.

'Umm… She said it was urgent, sir.' The DC held out his mobile.

Henwell sighed, reminding himself that the young officer remained a work in progress. 'Who is *she*?'

'A journalist.'

Bloody media, they hadn't left him alone since he'd taken the CAPPE role. Henwell stood and snatched the phone from Lidstone. 'Hello.'

'DI Henwell. Sally Jarvis from the *Heat* magazine crime desk.'

'How long has *Heat* had a crime desk?' Wasn't it just a celeb gossip mag?

'About as long as the Met's had a celebrity crime squad.'

Touché. Henwell guessed he'd walked straight into that one, like a cartoon character standing on the end of a broom.

'A little bird tells me that CRAPPIE's been called in to help out on the celebrity murders.'

'It's not CRA…' Oh, what was the point? 'That's not something I can confirm or deny. Speak to the press office.'

'The photos of you outside Mickey Morris's house have already confirmed it.'

She had him there again. 'The Metropolitan Police takes crime against people in the public eye very seriously.' It was a line he'd trotted out more times than he could remember. 'And my team is helping pursue a number of…'

'Yeah, yeah. Cut the crap, Inspector. You haven't got a clue, have you?'

'You should really be speaking to DCI Simpson.' He was the one who'd been running the investigation and should really be getting the grief from the media.

'I've heard that you might be easier to do business with.'

Ha! So she'd already been given the brush-off by Simpson. 'What exactly is it that you want?' Maybe it was worth seeing where this was going?

'An early heads-up on any arrests if I help you out.'

'Help us out?'

'I do come across a lot of information in my line of work.'

'And withholding that information from a murder inquiry would be a serious matter.'

'Which is why we're speaking right now.'

'OK. I'm sure we can come to some arrangement.' It wasn't strictly Henwell's offer to make, but again, what was the word Connor had used… latitude? 'But only when we actually charge a suspect.' He'd seen first-hand how too much early publicity around an arrest could destroy a case. 'And only if your information's good.'

'Works for me. But I'm not sure it's a discussion either of us wants to have on the phone. Shall we say eleven tomorrow morning?'

'How about we say this evening?' Henwell was eager to hear what she had to say right then.

'No can do. Deadlines to hit, parties to go to. And a female journalist and a male copper meeting up after hours… Tongues might wag.'

They might indeed.

She gave him the name of a café in Soho. 'Eleven tomorrow. Don't be late.'

And then she was gone.

Still not bad though. One day on the case and he already had a lead. Tomorrow would reveal if it was worth following. He checked his watch – just gone six-thirty. A bonding session in the pub would be good for team morale. Roberts and Lidstone could just as easily tell him if they'd found anything in the files over a pint or two.

Chapter 6

'Yes.' Anna snatched up the phone when she saw the extension number on the screen – the tech team. 'What have you got?'

'Err… Nothing yet. Sophie's coming up to talk to you about that. Said she'll be there in about five minutes.'

'OK, thanks.' Anna tried not to let the frustration creep into her voice. She'd handed the laptop over to the techs on her return from France, the best part of a day ago now. And they'd found nothing. Military-grade encryption, that's what they'd said yesterday. But then wasn't that exactly the sort of thing MI5's IT experts were meant to be able to crack in their sleep? And now today, having finally got past the security, it seemed they still haven't found anything. So the sainted Sophie Harper, the head of the tech team herself, was coming up to explain in person.

Someone had killed Olivier to stop him selling information to MI5. And with no other intel or online chatter, the laptop was the only lead they had. There had to be something.

Anna closed her eyes and stretched, remembering too late about the sore ribs where the dirty little coward had kicked her before doing a runner. She leaned forward, rubbing at the bruise. In the shower that morning she'd noticed it was already starting to bloom, nasty shades of purple and black. Anna reckoned she wouldn't be back on the judo mat for at least a week.

It had taken her a good chunk of yesterday afternoon and evening to smooth things over with Arnaud at the DGSI. But then the French had sanctioned the meeting in Lille, so he hadn't been able to come over all high-handed about how it had turned out. They'd started by dancing around the one subject they really needed to discuss, before Anna had finally put it out there.

How had Olivier's killers known? Had there been a leak about the operation?

Default positions had been duly stated.

Not us.

Not us either.

But MI5 and the DGSI would each need to run their own internal investigations before they could be sure. In reality, they both knew a leak was highly unlikely. When assets were exposed, it tended to be because they'd given themselves away. It was usually just a word or action, something slightly out of character.

And more often than not, it got them killed.

Arnaud had gone on to confirm that the apartment had been deserted when the French police had arrived. Apart from the body, that was. They'd failed to turn up anything of interest and were treating it as a robbery gone wrong. Which brought her back to the laptop again.

'Anna?'

If it didn't offer up any secrets, they'd have no way of following up on the terror threat.

'ANNA.'

She looked up, realising she'd been miles away.

'I've emailed you my report on Lille.' Felicity was leaning against the desk, smiling down at her. 'I'm going to grab some lunch.'

Anna looked around, noticing the place was already three-quarters empty. Even those charged with the nation's security liked to get out for lunch come Friday.

'Any plans for the weekend?' She wasn't really interested in what Felicity might be up to, but it was the kind of thing bosses asked their teams, wasn't it? And she had promised herself she'd try harder with the girl since Lille. Anna was still prepared to give Felicity the benefit of the doubt over her laughter in the taxi, putting it down to the stress of seeing a dead body on her first assignment.

'Oh, just the usual.'

Good. Anna wasn't going to be forced to listen to a blow-by-blow account.

'You know, drinks with some friends tonight. Lunch in town tomorrow and a bit of shopping. Opera in the evening. Then Sunday…'

It sounded like everyone's idea of the perfect little spook had the perfect little social life too. Anna half tuned out as she started to scan her emails.

'And you?'

'Sorry?' She realised Felicity must have finished the rundown of her action-packed Sunday. 'Oh, err, nothing much.' When she wasn't working, Anna's weekends tended to be based around judo, gym and a lot of reading. And that was how she liked them.

But this weekend was looking set to be as packed as Felicity's, not that Anna was about to share the details. Dinner at her friend Amanda's on Saturday then Sunday lunch with Jess and her family. Anna really did love her younger sister, even if the mother of two (and one on the way) found every opportunity to exude her own brand of contented marital smugness. Her husband, Gareth, didn't help matters. Yes, he was a successful surgeon, but there had always been something of the ferret about the man. And he wasn't above snatching furtive glances at Anna's chest when he thought she and his wife weren't looking.

'See you later then.'

Was there a hint of pity in Felicity's smile as she trotted jauntily back to her desk?

Christ, get a grip, woman. The girl was young and a little bit full of herself. That was all. A little like Anna had been at that age. And it was hardly Felicity's fault she actually had things to do at the weekend and people to do them with. Working for MI5 didn't mean you had to cut yourself off from the world entirely.

Anna checked the clock on her screen, wondering what was taking Sophie Harper so long. She couldn't see the conversation taking more than five minutes if the techs really hadn't found anything. So maybe she could test her ribs out with a gentle lunchtime jog along the river. It might help to keep her mind from the horrors that awaited on Saturday night. She always looked forward to catching up with Amanda, but how about just the two of them going for drinks? Why did it always have to involve dinner with her friend's banker husband and his city chums? Anna's single status meant an eager 'eligible' would have been lined up to sit next to her. He'd see himself as a thrusting go-getter who worked hard and played harder. He wouldn't ask her a single question about herself, preferring to tell her what a good judge of character he was, the ludicrous price he'd just paid for a new bike and how much he knew about wine. Anna's lack of interest would be evident to everyone but him before they'd finished the starters. He'd end up drinking too much, exposing some unsavoury right-wing views and assuming she was a lesbian.

Cancelling was a temptation rather than a real option though. Anna had kept in contact with few enough of her old friends as it was. Making her last-minute excuses to Amanda for a third time on the spin would be a step towards losing touch with another.

But couldn't her friend stop trying to fix her up? Yes, Anna knew it had been over eighteen months now since she'd split up with Scott. But she certainly didn't need any help getting over that lying tosser. And it wasn't as if she was short of offers. It had been Anna who'd decided to put her career first when things might just have got interesting with a certain old flame.

Whoa! She tensed as she pulled her thoughts up abruptly, bringing another sharp protest from her ribs. Where had that one come from? She'd lost very little sleep over the past months wondering what might have been with Dermot Jack. She certainly wasn't about to start thinking about him now.

The ping of the lift arriving brought her back to the present. The doors opened and what appeared to be a young girl, trying to pass as an adult, headed her way. Surely she couldn't be…?

'Anna? I'm Sophie Harper.' The child/woman reached her desk and extended a hand with a smile.

Anna knew everyone in tech was unfeasibly young, but Sophie looked like she was fresh out of university, as if she hadn't even started in fact. In reality, the new head of the tech team had already enjoyed a successful career in the private sector before she and her reputation had been poached to serve Queen and country around three months ago.

Sophie pulled up a chair without being asked and smiled at Anna. 'I'm sorry, but there's nothing on the laptop.'

'Are you sure?' Anna realised too late that her voice had been a little on the sharp side. Despite her age, the new tech team leader was at least two grades more senior.

Sophie eyed her for a second or two. Perhaps thinking she could do without the attitude. But when she spoke, her voice was calm and friendly. 'We've still got some drives to go through but we've done most of it. What exactly was it you were looking for anyway?'

'We're not 100 per cent sure.' In truth, Anna wasn't even one per cent sure. Just anything that told them more about the terrorist threat.

'My guys will keep going until it's finished. You'll have the full report first thing on Monday.'

'Thank you.' Anna smiled. 'And sorry for snapping.'

'That's OK.' Sophie smiled a tired smile in return.

Anna noticed the tiny lines around her eyes, and suddenly Sophie didn't look quite so young.

'If it's any consolation, it's as frustrating for us as it is for you.' Sophie stretched as she stood up, ironing out the kinks of another long day at her desk.

And Anna felt herself warm to the woman. A quick glance at Sophie's hands showed her ring finger remained bare. Anna had long given up trying to second-guess what men or women found attractive, but Sophie Harper, with her smiling eyes, long dark hair and delicate features, would probably tick the majority of people's boxes. Maybe she was just another slave to the job?

Had they met outside of work, they could well have become friends. And actually, perhaps Sophie might even fancy going for a drink sometime? It was time Anna tried to widen her social circle a little.

'Why have all that security on the laptop if there's nothing to hide?' A voice from over her shoulder interrupted Anna's plans to reboot her social life.

She turned to see Felicity. 'Oh, I thought you'd gone for lunch? Sophie, this is Felicity Diamond, one of my team. Felicity, Sophie Harper.'

Felicity's tone had been challenging at best, downright impertinent at worst, and Sophie had a reputation for not taking prisoners. Well, Felicity could certainly do with being taken down a peg or twenty. Anna sat back to watch the show.

But Sophie just smiled. 'Nice to meet you. I've heard good things.'

Jesus... Was there no end to the admiration for the golden child?

'The encryption was pretty high grade.' Sophie nodded thoughtfully. 'But the owner worked in IT security, right?'

'Yes.' Felicity nodded with a smile.

'I love your shoes by the way.' Sophie stood, smiling more widely now.

'Thanks.' Felicity seemed genuinely pleased at the compliment. 'They're Gemma Carrat. She hasn't really made it big yet. I like yours too. Rupert Sanderson, right?'

'Yes.' Sophie beamed from ear to ear.

'I adore Rupert's shoes.' Felicity was making a great show of inspecting them carefully now. 'I must have a dozen pairs at home.'

Anna took a sly glance at the women's shoes. Both were black and neat looking with a bit of a heel. Well trained in observation as she was, she still couldn't detect anything remarkable about either pair. But then nobody seemed to be saying anything about Anna's shoes, a pair of sensible numbers she'd picked up in last year's sales.

'I'm just heading out to grab some lunch.' All of Felicity's attention was on Sophie now. 'Do you want to come?'

'Yeah, why not?' She turned to Anna. 'We're done, aren't we?'

'Cool.' Felicity reached over to her desk and grabbed her bag. 'We could sit in at the veggie place round the corner.' With that, the two women headed away towards the lifts chatting like old friends.

Anna turned her computer off and bent down to grab the gym bag from under the desk. That lunchtime run was definitely happening now.

'Hello Anna, how are you?'

When she looked up again, it was into the big jowly face of Sir Richard Lawson.

'Great, thanks, Sir Richard.'

'It's always just Richard to you.'

The 'Sir' had come with Lawson's elevation to the Director-General's role last year. Anna's part in sorting out the situation with the Russian arms dealer had undoubtedly helped him to cement the top job. Her own promotion had followed swiftly. But his avuncular interest had started years before, a result of his close friendship with her late father.

Lawson's jowls quivered as he took a quick look around the almost empty office. 'Any movement on that French business?'

She shook her head. 'The techs don't think they'll find anything useful on the laptop.'

'Well, if you need anything let me know.' He smiled again. 'And say hello to your mother for me.' Even after the death of Anna's father, Richard Lawson had stayed close to the family. Cards at Christmas and birthdays and regular lunch invitations for her mum.

'You too, Sir… I mean Richard.'

He started for the door then stopped. 'I hear Felicity did well in Lille.'

'Great, yes.' Anna smiled as the silent scream echoed inside her head.

'Pleased to hear it. Well, the Home Secretary waits for no man.' He gave her a last smile as he turned to go.

Anna picked up her bag then fished in her pocket as her mobile started to vibrate. 'Hello?'

'It's Sophie, Sophie Harper.'

A belated invitation to join her and Felicity for lunch? Anna would rather gouge her own eyes out with a spoon.

'I'm heading back now.' Sophie sounded as if she was running, her rapid breathing set to the drumbeat of those fashionable shoes on the pavement. 'The guys think they might have found something on the laptop.'

Chapter 7

'Dermot, Mr Diesel is here.' There was more than a hint of distaste in Emilie's voice as she popped her head round the door.

'Great, send him in.' Dermot resisted the temptation to keep the chef waiting and tried to muster up some enthusiasm. Best to get it over with.

Emilie smiled and nodded, lingering that little bit longer than necessary in the doorway, all the more time to show off another figure-hugging T-shirt, white this time, and an even tighter pair of jeans.

'Dermot, how are you?' Marcus barrelled into the room, a wide smile on his big meaty face. He flopped down into the chair Anton Du Beurre had occupied so much more gracefully the day before.

Marcus liked to think he was known for his dress sense. He wasn't, at least not in a good way. Today, his jeans were even tighter than Emilie's. The effect was very different, of course, and he was far too keen on wearing orange for a man about to embark on the rapid downhill journey into his late forties.

'It's nearly one o'clock.' Marcus reached behind his back for a cushion. He looked at it disapprovingly for a second then threw it on the floor. 'You always used to take me to lunch.'

Well, yes. But that had been when he was a client who actually earned Dermot some money. They'd parted company the year before, after a public brawl outside a restaurant had landed the chef in the papers and a lot of hot water. Marcus had been sacked from *The Meal of Fortune* soon after, when a series of his tweets sharing his views about women had strayed rather too far over the line.

Jobless and apparently penniless, the chef had come crawling back, begging Dermot to take him back on as a client. Marcus had even displayed a remarkable lack of bitterness that Dermot was now working for the man he believed had 'stolen' his job hosting *The Meal of Fortune.*

Of course, Dermot had told him where to go. Not having to put up with Marcus's foul-mouthed tirades had been one of the bigger improvements in Dermot's life over the past year. He reckoned it ranked about third, behind not getting killed by a Russian hitman and seeing his daughter a little more often.

But Marcus was nothing if not persistent, mounting an on-going campaign of emails, texts and calls. Dermot had finally relented, figuring that representing Marcus and finding him some work would take up less time than constantly telling him to piss off. That had been six weeks ago, and it was a decision Dermot had regretted a little more with each passing day, as the offers had failed to materialise for the chef. Those tweets were just too current, the chef's 'brand' still toxic in the age of easy social media outrage.

'Tea, coffee?' Emilie opened the door and popped her head in again.

Dermot had been planning to offer nothing; the higher the level of hospitality, the longer Marcus would stick around.

'Coffee, please.' Marcus looked at her with a lecherous grin. 'And if you have any biscuits?' He turned to Dermot as the door closed. 'Well?'

'Well, what?' Dermot knew perfectly well what he meant but wasn't playing that game today.

'That little piece has got the hots for you.'

'Don't be a dick. And no one's referred to a woman as a "piece" since about 1976.'

'Come on, it's obvious.'

If a self-centred egotist like Marcus had noticed Emilie's crush, then it must be real. Dermot fought back a sigh as he thought again about the dinner with Anton that evening.

'She works for you. That means you've got a little leverage.' The chef gave him a big fat wink.

'Leverage? Jesus, Marcus, you've heard of Harvey Weinstein, right?'

The chef just shook his head.

'"Me Too"?' Where had the man been?

But Marcus was looking dangerously confused now. 'You don't know who he is either? Why are we talking about someone neither of us has ever heard of?'

'Forget it.' It would be far too hard to explain to a man who thought gender equality was simply a green light to try it on with all women.

There was a soft knock on the door and Emilie shouldered her way in carrying the coffees. 'Is there anything else I can do for you, Dermot?'

'No thanks.'

She gave him another lingering smile before turning slowly and swaying her hips as she walked from the room.

'Oooh… *Is there anything else I can do for you, Dermot?*' Marcus rolled his eyes. 'What are you waiting for? It's not like you're getting any action.'

'I might be.'

'You wouldn't be so touchy if you were.' Marcus shook his head. 'What happened to your MI5 girlie?'

A bloody good question. Anna Preston had strolled back into his life, turned it upside down then walked out again without so much as a goodbye. But Dermot had put that all behind him and hadn't thought about her in months.

Until now. Thanks for that, Marcus.

'Let's just get on to business, shall we?' They'd be here all day otherwise. 'I've made some calls, but things are a bit slow right now.'

'You mean you haven't found anything.' The chef's face darkened.

Dermot remembered how quickly Marcus could flip from genial bonhomie to foul-mouthed rant. 'I didn't say that –'

'Ten years as host of daytime TV's most popular show. Doesn't that mean anything?' Marcus's face was getting redder. 'I just want to be back on TV. I'm the bad boy of cookery, right?' Marcus puffed himself up in his chair. 'That's not a bad rep to have.'

Trouble was, it wasn't a reputation for being a hard-drinking, hard-partying, lovable rogue. More like an annoying gobshite, who nobody wanted to work with, ever again.

And again there were those tweets.

'And what about all those awards I won?'

TV's Worst Dressed Man three times and *Daytime TV's Most Annoying Man* four, if Dermot remembered rightly. Marcus had managed to bag a credible third place in the *Welsh Daytime TV Personality of the Year Awards.* An impressive achievement, as he was actually from Cornwall. But that had been way back in 2014.

'Look, there is something.' Dermot knew he'd have to sell it carefully. 'And it is TV.' He paused. 'An advert.'

'I don't want a sodding advert. I want a show.'

'It's good money.'

'What's the advert for?' Marcus suddenly sounded a bit more interested at the mention of cash.

Dermot tried not to wince. 'Tinned tuna.'

'You've got to be sodding joking.'

'Premium tinned tuna.' Dermot reached for the folder on his desk and pulled out the top sheet of paper. 'And it'll remind people who you are.'

'It'll remind them I'm in a fish advert.'

'They've even sent us the scripts, written especially with you in mind. But I can send them back if you're not interested.' He slipped the paper back into the folder. 'Not sure what else I'll be able to find you though.'

'OK, OK… Just read them.' Marcus sighed. 'Doesn't mean I'm saying yes.'

'So they're a Japanese company, hoping to break into the UK market.' Dermot pulled the papers back out again. 'It says the aim of the advert is to get people to think tinned tuna is a versatile and tasty food that they really enjoy.'

'They're only saying that to sell more tuna.'

'Well that is their job. Just listen.' He started to read from the script. 'We open on a man and a woman sitting opposite each other in an expensive-looking restaurant. A waiter appears with two plates and says in a French accent…'

Marcus held up a hand to stop him. 'You're not going to do the voices, are you?'

'Not if you don't want me to.' He'd always thought he'd been good at the accents when he read stories for Molly. 'He says, "The grilled sea bass for the lady and fillet steak for Monsieur." The man and woman smile, looking very pleased with their choices. Then you pop up from behind the table and say, "I'd sooner have tuna." The man and the woman look at each other and nod enthusiastically. They wave their food away and ask for tuna instead. Then it cuts to…'

'Sorry, hang on.' Marcus waved a hand in the air. 'It actually says I pop up?'

Dermot looked down at the script. 'Yes, you pop up.'

'Not really me, is it? Popping up. It's not very manly.'

'OK, let's just say you appear, then.' Dermot fought back a sigh. 'I can ask them to change it in the script.'

'But how will I appear?'

'Up from behind the table, I guess.'

'Won't that be the same as popping up?'

Dermot looked back at the script, wondering how tightly he'd have to roll it before he'd be able to stuff it up one of the chef's nostrils.

*

He finally managed to get rid of Marcus around half past one, with a promise that the chef would at least think about the tuna advert.

Dermot considered nipping out for a sandwich but decided against it. He clicked on a browser and opened up a celebrity news site. Predictably the Mickey Morris murder continued to hog the headlines.

The former sitcom star had been a client of Dermot's for a few months back in 2008 or 2009. Dermot had done his best for Morris, he really had. But it hadn't been easy, what with Mickey's reputation for drinking and drugs. Not good when you were trying to appeal to a family audience. The parallels with Marcus Diesel's current situation were all too clear. Maybe Dermot should just drop the chef.

Morris had ended up spitting the dummy and sacking Dermot, accusing him of not trying hard enough. Dermot clicked on the top story and started to read.

Police are declining to comment on rumours that TV funny man Mickey Morris, found dead in his home yesterday morning, had been beheaded with a battleaxe.

Jesus… He was glad he'd skipped the sandwich.

The Met is also still refusing to link the death of the star to the recent spate of celebrity murders.

Of course they were linked, nobody was falling for that one.

Experts are speculating about the harm the killings could do to the UK economy. Aaron Willis, Entertainment Industry Analyst at PDW Consulting, said, 'Celebrity culture contributes a huge amount to the economy. A threat to celebrities is a threat to the well being of the nation.'

Attendance at award shows and premieres is said to be down too as celebs stay at home fearing that they may be next. 'These events supply the gossip and pictures to fuel the public's obsession with celebrities,' said Sally Jarvis, Crime Editor at Heat *magazine. 'If celebs stop attending, the whole news machine will be in danger of drying up. There are even rumours that applications for the next series of Love Island are down. It's a real worry.'*

Dermot read the article to the end before copying the page link and pasting it into a password-protected document that he'd squirrelled away deep down among the archived folders on his computer. Best if Emilie didn't stumble across it.

Or anyone else for that matter.

Then he moved on to another website, scrolling down for more news of the police investigation into Mickey Morris's death. He read the article before moving on to the next, copying all the links and pasting them to the same file. Then on to another site and another until he had all the latest news of the murder filed safely away.

Chapter 8

You could have been forgiven for thinking DCI John Simpson was a little in love with himself, keeping everyone waiting as if he owned the place. But then it was his investigation, his briefing. He was still an utter tool though, if you asked Henwell.

The incident room was crammed full and stuffy, despite the November chill. The best part of sixty officers shuffling and muttering, almost as one, gathered for the afternoon briefing that Simpson had only called that lunchtime.

The room had an edge to it too. Essence of coffee breath nicely set off by stale sweat and more than a suspicion of egg sandwich. But there was something else too. Failure hung in the air like a cloud. The sour whiff of a case going nowhere fast.

But there was expectation here as well. Nerves to be sure, but adrenalin too. The daily briefing had already taken place that morning. Had there been some kind of breakthrough?

The text from DS Prim had made it clear Henwell was expected to attend in person. And usually that would have been fine. Any up-to-date info on the main inquiry could only help his little side investigation. But after his coffee with the *Heat* magazine journalist, he was itching to get back to base and get cracking.

Sally Jarvis couldn't have been more different than the hard-nosed hack he'd expected. Warm, funny and attractive in her busy northern way, she'd flirted outrageously before getting to the point. In other circumstances Henwell might have reciprocated, despite the rock the size of one of Jupiter's lesser moons weighing down her ring finger. Only after he'd repeated his promise of an exclusive on any charges had she shared her information.

Henwell knew it could be nothing. But it could also be the lead that cracked the case right open.

He'd felt his nervousness build as he'd ridden the Tube down to Putney and completed the short walk to the police station, where Simpson's MIT was based. The last thing he needed right now was to hear that the DCI's earnest band of plodders had unearthed the same lead. Because actually, they really should have been on to it by now. A dropped catch for sure, but one Henwell was hoping to benefit from.

The talk in the briefing room stopped as the door opened and Simpson's expensive shoes finally clippity-clopped their way across the floor. A different well-cut suit to yesterday; the hair neater, not having spent the best part of the morning under the hood of a sweaty scene-of-crime suit. A step behind to the left and right were DS Prim and Dr White, devoted acolytes to the high priest of criminal investigation.

'Thank you for coming, everyone.' Simpson reached the front and launched straight in. His sharp eyes swept the room, pausing briefly on Henwell before moving on. 'We've got a lot to cover.' His voice carried weight without being loud. It was one that was accustomed to being in command, to being heard. 'So I'm going to keep this as brief as possible.'

A sentence that usually meant exactly the opposite in Henwell's experience. And that was when he felt it, the little flash of jealousy. How often had it been him up there? DCI-ing it at the front, rather than hanging onto the back wall.

'I've got an important update on the case.' Simpson paused to let the words sink in. 'But first I'd like to welcome a few new faces to the investigation.' He launched into a list of names, various DSs and DCs seconded from other major investigation teams.

It was easy to spot the newbies: up at the front, competing to show their keenness.

'And I'd like to welcome DI Henwell from CRAPPIE too.' Simpson smiled, his eyes back on Henwell, pausing long enough to let the sniggers ripple out around the room.

Henwell smiled back politely, nodding to a couple of faces he knew of old. It was going to be a long time before people stopped finding that one funny. But he could take all the mockery they had to throw at him, as long as Simpson wasn't about to announce a breakthrough.

*

Forty-five minutes later, Henwell was out of the building and hurrying back towards the Tube. A few more nods of recognition and smirks as he'd pushed his way to the door, then he was free.

Normally he'd have been livid at having his time wasted like that. Not today though. After a few more platitudes, Simpson had stepped back and given the floor to none other than everyone's favourite waste of time and space…

Ladies and gentleman, Dr Neeeeillll White.

The psychologist was dressed as yesterday, crisp white shirt and chinos under a blazer with shiny buttons. Probably what all the smart profilers about town were wearing this year. To Henwell, he looked like a mildly successful country solicitor on his day off.

And the important update on the case? White had only gone and added more detail his profile.

Way to go Neil. Henwell had sensed the silent groans from his fellow disbelievers around the room.

Having consulted with several peers in the US, White was now leaning more towards the view that the killer was simply a man obsessed with celebrity. It wasn't an attempt to get himself noticed at all, apparently. In the killer's mind, murdering celebs brought him closer to them. Henwell didn't see what this new theory added. Or what actual evidence White had to back it up. But with the psychologist leading Simpson's team further and further down the crazed fan-boy route, Henwell would have a little more time to pursue his own very different line of investigation.

The District Line back to town was quiet and he managed to bag a seat on the end of the row. He pulled out the next case file from his bag, checking for prying eyes before he opened it and dived in.

Matt Street, victim number three.

Roberts had read the file the night before and found nothing. But it always paid to check, particularly as he remained unconvinced about the sergeant's work ethic.

Street's was a similar story to the others. No forensics from the scene and nothing from the neighbours in the busy block the victim had called home. What exactly had happened to the nation's curtain-twitchers?

The former England cricketer had been known for his flamboyance and flare with the bat. But he'd probably made more headlines for diving under the covers with a string of young actresses and models than he had for driving through them on the pitch. Who knew the sound of leather on willow would prove so alluring for the ladies?

Older, and significantly balder, now, he'd carved out a new niche for himself as a wildlife presenter. He'd recently been chosen to front a forthcoming Netflix show on native British mammals. That was until the killer had finished him off in a style that paid tribute to his careers old and new. Beaten to death with the cricket bat he'd used to score a century against the Australians at Lord's; an improvised gag made from a stuffed weasel and some gaffer tape had kept the noise to a minimum.

Henwell finished reading and slipped the folder back into his bag as he stood for his stop. Again, there was nothing new to be learned and nothing Simpson's team, or Roberts had missed.

*

'Sir. Sir.' Lidstone was up and out of his seat again the moment Henwell pushed the door open.

It has a habit that needed to be broken fast.

'You've got to see this.' The DC did a funny little dance as if he'd wet himself if he had to hold the news in for any longer.

'What is it, Danny?' Henwell held back a sign, remembering he was supposed to be encouraging the lad.

'Mickey Morris. I've found the murder weapon.'

'We've already got the murder weapon.' Roberts snorted. 'It was left at the scene, remember?'

'No. I mean, I know where it came from.'

DS Prim had given a short update on the Mickey Morris case once Dr White had finally finished spouting off. The ring-round of medieval re-enactment societies had drawn a blank. Turned out they all had modern-day armourers, who took great pride in their lovingly restored weapons. All halberds were present and accounted for, thank you very much.

'Look, there.' Lidstone pointed at his computer screen. It showed the home page of *A Hard Day's Knight*, the now-defunct medieval reality show, swiftly cancelled after Morris's death.

The cast were smiling nicely for the camera, all dressed up in ridiculous medieval garb: a knight, a nobleman, a jester, a monk, the predictable busty serving wench, etc., etc. And there, placed oh-so casually against the wall in the corner of the set, a dirty great halberd.

'I spoke to the props department.' Lidstone rushed to get the words out. 'They said they can't find it right now.'

Henwell just shook his head. They were missing a huge battle-axe and nobody had thought to tell the police. Unbelievable.

'Let's get down there. Find out who had access to the set.' Roberts managed to ease himself out of his chair. It seemed there was still a bit of old-fashioned copper's pride inside the man after all.

'No.' Henwell raised a hand. 'Great work Danny, but we need to give this back to Simpson's team.' It was how he'd agreed to play it. And given how careful the killer had been up until now, Henwell suspected the lead on the murder weapon would get them nowhere.

'But sir…' Lidstone's earlier excitement was quickly evaporating.

Henwell fished DS Prim's card from his pocket. 'Only right that you get the chance to break the news.' After all her team's work, Prim would be mortified that they'd been beaten to the murder weapon. And all the more embarrassing if the news came from a junior officer. 'Then I want you both to drop everything. Find out all you can about this man.' He fished into his jacket pocket for the picture that Sally Jarvis had given him, the name scrawled across the back in biro. 'Any links to the murder victims. Criminal record. If he's had so much as a parking ticket or farted when he shouldn't, I want to know about it.'

'Doesn't look like he fits the profile.'

'That's because he doesn't.' Henwell turned and headed for his office. 'I want everything you can find by five.'

Whatever they found was likely to be inconclusive. But it might just be enough to get an arrest warrant that evening, given the nature of the crimes and the potential flight risk. And then they'd have their man in custody for twenty-four hours. Henwell thought about how that might play out.

A cold, uncomfortable interview room.

Just a desk between them.

Some inept showbiz lawyer riding shotgun at the suspect's side.

Questions, questions, questions. Henwell probing, slowly picking away at any weaknesses and inconsistencies.

All manner of interesting things might come out.

He closed his office door and flopped into his chair. Less than two days on the job and he'd come further than Simpson's whole team in three months.

One phone call.

One tip-off.

Could it really be that easy? He ran it through his mind again, liking the odds that little bit more.

But still not quite enough. No harm in seeing what his old pals at the mobile networks could dig up. That word of Connor's came to mind again.

Latitude.

Chapter 9

'No!!!' Emilie took a sip of her wine and turned to look up at Dermot, her big eyes glassy and a little unfocused from the alcohol. 'Why didn't you tell me?'

Back in the day, Dermot had devoted a good part of his waking hours to telling pretty girls he was in a band. But that was all a long time ago. And it wasn't something he'd come close to sharing with Emilie.

For bloody good reason too. Now Anton had gone and spilled the beans all over the nice white tablecloth.

The evening had been going just fine right up to this point. As Anton had predicted, his name had been enough to secure a table at The Ivy, the long-time Covent Garden hang-out of the famous. They'd been treated like minor royalty on arrival before being shown to a table tucked away in a discreet corner. But not so out of the way that they couldn't be seen. That was the point of going to somewhere like The Ivy, after all.

'Tell her, my friend.' Anton leaned forward, his back to the room as he took another sip of wine, his smile twinkling playfully in his eyes.

'Please…' Emilie leaned in closer to Dermot. She'd pretty much hung on his every word through their starters and main course, those eyes rarely leaving his face. How much worse was it going to be now she knew he'd once been a pop star?

Thankfully, Anton didn't appear to have cottoned on to Emilie's behaviour: far too busy, ordering the best wine, quizzing the waiter about the menu and talking about himself.

'OK, OK.' It was probably best to get it over with and move on. 'I was in a band for a while. We had a few hits then we broke up.'

'I think you had more than a few hits.' Anton shook his head in mock admonishment. 'Four number ones, wasn't it?'

Five actually, but best to play that down. He just smiled back at Anton. 'I didn't know you knew so much about me.'

'Oh, I did my research.' Anton smiled knowingly.

'Come on, tell me more.' Emilie was jiggling about next to him in a way that could only be described as distracting. Her dress took the words 'low cut' to a different level.

'It was over almost before it began.' Dermot shook his head. 'We split up after eighteen months. Robbie Gray went solo. And the rest is history.' The words were out before he realised his mistake.

'OH MY GOD. You were in Robbie Gray's band.'

Well, no. It had never been 'Robbie's band,' not back then. But Dermot nodded all the same.

'I had posters of him all over my room.'

Yeah. Like every other teenage girl on the planet. Dermot had sung lead on four of their five number ones, with Robbie on backing vocals. But again that kind of information wasn't going to help matters right now.

'And you are still friends?' Emilie shifted round in her chair, leaning in to offer him the clearest view down her dress yet.

'Not really, no.' Dermot kept his eyes on her face. 'It was all a long time ago. You tend to drift apart.' That and the fact that Robbie Gray was the biggest bellend the human race had ever produced.

'Why didn't you go solo too?' Her eyes were even brighter and wider now.

'I did.'

'What happened?' Her smile faded away as a wave of crimson crept upwards from the top of her dress to her face. 'I'm sorry.' She grabbed for her drink, nearly knocking it over.

'Don't worry. It just didn't work out.' He tried for a sympathetic smile. 'As I said, it was a long time ago.' Hopefully the lingering stench of old failure would cool her interest.

'Well, let's drink to you and Robbie Gray anyway.' Anton thrust his glass across the table.

Dermot raised his glass to be polite, looking around for the waiter and wondering if he could persuade the Belgians to skip dessert. Then they could call it a night before Emilie drunk too much more or Anton jumped to any wrong conclusions. Next to him, he felt his assistant shift that little bit closer. And by the time he'd managed to spot a waiter, the chef was already calling the man over and asking for the dessert menus and another bottle of wine.

Great.

*

'Well, that was magnificent.' Anton sat back and surveyed the empty plates.

The extra bottle of wine the Belgian had ordered was all but gone too. Dermot had restricted himself to a small glass, leaving Anton and Emilie to polish the rest off. Maybe it was all that high-octane beer brewed by the monks, but these Belgians could certainly put it away. The only consolation was that Emilie didn't seem any more drunk or flirty than she had been after the first bottle. She flashed him a quick smile as she excused herself and headed to the ladies.

Anton took another long slug of his wine, those twinkly eyes not so twinkly anymore as they locked in on Dermot. If there was ever going to be a man-to-man talk about the chef's 'niece', it would be now.

But thankfully, Anton's thoughts were elsewhere. 'Tell me again why you British like to make your jokes about there being no famous Belgians?' It was one of his favoured themes, up there with the claim that his countrymen had actually invented French fries and the cruel mockery they endured in Britain for enjoying them with mayonnaise rather than ketchup.

Dermot just offered another shrug. It was definitely time to bring the evening to a close before Anton drank too much more.

'And do you know why so few Belgians find fame?'

He did, yes. Mainly because he'd heard the theory from Anton on many occasions.

'It's those Dutch bastards. And the French. They've got the whole entertainment business sewn up, worldwide. That's why we never get a look in. Take The Smurfs.'

Molly had enjoyed the movies chronicling the adventures of the little blue folk, but given the opportunity Dermot would have passed.

'They're Belgian I tell you.' Anton reached out for his glass of wine, which was nearly empty. 'Les Schtroumpfs. That's what they were originally called, until the Dutch came along and re-named them. De Smurfen… Ridiculous. Now the whole world thinks they come from Holland.'

Surely the opportunity to blame the Dutch for The Smurfs was a bullet well dodged.

'Zombies as well.' Anton was really warming to his theme now. 'It was a Smurf story that introduced the idea of the living dead, nine years before the first zombie movie. Nine Years! We lose the Smurfs we lose the credit for the whole zombie genre too.' The chef sat back in his chair with a sigh and a shake of his head.

It was a lot to take in, but if there was such a showbiz-wide Franco–Dutch conspiracy to keep the Belgians down, Dermot wasn't aware of it. He'd once made the mistake of asking Anton for evidence of this plot. The Belgian hadn't been able to provide any. But then that was the point according to Anton. The lack of proof was proof itself of how deep and widespread the whole vile plot ran. The chef figured that he'd only got his break because the French and their Dutch allies hadn't yet found a way to control YouTube.

But they would.

Dermot finally managed to catch the waiter's eye and made the sign for the bill.

Anton leaned further across the table, jabbing out a finger. 'Like I said, I checked you out. Made sure there wasn't any Dutch in you. Or French.'

'He's only joking.'

Dermot felt a hand on his shoulder as Emilie stepped up next to him. She didn't seem in any hurry to remove it.

'I most certainly am not, my dear.' Anton was too caught up by his theme to notice. Then he shook his head and smiled. 'Look at

Napoleon. Did you know Waterloo is in Belgium? He just did that to piss us off.'

Dermot didn't know a whole lot about European history but he suspected it looked a little different viewed through the distorted prism of an anti-Belgian conspiracy theory.

'They've always been out to get us.' Confident he'd landed his point, Anton stood and headed off unsteadily in the direction of the gents.

'I'm sorry.' Emilie slipped back into her seat next to Dermot. 'He's so proud of his country. All the prejudice really annoys him.'

'You think he's right?'

A dark cloud passed across Emilie's eyes for a second, but then the smile was back. 'I don't know, but he's convinced. Not that many of us are famous.'

'And the French fries?'

'We definitely invented them. There's a museum in Bruges.' For a second, the cloud was back. Then she smiled again and laughed. 'And we just like them with mayonnaise, OK?'

Dermot smiled back for a second then looked away, remembering he wasn't supposed to be encouraging her. The silence started to stretch towards uncomfortable, so he had a look round the restaurant, wondering where that waiter was with the bill.

Then Anton was back, riding a wave of bonhomie, all talk of conspiracies gone. 'This is on me.' As the waiter finally appeared, Anton handed over his credit card, not bothering to look at the bill. Then he turned back to Dermot and Emilie, his dark eyes twinkling mischievously. 'We could go on somewhere else? The night is still young.'

It was just about the last thing Dermot needed, but rescue came from an unexpected source.

'You have an early start tomorrow, Anton.' Emilie's face was all seriousness now.

'Oh yes.' The chef grinned sheepishly.

And Dermot remembered too. Anton had to be up by 6 am, to appear on one of the Saturday-morning cookery shows. There was even talk of a regular guest slot if things went well. Just one more step towards the culinary domination that Dermot was planning for the chef.

'Then we'd better call it a night.' Anton stood, waiting to embrace Dermot as he extracted himself from behind the table.

And just a few short minutes later, the evening Dermot had been so dreading was over. They parted on the pavement, Anton giving him a cheery wave and Emilie a final long lingering smile, as Serge held open the door to their car. Dermot gave a little wave of his own, before turning away to hail a passing cab.

Road works on the A4 ensured the journey back to Chiswick was longer than usual, but Dermot had plenty to keep his mind occupied. What to buy Molly for Christmas for one. And how he was going to deal with the other little problem on the horizon.

The cab dropped him off a little after midnight. Dermot paid the driver with a generous tip and headed for his flat. He was halfway up the path before he spotted the two men waiting at his door.

The last time he'd had an unexpected caller it had ended in a whole world of trouble and nearly cost him his life. But then the visitors weren't entirely unexpected this time. He paused as he noticed the car on the road and the van behind it. Another group of figures, all dressed in black were lit up by the streetlight. The taller of the two men started down the path towards him, something held aloft in his right hand. It seemed like Dermot's other problem had just got that bit bigger. The horizon a whole lot closer too.

Chapter 10

Sophie Harper hadn't been kidding about the laptop. A final sweep of the computer's deepest, darkest domains had finally hit pay dirt. Files and files of it squirrelled away in a set of encrypted folders that had actually been deleted. But fully recoverable if you knew what you were doing.

Anna and her team had spent the rest of Friday afternoon and a good chunk of the evening going trawling through all the information, trying to make some sense of it. Now, just shy of nine on Saturday morning, she was up in Lawson's office about to lay it out for him. And if the situation was serious enough to disrupt the DG's weekend plans, Anna would have no issue cancelling on Amanda that evening. Work came first and missing the dinner would almost certainly go down as a lucky escape.

Lawson grunted, eyes down, flicking through the short summary Anna had included at the front of the file like the diligent little spook she was. Finally, he looked up with a sigh. 'Economic terrorism then?'

'We think so.' It was the way all the evidence pointed. Pages and pages of modelling, showing a wide range of scenarios for the UK economy. The estimates showed reductions in GDP ranging from numbers in low single-figure billions to close to £500 billion per year.

Lawson turned the page and stared down at the rows of numbers before looking up. 'The recovery's still very fragile. Anything that wipes billions off the economy could tip us back into recession.' He leaned back in his chair. 'That could mean budget cuts for us. And God knows things are tight enough already.'

He shook his head. A Cold War veteran and a field man at heart, Anna knew he favoured good old-fashioned tradecraft over spread sheets and management speak. But that was exactly why MI5 couldn't have had a better leader right now.

'And there's no intel on the target?'

'No sir.' Anna shook her head. That was the problem, they had absolutely no idea.

'Physical attack or cyber?'

Again Anna shook her head. Nothing in all the files they'd recovered had revealed the specific details of the threatened attack; just all those economic scenarios.

'Where did your source get all this?'

'We don't know.' Sophie Harper's team were working on that but weren't hopeful.

'And there's no chatter?'

Another shake. Usually, they'd expect a bit of online chit-chat among the various groups and crazies GCHQ monitored, when something big was in the offing. But again there'd been nothing. 'Whoever's behind this, they're keeping it tight.'

And that was the other problem. The 'who' could be anyone. Islamists, Chinese, Russians, North Koreans? Climate activists even? An established organisation, a splinter group or an entirely new one? Without the first clue where to start, they'd need to look at all of them.

'And nothing from the Cousins?'

'No. We've spoken to Langley, the NSA, Secret Service, Homeland Security.' Given the Americans' reluctance to share intelligence among their own security organisations, it always paid to check in with all of them.

'Timings?'

'Nothing sir.' There were only so many times Anna could shake her head.

He looked back at the folder. 'These files are over three months old.'

'Or older.' That was only the date they'd been downloaded onto Olivier's laptop.

'So it might not even be happening anymore.'

'Except they just killed Olivier.' Someone had wanted to keep the information a secret. 'The techs think he must have left a trail when he stole the data.'

'True. We can't risk leaving it.' He shook his head.

No. But the real risk for Anna was that he might take it away from her. Not long ago she'd been stuck behind a desk reviewing and filing research reports. Nobody could say she didn't deserve to get where she had, but sometimes she had to pinch herself. Lawson could have been forgiven for thinking something this big should be handed on to someone with more experience. She held her breath as his eyes dropped to the file again.

'OK.' He finally looked up at her. 'I need you to run with this now. Find out what's going on, assess the actual threat level and deal with it.'

Anna breathed again.

'Keep sweating GCHQ. Get on to the Treasury too. The Economic Threats Unit needs to be aware of this. And the City of London Police. Get back on to the Americans and the counter-terrorism guys in Brussels. They're still prepared to share with us. For now at least.'

She nodded, even though she'd done all that already.

'And what do we make of this?' Lawson had flicked through to the last page of the file.

Anna leaned across the desk to confirm what he was looking at, her eyes running down the list of seemingly random letters and numbers. 'We're not sure yet, sir. Not even sure if it's relevant. It was saved in the same file. Sophie's team are looking at it again, and we've sent it to the cryptologists to see if its some sort of code.'

'OK, keep pushing them.' He grunted again as he closed the file and pushed it back across the desk. 'Everyone's got a lot on, and you need to make it clear to them all that this is a priority.'

'Will do.' Anna reached out and took the folder as she stood, taking it as her dismissal. It was unlikely that this was the only urgent issue that had brought Lawson in today. And she'd pulled the whole team away from their weekends. They were all downstairs, reading the intel while they waited for instructions.

Even Felicity Diamond.

The golden child had floated in around eight-thirty, carried by a gently scented zephyr of warm air. Birds had chirped merrily in her wake and pretty little flowers had bloomed every time her achingly fashionable shoes had kissed the ground.

'Just hang on a moment.' Lawson stood too. 'I need to talk to you about something else.'

'OK.' She looked at him warily now, sensing his discomfort.

'First I need you to promise me you won't get distracted. This terrorism thing has to be your number one priority.'

'Of course.' Anna tried not to show any sign of irritation. He'd given her the assignment; why question her professionalism now?

'That's what I thought.' He let out a deep sigh. 'The Met has made an arrest in connection with the celebrity murders. They're keeping it under wraps because of the level of media interest, but it's bound to get out sooner or later.'

'OK. Well, that's good, isn't it?' She'd been half following the case, mainly because it was impossible to avoid the wall-to-wall media coverage. Drought? War? Famine? Nah, who cared when real live celebrities were getting bumped off? But she didn't see what it had to do with her.

He looked at her for a long time then told her who'd been arrested.

Ah…OK. Anna could see now why he'd been so concerned about how she might react.

Chapter 11

Dermot looked around the grey walls of the windowless room. The clock on the wall was the only feature of any note. Right now it was telling him it was twenty past eight, exactly ten minutes since the sergeant had brought him up from his cell, saying his lawyer was here.

But still no lawyer.

Well… If this was some sort of little game to unnerve him, it wasn't going to work. Sitting up here with a nice hot cup of tea was nowhere near as bad as being down in the cell.

His night had been largely sleepless, on a thin mattress that would have served him better as a sheet. Someone in the next cell had insisted on shouting out each time Dermot had been about to drop off. But he must have slept eventually. One minute it had been pitch-black, and the next a dim light was filtering in through the high window. And however bad the cell had been, he'd been in worse places. They could play their little mind games, but that was fine. They had nothing on him.

They couldn't have.

Dermot yawned and stretched. Just keep it calm. There really was no need to panic.

He rubbed at the stubble on his chin, thinking how nice it would have been to shave. All he'd got was a cold-water wash in a bowl and an unnecessarily abrasive towel to dry himself. But then razor blades and prisoners were hardly an ideal combination.

'It's not a hotel, you know.' The custody sergeant had clocked the look of disgust on Dermot's face at the weak tea and plate of scrambled eggs he had been served back down in his cell.

He reckoned he'd actually stayed in worse hotels in his time. He just hadn't bothered with the breakfasts. But today he'd made sure he drunk the tea, cold but sweet, and even forced himself to eat the eggs, which had somehow managed to be runny and dry at the same time. It was likely to be a long day, and there was no way of knowing when they next planned to feed him.

Dermot sat back, drumming his fingers on the table, wondering what had happened to his solicitor. Thankfully, it wasn't his weekend to have Molly. Otherwise, he'd have had to use his one phone call to contact Sarah and rely on his ex-wife to sort out a lawyer, as she seethed over her own ruined weekend plans.

Instead, he'd called Emilie.

'Dermot?' Her sleepy Belgian voice had been edged with concern as she'd picked up the phone a little after two am. It had taken her a minute or so to wake up properly and the same again to calm down, once he'd told her about his arrest. After that, his first instruction had been to deal with any calls from clients. The second to get on to his lawyer first thing in the morning.

Terry Jackett had helped get a couple of his clients out of compromising situations in the past and had been paid well for his services. Dermot had no doubt that the layer would come through for him, even at the weekend. Although right now, it looked like he was doing it rather slowly.

The clock on the wall told Dermot he'd been sitting there for fifteen minutes now. He leaned forward, breathing in deeply as he felt the fear coming back at him, as it had at regular intervals throughout the night. He stared at the grey walls around him, thinking back to what he'd done.

Every last stupid thing.

The walls were probably similar to those of the cell where he'd spend the next thirty or so years if he was found guilty. Just a TV and some books to keep him occupied. Oh, and a big lifer called Tyson or Gerald for company. It was unlikely his cellmate would worry overly about the men Dermot had been convicted for killing. He'd probably have done far worse himself. But he might have a thing or two to say about the women. Along with plenty other inmates around the place. Cons were known for being traditional like that.

So, so stupid. But then they couldn't have anything on him. He'd been careful. Dermot took some more deep breaths and the panic started to ebb away, gone almost as quickly as it had come.

Calm, calm, calm. That was better.

But then he was thinking about Molly. What would they tell her? And how would she handle the playground shame of a murdering father locked up in prison? Would she visit? Would she hate him forever?

He tried to shake the thought away. Just keep it together, alright. They had nothing on him. Not really.

'Jesus.' He was up on his feet, jumping like a startled animal as he heard a key in the door. He really hoped that yelp had only happened inside his head.

The door opened slowly to reveal the figure of a woman. Five foot three at the very most but every inch of her radiating unmistakable confidence. She looked him up and down as she walked slowly into the room.

'You're not Terry.' Dermot was suddenly aware his mouth was still hanging open. That yelp hadn't been silent after all.

'I think that's lucky for both of us, don't you?' She kicked the door shut with the heel of what looked like an extravagantly expensive shoe, before walking to the other side of the desk and putting her bag down.

Dermot stood opposite her, unsure of what to say as she rifled around in the bag, finally retrieving a pen and notebook.

'Saturday mornings… They're not really Terry's best time of the week. Most mornings aren't these days, nor afternoons.' There was no hint of a smile at her little joke. Clearly not a woman who found it necessary to break the ice.

'But he's representing me.'

'No, I'm representing you. Saskia Torrance.' She thrust out a hand across the desk. 'Mr Du Beurre felt I'd do a better job than some washed-up has-been. Shall we sit?'

'Terry's a friend of mine.'

'That's nice for you both. You can buy him a drink once I've got you out. Make it several, to thank him for *not* representing you.'

He opened his mouth to protest, but his heart wasn't in it anymore. The idea of having this woman as his lawyer, rather than a renowned booze hound, was growing more attractive by the second.

'Good.' She opened her notepad. 'Now there's a couple of policemen upstairs very keen to put you away for murder. Let's see if we can stop them, shall we?'

*

'So don't answer any questions unless I say so. You understand?'

Dermot nodded; it must have been the fifth time she'd given the same instruction over the past forty-five minutes. Each time speaking slowly and clearly, as if to a small and rather dim-witted child. He might have gone and got arrested, but Dermot was pretty sure his IQ hadn't plummeted after a single night in the cells.

'This first interview is all about finding out how much they know. We'll get a view from the questions they ask. You don't need to answer anything if we decide it won't help.'

By 'we' she meant 'she' of course.

'At this stage, they're just trying to get enough to hold you for longer.' She leaned back in her chair, hard blue eyes still on him.

If he'd met her in different circumstances, he might have found her attractive, beautiful in a severe and totally unforgiving kind of way. Like a granite cliff face (albeit a small one) bathed in sunlight after a chance spring shower. But then it was difficult to imagine the kind of circumstances in which they might have met outside the police station. He certainly couldn't see her setting foot in the Soho drinking establishment Dermot tended to favour. And it was pretty clear that she came from money, from entitlement too. Probably the daughter of a judge, maybe two judges. Doing her best to prove herself to them and make up for a loveless childhood. One she'd inflict on her own children one day without even realising. Saskia Torrance probably knew that people called her a bitch behind her back. But to her, it would be a compliment. But then didn't that make her exactly the person he wanted in his corner?

'OK.' She leaned forward again and opened up the folder, reading out the charges against him.

Charlie McGee, Jane Holland, Matt Street, Zara Dunn, Nicole Berry, Kevin Story, Martin Crawley and Mickey Morris.

Eight celebrities. All dead.

And all Dermot's former clients.

Even he could see how it looked.

'If that's all they've got, they've got nothing.' She sat back again and fixed him with a stare. 'That's why you don't answer any question unless I say so.'

Was that the sixth time she'd said that or the seventh? He was beginning to lose count.

'Want to know something about me, Mr Jack?' It sounded like she was going to tell him anyway. 'I don't like losing.'

That had to be good.

'And because I don't like losing, I usually don't.'

Even better.

'To be honest, I don't really give a toss what happens to you.' The words jarred in her cut-glass accent. 'But I do care about my record. So don't say anything that helps them out. OK?'

Eighth time?

He nodded. The more skin his lawyer had in the game, the better.

'They'll come at you hard from the start.' Something in her eyes softened, if only a little. 'You need to be ready for that.'

'The old good cop, bad cop routine, right?' Dermot was fairly sure he'd be able to handle it.

'They don't really go in for that.' The first hint of a smile, along with a little shake of her head. 'That's only on TV.'

Oh.

'It's mainly just bad cop and complete arsehole.'

He could handle that too, far simpler if nobody was pretending to be his best buddy.

'Last question.' That hint of softness had gone from her eyes, the smile as well. 'Is there anything at all you haven't told me?'

Dermot tried to hold her gaze but couldn't. He let his eyes fall to the table, a guilty schoolboy caught in a lie.

Her sigh was like the north wind. 'If you did do it, I really don't want to know, OK? You're innocent until proven guilty, remember. Anything else, you need to tell me.'

He kept his eyes on the table, still weighing it up.

'I'm your solicitor. It's far better that I know now.'

He finally looked up.

And then he told her.

She did a bit of swearing then. Again the words sounding out of place in her polished accent. Her eyes stayed locked in on his. Cold, hard, determined. But somewhere, beneath all that perma-frost, something was stirring.

Doubt.

'You'd better go through it from the beginning again.'

So he did.

Then she made him repeat it once more before telling him exactly what she wanted him to say.

Chapter 12

That little rush of adrenalin, the tingle of electricity. Henwell felt it as he looked through the one-way glass into the interview room. Because this was what the job was all about. Taking the suspect and slowly, sometimes almost gently, breaking them apart. Until there was nothing left for them to do but pour it all out in confession. It often felt like a kindness in the end.

And it would be no different for Dermot Jack.

Henwell continued to study the man on the other side of the glass. He was leaning back in his chair with his eyes shut, pretending to be completely unfazed by his sudden arrest and night in the cells. Henwell doubted he was even fooling himself.

Dermot finally opened his eyes and stared right back at the glass. And now, with those eyes wide open, there was no real hiding it. The journey from being a normal person to a suspect was complete. Innocent or guilty, everyone who ended up here made that trip.

Next to him, the lawyer sat calmly looking at her papers. Saskia Torrance was Henwell's real opponent here, not Dermot Jack. Her slender, five foot three-ish frame, combined with her eye-watering fees, made the former Lord Chancellor's daughter about the most expensive criminal lawyer – pound for pound – that London had to offer.

Henwell had never crossed swords with her. Representing the kind of drug dealers he'd spent his career sending down wasn't the way to build a reputation for winning. It was all about the cases you took, the battles you picked.

And yet here she was, representing Dermot Jack. That alone made Henwell nervous.

He checked his watch again. Suspect and lawyer had been sitting in the interview room for about ten minutes. That was on top of the hour Saskia Torrance had insisted on spending in conference with her client. Add that to the time since they'd arrested Dermot early that morning and the initial twenty-four hours of custody was ebbing away fast.

But still, Henwell was being forced to wait.

'Sir?' Next to him, Roberts looked at his watch.

'Not yet.' He shook his head.

The sergeant let out a sigh of frustration. Lazy timeserver he may be, but like Henwell, he had the scent of a collar and was itching to get moving.

Sadly the same couldn't be said for Simpson.

The DCI had been keen enough on the arrest last night, practically wetting himself at the prospect of progress in his stalled investigation. And once the arrest warrant had been secured, he'd agreed that the threat to life and flight risk meant they should pick up Dermot there and then, rather than waiting for morning when they could have cracked straight on with the interrogation.

Now Simpson wasn't answering the phone or responding to messages. One minute he'd said he was on the way. The next, he was asking them to hold off until he'd contacted Dr White for advice to guide the interview.

Please somebody save us…

The profiler was certain to ask them to probe into the suspect's childhood, hoping for a record of bedwetting, animal torture, arson or any combination of the three. The Macdonald Triad as it was know, the three early signs of a psychopathic killer in waiting. Well… if you were a paint-by-numbers psychologist who thought all crime came out of a textbook and had never actually arrested anyone.

The only consolation was that the delay would be topping up Dermot Jack's levels of discomfort. His lawyer would be none too pleased either, although less easy to ruffle. Henwell took a minute to study her again, thinking she'd be genuinely beautiful if you could get past the scowl and the whole mini-ice-queen vibe. He kept his eyes on her for a second or so longer; then he was scrambling in his pocket as his phone started to buzz.

'Sir?' He resisted the temptation to ask where the hell his superior officer was.

'Hang on. I've got Dr White holding, bringing him on now.'

Henwell managed not to swear as the phone beeped.

'He's not your man, Detective Inspector.' White launched straight in, each and every one of his words reeking of smug self-assurance. But at least he'd got straight to the point. 'Doesn't fit the profile.'

'I thought profiles were meant to guide an investigation.' Henwell wasn't about to have his whole line of inquiry dismissed that easily.

'They do a bit more than that.' The good doctor sounded genuinely saddened at such an unenlightened attitude towards his work. 'They're a valuable tool that should shape every aspect of a criminal investigation.' He paused. 'We've all seen police officers go astray because they "like" a suspect without any real evidence.'

Yes, and they'd all seen investigations bogged down by the pedantic posturing of some idiot profiler.

'This is a solid lead, sir.' Henwell appealed directly to the DCI. 'They were all Dermot Jack's clients and all of them sacked him. It's a pretty strong motive.'

'But what else have you got?' There was a sharpness to Simpson's tone.

Well, there was the information from his contact at the mobile network. Inadmissible as evidence at best, illegally obtained at worst. Henwell wasn't going to share that with Simpson until he really had to. 'We need to interview him, sir. Sweat him, see what he gives up.' His hope was that this would give them enough to go back to the phone company and get the GPS location data the official way. Then they'd really be in business.

'We're under intense public and media scrutiny, as you know.' The DCI let out a long sigh. 'The Met simply cannot afford any more criticism.'

In Henwell's view, the Met was a pretty hardy institution, well used to having various shades of crap kicked out of it. A little more wasn't going to hurt. Simpson's career prospects were another matter.

'Your unit has operational independence in matters pertaining to the celebrity community.' The DCI continued before pausing.

Henwell kept quiet, experienced enough to recognise Met doublespeak when he heard it.

'The choice to progress with this is yours, but I won't have the main investigation sidetracked.'

The passing of the buck had never sounded so sweet. Henwell smiled at Roberts, resisted the temptation to punch the air.

'If there's no further evidence, and I mean real evidence, you'll need to release him.'

'Yes, sir.'

'And if there is anything at all, I want to know straight away. Understood?'

'Of course, sir.' It sounded a lot like cake and eating it. But Henwell would decide how much of that cake he'd be sharing. And exactly when he'd share it.

'One more thing.' Dr White jumped in again. 'You might want to find out about any childhood issues. Bedwetting…'

Henwell cut the call and turned to Roberts. 'Let's see what your interview technique's like, Sam. Time to prove that dick of a profiler wrong.'

*

Dermot Jack's gaze was on Henwell as he entered the interview room, trying to stare him out for one, two, three seconds. Then the suspect's eyes slid back down to the table in front of him.

A man with something to hide.

Beside him, the lawyer kept her own eyes on the papers in front of her. But as Henwell reached the table, she stood and looked up at him. A full-beam smile melted all the frost and ice clean away as she stuck out her hand. 'DI Henwell, I assume. Saskia Torrance.'

'Pleased to meet you.' He took her hand.

The shake lasted just that little bit longer than necessary. She blinked once, twice and then a third time. 'I've heard a lot about you.'

He doubted it. The smile, the compliment and that wide-eyed innocent-girl look were all part of the game.

One he wouldn't be playing.

'When your solicitor's quite finished, we can get on with it, Mr Jack.' He waited for her to sit then took his own chair, reaching out to hit play on the voice recorder. 'Interview commencing 9.46am. DI Henwell and DS Roberts in attendance. Suspect Dermot Jack. Also present, Saskia Torrance. Over to you, Sergeant?' He turned to Roberts, who was taking his time putting his papers and a half packet of biscuits on the table.

The lawyer let out a long sigh as her eyebrows climbed towards the ceiling, her frustration already evident. It felt like an early goal for the cops.

*

Little more than an hour later, the game seemed to be grinding towards a tedious draw. Roberts had proved to be a competent interrogator and every bit as irritating as Henwell had hoped. But still, he'd failed to get under Dermot Jack's skin. The lawyer had prepped her client well, it seemed.

Roberts paused to look down at his notes then leaned forward for another go. 'Tell us again about your relationship with Matt Street?' He'd already been through each of the murder victims one by one, asking that same question. Now he was having another go round, hoping to uncover any inconsistencies. Or even better, lies.

Dermot Jack looked across at his lawyer, as he'd done with each question. She gave him a small nod.

'He was a client.'

'When?'

Another look at his lawyer. Another nod.

'I can't really remember. Four, five years ago.'

'We can check the exact dates in his business records.' Saskia Torrance was still operating in 'my client has nothing to hide' mode, playing at being helpful.

Henwell wondered how long that would last once they really got going.

'And where were you on the night he was murdered?' Roberts carried on probing.

'Come on.' The lawyer shook her head. 'You don't expect him to answer that?'

'OK. Where were you on 17th September this year?' The sergeant took a biscuit and sat back to wait for the answer.

'Look. I don't know, do I? I've told you that already.' Dermot looked at Henwell then back at Roberts, the first sign of exasperation creeping into his voice.

Saskia Torrance noticed it too. She reached out and put a hand on his arm. 'As we've already said, we'll check my client's diary and get back to you with details of where he was on all of the dates in question.'

'OK. Jane Holland –' Roberts made to move on.

Henwell cut him short with a wave. The lawyer would be demanding a break soon, and they were yet to land a significant blow. There was always the possibility that Dermot Jack's DNA might come up at one or more of the crime scenes. Lidstone had the lab retesting for matches now they'd taken a sample. Or they could get something from the search of his flat and office. The SOCOs had started first thing, and two computers had already been sent to the IT team for closer inspection. But Henwell knew they were likely to need something from the interview.

'Where were you on the night of 14th October? The night Kevin Story was murdered at the Dominion Theatre.' He decided it was time to play one of his trump cards. 'It isn't that long ago. And it would really help if you could remember.'

'Listen.' The lawyer let out another long sigh. 'We've already established that my client used to work for all of the victims. That's not in doubt.'

'And that he was sacked by them all.'

'The exact circumstances vary in each case and – '

'Do you still work for any of them?' Henwell ignored her and turned to Dermot.

Eventually, the man shook his head.

'For the tape, Mr Jack.'

'No.'

'And did you decide to end these working relationships?'

Dermot looked to his lawyer again.

'You don't have to answer that.' The lawyer cut in.

'We'll take it as a no then.'

'You'll take it as a no comment.' A flash of anger lit up her eyes.

Henwell fought back a little smile at another point scored, however small.

'Back to 14th October. Can you tell us where you were that night?'

'No.'

'But you were at the theatre three days earlier, right? We have a witness and CCTV.'

They had neither actually. But the GPS data from Dermot's phone placed him at the theatre on the afternoon of the 11th. The CCTV and the witnesses might well follow once they'd had time to chase them up. 'What was it, a little recce?'

'Don't answer that.' The lawyer leaned forward, her hand on Dermot's arm again.

'No, it's OK.' Dermot looked at her then back at Henwell. 'I don't remember. But it's possible. I have a few clients doing theatre right now. Sometimes I go to see them at rehearsals.'

'OK. But someone you knew well was murdered three days later at a theatre you'd visited. That seems like the kind of thing that you'd remember.' Sadly, the mobile data didn't put Dermot back at the theatre on the night of the murder itself. But then any self-respecting serial killer would have the smarts to leave his phone at home.

'I didn't know him well. He was a client. It was years ago.'

'A client who sacked you.'

'Yes. No… I mean, things just didn't work out.' He turned to his lawyer, the frustration threatening to bubble over.

Things hadn't worked out for Kevin Story in the longer term

either. The eighties pop star had been found dead in his dressing room. Strangled with a microphone cord, the severed index finger of his right hand superglued to his lips. It was a crude nod to the scandal that had all but ended Story's career. Two albums in, and at the height of his fame, the rumour that he hadn't actually sung on his records had taken root.

Career over.

Well, until the attempt at a reboot, nearly three decades on, with a musical featuring his hits. The live show had seen Story doing all the singing in an attempt to prove the doubters wrong and secure his legacy.

The critics hadn't been kind, although a rush of inevitable revisionism had followed his death. Story was now being lauded as a giant of the eighties pop scene, as opposed to a dirty little cheat who'd just mimed along to some over-orchestrated backing tracks.

'You can see our problem, can't you, Mr Jack? We've got multiple dead celebrities, all directly linked to you. And now we have you scouting out one of the murder scenes.'

'And that seems like all you've got.' Saskia Torrance shook her head, letting him know her patience was wearing thin. 'We've made it perfectly clear that my client will cooperate. This aggressive line of questioning is quite unacceptable –'

A knock on the door cut her off.

Henwell turned to see Lidstone pushing his way in, embarrassment and three flights of stairs painting his face a deep shade of red. 'Sir… There's something you need to see.'

When Henwell looked back at the lawyer, she was puffing out her cheeks with a long slow shake of her head.

And well she might. The prearranged interruption with 'urgent news' had to be one of the oldest tricks in the police interrogation book. Designed to unsettle the suspect and the most gullible of junior lawyers. But it was never going to work with someone as experienced as Saskia Torrance. Which was exactly why Henwell hadn't planned anything of the sort.

'Interview terminated at 10.57am.' He stood and turned off the recorder. If Lidstone thought it was important, then Henwell wanted to hear it. Maybe it would give him enough to keep Dermot Jack in custody for another thirty-six hours?

The he'd be able to keep his remaining trump card up his sleeve for a little while longer.

Chapter 13

'We've looked at it carefully. If it is a code, we'd need a lot more to go on.'

Anna listened to her phone as the cryptologist explained how little help he was going to be.

'The only thing we can think of is that it could be a decryption key, even a set of keys to be applied sequentially. But without more information, we're shooting in the dark. Sorry. And if it is a key, we'd need the original text to apply it to.'

'Thanks anyway.' Anna scribbled the words *decryption key* on her notepad as she cut the call. Then she crossed them out. It was another dead end.

She slumped back in her chair and looked around the office. Sunday morning and she was about the only person there.

Saturday's effort had been a real team one, with everyone pulling their weight, even Felicity. They'd done just about all the liaising it was possible to do with police and intelligence agencies, both at home and abroad. But they'd come up with nothing. Anna had sent the team home at about 5pm so they could get on with their weekends, albeit on standby in case anything did come up. Not that it seemed likely.

And there was precious little reason for Anna to have come back in today. She could have waited for an update at home, or even over lunch at her sister's. She checked the time on her phone, just gone 10.30am, wondering how late it would be acceptable to phone and cancel. There'd be a bit of huffing and puffing, but ultimately her sister would understand. She was one of the few people who knew Anna didn't actually work for the Department for Transport.

Amanda had been slightly less sympathetic when Anna had pulled out of dinner the previous evening. But her friend's text earlier that morning suggested that Anna had already been forgiven.

OMG. Donal is HOTTTTT. I would if I was single. Not a banker (real or rhyming). Some kind of physicist. Has TWO dogs. FIT AS… Already said I'll set the two of you up 1-2-1. Axxx

Anna had made sure her reply was as non-committal as possible, although she'd already half decided to take her friend up on the offer.

But it was time to put Donal and his dogs (retrievers she imagined) out of her mind. Anna pulled her chair in and scanned over the set of numbers and letters from the email once more. In the absence of any other intelligence it was all they had to go on. Maybe she'd give it another hour then head over to her sister's house. The idea of a normal family Sunday lunch was beginning to seem more appealing as the text started to swim and blur before Anna's eyes.

She shook her head, bringing the page back into focus. Ten sets of letters and numbers. Processed by the most powerful computers in the land and then scrutinised by the ablest analysts and code breakers at MI5's disposal.

And nothing.

Anna had even done a bit of googling on the side because you never knew.

First up was CM069. The only reference they could find anywhere was to a kind of rifle used in Airsoft. It was a game like paintball but where the pellets didn't actually burst and make a mess all over you. Increasingly popular apparently, most likely with grown men who'd never seen real violence and laboured under the mistaken belief it held some sort of glamour.

Next, GC2610. The reference number of a replacement engine part for a hedge trimmer. Not really getting them anywhere, was it?

JH189 could refer to a type of wireless speaker or a distributor cap for a diesel engine. KS1410 was either the product code for an aircraft engine component or the reference for a two-bed rental apartment on a Croydon estate agent's website. Enquiries by local police had revealed the place was still vacant and not currently home to a bomb-making factory. Discreet background checks on the estate agent's staff were on-going.

MS239 could have been the flight number of Egypt Air's daily departure from Cairo to Luxor, although Anna failed to see how this could relate to a threat to the UK economy. The Egyptian security services had been informed of the potential threat but had reported no corroborating intelligence of their own. There was also a relatively unsuccessful indie artist from the US named Tiny MS239, whose 2015 release *Pop Off* hadn't troubled the charts on either side of the Atlantic. But it was unlikely that she was planning a terror attack in revenge for her poor sales.

MM0811 might have been a job-site reference code for a role as an accounts administrator in a small Birmingham engineering firm. More interestingly, it came up as the name of an anonymous profile on a popular gaming chat room. That was definitely something they were looking into further.

Another potential aviation reference was MDDJ1711. If you lost the numbers, MDDJ was the airport code for Dajabon airport in the Dominican Republic. But it was only a small domestic airport on the border with Haiti, with no international flights. They'd requested manifests to see if any passengers had joined or planned to join connecting flights to the UK at the country's main international airport. But that was likely to prove a slow process.

As far as she had been able to work out, NB0110 was the product code for a brand of insect repellent. They were coming up with nothing for RVP2411, and ZD299 was the reference number for a replacement ceramic disc for car brakes.

So maybe a crack team of terrorists planned to fly in from Egypt and the Caribbean and use the components to build a deadly device.

In a Croydon flat.

While protecting themselves from the police with a toy pellet gun and doing a bit of gardening on the side.

That was that then. They just needed to get down to the airport and arrest anyone who reeked of bug repellent (presumably in preparation for south London's fearsome insect population).

In short, they had nothing.

Anna's stomach chose precisely that moment to remind her that it hadn't eaten, and she thought about lunch again. It would take her mind off things for an hour or two, and hopefully, she could come back to it fresh later on. It might stop her thinking about Dermot as well. But yesterday's conversation with Lawson was already starting to replay itself in her head.

*

'It can't be him.' Anna had stared at her boss. She would have staked her life that Dermot wasn't a murderer.

'It does seem unlikely from what we know of him. Still, it's a police matter.'

'But he helped us… With Bukin.' The events with the Russians had played out in her mind. Lawson didn't know half of what Dermot had actually done.

'And we're grateful.' At least he'd had the decency to look uncomfortable. 'We simply can't be seen to be involved. Your judgement on this terrorism thing has been impeccable so far.' His eyes locked on hers. 'Don't give me any other reason to question it now.'

'No, sir.' She'd held his gaze.

He'd smiled as he stood, indicating that their meeting really was over. 'Your father would have been proud of you. You know that, don't you?'

Yes, she did. She also knew that David Preston wouldn't have sat on his hands when a friend was in trouble.

And Lawson did too.

'Very, very proud.' His voice had trailed off, eyes still locked on hers.

'*… can't be seen to be involved.*' She'd replayed his words in her head as she'd left Lawson's office. The message was simple. Just be discreet. And don't let me hear about it.

*

Anna had wrestled with the problem all through Saturday, too distracted by the terrorism threat to come to up with a plan of action, let alone actually do anything.

But her decision to sleep on it meant that she'd let Dermot spend a second night in the cells, and her guilt levels had grown rapidly throughout the morning.

She checked her watch, still plenty of time to get to her sister's place, so she opened up a news website and read the latest article about the celebrity killings. There was no mention of an arrest, which had to be good, didn't it? Maybe if she waited a few more hours, he might be released and she wouldn't have to get involved?

But could she really just stand by?

Dermot wasn't a killer, Anna knew that. The only thing he was guilty of was getting back into her head and her life.

Her choice had been simple that day eighteen months ago in St James's Park. A career with MI5 or another go at a relationship with her chancer of an ex-boyfriend? In the end, it had been a closer-run thing than she liked to admit. But it was a decision she'd never regretted.

And she still didn't regret it now. But that didn't mean that she wasn't going to try to help him.

Anna sighed as she reached for her phone. First up, she needed to hear what the gossip was in the Met. Who was running the case, what evidence they had and how strong it was? But she couldn't go via the official channels. The warning from Lawson played out in her head again.

She scrolled down her contacts until she found Charlie Gould's name. She'd worked with the anti-terrorism DI on an operation a few months back. Once the job was done, they'd taken the relationship outside of work.

But not that far.

A couple of meet-ups for early evening drinks and one rather awkward dinner later, Anna had made it clear that things would be going no further. Charlie still seemed to hold out hope though, if his periodic texts were anything to go by.

'Anna.' He answered on the first ring, not quite managing to hide the eagerness in his voice. 'How're things?'

'Good. Look, err… I need to ask you a favour.' She was fairly confident he'd share what he knew and keep quiet if it ever came out that she'd been asking.

'Great, let's have a drink in the week and talk about it.'

'It's a bit more urgent than that.'

'Well, let's have a drink anyway.'

'OK. How does Wednesday sound?' You couldn't fault him for trying. And it was a small price to pay.

'Yeah. Perfect.' He sounded surprised that she'd agreed so easily. 'How can I help?'

Anna quickly explained and rang off, after extracting a promise that he'd get back to her as soon as he'd made a couple of discreet enquiries.

He was back on the line less than ten minutes later. 'The investigation's being headed up by a DCI Simpson. Runs the MIT out of Putney. Solid copper, good record, destined for great things. Ambitious but won't cut corners to get results.'

So far, so good.

'He's not running this directly though. It's a DI Henwell. A bit of a maverick by all accounts.'

That was less good.

'Runs this new celebrity crime squad. Everyone thinks it's a joke. He'll want a quick collar to get himself out of there.'

Right now that collar looked like it belonged to Dermot.

'What evidence do they have?'

'Don't know. Enough to keep him in for more questioning after the initial 24 hours. I'll try to do some more digging.'

'OK, thanks. Call me if you hear anything else.'

'And Wednesday?'

'Oh yes.' Anna knew she wouldn't get him off the phone without a firm arrangement. 'Seven o'clock, same place as last time?' She said her goodbyes and rang off, still unsure what to do about Dermot. Any direct contact with the officers running the inquiry was out of the question. Even a sniff of MI5 trying to get involved would play very badly. All she could do right now was wait and see how it panned out.

Her eyes returned to the list in front of her. Anna decided to give it another half hour before heading to her sister's. But the numbers and letters started to swim again, as the late night and early morning in the office finally caught up with her.

*

She woke with a start, eyes focusing on the vibrating phone. Her sister's name lit up the screen. The time read 12.14pm.

Shit

'Hi, Jess, I'm really sorry…' Anna waited for some kind of excuse to pop into her sleepy brain. 'I…' Then she stopped herself as something else elbowed the excuse away. 'I… I've got to go.'

She cut the call and stared down at the paper in front of her, remnants of her dream still doing the rounds in her head. Somewhere in there was something she knew was important.

Dermot.

No.

But he chose that moment to pop into her head. Looking forlorn and lost in a police cell.

GO AWAY.

There just wasn't time for him right now.

Eyes on the paper again.

CM069, GC2610, KS1410.

The connection was there, floating tantalisingly out of range in her tired brain.

WAKE UP!

MS239, JH189.

But it had just been a dream. All her synapses firing at once, taking her waking thoughts and merging them into a warped new reality.

ZD299.

Or perhaps it was her subconscious putting it all together, getting to a place her waking brain hadn't quite managed.

MM0811. JH189. KS1410.

There was just something familiar. She reached out to grab it, but it danced out of reach.

MM0811. ZD299. NB0110. MDDJ1711.

Come on. She grabbed at it again, but again it slipped away. The thought of Dermot in his cell darted back in to take its place once more.

OK, OK, she'd help him. But could he please just leave her alone for now?

Her phone sprang to life. Jess again.

She could get lost too.

MM0811. KS1410. ZD299.

No, wait. Rewind. MM0811. That was the one that had sparked it. A job in Birmingham? Engineering?

And just when she thought she'd lost the connection, it was there, stepping confidently onto the stage in the centre of her brain, lit up by the spotlight and ready to do its party piece.

Of course…

But no, come on. That was just ridiculous.

Seriously, no way.

But her fingers were already flying over her keyboard and her brain was fully awake now, although still not quite ready to believe the evidence coming up in front of her eyes.

Chapter 14

Lidstone's interruption the previous afternoon had indeed been worthwhile.

Pay dirt. A jackpot of evidence.

Henwell's little team had worked late into Saturday evening and then on through Sunday morning going through it all.

The file, tucked away deep among the archived folders on Dermot Jack's office computer, had clearly not been meant to be found. They'd been looking for a smoking gun, and what they'd found was a whole arsenal, neatly gift-wrapped by the suspect. He might as well have sent it to them by special delivery. It had been more than enough to get custody extended for another thirty-six hours. And now with the clock ticking round towards 1pm, it was finally time to confront the suspect with the evidence. It was going to be a long day for Dermot Jack.

Henwell pushed his way through the interview room door, pressing the record button as he sat. 'Interview commencing at 12.57pm. DI Henwell in attendance, Dermot Jack and solicitor Saskia Torrance.'

'My client's whereabouts on the dates in question.' The lawyer pushed a sheet of paper across the table. It was a solid first move and one he'd entirely expected; the classic pawn-to-king-four opening in the chess match that was the police interview.

Henwell took the paper, folding it once and putting it on the table without even looking.

The lawyer nodded at him with a thin smile, acknowledging the equally predictable riposte. With the custody period extended, she must have anticipated that this morning wasn't going to be just about the alibis.

Well, now she knew.

Henwell looked across at her with his own smile. Today's outfit was far less severe than yesterday's. A blue top and linen trousers, instead of the dark-grey skirt and jacket. Maybe she was going for a softer, more conciliatory look. Or perhaps she had plans for later in the day that required a less lawyerly vibe.

Good luck with that. Henwell doubted she'd be going anywhere.

He turned his eyes onto the suspect. Dermot Jack managed to hold his gaze for all of a second, before looking at his lawyer then down at the table in front of him. He must have had a fair idea of what was coming too.

'On your own today, Detective Inspector?' It was the lawyer who finally broke the silence.

Henwell shook his head and nodded towards the door as it opened again. 'DS Roberts joining at 12.22pm.'

Again Roberts took a minute or two to settle, huffing and puffing as he arranged his papers and a new packet of biscuits that were already a third gone.

Saskia Torrance just shook her head, following up with her trademark eye roll; settling straight back into the 'expensive lawyer gets bored' routine she'd adopted for much of yesterday.

That wouldn't be lasting for much longer.

'I think it's time we talked about what we found on your computer, Mr Jack.' Roberts got straight to the point.

Dermot's eyes flicked towards his lawyer again then back down to the table.

'If you want my client to respond, you need to ask an actual question.' The lawyer sighed. 'But whatever you think you've found, it won't be enough to charge him.'

'You sure about that?' Henwell nodded to Roberts.

They'd printed out a selection of the documents from the laptop. All had been saved in different folders, each named with the initials of the victims. Not the smartest thing to have done, but you had to admire Dermot's filing. Roberts started to lay them out on the table, reading the headlines as he went.

'*McGee killer gets the last laugh.*

'*Matt Street killing: police stumped.*

'*Story microphone-cord strangling: No leads, say police.*' Roberts shook his head. 'Very droll, our friends in the press, aren't they?'

Roberts carried on laying out the cuttings. 'And it looks like you've kept your own little dossier on all of the murders. I'm sure you can see why we're finding that a bit suspicious.'

'It's all publicly available information.' Saskia Torrance reached out and picked up one of the articles, holding it up for emphasis. 'It doesn't prove anything.'

'Apart from an unusual level of interest in a series of violent murders.' Henwell leaned in to pick up his own cutting. 'Murders to which your client is already closely linked.'

'He has a perfectly plausible explanation.' She turned to Dermot with a nod.

Henwell couldn't wait to hear this one.

'It's like you said. I knew them.' Dermot sat forward in his chair. 'I was just trying to…' He trailed off as he turned to his lawyer.

'Go on. You've got nothing to hide.' Her eyes were on Henwell as she spoke. 'Tell them what you told me. Tell them the truth.'

That was a new one coming from a lawyer, but Henwell resisted the temptation.

Dermot swallowed, coughed and swallowed again. He wasn't sweating yet, but it wouldn't be long. Then he took a deep breath. 'It was after the third murder. That's when I realised they'd all been clients. Two could be a coincidence, but three?'

'OK.' Henwell raised a hand to stop him. 'So, let's get this straight. You're saying that you suspected you were the link between several high-profile murders and you didn't come to us?'

'Yes… No.'

'I think that's a no, because you didn't come forward, did you?' Henwell kept his eyes on the suspect. 'We could consider that as withholding evidence.'

'Or you could just listen to what he has to say.' The lawyer leaned back with another shake of her head.

'We're all ears.' Henwell propped his elbows on the table, eyes locked in on the suspect.

'Look, if word got out that my old clients were being killed, my business would have been finished.' The agitation was clear in Dermot's voice. 'You've got to see that.'

A fair-enough point, Henwell supposed, not that he was about to acknowledge that. He just fixed the man with his most dubious stare.

'And I thought you'd think…'

'That you did it?' Henwell couldn't resist a smile. 'That is what we think. So keeping quiet hasn't helped. In fact it's made it worse.' He kept his eyes on Dermot's, watching the anger build up and simmer away beneath the surface. It would bubble and bubble away until one final question brought it to the boil. Then Dermot Jack would say something he really shouldn't. Something he wouldn't be able to take back. And there'd be absolutely nothing his expensive little lawyer could do about it.

Saskia Torrance must have sensed the rising anger too. She raised a hand to stop Dermot as he made to speak again. 'You've got to ask yourself, Detective Inspector, exactly how much of a case you've got here.'

'Well, we've got motive for a start, opportunity too, and he's failed to explain why he's been following the murders so closely.'

'I've told you, I…' Dermot's voice rose a couple of notches, in pitch as well as volume. 'I didn't want my business ruined.'

'Tell them the rest.' His lawyer gave him an encouraging nod.

'Yes please. We can't wait to hear more.' Henwell smiled, sensing the anger getting closer and closer to eruption.

But when Dermot spoke, he sounded subdued, embarrassed even. 'I thought I could investigate it a bit, find the real connection. Then I would've come to you, I swear.'

'And how exactly are you qualified to investigate murder?' Henwell leaned back, encouraging Dermot to dig himself deeper.

'Look, I know it was stupid, OK.' His voice was rising once more. 'But I didn't kill anyone. It was just that… Last year, I got involved in something. With MI5. I helped them out with quite a delicate situation.'

'Go on?' Henwell smiled again as the hole got that little bit deeper.

'There was a Russian arms dealer. His daughter wanted to be a pop star. I can't really say any more. It's classified. But I guess working with MI5 sort of gave me a taste for it.'

'A taste for it? Wow. That's some story. Just when we were starting to believe you too.'

'Speak to them. They'll tell you.' The anger was back in Dermot's voice.

Henwell shook his head. 'If you really have worked with MI5, you'd know they like to keep things tight. Not really in the habit of giving character references. And you haven't explained your visit to the scene of Kevin Story's murder.'

Dermot's eyes flicked back to his lawyer. Another small nod.

'I went to warn him. Six of my former clients were dead. I figured he might be next.'

'And what did he say?'

'Refused to see me. Point-blank. Had the stage manager ask me to leave.'

'And there were witnesses?' This was getting better and better.

'Yeah, the stage manager, the ushers, couple of the cast.'

'Who can all testify that three days before he was killed, Kevin Story had you thrown out of the theatre?'

'No. I was just asked to leave. I wasn't thrown out.'

'OK.' Henwell nodded. 'Must have been humiliating though.'

'DI Henwell.' Saskia Torrance raised a hand. 'You're inferring things from what my client is saying.'

'That is kind of what we have to do. Spoiler alert, but not everyone we get in here tells us the truth.' Henwell gave her his best smile. Then he sat back again, watching Dermot Jack as the dam finally burst.

'You've got to believe me.' The man stood, slamming his fist down on the desk as he turned a shade of red that Lidstone would only ever aspire to.

'Sit down, Mr Jack.' Henwell kept his voice level.

'I've answered all your questions.'

'Dermot.' The lawyer reached out a hand.

'I've helped you as much as I can. Now you need to let me go.

I'm a busy man.'

'We don't *need* to do anything.' Henwell finally stood, nearly a head taller than Dermot. 'Now. SIT. DOWN.'

'Do as he says, please.' Saskia Torrance was standing too, reaching up to put a hand on her client's shoulder.

'Fine.' Dermot slumped back into his chair, the anger still in his eyes. 'I'll be making a complaint to your superiors. This is totally unacceptable.'

Henwell sat back down. Taking his time, letting the seconds tick by as he pretended to look at his notes. Then he raised his eyes to look at the suspect once more. 'Do you, err… watch many TV police shows, Mr Jack?'

'Yeah, sometimes.' There was confusion in Dermot's voice.

'Thought so.' Henwell paused for a beat or two. 'On TV you hear people saying things like you've just said all the time. Things like "I'm a very busy man", or "This is quite unacceptable", or "I'll be making a complaint to your superiors". They're often quite rude to the police on TV. Do you know why?'

Dermot shook his head, looking baffled.

'Care to enlighten him, Sam?' Henwell turned to his DS.

'It's just a plot device, isn't it? Makes the viewer think a certain character looks guilty or has something to hide.' Roberts smiled at Dermot.

Henwell waited a second or two, eyes on Dermot. 'And in your experience, Sam, do real suspects behave like that?'

'Nah.' Roberts snorted. 'Not the innocent ones, they're usually far too scared.'

Dermot Jack's mouth was slowly forming into a big wide 'O'.

'Glad we've got that one sorted.' Henwell stood. 'Let's leave it there for now while we check out these alibis.' What he really wanted to do was get upstairs and find out if anything had come back from the forensics lab. Frustratingly, they hadn't found any trace of Dermot's DNA or his fingerprints at the first six crime scenes. But there were still the last two results to come.

The lawyer nodded cautiously, clearly glad of the chance to calm her client down a bit, but equally wary of some kind of trap.

Best not to disappoint her then. He paused as he reached to turn off the recorder. 'And when we come back, I'd like to ask you about your visit to Portman Street Studios two days before the murder of Mickey Morris. Interview terminated at 13.32.'

It was the other trump card revealed by the GPS tracking on Dermot's phone. Henwell stood and left the room before the suspect or lawyer could say another word.

Chapter 15

'Interview recommenced at 14.02. DI Henwell and Sergeant Roberts, suspect Dermot Jack and his lawyer Saskia Torrance.'

Dermot watched as the big policeman leaned in, a self-satisfied smile across his face. It was the same smile that had been there throughout yesterday's interview and again that morning. 'Now, where were we?'

Henwell's eyes dropped to the notes in front of him, as he pretended to remind himself. It was all for show of course. The detective clearly knew exactly where they were.

Prick.

Dermot told himself to keep calm. It was all just to wind him up. That's what his lawyer had told him again during the break, before warning that they'd come at him hard this time.

'Oh yes.' Henwell finally looked up. 'We were getting on to your little visit to Portland Street Studios, where Mickey Morris was filming. Tell me about that.'

Dermot repeated the question word for word in his head, making sure there were no traps. Something else his lawyer had drummed into him. Then he turned to her.

She gave a small nod.

'I went to see Mickey Morris, to try to warn him.' There. He'd stayed calm, kept it simple. Just like she'd said.

'Like you did with Kevin Story?'

Another pause but he couldn't see any obvious pitfalls. 'Yes.'

'And let me guess. He refused to see you too.'

'Yes.' Dermot nodded. Calm, remember. Although that was easy for his lawyer to say. She wasn't one false step away from a multiple murder charge. But he felt like he was getting the hang of it now.

'Did you try to warn any other former clients?'

'No. Just him and Kevin Story.' He'd forgotten to pause that time. No harm done, but it had been sloppy all the same.

'OK.' Henwell pulled a face as he sat back, looking puzzled or pretending to. 'Just seems like a coincidence. The two ex-clients you say you went to warn end up dead.'

'I haven't been sacked by *that* many people.' Dermot tried to keep it light, pleased with his reply. Truth was, he'd never been hired by that many in the first place.

Henwell nodded without looking convinced. 'And after Morris refused to see you? What happened then? Did he have you thrown out?'

Dermot shook his head. 'No. It was all quite chilled.'

'What did you do then?'

'Just hung around the set. I know a couple of the production team, and I thought maybe I could catch a word with Mickey if he changed his mind.'

'So you'd describe the security arrangements as relaxed?'

'Yes.' Dermot turned to his lawyer, not sure where this was going. She shot him a warning glance.

'Sam?' Henwell turned to the fat policeman next to him.

The man made a show of wiping biscuit crumbs from his mouth then picked up an envelope from the desk. If Dermot had come to hate Henwell over the past couple of days, he loathed the fat sergeant even more.

Roberts reached into the envelope and slid out a photo. 'Did you see this on the set?'

It was a battleaxe, big and nasty looking. Dermot shrugged. 'Maybe. There were lots of weapons. It was a medieval reality show.'

'Well, this one was stolen from the set on the day you visited. And then it was used to kill Mickey Morris in his home two days later. You took it, didn't you?'

'No.' Dermot stole a quick look at his lawyer, trying to keep his voice steady. 'Of course not.'

'It's a bloody great battleaxe, Inspector.' Saskia Torrance suppressed a sigh. 'Do you really think my client could have just walked off the set with it?'

'Someone did.' Henwell ignored her, keeping his eyes on

Dermot. 'And you did just say that security was pretty lax.'

'I meant it was just normal.'

'But you definitely agreed it was "relaxed."'

'I'm not sure my client is qualified to comment on the security arrangements.' His lawyer was starting to sounded a little testy. Maybe she was the one who needed to calm down.

'I'm sure he's been on enough TV sets to have a view.' Henwell was still glaring at Dermot. 'Now let's talk about your alibis.'

Again his lawyer had warned him about this, the sudden change of tack to catch him off guard. They'd been through his diary together and managed to come up with his whereabouts at the times of all the murders.

'The night of Mickey Morris's murder, you were at home on your own.'

'Yes.'

'Not really an alibi then, is it?'

'Most people do tend to spend their evenings at home, Detective Inspector.' His lawyer took over. 'And Mr Jack does live alone. It is down to you to prove he committed the crime, not for him to prove he didn't.'

'Agreed.' Henwell nodded his head. 'But with the other evidence we've got, the lack of an alibi isn't going to play well in court.'

'We're a long way from this going to court.' The lawyer shot back.

'Are we?' Again the policeman kept his eyes on Dermot.

A wave of dizziness washed over him then, even though he was sitting down. All along he'd assumed he'd get out of this. There simply wouldn't be enough evidence because he hadn't done it – any of it – despite what they were trying to prove. How had it gone so quickly from questions about his whereabouts to talk of court?

'And on 14th October? You were working late at your office?'

'Yes.' But not working. One of the nights he'd stayed late looking at the connections as he tried to crack the case himself. All the time thinking he was some kind of super-sleuth.

Stupid.

He'd planned to delete his secret stash of press cuttings after Kevin Story's killing, knowing how bad it would look if the police linked him to the murders and found them. But then he hadn't deleted them had he? Still desperate to solve the case. Wondering why he seemed to be the only link.

Stupid, stupid. STUPID.

'And 1st October? Working late again?'

'Yes.' Another night when nobody could vouch for him. He could get Emilie to say she'd been there too, but he doubted she'd be a convincing liar.

The policeman shook his head. 'You don't actually have real alibis for many of the nights in question. You had grievances against all of the victims and had been snubbed by at least two of them just before they were murdered. Then there's your little treasure trove of press cuttings.' He kept his eyes on Dermot for a few seconds before shifting to look at the lawyer. 'That's enough for us to charge him.'

'But I didn't do it.' Why couldn't they see that? He turned to his lawyer. 'You've got to make them believe –'

He was cut off by a knock at the door.

'Oh please. You played this one yesterday.' Saskia Torrance didn't even bother rolling her eyes this time.

The door swung open to reveal the same red-faced young policeman as yesterday.

'What is it, Danny?' Henwell was already on his feet, heading for the door.

When Dermot turned to his lawyer, she was looking at him coldly, perhaps wondering what else he hadn't told her.

But there was nothing.

'Sir, I couldn't stop her…'

'Please let me in.' The voice that came from behind Lidstone was female and irate.

'She just –'

'Let. Me. In!'

Female, irate and familiar.

A figure ducked around the big policeman and stepped into the room.

'Anna?' Dermot was on his feet now.

She gave him a quick nod and half a smile before turning to deal with the six foot five of angry detective inspector who was moving to intercept her.

'You can't just barge into my interview room.' Henwell stepped in front of her, blocking Dermot's view.

'DCI Simpson said I could. He's your boss, right?'

'Anna?' Dermot waved his arms about, leaning to one side to see around Henwell and catch her eye.

'Not now.' She kept her attention on the policeman.

Instead, it was Henwell who turned to him.

'You know her?'

'Anna Preston, MI5.' She stuck out a hand towards Henwell as he spun back to face her.

Dermot felt his confidence start to return. 'I told you I had helped them out.'

'That's classified, remember.' Anna gave him a hard stare.

'Yeah,' Henwell scoffed. 'That's what he said.'

'Because it is. But he did help us.' Anna's eyes were still on Dermot, but her look had softened. Then she was back to dealing with the policeman. 'Hard to believe, I know.'

'Anna. I didn't do it. You've got to tell them –'

'Just be quiet and listen.' Her eyes flicked quickly around the room then back to Henwell. 'I think we need to have a little talk, Detective Inspector.'

'Which we'll be doing outside.' The policeman tried to usher Anna towards the door.

'Dermot needs to hear it.'

'Not before I've had a word with my client in private.' Saskia Torrance was standing now too, looking a bit peeved at no longer being the alpha female in the room.

'I'm here to help your client.' Anna seemed to notice the lawyer for the first time. 'That's something you clearly haven't managed to do.'

Meoouuwww.

The lawyer stared daggers back at Anna, for once lost for words.

'Whoa, whoa, whoa.' Henwell held up his hands. 'This is a police matter. You can't just waltz in here and ask us to drop the charges because he once helped the security services.'

'You're right. I can't. We don't really go in for that sort of thing anyway.' Anna gave Henwell an insincere looking smile.

Oh. It was kind of what Dermot had been banking on.

'I'm glad we've got that straight.' The policeman sounded a little happier now.

'But I can ask you to drop the charges…' Anna looked at Dermot for a second before her eyes returned to the policeman '… because he didn't do it.'

Now that was more like it.

'We've got quite a lot of evidence that suggests he did.'

'All of it circumstantial,' Saskia Torrance piped up again.

'Are you still here?' Anna seemed genuinely confused the lawyer hadn't gone. 'I doubt he'll be needing your services anymore. And some of what I'm about to say is classified.'

'Mr Jack?' His lawyer looked at him coldly. 'It's up to you.'

'No it isn't.' Anna shook her head.

Dermot looked at her then back to the lawyer with a nod. 'Thank you. I think I'll be OK now.'

'Fine.' She gathered up her papers and stuffed them into her bag. 'I'll be sending my bill directly to Mr Du Beurre. If you need a lawyer again, make sure not to contact me.' With that, she slipped on her jacket and left the room, about as elegantly as possible under the circumstances.

The fat sergeant was the only one still sitting. He reached for a biscuit with a grin as he watched the lawyer leave.

'You too.' Anna wiped the smile straight off his face. 'Out.'

God, wasn't she magnificent? She'd just taken on and beaten a top lawyer and two policemen single-handed.

'Sir?'

Henwell nodded.

The sergeant stood and stalked out of the room a lot less gracefully than the lawyer, even forgetting to take his biscuits.

'We don't need that either.' Anna reached out and turned off the tape recorder. Then she sat in the lawyer's chair, reaching out to help herself to one of Roberts' biscuits before offering the packet round.

Dermot took one to celebrate his imminent release, but Henwell declined with a sour little shake of his head. A bad loser as well as a prick.

'This better be good.' He gave Dermot an evil look before turning back to Anna.

She kept them waiting as she finished her biscuit. Was it another way of showing the policeman who was in charge here now, or simple good manners? Maybe even a bit of showboating? Dermot didn't care, because Anna was about to get him out of here.

'We've found something that calls whatever evidence you think you have into question. Something relevant to one of our own investigations.'

Dermot would be having more than a biscuit to celebrate that. Maybe he could even persuade Anna to let him buy her lunch.

'We think this is the work of a terrorist cell.'

Henwell barked out a short laugh. 'You're saying that a bunch of terrorists is going round killing celebrities? Seriously.'

The policeman had a point. Dermot had come up with enough wacky scenarios in the course of his own amateur detective work. But this beat them all. He put down his half-eaten biscuit. That celebration lunch was going to be on hold too. Anna didn't deserve it, not with crackpot theories like that.

'We think it's a plot to weaken the entertainment industry and cause a knock-on effect across the whole economy.'

Jesus, it just got worse. Dermot wondered whether he could persuade his lawyer to come back.

'And you've got evidence of this?' Henwell let out a long sigh.

'A list of the initials of all the victims and the dates of the murders.' She pulled a piece of paper from her jacket pocket and handed it across the table to the policeman.

'Come on.' Henwell looked down at the list. 'Anyone could have written that. It's been all over the press.'

'Before the first murder took place?'

OK, maybe it wasn't such a crackpot theory after all. Dermot reached out for the biscuit again.

'Where did you get this?'

'I can't tell you that, I'm afraid.'

'That's convenient. Let me guess, classified, right?' Henwell shook his head dismissively.

'Yep. Looks like you're a quick learner.' She flashed Henwell a smile. 'But I can tell you Dermot didn't write it.'

'Doesn't mean he's not involved.'

'Oh, I think it does.' She turned to Dermot, but the smile had gone now and the look in her eyes held no hint of triumph. 'I'm sorry…'

Sorry? What did she have to be sorry about? She was about to get him out of here. He was going to buy her lunch.

'There.' Anna reached out and grabbed the paper from the policeman's hand and laid it out on the table in front of Dermot.

'What?' It was just a load of letters and numbers.

Her finger moved down the list until she was pointing to the second line from the bottom. 'It looks like you're next.'

Part Two

The Chemistry Between Us

Five days (but no more murders) later…

Chapter 16

Come on, come on. Anna stared up at the red light, willing it to change. They were exposed enough out here when they were moving. But sitting still was worse.

The filter arrow finally turned green and the car in front moved off, turning across the three lanes of waiting traffic. Anna followed, keeping close enough to stop any vehicles pulling in between, her eyes flicking to the mirror then back to the road in front, alert for any hint at danger.

Three long and boring days had slunk by since they'd started this. Three long and boring days, with absolutely nothing out of the ordinary happening.

But then that was surveillance for you.

And it was hardly surprising either, with the date on the list for the next killings still two days away. If they knew anything about these terrorists, whoever they were, it was that they liked to stick to their schedule. Sadly, this was about the only thing they did know about them. All that monitoring, tapping-up of sources and liaison with intelligence services and police forces, both domestic and international, had turned up precisely nothing.

So the only option they had was to watch and wait.

Dull yes, but hardly stress-free, not with all those doubts doing the rounds inside Anna's head. But it was she who'd come up with the plan and then persuaded everyone else to go along with it. So she really didn't have too many grounds for complaint.

Lawson, of course, had needed little convincing to go along with her idea. This kind of thing was meat and drink to a man who'd spent the Cold War years running agents on the wrong side of the Iron Curtain.

Just the police to persuade then.

Anna had known that the plan would never work without the Met's buy-in and full support. DI Henwell had been bang up for it from the off. With Dermot off the hook, he was minus a suspect and short on other leads. Moving it up the Met's chain of command had proved a little trickier though. DCI Simpson, for one, hadn't been keen.

Terrorists? Really? His profiler wasn't having that. And anyway, such an approach was hardly by the book.

If MI5 had such a book, nobody had ever told Anna where to find it, or which bits to read. So upwards she'd gone to Deputy Assistant Commissioner Connor.

Now there was a piece of work.

He'd been at pains to make it clear that the Met wouldn't normally plan such an operation themselves… But of course they'd go along with any decision that MI5 made on the matter. It was a great way of ducking responsibility without actually saying no. Easy to see why the man had risen so high.

Anna's eyes scanned around as she followed the car in front up a short hill then round a sweeping bend, the tension inside rising a little more. With those three long and boring days behind them, today had brought something a little different.

Out here in the open.

Isolated.

Exposed.

At least as exposed as you could get in west London. Still, it felt like ramping the risk up to a whole new level.

Their little convoy had headed west out of the city centre on the A40, before pulling off at Gypsy Corner and heading on into the depths of the Park Royal Industrial Estate. She checked the mirror again, relieved to see the dirty white van packed with SCO19's finest firearms officers was still behind her. Then she flicked her eyes back to the road in front, wondered again what she might have missed. And whether she'd led them all into making an awful mistake.

'Sierra Oscar Two, Sierra Oscar Two, this is Sierra Oscar One. Do you copy?' DI Henwell's voice came over the radio from the car ahead.

'Copy, Sierra Oscar One,' Anna replied, still getting used to the police call signs they'd adopted for the joint operation.

'We're about ten minutes out now. Over.' His voice was calm and controlled, as it had been since they'd started this.

Anna smiled to herself, remembering how she'd thought he was a bit of a tool when they'd first met. A bit rich, given that *she* was the one who'd barged into *his* interview room. But it was fair to say that he'd impressed her over the past few days. A little part of her had even wondered whether the two of them might…

But no, she'd quickly put that one to bed. The three awkward hours Anna had spent with Charlie Gould on Wednesday night had only reinforced her views on the perils of mixing work and pleasure.

'Sierra Oscar One to all units. In position? Please confirm.' Henwell's voice came on the radio again. He was being thorough, making sure they had everything covered, even though none of them really believed anything would happen today.

Anna listened as each of the surveillance teams responded. Maybe this was the real cause of her unease. While Henwell was leading the undercover team, Anna was just another of those 'units', tasked to watch discreetly from the sidelines. The whole point of the operation was to create the illusion of business as usual. Little point in setting a trap the intended prey could see a mile off.

But again she had nobody to blame but herself. It had been Anna's decision to take on the surveillance role rather than going undercover, believing that it would provide a wider operational perspective. And besides, Felicity Diamond was a lot more suited to the second undercover role than she was. In fact, it was hard to tell exactly what special preparations the girl had made. Maybe her skirt was a little shorter and the heels higher, but otherwise Felicity looked pretty much the same as she did every other day at work.

Now though, firmly on the outside, Anna just felt remote. Certainly much too far away to make a difference if anything did go wrong.

The car ahead slowed as Henwell indicated right, turning deeper into the industrial estate. It was a hotchpotch of factory units, warehouses and the occasional ageing office block, which sprawled from the fringes of Shepherd's Bush up towards Wembley. The regeneration that had turned much of London into million-pound plus apartments for absent overseas buyers had taken one look at this part of the capital and hurried back off to Kensington and Chelsea, before it caught anything nasty. The light drizzle of a gloomy November afternoon wasn't doing the place too many favours either.

Anna checked the mirror again, still unable to shake her unease as they headed round another long bend then across a roundabout. She sped up a little to keep close behind Henwell's car, her mind drifting back to the events of last Sunday that had brought them here.

*

The walls of the bleak little interview room seemed to close in around them as Anna watched Dermot staring down at the list. Part of her was still mad at him for worming his way back into her life again. A little harsh perhaps? It wasn't as if he'd chosen to be on a terrorists' death list.

But any qualms she might have had at the prospect of seeing him again had dissolved the moment she'd stepped through the door. There could never by anything between them. Anna had made that abundantly clear last year when she had disappeared from his life without so much as a goodbye. Ghosting… That's what they called it now, didn't they? She was doing her job now. That was all.

His eyes stayed on the list, focused in on the letters and numbers on the second to last line.

MDDJ1711.

Not a provincial airport in the Dominican Republic after all.

He stared at it for a moment longer then looked up at her. 'November the 17th. That's next Saturday.'

'Yes.' She nodded, keeping her eyes on his. 'Six days.'

'And you really think it's Marcus and me?'

It felt like an age since she'd broken the news that Dermot and the chef were next on the list, but in reality it couldn't have been more than a couple of minutes.

He looked down at the paper again then up at her with a shake of his head. 'It could be anyone.'

'Well, anyone with the initials MD and DJ,' Henwell chipped in.

Not helpful. Anna threw him an unfriendly look. 'We ran it through a rather advanced piece of software. There's no single person we can find with those initials.

'What, you've got computers that can work out which celebs are going to get killed next?' Dermot didn't sound convinced.

'That's not actually what they're for, but we can programme them to look at pretty much anything. Given the celebs they've been targeting, the chances of it being any other combination of two people are extremely low.'

'How low?'

Anna saw the hope in his eyes. He'd probably take his chances at fifty-fifty. Maybe sixty-forty even. Sadly she was about to take that away. 'Nought point three per cent.'

Dermot didn't respond, leaning forward instead and putting his head in his hands.

Anna kept her eyes on him as he sat there, adjusting to his new reality of being the hunted rather than the suspected hunter.

'But why two of them?' Henwell reached over and grabbed the piece of paper, turning it round. 'All the others have been single killings.'

'You have a word for it with serial killers, don't you?'

Henwell nodded grimly. 'Escalation.'

'Except these aren't your normal serial killers. They're trying to damage the entertainment business and create a knock-on effect that will cripple the whole economy.'

'Is that even possible?' Henwell looked sceptical.

'We think so, yes. The Economic Threats Unit at the Treasury is looking at it now. For the terrorists, escalation is all about getting more and more publicity to get celebrities running scared and stop them from working. Each murder needs to be more horrifying than the last to keep the headlines rolling.'

'Hence Kevin Story with the finger, Mickey Morris with the battleaxe.' The policeman nodded, catching on fast. 'And RVP2411, the last one? That's got to be Raymond Van Perrie, right?'

'Yes. We ran that through the software too.' The former Dutch footballer and manager had made quite a name for himself on the reality TV circuit since quitting the dugout. 'Very few people with those initials. Over 99 per cent chance.'

'But why am I even on the list?' Dermot sounded more indignant than frightened. 'I'm not a celebrity anymore.'

Anna turned back to him with a shake of her head. 'But you are an agent?' She was speculating here; there simply hadn't been enough time to think this through. 'If you were trying to harm the showbiz economy, scaring off agents wouldn't be a bad approach. Marcus is probably the main target, but the two of you make a nice double whammy.' She cringed a bit inside, realising how insensitive her words had sounded.

Opposite her, Henwell sat back, a puzzled look on his face. 'Why not go for the really big stars? None of this lot are exactly A-listers.'

Again it was a question they hadn't really had time to consider. 'The bigger the star, the better the security. Maybe they're going for soft targets? They're getting enough publicity as it is.'

'True.' Henwell paused for a moment, deep in thought. 'Still doesn't explain why they're all his ex-clients. Have you ever worked with Raymond Van Perrie?'

'No.' Dermot shook his head. 'And for your information, Marcus Diesel is a current client.' He turned to Anna. 'It's obvious, isn't it? Someone's trying to make it look like it was me, to cover their tracks.'

'And *you* did a pretty good job of helping them.' Henwell cut in.

'What?' Anna turned to the policeman.

'You couldn't make it up. He decided to run his own little

investigation. Said he got a taste for it after helping you guys.'

'I was only trying to prove it wasn't me.'

'Dermot you nob.' Anna shook her head, throwing him a withering glance. But the idea that someone was setting him up wasn't a bad theory. She turned to Henwell. 'I think we all agree that it wasn't Dermot. Yeah?'

The policeman held her gaze for a second. Then he let out a long sigh. 'Mr Jack, on behalf of the Metropolitan Police, I'd like to apologise for any inconvenience caused by our investigation.' He reached a hand out across the table. 'You're free to go. Not that I'd recommend it just yet.'

Dermot shook Henwell's hand, turning to Anna with a rueful grin. 'I think I preferred being the suspect rather than the next victim.'

She knew that he was trying to be brave, but it wasn't hard to see the fear lurking in his eyes.

'We'll get protection, right?' His grin was already fading fast. 'You'll put us in a safe house until you catch them. Armed guards, everything. Right?'

'If that's what you want.' Anna knew she was going to have to play it carefully. She'd only come up with the plan on the cab ride from Thames House and didn't have all the details worked out yet.

'Of course it's what I want. Marcus will too. A guarantee we'll be 100 per cent safe.'

'There's no such thing. Whoever these guys are, they're good. They'll keep on coming until they get you or we catch them.'

'Well, bloody catch them then.'

'We're trying. But right now we don't have any intelligence, and the police don't seem to have any leads.' She flashed a smile at Henwell, before turning back to Dermot. 'They arrested you, for God's sake.'

'There was clear evidence…' Henwell trailed off.

Anna decided it was time to get to the point. 'You really helped us out of a hole last year. And I'm sorry I never got the chance to thank you properly.'

'That's OK.' He nodded, a half smile back on his face.

She doubted he'd still be smiling when he'd heard what she had to say. 'We can help protect you. But, well… you could help us catch them. We know they're coming after you and we know when.'

'Oh no.' He shook his head as realisation crept in. 'No way.'

*

Fast forward four days, and Dermot Jack and Marcus Diesel were going about their daily business as if a bunch of terrorists weren't planning to kill them. Bait in the trap that Anna hoped would soon spring shut.

And the only reason Dermot had agreed to go along with it was… Well, it was because of Anna, wasn't it?

She'd seen it in his eyes back in the interview room, along with the anger and the fear, when he'd finally stopped arguing and said yes.

Hope.

After this was all over, he was hoping there'd be another chance for the two of them. Well there wouldn't, however brave he proved himself to be. Anna was very clear on that point.

But she'd realised with more than a touch of shame that this forlorn hope of his was exactly what she'd been banking on to persuade him all along.

'Sierra Oscar One to all units. Five minutes now.' Henwell's tone was still calm and controlled.

'Roger that.' Anna wasn't sure her own voice had been steady enough to hide all the doubt that had just come flooding back in.

Or the guilt.

Chapter 17

'You really think we should be doing this?'

'Sorry?' Dermot had been staring out of the car window as Marcus bored everyone with a tedious anecdote about how he'd once borrowed a pair of trousers from a breakfast TV presenter. But at some point, the chef must have finished and moved on.

'I said, are you sure this is a good idea?' Marcus sounded more than a little testy.

What, acting as bait to trap a bunch of murdering terrorist? No, Dermot wasn't sure at all. They'd cut Mickey Morris's head off with a bastard axe for God's sake. What would they have planned for him and Marcus? Dark terrors had stalked his every waking moment and most of his sleeping ones for the past few days.

But every time the fear threatened to overwhelm him, he reminded himself of all those policemen with big guns hiding around the place. And what was the alternative anyway? Sitting round in a safe house with Marcus getting on his tits until the police caught the terrorists? Or the killers finally managed to get to them?

And this way, Anna would see first hand, how brave he was. Then just maybe they'd get to give things another go.

'You'll both be perfectly safe.' Henwell spoke from the front seat.

Dermot still hadn't forgiven the big policeman for the arrest. But he had to admit having him so close at hand was reassuring right now.

'Oh I'm not worried about that.' Marcus turned to look at Dermot, confusion clouding his face. 'I meant the tuna deal.'

'We agreed.' How typical of the chef to be prioritising his profile over the threat of violent death.

For the past few days, business as usual had meant hanging round the office or going to the odd meeting in town, sticking to the routine and keeping appointments. Today it meant driving out to west London to the UK HQ of the Hanku Canned Fish and Seafood Company to sign the contract for the tuna advert.

But then this wasn't quite business as usual. More like securing a huge endorsement deal that would bag Marcus a load of cash and might get the chef off his back for a while. That felt like a win-win, as long as no one killed them along the way.

Henwell steered the car round a long bend then turned left. He was undercover as Marcus's driver, with the woman from MI5, Felicity Diamond, playing the part of the chef's personal assistant. She was in the back seat of the people carrier, getting right into character, retouching her make-up. Next to her, Emilie completed their little party.

'It's just not me.' The chef sighed sulkily. 'You know, fish.'

For some inexplicable reason, he'd chosen to wear a beret today. He took it off and replaced it at an angle he must have thought was a little jauntier, leaning forward to check his look in the mirror. Along with the beret, he'd chosen to wear a slightly tight suit the colour of fresh dog turd and a canary-yellow shirt. His feet were decked out in bright red trainers with little white ankle socks beneath. Cutting-edge hipster chic or a fading celebrity dressing like an arse? It was so hard to tell these days. Hopefully, the Japanese fish marketing executives would see a larger-than-life character, who'd help them sell truckloads of tuna to the eager British public.

'This will get you straight back on TV.' There was no way Dermot was letting Marcus back out of the deal now.

The chef gave the beret another little tweak. 'They don't still expect me to pop up? I told you I'm not doing that.'

This brought a loud snort of derision from the back seat.

Dermot turned and gave Felicity Diamond a sharp look. Fair enough, she was putting herself in harm's way to protect them, but her attitude was hardly helping.

She just smiled back at him innocently, the sort of butter-wouldn't melt look that he suspected would get a girl like her a rather long way in life.

'I've spoken to them.' He turned back to Marcus. 'They've changed the script. You stroll in "manfully" now.'

'Really, it says that, "manfully"?'

Dermot nodded. It said nothing of the sort, but that was a bridge they'd cross once Marcus had signed the contract.

'Cool.' The chef turned to stare quietly out of the window, leaving Dermot to get back to worrying about being a terrorist target.

'Everything's going to be all right.' Emilie leaned forward, speaking quietly into his ear, a hand on his shoulder.

As if he didn't have enough to worry about. Her hand lingered on his shoulder and he caught the scent of her perfume as she leaned in closer. If anything, Emilie had been making her feelings even more obvious since his release from custody. Little touches of his hand and shoulder, generally standing too close and smiling up at him with those huge eyes.

One thing he couldn't fault was her loyalty. Or her bravery. Dermot had been totally straight with her about the death threat, practically ordering her not to come into work until it was all over.

She'd refused point-blank, saying that now more than ever was the time when she needed to stick by him. MI5 and the police had considered it and agreed.

Business as usual, remember.

There was no guarantee that the terrorists weren't keeping tabs on him already and Emilie's sudden disappearance might have set alarm bells ringing. Besides, there was plenty of protection.

But it didn't stop him feeling guilty as hell at dragging her into this. Or worrying that Anna might get the wrong idea and think something was going on between him and Emily. Dermot didn't typically believe in fate, kismet, destiny or whatever it called itself these days. But he'd messed up his first chance with Anna, then failed to make amends when a second opportunity had unexpectedly leaped into his lap. And now someone somewhere had decided that he would get a third go. It was a chance he was determined not to waste. But taking that chance would have been a whole lot easier if he'd got to spend any length of time with her. That visit to rescue him from the police interview room had been the only time he'd actually seen her over the past few days. There was a debrief planned after they returned from the fish company though, and he was hoping she'd be there.

'OK, this is it.' Henwell turned right and swung into a car park in front of a squat, ugly office building.

'What a dump.' Marcus looked across at Dermot. 'Why did we have to come all the way out here?'

'It's their head office and they're about to pay you lots of money. So just be nice, OK.' But Marcus had a point. The building looked as if it had been hastily built sometime in the seventies out of second-hand materials. It was certainly in need of a spruce-up to match the brand new sign with the fish company's name and smiling tuna logo, which had been placed above the front door.

Henwell guided the car to a stop in one of the parking bays marked for visitors, before switching off the engine and turning to face them.

'OK, let's go. Me first. Felicity, you're at the back. We're not expecting any trouble today, but let's just stay alert.' He climbed out and walked round to open the door for Marcus.

The terrorists had never deviated from the schedule on Anna's list, which meant they should be safe for another two days. But Dermot felt a stab of anxiety as he opened his own door and hopped out into the deserted car park. He turned to Henwell. 'Shouldn't you maybe… err, you know, case the joint?'

'Case the joint?' Henwell gave him an odd look.

'Yeah, you know, have a look round, a recce.'

'I am familiar with the phrase, thank you.' The policeman came closer, lowering his voice as he nodded towards Marcus. 'Does his driver normally do that?'

'No.' Marcus didn't normally have a driver, but Dermot got the point.

'Exactly. We're acting normally, remember.' Then Henwell leaned right in, his voice dropping even lower. 'And for your information, the joint was fully "cased" two hours ago. We know what we're doing, OK. Just concentrate on your fish deal and leave the proper work to us.'

Well, that had told him.

Felicity Diamond threw Dermot a withering look as she put her hand on Emilie's shoulder, gently guiding the Belgian girl forward.

His assistant gave him a nervous smile. He fought back a pang of guilt as he smiled back, hoping it would reassure her without giving her any other sort of encouragement.

Then they were heading off in a line across the car park. Dermot breathed in deeply, trying to walk as tall as he could behind Henwell. Because actually, sod it… He was the one about to clinch a huge deal. Possibly the biggest celebrity endorsement in the history of tinned fish, or any canned produce for that matter. Who exactly was doing the 'proper work' now?

Henwell pushed through the glass door then held it open for the others. The reception area was large and minimalist in design, white walls and just the odd plant, along with some pricey but uncomfortable looking chairs. All were empty.

'Mr Diesel's party?' A pretty young woman behind the desk smiled as she greeted them and took their coats, doing her best to ignore Marcus's leering gaze.

Dermot shot the chef a look… *Behave.*

The receptionist finished with their coats and called to tell the waiting seafood executives that their guests had arrived. Then she led the way through a set of double doors. Dermot followed her down a short corridor towards a door at the end marked 'Boardroom'. Marcus came next with the two women. Henwell had stayed back in reception, keeping in character as the driver. Because who took their chauffeur into meetings? Maybe he could nip out and give the car a polish while he was waiting?

'Just in here, ladies and gentlemen.' The receptionist pushed the door open.

'After you.' Dermot stepped back with a smile and gestured for Marcus to go first. The chef was the man of the moment after all.

Marcus adjusted his beret one last time then headed into the room. Dermot made sure he followed right behind. It was one thing to let the chef make his big entrance, but best not to let him say too much.

'What the…?' Dermot walked straight into Marcus, who'd stopped dead in front of him.

The receptionist had clearly made some sort of mistake. Maybe she was new?

There was no bunch of eager tuna marketing executives waiting for them. And it didn't look like the sort of place where record-breaking seafood endorsement deals were thrashed out.

In Dermot's mind a penny tottered precariously on the edge of a precipice before plummeting over the edge.

Chapter 18

Henwell shifted forward in his seat and tugged at the collar of his shirt as his eyes flicked around the reception area. Then he looked down at his watch for what must have been the fiftieth time.

Exactly ten minutes and seventeen seconds had elapsed since Marcus, Dermot and the two women had gone into the offices. With the meeting scheduled to last for a good hour or so yet, there was absolutely nothing to be worried about.

Still, he felt anxious.

But then that was his job, wasn't it; to worry about the detail? He pulled at his collar again. The thing was just too damned tight, the new suit he was wearing a little too snug across his shoulders as well. The two suits he owned and rotated for court appearances and the odd wedding were loose-fitting and comfortable. Otherwise, it had been fifteen years since Henwell had worn a police uniform. But a return to that uniform would be the least of his worries if things didn't go to plan.

Simpson had made it clear from the start that he wanted no part of this. In the DCI's view, Henwell had already been wrong about Dermot Jack being the killer. And while MI5's evidence of a terrorist plot was worth investigating, it was best to keep an open mind. So the MIT would continue to progress other lines of enquiry while Henwell's team worked with the spooks.

But if you stripped away all the bollocks, it was clear that Simpson just wanted to pass the buck for a risky operation using civilians as bait. He could always step in and claim the credit if it worked. And it wasn't hard to see the influence of the good Dr White behind the DCI's thinking. The profiler was a man in a hurry to build a reputation by helping catch the celebrity killer. A gang of terrorists just didn't fit his profile.

Henwell's eyes flicked around the room again. Then, in the absence of anything else to do, he stood and did a little pacing, all the time telling himself to relax. But that wasn't going to happen. Not until the meeting was over and they were all safely back in the car. He watched as the receptionist stood with a little smile and then disappeared through the door behind her desk.

'Sierra Oscar Two, this is Sierra Oscar One. Status please?' He headed back to his chair, waiting until the door was closed before speaking quietly into his lapel mic.

'All teams in place. Nothing to report.' Anna Preston's voice came back calm, clear and confident.

'All quiet in here too. They're all in the meeting.'

'Well, we're ready if anything happens.'

'Roger that.' He looked through the windows in front of him, spotting her car parked up discreetly beside the warehouse over the road. And he knew that the dirty white van that had just cruised past was full of firearms officers.

With four more surveillance vehicles strategically placed to cover each of the roads that led to the building, they had all bases covered.

And he hadn't been lying when he'd told Dermot they'd done a full check of the building. Two officers, grudgingly loaned by Simpson had dropped in for an unscheduled visit to the fish company offices that morning, posing as fire safety inspectors. They'd found two meeting rooms and a selection of offices with eight staff, as well as box upon box of freshly printed marketing materials for tinned tuna.

'Sierra Oscar Four to all units.'

Henwell tensed as the voice of one of the surveillance officers sounded in his earpiece.

'Van coming from the left. Fast.'

He heard the sound of the engine first. Then the van came into view, before speeding by without slowing. He leaned back, letting out a long breath. Just a bloody van. Hardly surprising in the middle of an industrial estate.

'All clear.' Anna Preston's voice came through his earpiece, still calm and in control.

Typical bloody spook. That's what Henwell had thought when

she'd barged her way into his interview room. Stuck-up and snooty with it too.

His view had changed somewhat over the past few days. Professionally and well… In lots of other ways. But Henwell wasn't about to go there. He'd witnessed enough trouble over the years when colleagues had got that little bit too close. And anyway, he suspected Anna would be far too professional for that sort of thing.

Then of course there was the thing between her and Dermot Jack he hadn't quite been able to work out. There was history between them for sure. And it was something that went deeper than the 'help' he'd given MI5 with the Russians.

Henwell stood again, still unable to shake off his feelings of unease, wishing they'd come up with a cover role that hadn't left him stuck out here in reception.

'Sierra Oscar Two. This is Sierra Oscar One. I might take a quick look round. Just to be sure.'

'Copy that.'

He scanned the reception area once more then headed for the door to the offices. As he reached for the handle, the door opened. The receptionist jumped back in shock when she saw Henwell standing right in front of her.

'Sorry.' He conjured up an embarrassed smile. 'I was, err, just looking for the bathroom?'

'Of course.' She stepped forward to block his way, pointing back towards a door near the main entrance. 'Visitor bathrooms are over there. We haven't had a chance to put the signs up yet.'

'Thank you.' He turned and headed for the toilets, his plan to have a snoop around thwarted at the very first step.

There was no sign of the receptionist when he returned. So plan B, a bit of small talk to see what he could find out, was a non-starter too. He headed back to sit down, telling himself once again to relax. He was just trying to get comfortable when his phone rang, Lidstone's name on the display.

The DC knew Henwell was undercover, so he really shouldn't be calling. 'Danny, hi.' He checked the doors. There was still no sign of the receptionist, so it was safe enough to take the call. 'I'll probably need to keep it brief.'

'Sir.' Lidstone sounded breathless, but then that was nothing new there. 'You've got to get them out now.'

'Calm down. Take it slowly.' Henwell got to his feet, eyes on the door. The big DC might have been green, but Henwell was already learning that his instincts tended to be spot on.

'The tuna company, they've got a website and everything, but there's no evidence of an actual company registration.'

'They'll be registered in Japan.'

'No. That's what I mean. It was registered over here a few weeks ago. But there's no evidence of a parent company in Japan.'

Oh, for God's sake. Henwell wondered whether his faith in Lidstone's instincts might be misplaced after all. As far as he knew, the DC didn't speak Japanese or have a working knowledge of the country's corporate registration rules. 'Danny, I don't think –'

But the DC cut him off. 'Nearly all tinned tuna eaten in Britain is imported. But none of it comes from Japan.'

'They're trying to break into the market.' He'd overheard enough about the deal over the past few days to get the gist of it. 'That's why they want Marcus.'

'No, sir, you don't understand. Japan's never exported tuna to Britain. They eat more than they catch and end up importing a load.'

What was this, a lesson in the history of the international fish trade? And surely MI5 would have checked the company out. But the last thing Henwell wanted to do was discourage the lad. 'Danny, I'm sure –'

'No, sir, you need to listen. NOW!' Lidstone cut him off a second time, his voice rising in anger. 'The company doesn't exist. OK?'

If a shy junior officer like Lidstone was prepared to shout at a superior like that, he must be damned sure.

'Thanks, Danny.' Henwell cut the call as he stood and then

started towards door behind the reception desk. He had to at least check things out.

But then he forced himself to slow down, trying to think it through. There could be a million and one reasons why Lidstone hadn't found any evidence of the company. He pulled out his phone and called Felicity Diamond, waiting while it rang three times before going to voicemail. She'd been told to keep it on at all times and always to answer.

He reached for the door then stopped again. If Lidstone was wrong, he could be about to blow his cover, along with a highly lucrative tinned fish endorsement deal.

A million and one reasons.

'*... you need to listen. NOW!*'

He reached out and pushed on the door, but it didn't budge. So he tried again.

Locked.

He paused again, running over it in his head one last time before speaking into his mic. 'All units, this is Sierra Oscar One. Get in here now.'

'What's wrong?' There was a real edge to Anna's voice.

'The company's a fake. I think it's a trap.'

Then he took a couple of steps back, lowered his shoulder and charged the door.

Chapter 19

Anna was out of the car and running, the sound of Henwell crashing through the door in her earpiece. 'What's happening?'

But there was no reply.

She remembered how clever she'd felt as she laid out her plan to Dermot.

Not so clever now. How had they not known that the fish company was a fake?

She reached the road, heading straight across without even looking. Off to her left, the SCO19 team were piling out of their van, fanning out as they headed for the building. One of them broke off and came her way, shouting as he gestured wildly for her to get back.

No chance.

Anna pushed on harder, sprinting along the pavement for another ten yards before cutting over the grass and on across the car park. She kept going, stretching her lead on the firearms team, weighed down by their big guns and body armour.

'Sierra Oscar One. Status.' She spoke into her lapel mic as she ran.

No response.

Come on, come on.

She willed herself forward across the car park, ignoring the burning in her legs.

The terrorists were here.

The trap had been sprung.

They could end it now.

But this wasn't how it was supposed to go down.

Fifty more yards to go. She could see straight into the reception area behind the big glass windows.

Empty.

But then she saw movement, just a blur at first, turning into a tall figure.

Running.

Henwell.

Stooped but moving fast towards the front door, something in his arms.

No, not something, someone.

Anna powered on as the big policeman shouldered the glass door open without breaking stride and ran on towards her. The someone in his arms flopped loosely, her head lolling and rolling.

Emilie Pieters.

The door swung shut behind him.

Nobody else followed.

No Marcus.

No Felicity.

No Dermot.

Henwell straightened up to something like his full height as he ran towards Anna, the weight of the girl in his arms not slowing him unduly. He shouted, but his voice was drowned out by Anna's own footsteps and thudding heartbeat.

The reception area behind the glass was still empty.

The others? Where were they? Why weren't they coming? Why was he leaving them behind?

'Get back.' Henwell was twenty yards away, the strain clear on his face.

NO!

She had to get in there. Had to find them.

Henwell closed in on her, trying to cradle Emilie's head as best he could with one elbow.

Anna picked up the pace some more, adjusting her path to go round him.

'Get…' Ten yards away Henwell stumbled and went down in a heap, somehow managing to twist his body so that the girl in his arms didn't take the full force of his weight.

'GET DOWN.'

This time the voice came from right behind Anna, just as something took her legs out from under her and the tarmac came rushing up. Then she was rolling once, twice, three times, kicking against the arms wrapped tightly around her legs.

Finally, she managed to look up.

Dead ahead, Henwell on the ground, head down, his arms wrapped protectively around the Belgian girl.

Behind him, the headquarters of the Hanku Canned Fish and Seafood Company had disappeared behind a writhing mass of red, yellow and orange flames. Then came the noise, crashing over Anna like a collapsing wall. Next, the searing heat and the smell of smoke in her nostrils.

And as the heat and the noise and the smoke rolled over her, she buried her face in the tarmac, thinking just how badly she'd gone and messed things up.

Chapter 20

'Sir? Sir? SIR!'

Henwell knew he'd gone well past the point where he could credibly pretend to be so engrossed in his work that he hadn't heard. He looked up, wondering whether it was worth attempting to pull his face into some kind of smile.

But it was well past the time for that.

'I'm heading off now.' Lidstone was loitering nervously in the doorway, running a hand through his blond hair as he shifted from one foot to the other.

'Good night, Danny. And listen…' He'd never been good at this bit. 'Thank you again.'

'Sir, I'm really sorry. If I'd checked sooner…' The DC's voice trailed off, his bottom lip starting to quiver.

*

The door in the fish company reception had flown open at the second time of asking by Henwell's shoulder. On the other side, Emilie Pieters had lain still on the polished linoleum floor of the corridor, blood seeping from a wound on her right temple. He'd started to move towards her before his training kicked in.

Make sure the area's safe first.

A good choice as it turned out, a few seconds of misplaced CPR would have been enough to kill them both.

He'd heard the faint beeping first, then spotted what looked like a detonator on the floor by the wall, the wires going into a large black holdall. He'd gone to the young Belgian woman then, bending to scoop her up without pausing to see if she was breathing. Then he'd started to run. No time to worry about the others.

*

It had been well after 6pm when Henwell had made it back from the hospital, after a thorough examination and quick stop to check on a sleeping Emilie. The cuts on his hands from where he'd hit the tarmac were superficial and there was nothing else wrong with him according to the junior doctor, who looked as if he should have been at home playing with the plastic stethoscope he'd got for Christmas.

Lidstone had been waiting in Henwell's office, his letter already typed up. So instead of dealing with the urgent messages from the SOCOs, Anna and of course Simpson and Connor, he'd spent the first half hour talking Lidstone down from a resignation.

Now, just short of two hours later, it looked like the DC was shaping up to have another go.

'Danny, listen.' Henwell stood and walked around the desk. 'You've got nothing to be sorry for.'

'But I should have checked the company registration earlier.'

'No, Danny, you shouldn't have. We'd already checked that they were registered in the UK. MI5 had checked that too. Nobody else would even have thought to look any further. If it wasn't for your ridiculous obsession…' He paused and shook his head, producing a smile this time.

Lidstone managed a smile of his own. He'd revealed that he was fixated with the origin of the food he ate and couldn't ever remember seeing a tin of tuna from Japan. That's why he'd dug a little deeper into the company.

'Attention to detail, Danny. That's what good police work is all about. It saved my life today. And Emilie's.' Of course, he'd said all of this earlier, more than once.

The young man reddened and looked at his feet. 'Thank you, sir.'

'No, thank you.' He put a hand on the DC's back. 'Now it really is time you got yourself home. I need you fresh tomorrow.' Henwell knew he should probably have been taking Lidstone for a drink.

Several drinks in fact. It wasn't every day you had your life saved by another officer.

But not today.

Not with three people blown to pieces and the operation gone to shit. And with one of the dead a serving MI5 officer, said shit was only going to get thicker, deeper and a whole lot shittier.

'I can stay longer if you need me to do anything else.'

'No.' It was survivor's guilt that Lidstone was experiencing. The very same that Henwell was feeling right now. 'I'll be off in ten minutes myself.' Not true. He knew he'd be there for hours yet, going back over it all for any tell-tale signs they'd missed anything.

'If you're sure, sir.'

'I'm sure.' He guided the young man to the door. 'Thanks again, Danny. I owe you.'

Lidstone headed off slowly across the outer office as Henwell walked back around his desk and slumped in his chair. He and DCI Simpson had been summoned to Connor's office the next morning. It was going to mean his job most likely, unless he could find some sort of lead on the terrorists before then. Simpson's officers who'd checked the place out were sure to get a roasting, but there was no doubt where the buck was going to stop.

And hard.

He stared at the papers in front of him again then took his phone out, scrolling down his contacts to Anna Preston's name. His finger hovered over the call button. Then he slipped the phone back into his pocket. She'd left a message while he was in the hospital. Ever since, he'd been fighting the temptation to call her back, to compare notes and see what they could work out together. But who was he trying to kid? He just needed sympathy, company too. If they spoke now, he'd end up suggesting they meet for a drink.

Or maybe she would?

And that wouldn't be a good idea. Not tonight. He craned his neck to look through the open doorway, checking that Lidstone really had left. Then he turned back to the incident report on his desk, scanning for that elusive connection. But his thoughts just kept coming back to the way he'd handled Dermot's suggestion that they 'case the joint.' How patronising he must have sounded, how dismissive.

Not so dismissive now.

Three dead and it was all his fault.

Chapter 21

Three dead and it was all Anna's fault.

Dermot.

Felicity.

Marcus.

The names had gone round and round in her head, all through the long night of broken sleep and into the morning. She was the one who'd wrapped Dermot around her little finger, persuading him to risk his life to snare the terrorists. And then there was Felicity. Yes, the girl had welcomed the chance to go undercover. But it was Anna who'd sanctioned it. After those two, she had little capacity for guilt over the chef's death. But someone would soon be mourning him. And that was down to her too.

Dragging herself out of bed before it was light, she reached Pimlico Station a little after 7am, stepping out into the cold air of a perfect late autumn morning; the sun just coming up in a crisp blue sky. The mocking irony of a day to rejoice, coming hard on the heels of a soulless week of grey drizzle.

A day to make you fall back in love with life again.

Unless your name was Anna and everything was your fault.

Head down, she cut her way between the early commuters, forging on towards the river, Millbank and Thames House.

The walk would do her good; at least that's what she'd told herself. Help her calm down and clear her mind in advance of the meeting, maybe even stretch some of the stiffness from her left thigh. The firearms officer had taken her down with a textbook rugby tackle. The bruise where she'd hit the ground had come out overnight, just as the ones on her ribs from Lille were fading. She'd studied it in the shower that morning, poking at it until it hurt, for some reason thinking it was shaped a bit like Africa, just the wrong way round. The bruise was just about the only part of her that didn't feel numb. Self-pity wasn't an outfit that suited anyone, but it was the only one that would fit Anna today.

*

The noise, the heat, the smell.

Anna had just lain there, the grit of the tarmac stinging her cheeks as she tried not to cry. Things had rather run away with themselves after that.

Her minor cuts and bruises had put Anna towards the back of the queue for medical attention, so Henwell had already left the hospital by the time she'd been pronounced fit to go. With his phone going straight to voicemail, there'd been no way to get any sort of info out of him. So she'd tried to talk to Emilie Pieters instead. A polite young doctor had firmly told her Emilie was awake and doing OK, but in no fit state to deal with questions.

People were dead and he was worried about whether she was up to a bit of a chat? But he was just doing his job and didn't deserve to be the target of the anger Anna knew she should be reserving for herself.

In the absence of anything better to do, she'd headed back to the scene of the explosion. But with parts of the building still burning, the fire brigade were maintaining a cordon around the whole area. It would be another couple of hours before the fire investigation team could get to work and only after that would the Met's SOCOs get the run of the place.

Not that there'd be much to investigate by the looks of it.

So she'd headed back to base, a cold determination settling inside her. All her thoughts, all her waking hours would be devoted to getting these bastards. Far better than sitting at home and thinking about the dead. The police would be all over the CCTV cameras, but Anna could check up on any chatter that GCHQ might have picked up and see if any of the other intelligence agencies had come back with anything.

She'd stepped out of the lift doors, the buzz of the office slowly fading as colleagues looked up, already knowing.

Then she'd seen it, Felicity's chair. Empty, except for one of her ridiculously small and expensive handbags slung over the back.

She'd turned and walked straight back out.

Gone home.

Drunk wine.

One glass. That's what she'd told herself. Just enough to take the edge off. Best make it a large one though. The glass had been virtually empty by the time she finally moved on from Felicity.

The old photo album from school was on the top shelf of the cupboard under the stairs. It was that grin which got to her more than anything else, fixed across Dermot's face in each and every photo. He'd never hammed it up for the cameras. Never smug, mocking or anything else.

Just a grin.

Whatever he'd become, that was how he'd been back then. And she realised that the guilt over Felicity had been little more than a self-defence mechanism, her brain's way of keeping her away from this. Tomorrow the fingers would point.

Tonight though, more wine.

Because nobody else could ever blame Anna as much as she blamed herself.

*

She stepped out of the lift into the foyer outside Lawson's office, thankful that last night's drinking hadn't delivered the crushing hangover she fully deserved.

'Go straight in, please. Sir Richard will see you now.' Despite the early hour, Lawson's PA was already behind her desk.

The woman's name was Rose. Her parents must have been thinking of the thorny bits on the stems rather than the fragrant flowers at the end. She looked about sixty but was reputedly far younger, her face etched with lines from over twenty years of constant scowling in service of Queen and country. But today the only thing Anna saw in the secretary's gaze was sadness. The same sadness they all felt when the service lost an officer.

'We were all so sorry to hear about Felicity.' The woman's tone was probably about as soft as she was capable of making it.

'Thanks.' Anna nodded as she made for the door, keen to get it done. Hopefully, she'd be back out before the office started to fill up. She wasn't sure she could bear any more sympathy. At some point during the long and sleepless night, she'd realised there was only one course she could take – bring an end to the only career she'd ever wanted. The only consolation was that her father wasn't still around to see it happen.

'Anna, thank you for coming.' Lawson stood as she entered, his face grim, jowls behaving themselves and not wobbling too much, perhaps in recognition of the gravity of the situation.

'Sir Richard, I…' She was only halfway to his desk, but suddenly she wanted to get it all over with. He would refuse her resignation of course, try to protect her. But Anna wouldn't have that.

Couldn't have that.

'Come and sit.' He reached down and picked up his phone. 'Rose, dear, please could you rustle us up a couple of teas.'

Anna doubted she'd be staying long enough to drink hers. Somehow, she made it to the chair and sat. Lawson lowered his bulky frame back into his own chair, eyes still on her.

'After yesterday, sir, I need to…' She trailed off as she saw the hardness in his eyes.

Maybe he wasn't going to argue after all.

But then his look softened. 'I know what you're going to say. But we always have to carry on, whatever happens. You know who taught me that?'

Yes, Anna knew, her father. She felt a sudden surge of anger. Lawson knew about Dermot and her, about their past. And he knew how she'd be feeling at losing Felicity too. How dare he use her father's memory like that?

'Maybe we were a little hasty with the operation.'

He was trying to share the blame when they both knew she'd been the one who'd rushed into it. Those old jibes came back again.

Headstrong. Impulsive.

And they were true, weren't they? What was needed now was

someone far better than Anna to sort out the mess. Someone calmer, more measured. 'Sir. I can't –'

He raised a hand to cut her off. 'There's a lesson to be learned here. Then we move on. Nobody's blaming you for this, Anna.'

'No. I'm sorry, sir. I can't. I've got to –'

'Just hold on a second.' He leaned forward and pushed a piece of paper across the desk. 'At least take a look at this before you make any decisions.'

Chapter 22

Dermot emerged from sleep into a few seconds of blurriness and contentment, an odd but strangely pleasant dream slowly slipping away.

But it didn't last. Soon enough everything that had happened came crashing back at him. He pulled himself upright, his heart accelerating up through the gears and his breaths coming in ragged gasps, as the panic built inside him.

Kidnapped…

And MI5 had just stood by and let it happen. The police too.

He stoked the anger, letting it burn hotter and brighter until it outshone the panic and the fear.

Shining on the terrorists.

Bastards. Bastards. Bastards. Whoever they were.

But lighting up DI Dicksplash Henwell brightest of all. If he'd actually bothered to check properly, like Dermot had suggested, then none of this would have happened. But there was plenty of anger left for Anna, who should have been there for him.

And for himself. The idiot who'd agreed to go along with the whole plan in the first place.

Stupid, stupid. STUPID!

He wanted to close his eyes and scream it all out. Instead, he breathed in deeply, trying to calm himself as he sat up straighter and scanned around. He seemed to be lying on some kind of camp bed. The dirty window high on the opposite wall gave just enough light to make out the details of his improvised prison cell, which looked more like a storeroom. He scanned some more, eyes becoming more accustomed to the gloom as he fought back against the panic again. Shelving units filled with boxes ran up the far wall. He felt a surge of hope as his eyes darted upwards. But the window was a good ten feet above the highest shelf. A bid to escape that way would offer little more than the prospect of a broken neck.

The door then? He swivelled to his left, eyes homing in on a crack of brighter light along the floor as his other senses finally kicked in.

What on earth was that smell?

Jesus… Stench more like. It was as if something already rotten had finally done the decent thing and decided to die. The noise that went with the smell was like a rusty chainsaw chewing its way through a particularly stubborn piece of wood.

He rolled over and looked across towards the other side of the room.

In the faint light, he could just make out another camp bed and a sleeping figure.

Marcus Diesel.

The rasp of the chef's snoring stopped as he rolled over and let out a loud fart. It was far from his first if the smell was anything to go by.

'Marcus.' Dermot tried to call out but his dry throat could only produce a low croak. He coughed and had another go, getting a little more volume this time. 'Wake up.'

But the chef just swore in his sleep and then started to snore more loudly.

Another memory came back to Dermot. The door to the meeting room slamming shut behind him, then rough hands holding him down. A cold scrape on the back of his neck. And then nothing until now.

No wait, that wasn't quite right. Another memory tiptoed in.

Darkness, the faint shape of a figure standing over him then slowly bending down. Dermot had felt that same cold scrape again, this time on the arm.

And again nothing.

He let the fingers of his right hand roam over his left forearm until he felt a tender spot just above his wrist, and then he felt around the back of his neck for another.

Injected. Drugged, twice at least.

He climbed to his feet, a hand on the wall to steady himself as dizziness threatened to send him crashing back to the bed.

One, two, three, four, five, he counted. The spinning room slowed and finally stopped. He started to move tentatively in the direction of the chef's bed, trying to keep his breathing under control.

Another wave of dizziness struck and he stopped for a second, noticing a dark shape on the floor in front of him. It was a plastic bucket, upgrading their cell to an en suite. Beside it sat a neat little pyramid of toilet rolls, thoughtfully placed there by their kidnappers. It was always those nice little touches… He kicked out, sending the toilet rolls bouncing off around the room. If there was a Tripadvisor for kidnappers, they'd only be getting one star. He stepped around the bucket and leaned over the sleeping chef.

'Wake up.' He gave Marcus a prod and a shake.

But the chef just farted again and rolled over onto his other side.

They needed to get out of here, and all Marcus could do was sleep. Unbelievable. Dermot thought about a kick, or even tipping the lazy tosser off the bed. But years of experience had taught him that a problem shared with Marcus was a problem doubled. There'd be ample time for bitterness and recrimination when the chef finally woke up. Best to let him sleep for now, while Dermot did his best to work out a way to escape.

More pressingly, the sight of the bucket had made him realise how desperate he was to pee. He unzipped as he turned round, then leaned back contentedly as a long steaming flow hit the bucket, relief finally bringing a bit of clarity.

The whole fish company had been a trap from the start; that much was clear. But they were still alive, which meant the terrorists must be planning to stick to their timings. The kidnap had been on Thursday afternoon and he'd been drugged once at the start and then a second time when it had been dark. So maybe that had been Thursday night. And he'd been desperate for a pee but not that desperate. So he couldn't have been asleep for two whole days. That meant it was probably Friday. There was still time for them to be rescued – maybe as long as 24 hours? Anna had been there for him with the Russians and she'd be here for him now. Not that Dermot was going to sit around and wait for that. He finished peeing and zipped himself up before stepping carefully across the room towards the chink of light. His hand fumbled in the dark, finally locating the door handle. He gave it a twist and then a pull, but it didn't budge.

Never going to be that easy, though, was it?

The rage started to build inside him, making him want to kick out at the door or charge it with his shoulder. But no, he breathed in deeply again, trying to stay calm. Even if he could break through the door, there were bound to be guards. Best to bide his time and come up with an actual plan.

He headed back to his bed, forcing himself to think. Then he sniffed. And again. There was another smell in the room, one he hadn't previously picked up on over the stale reek of Marcus's farts. It was then that he noticed the tray on the table beside his camp bed, a similar one sat next to the snoring chef. He hurried back across and stared down at the tray as the smell of curry tickled his nostrils. Chicken tikka masala if he wasn't mistaken. A generous-looking portion of rice and even a tasty-looking mini naan bread on the side. A bottle of water too.

He reached out and touched the plate. Still hot. That meant someone had been here while he'd been sleeping. And recently too. Perhaps that was what had woken him.

Dermot felt the rage inside start to curdle. That might have been their best chance to surprise their kidnappers, to overpower them.

And they'd slept right through it.

He reached out for the plate, ready to hurl it as hard as he could against the wall. Show the bastard terrorists what he thought about their bastard terrorist food. But the anger ebbed away as his stomach gave a little rumble of protest. So he sat down and started to shovel the food into his mouth with the plastic fork. The sauce was thin and the meat a bit sinewy, but the curry was warm and even had a bit of a kick. Less than two minutes later, the food was all gone, the water too.

He eased the tray back onto the table, keeping hold of the fork and slipping it into his pocket. It might be plastic, but you never knew; a jab in the eye would still be painful.

His stomach rumbled again, and he wondered about nipping across and helping himself to Marcus's curry. It was only going to go cold otherwise.

But as he looked over, he saw the chef's eyes finally opening.

'Marcus, listen to me. I want you to stay very, very calm.'

Chapter 23

Henwell cradled the phone under his ear and listened as Anna's words tumbled out, not quite believing what he was hearing. But the same words were right there in front of him on his computer screen, highlighted in bold and underlined, in the first paragraph of the fire investigation report she'd just emailed over.

Part of him wanted to leap out of his chair and jump around his tiny office, screaming and shouting. But he managed to keep it all inside. 'We're still working on the CCTV. I'll get straight back if we find something. *When* we find something.'

'Thank you.' There was something in her voice, a slight hint of a tremble. But then it hardened. 'Let's get those wankers.'

For a second, Henwell thought she was about to say more, but she'd already cut the connection.

'Roberts, Lidstone, get in here.' He stood, not so worried about sounding calm now. 'There was no evidence of human remains at the fish company building.' The words came out while the two officers were still jostling in the doorway.

'You mean, they're not dead.' Lidstone's eyes opened wide, his mouth wider.

'Bollocks.' Roberts shook his head. 'They were just blown to bits, that's all.'

'No.' Henwell thought back to the note of exhilaration in Anna's voice as she'd shared the news. 'The bomb was just an incendiary device, a big firework really, lots of smoke and flames but no real power.'

'Well, the fire then, it must have incinerated the remains.' The sergeant still wasn't having it.

Henwell shook his head. 'Nowhere near hot enough.'

Lidstone kept on gaping.

'There was nobody in that building when it exploded.' He sat back in his chair and turned the computer screen so the others could see the fire report. 'One hundred per cent.'

'Doesn't mean they're not dead.' Roberts still seemed keen to rain on everyone's parade.

'True.' Henwell had already discussed that with Anna, both quickly coming to the same conclusion. 'Why go to all that trouble of blowing up the building and then just kill them? It was a decoy to give them enough time to get the hostages away. They're sticking to their timings. And they've got something big planned.'

'So we might have time to find them?' Roberts still didn't sound totally convinced.

'How are we getting on with the CCTV and ANPR footage?'

'Still going, sir. There's a lot of cameras. We'll crack on.' Roberts turned and hurried from the room about as fast as his bulk would allow him.

Lidstone waited, mouth wide, eyes unfocused.

'Danny?'

The DC just stared straight past him.

'DANNY!'

Lidstone shook his head, his eyes refocusing on Henwell.

'No one's dead, Danny. Let's see if we can keep it that way.'

'Yes, sir.' Lidstone nodded and headed out of the office.

Henwell just prayed the CCTV would give them a break. Any sort of break. The hostages may not be dead yet but they would be in twenty-four hours. And right now, he had precisely nothing to go on.

*

Make that twenty-four hours minus around forty-five minutes as Henwell's call with DCI Simpson ran on and on. Not all the time had been wasted, just most of it. The useful bits could have been crammed into five minutes tops. At least he'd been spared the visit to Connor's office, on account of the fact that nobody was actually dead yet.

'So to recap, Detective Inspector, you're still running this for now.'

That was the most the useful bit, Henwell was still in charge. But that was likely to change swiftly if they didn't manage to stop the murders, and it was the third time Simpson had recapped it.

'MI5 are liaising with Counter-Terrorism, but DAC Connor feels your experience of the case means you're best placed to lead on the search for the hostages.'

Which meant Simpson had passed on the whole poisoned-chalice, giving the DAC little choice but to stick with Henwell.

'I can give you whatever resources you need. DS Prim, DS Chandra, four of our DCs and twenty uniforms. Shout if you need more.'

'Thank you, sir.' They'd been through all this too. But Simpson was just making damned sure he couldn't be accused of being unsupportive.

'They'll work out of Putney. DS Prim's already setting up an incident room.'

Henwell suspected that Prim, given her by-the-book attitude, would be good at that, as well as marshalling the uniforms. Interestingly, there'd been no offer of any help or advice from Dr Neil White. Most likely, the psychologist had been quietly told his services were no longer required, now that he'd been proved himself to be an incompetent idiot.

'Up to you how you deploy them, of course.' Simpson was still banging on. 'But I got Prim leading the door-to-doors around the explosion site, yesterday. They're carrying on with it now.'

'Thank you, sir.' It was a good call, to be fair. With all that ambition and pomposity going on, it was easy to forget that the DCI was a more than capable copper.

'She's got good instincts. Keep her close.'

Hmmm. Which would mean keeping Simpson close too. But there was no avoiding that.

'Oh, and the media are sticking with the gas explosion line we gave them.'

For now... News of the bomb was bound to leak out eventually. That was probably another thing Henwell would end up taking the rap for. But no matter. He had twenty-four hours to turn things round. And that was a far better hand than he'd been holding a few hours earlier.

'If that'll be all, sir?'

'Of course. I just wanted to say…'

Bloody hell, couldn't the man just let him get on with his job?

'This whole operation – it was ill-conceived, but…' Simpson paused again. 'You did save that young woman's life yesterday. Remember that.'

Wow, who knew? The DCI actually had a streak of humanity.

'It may be all you've got left to hold on to when this is done.'

Or maybe not.

Henwell wondered whether he was expected to respond, but before he could the DCI ended the call.

Chapter 24

'I didn't want it anyway.' Marcus sat on his bed, staring sulkily at the chicken curry dripping slowly down the far wall. The plate lay on the floor below with the tray, the water and the naan bread.

'I'd have eaten it.' Dermot looked at the mess. The naan bread might still be salvageable.

'I should have thrown it in your ugly face. Seen how you liked that.' Marcus climbed to his feet. 'Everything will be all right, you said. They'll look after us, you said. How is this looking after us?'

'OK, OK, they messed up.'

'No, you messed up.'

'You think this is *my* fault?'

'You're the one who fell for that whole fish deal. "I'd sooner have tuna."' Marcus put on a childish sing-song voice.

'And I was supposed to have known?'

'Well, yeah. You're my agent. You're meant to know if a deal's genuine or not. Or maybe you could have just got me some decent offers. Then we wouldn't have had to bother.'

Except that Marcus particular brand of old school toxicity meant there hadn't been any other offers. But then Dermot suspected the terrorists would have found another way to get at them, even if they'd passed up on the fish deal. He lay back and closed his eyes. It was best to just let the chef rant on when he got like this. But thankfully Marcus seemed to have had enough too. At least that meant Dermot would have some peace to think about how to formulate an escape plan.

The brief silence was broken by the sound of pee hitting the bucket. Dermot opened his eyes and immediately wished he hadn't.

'Could you maybe turn round?'

The chef just carried on peeing, so Dermot stared up at the ceiling. At least the sound was preferable to listening to the man's whining.

Marcus finally finished, zipped up and flopped back on his bed. 'They're going to kill us. You do know that, don't you?'

Yes, he was aware of that.

'DERMOT?'

He counted to ten in his head.

'Are you listening?'

'No. I'm trying to think about how to get us out of this.'

'If you'd thought in the first place, we wouldn't be in "this."'

'And that's supposed to help, is it?' Dermot propped himself up on one elbow. 'Look… The police, MI5, do you think they're going to let anything happen to us?' But it didn't sound any more convincing out loud than it had inside his head.

Marcus snorted. 'They got us into this.'

'Sorry. I thought that was all my fault.'

'And theirs. Especially that big wanker of a policeman.'

At least they could agree on something.

Marcus lapsed into silence once more, staring sullenly at the curry-spattered wall. Then he turned back to Dermot with a shake of his head. 'I don't know why I ever agreed to work with you again. I guess I wanted to give you one more chance, for old times' sake.'

It wasn't quite how Dermot remembered it, but he really didn't see the point of arguing.

'You know what I'm going to do if we get out of this? I'm going to sack you. We're finished.'

'You can't, because I just quit. We didn't have a contract anyway.' It was true. Dermot had never got round to working up a new one when he'd taken Marcus back on.

'Then you're still sacked from last time. Remember?'

How could he forget? The satisfying memory of the fillet steak he'd thrown, hitting the chef square in the eye made him smile to this day.

Or it had done.

'Yeah… Sacked.' The childish, sing-song tone was back in Marcus's voice. 'How does that make you feel, Mr Big Shot Agent?'

Pretty good actually. Well it would have done if a gang of terrorists hadn't been planning to kill him.

'Dermot?'

He lay back and closed his eyes, hoping Marcus would just leave him alone.

'Dermot?'

He rolled over to face the wall.

'DERMOT!'

He stuck his fingers in his ears, fading out Marcus's voice to a dull hum, as he desperately tried to think of a way out.

Chapter 25

'Any news?' Emilie Pieters' question was out before Anna had made it through the doorway of the hospital room.

'Not yet, sorry.' Anna shook her head.

'But you think he is still alive?' the Belgian girl pulled herself upright in the bed.

Anna nodded. The police had already broken the news to Emilie that nobody had died in the explosion.

Interesting choice of words though.

'*Him*' not '*they*'.

Maybe the Belgian girl was just worried about her short-term job prospects? Or perhaps what Anna had heard from Felicity was true; Emilie Pieters was more than a little bit in love with Dermot.

The girl sniffed as she looked up at Anna. Her big eyes were red and tired looking, her face puffy and pale. But despite everything; her scrape with death, the bang on the head, the bandage and a no-doubt-restless night in hospital, she was still managing to rock the whole fragile-beauty look.

And rock it well.

If Felicity was right about Emilie's crush, Dermot was a lucky man. Although frankly, the whole age-gap thing was a bit gross.

Anna shook the thought away. Right now, she had to focus. 'Are you OK to answer a few questions?'

'Yes, I'm fine.' The girl sniffed again.

'I know you've already spoken to the police, but you might remember something else.' In truth, it was a long shot. But with GCHQ still reporting a dearth of online chatter and the police chasing down all other leads, there was little else for Anna to do right now. And it wasn't much of a walk from Thames House to St Thomas' Hospital.

Emilie tried a little smile. 'My cousin is coming to collect me. He won't be here for a little while.'

That would be the famous Anton Du Beurre. Anna hadn't yet had the pleasure and wasn't in any hurry to meet him. The Belgian chef seemed intent on making a nuisance of himself. All day he'd been bombarding Henwell's team with calls, demanding updates on the investigation and even threatening legal action if his agent wasn't found.

'Just start at the beginning and tell me exactly what you remember.' Anna sat down on the end of the bed.

'I'm sorry.' Emilie shook her head. 'It's just all a blank. One moment we were walking into the room, then bam.' She made a chopping motion with her hand. 'Something hit me on the head.'

'And you definitely didn't see anyone, any faces?'

The girl shook her head again as she sat up straighter in the bed. 'The next thing I remember, the policeman was carrying me out of the building. Then boom.' This time she made an exploding gesture with her hands.

And Anna couldn't help but notice how delicate those hands were.

'Without him…' Emilie trailed off, looking small and lost in her big hospital bed. Beautiful still, but that vulnerability went deeper, a fragility and lack of confidence that Anna hadn't truly appreciated before. Other girls would have played Emilie's looks for all they were worth, but Anna doubted Emilie understood the effect she had on men. It was perhaps why she'd fallen for someone like Dermot. To her he was probably part boyish rogue and part self-assured charmer, with more than a hint of father figure thrown in for good measure.

Anna blinked, realising she was still staring at Emilie's delicate little hands. When she looked back up, tears were rolling down the girl's cheeks. 'I know this is hard for you, but did you hear anything. Anyone speaking?'

'No.' Emilie's forehead creased into a little frown. 'Nothing.' Then she slumped back onto the pillow and wiped away the tears. 'I'm sorry. I didn't help them back there, and I can't help them now.' The words dissolved into a series of little sobs.

'You've done your best.' Part of Anna wanted to lean in and

give the girl a hug while the rest wanted to give her a damned good shake and scream at her to try a bit bloody harder. But she regretted the thought immediately. The tears reminding her again of the fragility beneath that beautiful surface. The girl was a civilian too, not trained to pick up on little clues while someone was bashing her around the head.

'The investigation, do you have any…' The Belgian wiped her tears away again as she searched for the word. 'Leads? Is that the right word?'

'I can't really say.' Anna wasn't about to share details of an active terrorist investigation. Not that there was much to tell.

'OK. I understand.' She looked at Anna as if appraising her fitness for the task at hand. Then she lowered her eyes to the bed.

But not before Anna had seen a flash of something else. Hardness? Determination? Steel even? Maybe Emilie wasn't such a pushover after all.

'He means a lot to you, doesn't he, Dermot?' The words were out before Anna had time to think them through.

'Yes.' Emilie looked up again with a sad little smile, all that vulnerability back in spades. 'He has been very kind to me.'

'He can be like that.'

'The two of you were close once. Yes?' Emilie was watching her closely now.

'He told you that?' Anna wasn't sure she liked the idea of Dermot discussing her with his latest squeeze.

'No. Marcus did.'

That figured. The chef was known for his loose lips almost as much as he was for his wondering hands. 'It was all a long time ago. And the of you two are…?' Anna stopped herself, feeling her face start to redden.

'No, no. Nothing like that.' Emilie's eyes dropped down to the bed again. 'A man like him and someone like me. I do not think that would be possible.'

Oh, it would be more than possible. Anna wondered what was stopping Dermot. She stood to leave, giving Emilie a smile. 'We will find him.' Again she hoped she sounded more confident than she felt. 'As soon as we've got any news, we'll let you know.' She turned and found herself staring straight into the dark eyes of Anton Du Beurre.

'Hello, my dear.' Anton looked past her to Emilie.

The Belgian chef looked older than he did on TV, but taller too and broader. And something in his eyes suggested he wasn't quite the amiable buffoon he liked to portray on screen.

'You are with the police?' His voice was friendly enough as he turned his attention to Anna, the accent less thick than the one he used for TV.

'No. Not exactly. Anna Preston.' She stuck out a hand, unwilling to elaborate further

He took it, throwing a little bow and a smile. Something in that smile seemed forced though, and she sensed an anger lurking just below the surface. But then everyone was feeling the strain today.

'So MI5 then? British intelligence?' Whatever had been hiding behind his smile was gone now.

'Something like that.' Anna kept it non-committal.

'The police are going to take us home now, Emilie.' Anton looked over at the woman in the bed before turning back to Anna. 'That is if you've finished your questions, Miss Preston.'

She nodded.

'Then why don't we wait outside while Emilie gets herself dressed?' He stretched out an arm to guide Anna from the room.

She shot him a warning look that had the arm quickly pulling back again. The Belgian stepped aside with another little bow then followed her out onto the main ward.

'OK, let's cut the crap.' The words were out as soon as the door had swung shut behind them. They would have sounded comical in his Belgian accent, but this seemed to have receded even further. 'Are you any closer to finding them?'

'I can't say anything right now.'

'Can't or won't? I have a right to know. Dermot's my agent, for God's sake.' His anger wasn't lurking under the surface anymore.

'Dermot's my friend and Felicity's my colleague.' Anna managed to keep her voice level. 'So we're all doing everything we can. The best thing you can do is take Emilie home and make sure she's OK.' She followed up with a tight little smile then turned and walked away without waiting for a reply.

And if Anton Du Bloody Beurre did say anything more, she didn't hear it because her phone was already ringing. The name lighting up the screen suggested it was a call she really ought to take.

*

'Anna.'

He'd spotted her when she was perhaps fifty yards away, watching her approach through the late afternoon gloom for a few seconds. Then he'd turned away to look back across the river towards the lights of the Houses of Parliament on the far bank. Now Sir Richard Lawson turned again as she reached his side.

'Any more news?'

She shook her head.

'Well, thanks for coming.' He smiled warmly, but there was a tiredness in his eyes, his face the colour of a heart attack. One good lunch away from the big one. That was the consensus back at Thames House. But then Lawson had looked that way ever since Anna had known him. And he was still going strong when so many others were already in the ground, her own father included. The day Anna had joined her mother and sister to scatter David Preston's ashes on the South Downs was more than a decade ago now, remote and raw in equal measure.

Lawson looked away, seemingly composing his thoughts as he gazed out across the Thames again. Was this the bit where he pointed to Parliament and told her that they did what they did to protect freedom and democracy? That the politicians over there would throw people like them to the wolves if they knew the half of it?

Probably not, because that only happened in spy movies. If

Lawson wanted to meet here, it had to be important. It wasn't just the chill of the November afternoon that made her shiver.

'Just had lunch at the House with the Home Secretary, always like to stroll back.' He turned to her again.

Maybe it was these regular walks between Westminster and Thames House that kept any cardiac trouble at bay. Anna relaxed. With his diary likely to be full when he got back to Thames House, he was just finding a way to fit her in.

'Shall we?' He pointed towards Lambeth Bridge and started walking. Off to the left, Anna spotted movement and recognised one of his bodyguards. She knew that somewhere two, possibly three more, would be hovering, wondering why the boss couldn't make their lives easier by getting a car.

'There's something I need to tell you.' They'd walked on another fifty yards before he spoke again. 'You've heard of Occam's Razor, I take it?'

Whatever Lawson had to say, it was going to come on the other end of a lecture. One that would probably last the length of the walk to Lambeth Bridge and across to HQ on the other side. But with the things he'd done for his country, he'd earned the right to wax lyrical, even with the clock ticking down fast.

And yes, she'd heard the theory. It had been one of her father's favourites, probably where Lawson had picked it up in the first place. 'The simplest explanation is usually true.'

'Not quite.' He gave a little shake of his head. 'More accurately, the explanation that requires the fewest assumptions is normally correct.'

OK, if he was going to split hairs. Anna waited, but he walked on in silence.

On the river, a small boat was straining against the tide, while to their left, the traffic on the road was at a standstill. They'd walked more than halfway to the bridge when he spoke again.

'The whole tuna-company thing. It would have taken a lot of planning. They must have set that up a while ago. So they'd always been planning to snatch them ahead of time. But the bomb? That just feels like a hasty improvisation. They must have found out that we were on to them and decided they needed a diversion. Otherwise, why bother? Just take them.'

Anna had been thinking along similar lines.

'The question though, is how did they find out?' He stopped and turned to her.

'The terrorists would have been watching Dermot and Marcus for days. One of our surveillance team probably gave themselves away.'

'That's one assumption for a start; a highly trained surveillance officer got sloppy. It happens, but then we'd also have to assume the terrorists were watching at the right moment. That's two. And that they'd know enough to recognise what they were seeing. That makes three in all.'

Anna nodded slowly, doing her best to keep up with all of the assumptions as he started walking again.

'Or perhaps someone just told them.' They'd reached the foot of the steps up to the bridge. He stopped again and turned to her. 'Just the one assumption there.'

'You're saying we've got a mole?' Anna's shivers were back.

'I've been doing this long enough and know a leak when I see one.' He started to climb the steps. 'Well-planned operations like this don't go south for no reason. So it's either our friends at the Met or us. And it's not as if we've got the best reputation in that regard.'

'The Met can hardly talk either.'

'True.'

But Anna knew what he was thinking. The police might leak like a sieve, but unlike the intelligence services, they didn't have the ghost of Kim Philby hanging around and generally stinking the place out. They didn't have Blunt, Burgess or Maclean either. All years ago now, deep in the chilly depths of the Cold War. But the echoes of those names still haunted the intelligence community half a lifetime later.

'I want to keep this in-house for now. The last thing we need is the Met crying blue murder.' He paused for breath at the top of the steps.

'Felicity.' The thought hit Anna like a punch. 'If there's a mole, they may know about her too.' They'd been working on the premise that the girl's cover hadn't been blown. Their one shred of comfort from the whole sorry mess was that they had an officer on the inside. An officer who might just be able to get the prisoners out.

'I'm sorry, Anna.' Lawson shook his head sadly.

She felt her stomach fall away. 'You think she's dead?' It was more than likely if the terrorists knew she was MI5. But Anna wasn't going to accept it until they had a body.

Lawson reached out to touch her shoulder, his eyes sadder than she'd ever seen them.

She stared back, unable to ask the question on her lips as cold tears formed in her eyes.

They *had* found Felicity's body.

She wanted to put her fingers in her ears, to shake her head and block out his words. If she didn't hear him speak them, then they wouldn't be true.

But that wasn't it. When he started speaking, he told her about the series of large and highly irregular payments that had made their way into Felicity Diamond's bank account. 'I'm afraid it rather looks like she's their mole.'

Chapter 26

'Sir, we think we've got something.' Roberts stuck his head round Henwell's door, breathless with excitement and exertion from the short walk across the office.

Henwell jumped out of his seat and followed Roberts back into the main office. The team had worked all through Friday morning and deep into the afternoon without a sniff of a break. So if they thought they'd found something, however small or insignificant, Henwell definitely wanted to hear it.

The sergeant's habitual surliness had largely melted away, and he'd grafted hard all day, supervising Lidstone and a team of uniforms as they scoured the CCTV and traffic enforcement cameras for any clues. DS Prim was still out leading the uniforms on the door-to-doors but so far had turned up nothing. And Henwell had spent the day sweating the network of informants he'd built up during his time in the drug squad. It seemed more than inconceivable that something this big could have gone down without word getting round the criminal fraternity. But nobody was saying anything. MI5 and GCHQ had come up empty-handed too, even with the far greater freedoms to snoop and pry that they enjoyed.

Roberts lowered himself into his long-suffering chair with a groan, a hand easing an empty pizza box aside then reaching for the pack of biscuits next to his keyboard. Not until another of the custard creams had safely passed his lips did he reach for the computer's mouse. Emergency or not, a man had to keep his strength up. A couple of clicks later, a still image of a dark-blue Ford Transit van with blacked-out windows filled the screen. Another click and the image started to move.

'This camera's about 150 yards from the fish company building. The van drove past about five minutes before the explosion.' Roberts was still finishing the last of the biscuit as he spoke.

'Why are we only seeing this now?' Henwell felt his anger flare.

If it was that close to the building, it was one of the first cameras they should have checked.

Roberts sucked his teeth. 'It was listed as out of action. Danny… I mean we… didn't double-check until just now. Sorry, sir.'

Henwell took a long, deep breath. If the mistake had been Lidstone's, as Roberts had just let slip, then it would have been a genuine one. No point shouting the odds about it now. It was only yesterday that the DC had saved his life. And if Roberts was covering for the DC it might mean a bit of team spirit was developing between the pair of them. That had to be a good thing. But still, time had been lost. 'OK, what else?'

'We got them again here too, joining the North Circular.'

On screen, the image changed to show a traffic light. A red people carrier drove by, followed by the same van.

'And again here.' Roberts clicked his mouse and the image changed again. 'Heading east. First near Wembley, then again at Brent Cross, then Finchley. Nothing on the cameras from Woodford onwards or on the A1 or M11.'

'Run it all the way.' Henwell watched as the van was picked up by a series of cameras around the North Circular Road.

'Must have turned off on one of the minor roads. It doesn't look like they were going far.'

'Not all the junctions have cameras. We're checking the ones that do now.'

'Anything on the van's owner?'

'Rental sir.' Roberts grimaced. 'Picked up two days ago, not due back until next week.'

At least it wasn't stolen. That would have meant a dead end. A rental meant a driving licence at least.

'We're chasing the hire company now, some place in Wembley.' Lidstone's head popped up from behind his computer screen. 'They've said they'll check and get straight back.'

'Tell them if they don't get back to us within ten minutes, we'll be out there with a warrant. Keep the team on the CCTV.' Henwell turned back towards his office then stopped. 'And well done.' Despite the lost time, it was a lead, the only one they had right now. Hundreds of vans must drive in and out of the industrial estate every day, but the timing was bang on. Henwell felt that familiar tingle down the back of his neck, the feeling of being on the scent.

He was heading back to his office when Lidstone gave a yelp. 'Got them.'

Henwell spun round, jostling with Roberts to get behind Lidstone's desk for a better look.

'There.' The DC pointed at the screen. The same van was turning off into a side street. 'Edmonton, just before the underpass.' He clicked on his mouse, and a map came up on his screen. 'It's all residential streets there, sir, not many cameras.'

'OK, get the locations of all the ones nearby and get them checked. I'll call DS Prim, get her to move her team down there, start door-to-door with photos of the van and the registration. Pics of Dermot and Marcus as well. Someone must have seen something. I'll tell her you'll email it all over to her.'

'Yes, sir.'

Roberts hurried back across the office as his desk phone started to ring. He picked it up, grabbing a pen and starting to write as he listened. 'OK, thank you.' He put the receiver down with a smile. 'Van was hired by a Mr Giles Parker from Hastings. Got his licence number and address.'

'Right, get the local plod to pull him in straight away.' Hastings was hardly a hotbed of international terrorism, but Henwell could feel the adrenalin buzz growing as he pulled his phone out and scrolled down to DS Prim's number. It was often the way of it with an investigation, one small find leading to another and everything quickly falling into place. If things carried on moving this fast, they might still have a chance. But they'd get nowhere if they couldn't find that van.

*

'Thanks, we'll be waiting for him.' Henwell ended the call from DS Warren of Sussex Police and sat back with a sigh. Just as things could start to move quickly, they could equally slow down again. And all in the space of an hour.

Nothing from Prim on the door-to-door, nothing more from the CCTV and now the van hire looked like being a dead end. Giles Parker had been up in London on business three days earlier when his wallet had been stolen. One minute it was there, the next gone. A pickpocket, he reckoned, outside a hotel in Covent Garden. He'd reported the theft at the closest police station, which just happened to be Charing Cross, where Henwell and the team were based. So it would be easy to check the details of the crime, although he doubted the local beat officers would have had the resource or the inclination to follow it up.

But the stolen ID was at least another indication that they had the right van. And with a location for the theft of the wallet, they could get straight onto the CCTV outside the hotel to try to ID the pickpocket.

Henwell stood up and tried to stretch out some of the kinks in his back. Just shy of 7pm and time was very much against them. But this wasn't over yet; he wouldn't let it be. Not with two people due to die tomorrow. He pulled out his phone and hit Anna's number; keen to share his findings and hoping she might have news of her own.

Chapter 27

'Dermot?'

He kept his breathing as steady as possible, hoping Marcus would think he was asleep.

'Dermot?'

Couldn't the man just leave him alone?

'Wake up!'

'What is it?' He finally relented.

'Do you think they'll bring any more food?'

'No. It's night-time.' The light from the high window had long since faded, leaving them in total darkness. He reckoned it must be well past ten o'clock. 'Maybe in the morning.'

'But I'm hungry.'

'I don't care. And I don't have to listen. I'm not your agent anymore, remember.'

'Look… I'm sorry. I was upset. I didn't mean what I said.'

'Seriously, don't worry about it.' The last thing Dermot wanted was the chef reversing his decision. If he did get out of this alive, not having to work for Marcus would be one of the few positives from the whole sorry episode.

The chef was silent for a few minutes, and Dermot hoped he might have fallen asleep.

'What do you think they've got planned?' Marcus's bed creaked in protest as he shifted his weight.

'No idea.' All he knew was that it was certain to be bigger than Kevin Story with the mic cord and the finger. Bigger than Mickey Morris and the dirty great axe too. Bigger and far more nasty.

'The police, MI5, they will find us, won't they?'

'Yes.' But every minute that ticked by made Dermot doubt it more.

'I can't die now. My obituary would say "former TV host."'

Was that all the chef cared about? But then maybe Dermot could use that to his advantage. 'Let's do something about it.'

'There's nothing we can do. We're trapped.'

'That's not the attitude that got Marcus Diesel to the top.' Dermot had been going to wait until morning to share his plan. But now seemed as good a time as any. 'Ten years as host of *The Meal of Fortune*. You remember that celebrity special in 2013?'

'Christ, yeah. That bird from Corrie was hot. Afterwards we –'

'I don't want to know. But it still holds the record for the highest audience for a daytime TV cookery show in the UK.'

'It does?'

'Absolutely.' Dermot had no idea about the audience figures, but he did need Marcus fired up and ready to go. 'That's why they targeted you. They'll be thinking if they can bring Marcus Diesel down, they can bring anyone down.'

'Yeah, that's right.' Marcus's bed creaked again. It sounded as if he was sitting up now. 'And I'm not going to let that happen.'

'Good, 'cause I've got a plan to get us out of here.'

Last year, with that business with the Russians, everyone had expected Dermot to hide in a corner and wet himself when the going got tough. But he hadn't.

A brave man. That's what the little Russian mafioso with the bad blond hair had called him at the end.

Brave or lucky.

He just needed to be brave or lucky again. Or maybe both? But he couldn't do it on his own.

'OK, this is what we need to do.' Dermot sat up, staring out into the darkness as he started to speak, knowing the chef would be looking right back at him. And if their eyes could have met, something special would have passed between them. Like in a movie, where two rivals put their differences behind them to battle a common enemy; lasting friendship forged as they fought together, eventually winning out against the odds. Except the Hollywood version probably wouldn't have had a half-full bucket of stinking piss on the floor between them. Dermot wrinkled his nose, trying to ignore the smell as he laid out his plan.

When he'd finished he sat quietly, listening in the darkness to Marcus's breathing as the chef took it all in. Maybe they *could* do this? Maybe there was hope after all?

'That's the stupidest plan I've ever heard. It's not even a plan at all.' Marcus's camp bed creaked as he rolled over. 'Oh, and you're still sacked.'

There was no way back for the whole buddy-movie shtick after that.

Chapter 28

Henwell checked his watch again, 11.40am, bang on time. He made his way slowly up the pathway towards the cracked front door, turning to nod to Roberts and the two uniforms behind him. All three nodded back silently, Roberts and one of the uniforms giving him the thumbs-up. The other one's thumbs were a little too busy with the big red battering ram in his hands.

Henwell reached the door and stopped. Up close it looked in even worse condition, half-rotten, the faded green paint cracked and peeling. It certainly wouldn't take much more than a shoulder. Henwell's was still feeling a little tender from being thrown halfway across a car park though, and there were all sorts of health and safety rules these days. So the battering ram it would be.

He checked his watch again. Lidstone, Prim and the second team would be in place at the back entrance by now. He held up his hand, silently counting down from five with his fingers.

*

Sometimes you just copped a break. It was one of the rules of police work. Maybe even the first rule. And sometimes those breaks just took their time to get copped.

Like all night and into the next morning.

But finally, it had come, which meant they were still in the game. Except that today was the day Marcus and Dermot were supposed to die. So it might already be too late.

They'd had no luck finding where the van had gone. Nothing from MI5 or GCHQ. And nothing from any of Henwell's sources either.

But the CCTV outside the hotel had come good. Giles Parker, emerging from what had been a successful business meeting only to fall for the classic brush-past. A minor collision for which he'd done all the apologising. It wasn't until a couple of seconds later that he'd realised he was a wallet lighter.

Plying your trade as a pickpocket in broad daylight in a city with the world's greatest concentration of cameras? That was just asking for it, surely? Well, not if you kept your hood up. A simple, low-tech approach that aced the best that CCTV had to offer every time.

And almost any other time, the pickpocket would have got away with it. Nobody hurt, credit cards cancelled, one punter a few quid out of pocket. Nobody was going to take the time to isolate the clearest image of the man in the hoodie. Then check and double-check every single frame for a potential match – on every single camera in a slowly expanding circle. And nobody was going to keep a whole team of detectives, uniforms and civilian staff at it all night. Not for an everyday street robbery that could be massaged away in next month's crime report.

But when there was a little more at stake and you did throw everything at it? Well that's when you got the results.

Slowly, painstakingly, they'd managed to track the hooded pickpocket as he'd taken a roundabout route away from the crime scene.

Down Long Acre and onto Shaftesbury Avenue. Then winding up through Soho. Rupert Street, then Berwick Street and Wardour Street. Finally emerging on Oxford Street, then heading along to Tottenham Court Road Tube Station. Which was where they'd almost lost him.

Tracking a man in central London, with its wall-to-wall CCTV coverage, was one thing. But once he made it onto the Underground, he could have emerged from any of the network's 270 stations across the capital and been lost forever.

But they'd got lucky. Maybe he'd thought he was safe? Or perhaps he'd just got a bit hot? But the hood had finally come off as the pickpocket entered the station, his eyes looking straight into a conveniently placed camera as he'd jogged down the steps. The facial recognition software had done the rest.

*

'Go, go, go.' Henwell gave the signal and the whole team started to move.

The 'big red key' as the battering ram was affectionately known, sent the whole door flying back up the hallway, and they were in.

The struggle, if it could be called that, was over before it began. The suspect was sitting on the sofa watching daytime TV in his pants. Next to him, a woman in a panda onesie was rolling a spliff.

The man's efforts to get to his feet were swiftly hampered by eighteen stone of police constable, who soon had him face down on the sofa with a knee in his back.

'Murghhhhggg.' Whatever he was trying to say, the cheap upholstery was doing a good job of muffling it.

'What we supposed to have done?' Panda woman was left to do the talking, or rather shouting.

'Just need a little word with your fella.' Henwell nodded to the female PC in the doorway. 'Take her into the kitchen, please. Try to calm her down.'

The constable relieved the woman of the drugs and started to lead her out of the room.

'Effin' Pigs… This is harassment, this is.' A steam of colourful language followed, the words shouted even louder.

Classy lady. The lad had done well for himself there.

'OK, let him up.' Henwell stood over the man on the sofa as the uniform let go. 'Sit there and don't move.'

The man sat.

'Darren Coyle?'

He nodded his head sullenly.

Nobody's idea of a terrorist. But that was because he wasn't. Coyle was just your common or garden toe rag, a petty thief with a string of convictions as long as the arm he used to dip into people's pockets and bags. With so many appearances in the Met's database, he probably deserved a subscription. It hadn't taken long to come up with an address.

'Where's the wallet, Darren?'

'What ya talking about?'

'We don't have time for this. The wallet you nicked in Covent Garden on Tuesday. The driving licence was used to commit a serious crime. That puts you in the frame for conspiracy.'

'I don't know about any wallet. Police brutality this is.'

If Coyle thought a knee in the back represented any sort of brutality, Henwell would be happy to hand him over to MI5. They'd have people somewhere in the dark bowels of Thames House who'd view their particular brand of persuasion techniques as little more than basic people skills.

And he'd be doing that soon if Coyle didn't start talking.

'You can really help us out here, Darren. Then we won't need to take it any further.' Henwell watched, seeing the calculation in the man's eyes. Not the sharpest, but there was a low cunning there, common to many of his kind.

'Let me get me clothes on first.' The man shivered as he looked down at his scrawny arms and chest, all covered in cheap-looking tattoos.

Henwell nodded again, and Roberts headed through the doorway, coming back a few seconds later holding up a fluffy pink sweatshirt and another onesie, this one covered in pineapples.

'All I could find.' He gave Coyle a nasty smile. 'Take your pick.'

'You taking the piss? Them's Nadine's.'

'Just put it on.' Henwell grabbed the sweatshirt and tossed it to the man on the sofa, fixing him with a hard stare.

Coyle stared back sullenly before slipping it over his head.

'Good.' Henwell bent down and picked up a neat white box from the coffee table as the sound of breaking crockery came from the kitchen. That would be the lady of the house calming down.

'iPhone 12 Pro.' Henwell held up the box. 'Not bad. Where did you get it?'

'It's mine.'

'All of them?' He nodded at the table where there must have been thirty identical boxes. 'And I'm guessing we'll find all sorts if we have a proper look round.'

'So?' Coyle sniffed and looked down.

'Just seems like a lot of stuff for one person.' He let his eyes wander around the sitting room, at the peeling paint, the damp on the wall and worn and mismatched furniture. 'You know, living somewhere like this.'

'They're all kosher.'

'Then it wouldn't be a problem if we took them away to check. The person you're holding them for wouldn't come round asking difficult questions.'

Coyle bowed his head, and Henwell knew he had him.

And right here was the flaw in the terrorists' plan. They must have had their reasons for freelancing the theft of the wallet to such a low-life scrote. But however well they'd covered their bases up until now, Coyle was the weak link in the chain. A chain Henwell was about to break apart.

'You ready to tell me about the wallet now?'

Coyle looked up. 'There was this guy in the pub –'

'Sir, you need to see this.' Roberts stepped forward, cutting the man off.

Henwell turned to see the sergeant holding up his phone. A video was starting up on the screen. Whatever Coyle had to tell them, it looked like it would be too late.

Chapter 29

Noon, the day already half over. Did that mean there was a fifty per cent chance Dermot and Marcus were dead already? Anna looked down at her phone, willing Henwell to call with news of the raid on the pickpocket's home. She knew that the longer the wait, the greater the chance the police had come up empty-handed.

She sat back with a yawn, rubbing dry eyes that hadn't seen sleep in well over twenty-four hours, then running a hand through her unwashed hair. Around her, the office was Saturday-lunchtime quiet. Her team were in of course. At least all the ones who weren't filthy traitors. But they were keeping their distance, heads down as they continued to sift for intelligence that in all likelihood simply wasn't there.

Fifty-fifty.

Anna's eyes flicked up to her computer screen, hoping for something from GCHQ, any chatter about the kidnapping they'd managed to intercept. Or maybe something from one of the obscure noticeboards that all the cranks and extremists thought were so secure?

But there was nothing. This group, whoever they might be, were watertight.

Fifty-fifty at best.

But no. The terrorists, in their own warped way, had shown a taste for the theatrical every time. Whatever they had planned, it was going to be big. Anna didn't believe Dermot and Marcus were dead.

Not yet.

She yawned again. Maybe she could close her eyes, just for a few minutes. She shook her head, trying to chase the tiredness away. There'd be no sleep for her until this was over.

Next, she stood up and walked across towards the window. Outside, the day hadn't got itself properly started, yesterday's crisp sunshine giving way to angry dark clouds hanging over the sluggish grey-brown river. Anna stretched, her eyes following a half-empty tourist boat gliding along serenely. And that's when her uninvited guest came, edging its way along one of the darker and most twisty pathways in her brain, hoping it wouldn't be spotted until it was too late to send it back into the gloom.

Felicity Diamond.

The mole.

In Anna's mind, the girl had already taken on the qualities of her animal namesake – sniffing, snuffling and scurrying.

Furtive.

She let the creature come, all the better to examine it. A single word shouted out on repeat in her head.

Why? Why? Why?

But she knew the answer wouldn't come until she had Felicity sitting opposite her, or preferably tied down to some kind of workbench.

The first payment had gone into the girl's bank account the week before. Sizeable but nothing that would have raised suspicions. Then the big one, the day of the ambush. Four hundred and seventy-ninety thousand pounds in all; the terrorists seemingly not prepared to stretch to the full half-million to buy the loyalty of an MI5 officer.

The money hadn't been touched or moved, and now Felicity's account was frozen. At least the greedy little bitch would never get her hands on the cash. Anna thought back to the guilt that had washed over her with the heat, smoke and noise of the explosion. Even later, after they'd established that nobody had died in the building, that guilt had refused to shift.

There was no more guilt for Felicity now though. Just rage, bubbling and boiling away.

She turned from the grey afternoon light and headed back to her desk, checking her phone again for any word from Henwell.

Still nothing.

It was the source of the money, more than anything else, which proved Felicity's duplicity. Or rather the lack of a source.

They'd chased the payment back up the line as far as they could, via a Swiss bank to a shell company in the British Virgin Islands. Then nothing. Payments like that were rarely legitimate.

Anna checked her email again then her phone, the filthy little mole with Felicity's features still snuffling about inside her head.

Should she have known? If she'd spent a little less time disliking the girl, a little less time being jealous, would Anna have noticed?

The only clue, the only possible hint, was the laptop Felicity had missed in Olivier's apartment. Maybe Anna should have picked up on that, rather than putting it down to Felicity's inexperience? Expecting people to be sneaky, conniving bastards was part of the MI5 job description, after all. Thinking the best of them until they proved you wrong was not.

But a junior officer on her first mission had failed to spot something in a hurried search, with hostiles closing in fast. It was a bit of a stretch to go from there to a full-blown traitor in one bound.

In her mind, Anna stamped her foot, and the mole went scampering back into the darkness. There'd be plenty of opportunities to worry about Felicity after this was done. Right now, it was time to get a coffee, splash some water on her face and chase up GCHQ again. She was just heading for the bathroom when her phone started to vibrate in her pocket. She whipped it out, juggling it in her hands for a second.

It was Henwell.

'Any news on the pickpocket?' Anna answered, hoping her voice didn't give her away. Only she, Lawson and a select few in MI5 knew about Felicity's treachery. It felt wrong to be holding it back from the policeman, but that's how it needed to be for now.

'Yes, but you've got to see this. I've emailed you a link.'

She turned back to her computer and opened up her email, just as her desk phone started to ring. Her mobile beeped to tell her there was another call waiting and then a different alert came, heralding the arrival of a text message. Another loud ping cut across the sound of the phone, and the lift door slid open.

'Anna.' Sophie Harper was running across the office towards her, phone in her hand. 'They've posted a video…'

Just like after all the murders. She felt her head spin. It was too late.

'Are you seeing this?' Henwell's voice was back in her ear.

One click, and the email was open. Another and the video started playing.

It wasn't until she'd watched it to the end that Anna realised her phone had stopped ringing.

First came the relief, because they were still alive. The video wasn't showing the murders, it was advertising them in advance. That would be the terrorists raising the already high bar again.

Then came the cold anger, stoked by the mocking tones of the masked man in the video.

She turned to Sophie. 'Can you track this? Find out where it was uploaded? Take it down?'

'Yes. But they'll just keep putting it up again.'

'We need to try.' On the screen, the number of views had already hit 100,000. That was the news blackout gone. The truth that MI5 and the police had let two men be kidnapped was well and truly out there now.

She started to watch the video again, this time looking more carefully for clues, as the man behind that latex mask laid out the details of what was to come later that afternoon.

'Anna, can you hear me?' Henwell was still on the line.

Then she remembered. 'The pickpocket.' There had to be something…

Otherwise, they'd be watching, along with everyone else with a decent broadband connection, as the murders of Dermot Jack and Marcus Diesel were streamed live to the whole world in a little under four hours' time.

Chapter 30

'What time do you think it is?' Marcus eased himself up off the camp bed and stood. 'I'm starving.'

'Must be the afternoon.' Dermot looked up at the window as his stomach rumbled. Hours had gone by since the first light had crept back into the room, but there'd been no sign of a hearty breakfast or lunch for the condemned men.

'You think it'll be soon?'

Dermot shrugged. 'Don't know. But you need to be ready. We agreed, yeah?'

'Yes. I said I'd do it, didn't I?' At some point during a night of broken sleep, Marcus had stood up, peed in the bucket and sulkily agreed to go along with Dermot's plan. 'I still don't see why it has to be me, not you?'

Dermot fought back a sigh; they'd been through this. 'You're the star here. If anything happens to you, whatever they've got planned gets ruined. They're not going to risk that.'

'And MI5 may still find us, or the police.' But Marcus didn't sound optimistic.

Neither was Dermot. All night, his hopes had been growing and then receding again, almost with every breath. Anna would never give up on him. But not giving up wasn't the same as succeeding, was it? They had to assume they were on their own.

He stood and walked over to the door, putting his ear up against the wood and holding his breath as he listened, but there was no sound from the other side. He paced back to his bed and sat down. Then he lay back, trying to keep his breathing steady. Marcus was right, of course; it really wasn't much of a plan. But then he hadn't heard any bright ideas from the other side of the room.

He closed his eyes, and Molly came to him again. All night he'd been fighting a losing battle to keep thoughts of her at bay.

'Daddy.'

She smiled up at him, five years old and wearing the pink anorak from the photo in Kew Gardens.

'Daddy?'

Next came the Puffa-jacketed seven-year-old.

'Daddy.'

And finally, the girl he'd seen just last week, nine years old going on thirteen.

DAD!

He chased all three of them away, wondering whether his daughter knew about the kidnap. And whether she knew that he was meant to die today. He could only hope his ex-wife had managed to keep it from her. Then he stiffened, eyes flying open as he heard a noise from the corridor outside.

He jumped up, catching Marcus's eye and nodding towards the door as the echo of footsteps got louder. The pair of them wouldn't be many people's idea of heroes, but then that might just be their one advantage. And despite all Dermot's doubts, the chef's face was set in a look of grim determination.

'Remember, they won't risk anything happening to you.' Dermot stood.

'Come on then.' Marcus positioned himself on the spot they'd agreed, between the two beds.

Dermot ran round behind him, pulling the plastic fork from his pocket. It suddenly looked very small in his hand.

And very plastic.

'You ready?'

'Ready.' Marcus nodded.

He held the fork against the chef's throat as a key turned in the lock and the door swung open.

'Owww. Don't press so hard.'

'Sorry.'

Bright light flooded the room. Dermot squinted, managing to make out two figures. They stepped through the door and then stopped dead.

Right... Now he had their attention. Dermot blinked, forcing himself to keep his eyes open despite the brightness.

Both figures were decked out all in black. Black sweatpants and hoodies, black balaclavas over their faces and wrap-around sunglasses for good measure.

'Come any closer and he gets it, OK?' His voice had sounded a bit high, but otherwise, he felt he'd done a good job of showing he meant it.

The one on the left took a step forward.

'Your little game's over if he's dead.' Again, he thought he'd done all right on the voice front, showing them how deadly serious he was.

The one on the right took a step to the side, fanning out.

'Please. He means it,' Marcus whimpered, a decent effort at sounding scared, but then he probably was.

Lefty moved forward again. He was the bigger of the two but looked agile enough on his feet. The other was smaller, lean, maybe even a woman? He/she took another step forward too.

'One more step and I'll kill him.' Dermot dug the fork harder into Marcus's throat, hoping it didn't snap.

'With that?' A dry chuckle came from the larger man's throat. He took another step forward. 'There is a reason we gave you plastic forks, you know.'

That voice? It seemed familiar. But there was no time to worry about it. They had to move fast. The fork had only ever been a bluff.

'Now.' Dermot pushed Marcus towards the door and followed, kicking the bucket over as he went.

Was there an old proverb… *'Anyone who leaves a bucket full of piss shouldn't be scared to get their feet wet?'*

Well, there should have been, because it worked a treat. The smaller figure jumped back instinctively as the bucket's contents spilled across the floor.

And that was all they needed. Marcus and Dermot ran between their captors and out through the door, Dermot slamming it shut behind him as he went.

'Come on.' The chef turned left, sprinting off down a long corridor lined with doors.

Dermot kept pace, listening for signs of pursuit. But there were none that he could hear.

They reached a right turn, then barrelled round it into an identical-looking corridor, lined with more doors. Some sort of self-storage place by the look of it.

Marcus slowed, trying the handle on the first door. It opened to reveal an empty storeroom.

'No, keep moving.' Dermot shoved him in the back. 'We need to find the way out.'

Marcus headed off again, already breathing hard.

Dermot risked a glance over his shoulder, but nobody was coming. It looked like the door might have locked behind them, trapping their captors in the little room. Part of him wanted to laugh out loud.

How easy had that been? No help from MI5 or the police, but they'd done it all the same.

Ha! Up yours, DI *'I Don't Need to Case the Joint'* Henwell.

And Anna? Maybe now she'd see Dermot for who he really was now?

They reached the end of the corridor; the only option was to turn right again into another identical passage way. He checked behind again, still nobody giving chase.

Marcus tried another door to the left. Another storeroom.

Then Dermot tried one to the right with the same result.

'Come on.' He took the lead now, running to the end of the corridor, another right turn the only option.

One more right, and they'd be…

He was starting to have a bad feeling about this. He looked around wildly for any sign of an exit. But there were none to be seen. So he started to move from door to door, trying the handles on every one. All opened to reveal more empty store-rooms.

Marcus was doing the same on the other side of the corridor.

All empty, all dead ends.

'We could hide?' The chef sounded dangerously short of breath now.

'No, they'll find us.' Dermot looked behind him again. Still nobody there. 'We've got to get out of here.' He headed on, just a fast walk now, trying each door he passed.

More storerooms.

They reached the end of the corridor, with no option but to take their fourth right. Dermot walked round the corner then stopped. Twenty or so yards ahead of them, the larger of their captors leaned casually against the wall outside their cell.

'Err… Dermot.'

He felt a tap on his shoulder and turned to see Marcus pointing back the way they'd just come. The other black-clad figure was walking slowly along the corridor, an ugly-looking handgun with a silencer pointed at them.

'It's this way.' The big guy called out.

Dermot swivelled back round to see him pointing to an exit sign on the ceiling.

'You didn't need to go all the way round.' That little chuckle again.

Why couldn't Marcus just have turned the other way out of the cell?

'Come on then.' The man pushed himself off the wall.

What was it about that voice?

The answer became clear as the man took off his sunglasses and hood. Then he slowly removed the balaclava, revealing a latex mask beneath. The likeness was passable at best, the painted mouth pulled into a half-smile, half-sneer. But it was clear enough whom the mask was meant to depict.

'What's going on?' Next to him, Marcus was shaking his head.

Things were moving a little too fast now, and Dermot didn't have any kind of answer. The masked man stripped off his hoodie and black sweatpants to reveal a pristine set of chef's whites beneath.

'Did you really think we wouldn't have cameras in there? Microphones too. We knew what you were planning all along. Thought it might be fun to get it on film, maybe cut it into the video.'

'You won't get away with this.' Dermot stepped forward but stopped as he felt the gun pressing into his back.

'We'll see.' The masked man shrugged. 'This way, please.' Then he unlocked a sturdy-looking door.

Even if Marcus had turned right, they wouldn't have been able to get away. The kidnappers had it all worked out from the start.

'Get moving.' He waved them through in front of him. 'Don't want to be late now, do we?'

For what? Dermot walked as slowly as he could. Every extra second gave the police and MI5 a little more time. That felt like their only hope now.

'Stop there.' The man barked out the order as Dermot reached the third door on the left. This one bigger than the rest. 'Backs against the wall.' He edged past them on the other side of the corridor and put another key into the lock.

'You'll never get away with this.' Dermot looked the masked man in the eye, then realised the eye holes were probably in the mouth, so he looked him in the mouth instead.

The man just ignored him. 'In here, please. You first, Marcus. You are the star of the show, after all.'

The chef paused then stepped into the room. Dermot turned again to see the gun still pointed at him. Probably best to follow.

The room was much bigger than the one where they'd been held. His eyes darted around, quickly recognising the parody of a familiar TV set in the far corner. And then the music started; the familiar theme he must have heard a thousand times down the years. And finally he heard the big booming voice of the announcer with those oh-so-familiar words.

'Ladies and gentlemen. It's time to spin…'

Chapter 31

'... *The Meal of Fortune.*' The announcer's voice boomed out from the speakers, echoing all around the grey walls of the situation room.

Anna stood, despite all the empty chairs down either side of the long conference table, her eyes locked in on the huge TV screen on the wall. On other days, it might have displayed satellite images of terrorist facilities in the planet's most isolated areas or real-time drone surveillance footage of targets. Right now, it was showing a daytime TV cookery show.

Of sorts.

The camera panned round the set. First the big wheel, then the two brightly coloured podiums awaiting the contestants. Finally, the kitchen area where the cooking would take place in part two of the show.

'OK, there might be a slight delay, but it's definitely a live stream.' Sophie Harper sat at the end of the table nearest the TV furiously typing away at her laptop, a headset keeping her in touch with her tech team in their basement bunker. She turned to Anna with a nod. 'We've started tracing.'

The video trailer had been running all afternoon. Subtle it was not, the masked man in the chef's outfit promising a new and deadly take on *The Meal of Fortune*, starring Marcus Diesel and Dermot Jack.

Live at 4pm, this was daytime TV after all.

Every time the tech team had taken the trailer down, it had just popped up again, posted remotely from IP addresses in Cairo, Kiev, Bucharest, Baku, Kazakhstan, Mumbai, Grimsby, you name it. And each time the video had racked up thousands more views. Ten million hits and counting, only God and Google knew how many people would be watching now the show was live.

But that was the key – *live.* This was the terrorists' next level of escalation, designed to send the publicity stratospheric.

But *live* meant a continuous signal, coming directly from wherever they were filming. Yes, they were bouncing it around the world to hide their location. But as long as that stream was up, they were traceable.

Anna looked across at Henwell. He'd opted to stay standing too, planning a swift exit as soon as the location was confirmed. He'd come across to Thames House as part of a small group from the Met to ensure a coordinated response. DCI Simpson sat at the table in front of Henwell, next to an uptight-looking female detective sergeant. Anna had forgotten her name the second they'd been introduced.

Deputy Assistant Commissioner Connor completed the police party. He'd sat himself down right next to Sophie Harper, all the better to badger her for updates presumably. Despite his promise to be there, Lawson had so far failed to show. But there was every chance that even a situation like this wasn't his main priority right now.

On screen, the camera swooped around the studio audience, who clapped and cheered enthusiastically. An edit ripped straight from the original show, Anna guessed. Unless the terrorists really had enlisted a live audience. Not that she'd put anything past them.

'How accurate can you be?' She stepped up behind Sophie.

'Not sure. Depends how good their encryption is.'

'Anything on the cabbie yet?' Connor looked over at DCI Simpson.

That was their other remaining hope. Henwell's pickpocket had revealed he'd been asked to steal the wallet, any wallet, by a man in a pub. Coyle's description had been vague – thirties, tallish, no real distinguishing features. All sounded a bit dubious. But CCTV outside the pub had a man fitting the description getting into a black cab at about the right time. Tracing the driver via his number plate had proved simple. But tracking him down while he was out on shift wasn't quite so easy.

'Not yet, sir. He's been out working since ten this morning.' It was the DS next to Simpson who answered.

Prim, that was her name, Anna remembered now.

'Phone just goes to voicemail. Turns it off when he's driving, according to the wife. Normally covers Waterloo Station. We've got a team at the rank, and we're monitoring all the cameras in the area.' Her voice was clipped, officious and full of self-importance. 'We'll find him, sir.'

Henwell caught Anna's gaze with a small shake of his head. He'd already made it clear to her what he thought of Simpson and his team. And it sounded like they were positioning themselves to take the credit, even though it was Henwell who'd done the heavy lifting with the van and the pickpocket.

But all of that felt like a long shot now. Tracing the signal had to be their best bet. Anna looked back up at the screen as the camera finished panning round the set and returned to the two podiums, which were now occupied.

Dermot first.

Unshaven.

Harried.

The dark bags that shaded his eyes looked like they'd been drawn on in crayon by a child in a foul mood, with only a few minutes left before bed time.

Anna took a breath, fighting hard against the impotent rage welling up inside her.

She was the one who'd put him there.

The camera didn't linger on Dermot for long, moving round to Marcus Diesel. Because the TV chef was the real draw here. If anything, he looked worse than Dermot. His three-day stubble was streaked with grey, skin puffy, hair greasy and lifeless. He'd lost that jaunty beret somewhere along the way too.

'Anything yet?' Connor leaned in close to Sophie. If he was trying to hide his impatience, he wasn't doing a very good job.

'No.' Her eyes stayed glued to the laptop screen.

On the big TV, the camera was settling on the show's host.

Anton Du Beurre. Or someone wearing an Anton Du Beurre mask, to be precise.

The police had been tracking down suppliers and stockists of the mask ever since the trailer had gone live. Turned out though that the chef was a hugely popular fancy-dress option and it was available at literally hundreds of shops and online stores.

The masked host raised his arms as the canned applause faded away. 'Welcome to *The Meal of Fortune*. My name's Anton Du Beurre.' The impersonation was poor, the Belgian accent far too pronounced. He strolled across the studio, stopping in front of the two contestants.

Cue more wild applause.

They'd already run recognition software on the voice from the trailer but nothing had come up.

'You join us this afternoon for a special live edition of the show. And we're delighted to welcome back a familiar face, our old host Marcus Diesel.'

The camera panned back to Marcus who was sweating under the bright studio lights. No flattering make-up for his big red face on this edition of the show.

'And we've also got Dermot Jack. Not such a familiar face these days. A long time since you were such a screaming little wannabee. Does anyone even remember the Newboyz?'

A sore point for Dermot, Anna knew. But she suspected getting prickly over his long-dead pop career wasn't his priority right now.

'Why don't you come a bit closer? Stop hiding behind that fucking mask.' Dermot's voice was dry and cracked. Scared for sure, but there was anger there, defiance too.

Good, because Anna needed him to be angry. That way, he might keep himself alive long enough for them to find him.

'Please, this is a family show.' The host's tone was all mock outrage now. He turned to stare directly into the camera. 'Apologies if you picked up some bad language there. You just can't get the contestants these days.'

'OK.' Sophie Harper stopped typing and sat back. 'It's not the best encryption I've seen, but it's pretty good. They're using various VPNs and at least one onion server, bouncing the signal off multiple points too.'

'But can we track them?' Simpson was as bad at hiding his impatience as his boss.

'Doing it now.' Again, Sophie didn't rise to it.

On screen, the host gave a little laugh. 'Don't forget to tweet us @MoFLive using #celebsmustdie.'

'Jesus.' Connor thumped a hand down onto the desk. 'The man's a nutter.'

Anna doubted the term appeared in the Met's inclusiveness handbook. And the DAC was wrong. This was a calculated plan to destabilise the economy, not the work of a psychopath.

'Well, you all know the game by now.' On screen, the host was moving things on, perhaps mindful of MI5's tracing abilities. 'We spin the wheel and it lands on an ingredient. The contestants buzz in and answer a cookery question. A correct answer means they can take the ingredient themselves or give it to their opponent. Then after the break, they'll both be cooking up a tasty meal with everything they've won.'

But what was the catch?

'OK, we're closing in now.' Sophie's eyes were still on her screen. 'They're definitely in London.'

'But for today's special edition we've added a couple of new ingredients. Let's give a big *Meal of Fortune* welcome to sodium hydroxide and hydrochloric acid.'

A gasp rang round the audience.

'You don't need a degree in chemistry to know that on their own either will be just as deadly as any poison, especially when consumed in the quantities we'll be using tonight.'

Another gasp from the canned audience.

'But instead of me tasting the dishes and choosing a winner, our contestants will eat what they've cooked. Then one of them will walk away with our coveted *Meal of Fortune* trophy.'

The camera cut away to an image of what looked like a gold frying pan on a plinth.

'And the other…? Well, they won't be walking anywhere.'

'What if we refuse?' The anger was even clearer in Dermot's voice but there was fear there too.

'Then you'll both die.' The host shrugged. 'And it'll be less fun for our audience.'

The camera panned to Marcus Diesel, who was struggling to keep a little smile from his face. And who could blame him? Ask a chef to choose his weapon of choice in a duel to the death, and a cookery quiz had to come somewhere near the top.

'We've got to shut this down now.' Connor's face was lit up with barely suppressed rage. 'There must be millions of people watching.'

'Not yet. We're getting close now.' There was a hint of excitement in Sophie's voice. 'It's East London, definitely. Just need a few more minutes.'

They may not have a few more minutes. Anna took a deep breath and looked across at Henwell, but his eyes were glued to the screen.

Then the phone on the table in front of Simpson sprang to life. He put it to his ear and listened for a second or so. 'OK, put him on.' He switched the phone onto speaker and placed it back onto the table, an edge to his voice. 'We've found the cabbie, they're putting him on now.'

Anna ran around the table to join the others who were all clustering around the phone.

'What's this all about? I had a bleedin' fare.' The surliness in the cab driver's voice was clear even over the tinny speakers of the phone.

'Mr Harris, is it? This is DCI Simpson of the Metropolitan Police.' The policeman was suddenly all charm. 'You're not in any trouble. We're sorry for the inconvenience. We have an active criminal investigation we think you can help us with.'

'Oh, OK.' The cabbie's voice softened a little.

'You picked up a passenger outside the King's Arms pub in Kennington on Tuesday. About 3pm. We need to know where you took him.'

Silence from the other end of the line.

Hardly surprising, he must pick up dozens of fares each day. What were the chances of him remembering?

'Yeah, that was a funny one. All the way out to Leyton. Big fare, nice tip too.'

'Mr Harris.' Simpson leaned in close. 'Can you remember exactly where you dropped him?'

'That's what I mean, a funny one. Some big old abandoned warehouse. Looked like they were about to knock it down. Temple Mill Lane, just off the A12.'

Prim was already looking the place up on her phone.

'Anything else you can remember about the passenger, Mr Harris?'

'It was a guy, thirties. Think he might have been foreign. Didn't speak much, gave me a piece of paper with the address.'

'OK, you've been very helpful. Thank you.' Simpson cut the call without further niceties.

'Got it, sir.' Prim had a map up on her phone.

'It's East London too. The tracking's spot on.' Simpson was on his feet, phone to his ear again and tension in his voice. 'Get SCO19 out to Leyton. Sending the exact location now.'

'Let's go.' Henwell was already heading for the door.

'Not you, Detective Inspector.' Simpson held up a hand. 'Your team's been very helpful, but we'll take it from here.'

'Sir?' Henwell turned to Connor.

The DAC shrugged. 'This has always been DCI Simpson's case. He makes the operational calls.'

Anna saw the anger in Henwell's eyes as Simpson and Prim headed for the door. She gave him an apologetic shrug as she started to follow. No one was telling her to stand down. Then she stopped, doubt started to niggle away at the back of her mind. Something just felt well off. Hadn't it all been just that little bit too easy?

On the screen, the masked host was laughing again. 'If you want Marcus to live, tweet us with #TeamMarcus, and #TeamDermot if you don't want to see Mr Jack's insides burned away by corrosive industrial chemicals.'

'Get that signal taken down now.' Connor was almost shouting.

'No.' Anna headed back round the table. 'Can you get any closer, Sophie, just to be sure?'

'Should be able to.' The tech team leader turned back to her keyboard and started typing again.

'How sure do we need to be?' If anything Connor's voice was louder this time. 'You heard what the cabbie said. We got them. Take it down now.'

'NO!' Anna stepped up close behind Sophie, the doubt in her mind growing stronger with every passing second.

Too easy...

'We can't let people see this.' The DAC was on his feet, face reddening.

'Nearly there.' Sophie didn't even look up. 'Triangulating now.'

'Take it down.' The DAC took a step closer.

'Sir.' Henwell was next to Anna now. 'She's right. Let's just be sure.'

'With respect, I am a deputy assistant commissioner of the Met, and I am telling you to take it down.'

Sophie's eyes stayed locked on her screen.

'TAKE IT DOWN.'

'Ahem.'

They all spun around at the sound of a cough.

'And with respect, MI5 don't answer to the Met.' Sir Richard Lawson's voice was like sharpened flint. 'I think my team are probably right on this one.' He stood in the doorway, eyes fixed on Connor. 'And just for future reference, if the Met wants to bully my people, they'll need to send someone a lot more senior than a deputy assistant commissioner.'

Connor returned the stare, his face reddening further. Then finally he turned away with a long sigh and a shake of his head. 'Have it your way.'

'Sorry I couldn't get here earlier.' Lawson's voice softened as he turned to Anna. 'On the phone to the Home Secretary. We have her full support.'

'OK, we're getting closer.' Sophie turned to Anna. 'But they're not in Leyton.'

'It must be some kind of mistake.' Connor's head snapped back around towards them.

'The signal's coming from further north. Looks more like Edmonton.'

'That's where the van turned off the North Circular.' Henwell stepped towards his boss.

'You said you didn't know how precise you could be.' Connor's voice rose as the anger threatened to get the better of him again.

In Anna's mind the doubt just grew that little bit stronger again. Nagging, nagging, nagging. She tried to tune out all the voices and think.

'If Miss Harper says the signal's not coming from Leyton, then it's not coming from Leyton.' Lawson pulled out a chair and sat down slowly.

'But the cab driver was certain.' Connor still wasn't having it. 'The guy even wrote the address down. They must have done something to the signal to make it look as if it's coming from somewhere else. It's all just a false trail to throw us off the scent so they can finish their live show.'

Anna ignored him, turning to Henwell instead. 'All the other murders? How close have you come to getting a break?'

'Nowhere near.'

'Exactly – they were careful. But this has been sloppy all the way. You found the pickpocket. He tells you all about the guy in the pub. Then you got the guy getting into the taxi and the cabbie remembering him because he gave a big tip and got out somewhere odd. He even wrote the address down so the driver would remember it. That's the false trail.'

Connor snorted. 'Seems like a lot of effort. Why bother?'

'You just said it. Because this is live.' Anna pointed to the screen. 'They know we can track them. They're just trying to buy enough time to finish the broadcast.'

'Why not lead us to the other side of London? Or somewhere else?' The DAC still didn't sound convinced.

'They'd know our tech is a bit better than that.' Sophie cut in, looking up from her laptop. 'Too far away and they'd know we wouldn't fall for it.'

'I'll get another firearms team to Edmonton.' Henwell already had his phone out.

Back on the screen, the camera was on Dermot, a haunted look in his eyes. But the anger was there still, determination too.

Anna just needed him to stay strong for a little longer.

'Got it.' Sophie's voice was edged with triumph. 'Just off the A406. Looks like another disused warehouse, right down by the River Lee.' She read out a postcode.

'Let's go.' Anna was already heading for the door, Henwell's big footsteps echoing behind her as he relayed the new location to the firearms team. And Connor was saying something too, but his words were drowned out by the voice booming out from the TV.

'Ladies and gentlemen. It's time to spin… The Meal of Fortune.'

Chapter 32

The big wheel started to spin, just like the one from the real show. The jaunty electronic tune was the same as the original too.

Dermot's heart hammered along with the beat of the music, as if it was trying to find a way out between his ribs. He closed his eyes, falling back on the last little scrap of hope he could find. The show was going out live. Surely MI5 would be able to track the broadcast. He just had to make the game last as long as possible to give them time.

He opened his eyes again, focusing on the wheel, willing it to spin on and on, but it was already slowing. He looked over at Marcus. This would have been the time for something to pass between them, a silent pact that they'd win through together or go down fighting.

The chef turned and their eyes locked. Marcus gave him a nasty little smile and turned away.

Well, if that's how he wanted to play it.

Dermot tensed as the wheel clicked towards the hydrochloric acid, and then relaxed again as it spun on past. Up against a chef in a cookery quiz to the death? It shouldn't have been a contest. Except that Marcus wasn't a chef, not really. Over a decade earlier, a string of high-profile celeb chefs had turned down the chance to present *The Meal of Fortune.* Too low-brow, too cheap and too daytime. Back then Marcus had been a bits-and-pieces TV presenter, but for some still unexplained reason the show's producers had liked his screen test. *The Meal of Fortune* had gone on to hold down Channel 5's popular teatime slot for twelve years and had been syndicated to the likes of Germany, Belgium, Uzbekistan and Samoa. Marcus had spent the time milking his new-found fame while living on takeaways. The man still didn't know either end of a spatula from a baboon's arse.

'And it's carrots.' The Anton impersonator's voice cut in as the wheel came to a halt. Wild canned applause followed.

'A hugely popular vegetable, the eighty-seventh time carrots have come up on *The Meal of Fortune.* Here's the first question. Cultivated as long ago as 1,000 BC, carrots were first grown in which Asian country? A, Japan; B, India; or C, Afghanistan?'

India, it had to be? Although Dermot couldn't remember ever having them in a curry. He pressed down hard on his buzzer, but it was Marcus's light that flashed on.

'Afghanistan.'

Nah… What was the man on?

'That's the correct answer.'

What?

But the chef had fluked it. That was all. No need worry

'I'll take the carrots.' Marcus sounded very pleased with himself.

He was welcome to them. In the race against time that was the show's second half, there was no time for vegetables that required peeling. The wheel began to spin again, breezing on past the sodium hydroxide and the hydrochloric acid before stopping on some chicken fillets.

'Another favourite on *The Meal of Fortune.* Tasty, versatile and quick to prepare. Would go well with a wide range of industrial chemicals too. Fingers on buzzers… The most popular Indian dish in Britain is?'

Marcus's buzzer sounded before Dermot could even react.

'Chicken tikka masala.'

'Well you didn't let me read the options but that's the correct answer.'

'I'll take the chicken too.' The chef glanced over with a superior sort of smile.

A bead of sweat broke free on Dermot's neck and started to make the long and ticklish journey down his back, as the wheel was spun once more.

'Now we've got the first results from our Twitter poll in. It's currently #TeamDermot 60%, #TeamMarcus 40%.'

The wheel avoided the two killer chemicals again, landing on some fresh coriander.

Right, no pressure. Marcus was welcome to the coriander; the man wouldn't know what to do with it anyway.

'Name three other fresh herbs.'

Easy, Dermot buzzed in first. 'Parsley, rosemary and… errr.' The names of all other herbs he'd ever heard of seemed to have been erased magically from his mind.

'I'm going to have to hurry you there.'

'Sage.'

'Correct.'

He took the coriander, happy just to be on the board.

On and on the wheel span, each time nudging past the two deadly ingredients. Marcus bagged a selection of chillies before Dermot struck back strongly to claim some handy stir-fry veg, two salmon fillets and an avocado.

'Well, gents, still no sign of our two guest ingredients. Maybe you'll get lucky?'

Somehow Dermot doubted that.

'Let's have a look at some of your tweets.' The man in the Anton mask spun the wheel again. '*"Kill them both. Talentless money-grabbers"* That's from Lydia43, a sentiment I think we all concur with. And DiscoDingo21 has got some ideas about what Marcus could do with those carrots. But again, I do have to remind you all this is a family show.'

The wheel spun on, past the leeks and the courgettes.

Slowing, slowing, slowing.

Tin of tuna, spaghetti.

Slowing.

Olives, garlic, cauliflower.

Finally stopping.

Dermot closed his eyes.

'Ladies and gentlemen, it's what you've all been waiting for. Hy-dro-chlor-ic acid.'

A stunned gasp ran around the canned audience.

Right then… Focus. Nothing that had gone before mattered.

Marcus turned to him with another little smile.

Tosser.

'A versatile and popular industrial chemical used in a range of manufacturing processes and, of course, highly poisonous to humans. But this is a cookery show, so we've got a question about puddings. What are the three main ingredients in crème brûlée? No multiple choice this time.'

Egg yolks were definitely one. But the other two…? Dermot tried to think of the last time he'd eaten one, in a café with Molly in Edinburgh. Then he tried not to think about Molly.

'Clock's ticking, gentlemen.'

Marcus pressed down on his buzzer, turning to Dermot with a look bordering on glee. 'Is it cream, sugar and eggs?'

The man in the mask made a show of inspecting his card then looked up. 'Egg yolks actually, but I'll give you that one.'

Hang on. NO! It was egg yolks… Dermot had known that, and Marcus had got it wrong. He opened his mouth to protest.

But Marcus was already speaking. 'I'm sorry.' At least the chef had the decency to look genuinely apologetic.

Dermot closed his eyes and let his head slump forward.

'But I'm going to have to take that ingredient.'

What? His eyes snapped open again and he turned to the chef as the words sank in.

Silence.

From Dermot, who had no idea what to say.

From the masked host, who was similarly lost for words.

And from the audience, because no canned sound had ever been invented to respond to what Marcus had just done.

'No, wait…' Dermot stopped himself. If the chef was going to take the acid, then he wasn't about to talk him out of it. And he'd got the bloody answer wrong.

'You do understand the rules here, Marcus?' The man in the mask finally found his voice. 'You can give it to –'

'It's my bloody show. I understand the rules.'

'*Was* your show, actually. But if you're sure?'

'You know what they say.' Marcus looked across at Dermot again. 'Whatever doesn't kill you makes you stronger.'

'We've always been keen on a little nineteenth-century German philosophy here on *The Meal of Fortune.*' The masked host nodded appreciatively. 'But I think you'll find it will kill you. Your choice though.' He shrugged and then pressed the button again to spin the wheel before Marcus could change his mind.

Two, three or maybe even four more spins went by in a blur. Dermot got nowhere near answering any of the questions, with Marcus buzzing in to claim some rhubarb, stock cubes and a handy balsamic salad dressing.

All Dermot could do was grip the podium in front of him tightly, trying to focus. He wasn't going to die, not unless the sodium hydroxide came up. So he needed to be ready if it did.

'OK, gentlemen. Just time for one more question. But let's have another quick look at our Twitter poll first. #TeamMarcus now up to 64% with #TeamDermot at just 36%. It looks like imminent death's doing wonders for your reputation, Marcus. Here we go, one last time.'

The wheel started to spin, racing on then starting to slow.

Why had Marcus taken the acid? It didn't make any sense. Dermot tried to force the question from his head as he watched the wheel.

Aubergine.

Asparagus.

Macaroni.

As long as it didn't land on…

An assortment of spices.

Slowing, slowing, slowing.

A turnip.

The wheel finally stopped. Dermot stared at it for a second or so, then closed his eyes. Puff pastry – he wasn't going to die.

But when he opened them again, he saw that the wheel had somehow crept on past the pastry.

'Well, well, well. We've only gone and landed on sodium hydroxide, ladies and gents.' The man in the mask was hooting with malevolent joy as savage applause echoed all around. 'Another ingredient making its debut on the show. Commonly used in the manufacturing of pulp, paper, soaps and detergents, this popular industrial chemical is also known as caustic soda and can be deadly even in the smallest of doses.'

Dermot turned, trying to catch Marcus's eye. The chef already had one poison. He might as well let Dermot answer this one and give him the second. But Marcus just stared straight ahead, his face set in harsh resolve.

'OK, a dairy themed question for you. Made from ewe's milk, pecorino cheese is produced in which country? France, Italy or Spain?'

Two buzzers sounded at the same time, but when Dermot looked down, it was his light that was on.

'Italy.'

The man in the mask looked at him for a second.

Come on, it had to be Italy.

'That's the right answer.' The host sounded like he was smiling behind the mask. 'Do you want to take the ingredient or give it away?'

Give it away of course. That was a no-brainer.

'We're all waiting.'

Dermot realised he hadn't actually spoken the words.

'Yes, I'll…' Then he stopped. Maybe if they got one poison each, they could both survive?

'Not thinking of playing the hero too?'

'Give it to me.' Marcus turned to him. 'No sense in us both dying.'

Exactly.

'How touching, but we do need an answer.'

'You've got to give it to me.' Marcus sounded desperate now.

But one poisonous chemical each? That seemed kind of fair didn't it? And they still had the whole second half of the show for the police and MI5 to come riding to the rescue.

'I'll give it to Marcus.' Then again it was best to err on the side of caution. But Dermot felt a hole open up inside him as he looked over at the chef. 'I'm sorry.'

'No. It's the right decision.' Marcus gave him a little nod as he turned away.

'Well, I think you'll agree, ladies and gentlemen, that was the most amazing first half we've ever seen here on *The Meal of Fortune.*' The host started to wrap things up. 'Over fifty million viewers round the world too. Just time to check in on our Twitter poll again. #TeamMarcus 79%, #TeamDermot 21%. Join us after the break when our contestants will cook up *The Meal of Fortune.*'

Dermot leaned back and closed his eyes, letting out a long breath as the canned applause started up. When he finally mustered the courage to open them again, Marcus was staring up at the big video screen where the Twitter poll numbers were changing once again.

#TeamMarcus 90%. #TeamDermot 10%.

And it was only when the chef turned to him, a broad grin spreading across his chops, that Dermot finally started to suspect what was about to happen.

Chapter 33

Jesus, this woman could drive. Henwell put his hand against the door to steady himself as the car swung round another corner.

For some reason, he'd assumed that he'd be the one behind the wheel. Maybe he did need to do that unconscious bias course he'd been avoiding for so long? But Anna's little red car had been closer than his, and Henwell had soon realised he'd have struggled to get around the corners as fast as she was currently doing. Probably wouldn't have run quite as many red lights either.

He looked up at the road ahead then back to the screen of Anna's phone in his hand, but the video was still buffering.

'Five more minutes, I reckon.' She forced the car on through the darkening streets. 'What's happening?'

'They're still cooking.' Or at least they had been when the video stopped.

He felt himself pushed further back into his seat as she got busy with the accelerator. They could still make it… As long as she didn't wrap the car around a lamp post, or take them under a bus.

The video started again, and Henwell watched as Marcus Diesel hacked away at a carrot with what looked like a bread knife. Next to him, Dermot was calmly tending to a stir-fry.

Then his own phone was ringing. He answered, eyes still on the screen where Marcus Diesel had finally finished peeling the carrot and was throwing it into a frying pan with what looked like an egg. He listened for a few seconds then cut the call. 'SCO19 are four minutes out. Medics are just behind them.'

Anna gunned the engine harder.

Henwell looked up, regretting it instantly, as they shot past a bus on the wrong side of the road.

Eyes back to the phone. There was still time, just about. But then he noticed the clock in the corner of the screen. Only two more minutes until the contestants finished cooking.

He looked up again as they shot under the flyover that carried the North Circular Road, the traffic lights ahead of them already turning to orange. But Anna just accelerated on across the junction before anyone had time to get in the way.

Back on the screen, Marcus seemed to be adding an unfeasible amount of soy sauce to his pan; maybe hoping it would mask the taste of the deadly chemicals. Henwell still couldn't figure out why the chef had chosen to take the chemical for himself. It meant certain death surely, and he didn't seem the self-sacrificing type.

He'd broken the news to Anna that Marcus had both the poisons and Dermot looked set to live about ten minutes earlier, choosing a moment when she wasn't running a red light or on the wrong side of the road. Henwell had felt a little sting of jealousy as he saw some of the tension draining from her face. What was it between her and Dermot? But if she was relieved, it had done nothing to slow the speed of her driving.

Anna hit the horn and flashed her lights, negotiating her way around a slow-moving van, ducking back into the correct lane temporarily to let a car pass the other way before overtaking a taxi and a motorbike in one go.

'OK, next right.' Henwell gave the instruction in plenty of time for her to slow for the corner.

But Anna didn't slow. Instead, she tugged fiercely at the wheel, taking them into the bend far too fast, and the car started to slide sideways. But just as it felt like they were going to mount the pavement and hit the wall beyond, she pulled the car out of the skid and sped off down the road.

On screen, Dermot and Marcus were transferring their meals onto plates as the audience counted down the last ten seconds.

'Come on, come on,' Henwell shouted as the phone in his hand buffered again.

Anna took the car around a sharp left turn, again without troubling the brakes. And then the video was back and the clock had reached zero. He lifted the phone closer, struggling to hear over the snarling engine. The man in the Anton Du Beurre mask was saying something before raising a finger to point at the big screen behind him.

The video stopped again.

And when it jerked back into life words and numbers were forming on the screen.

#TeamMarcus 97% #TeamDermot 3%

Henwell brought the phone close, trying to hear.

'What's going on?' Anna turned, trying to snatch a glimpse of the screen as she took another bend, only looking away as the car started to drift to the right.

More buffering, then the video was back again.

'What's he saying?'

The sound was suddenly clearer as Anna was forced to concede defeat and actually brake for a particularly sharp corner.

'Well that's the final result of our poll. Amazing. And we've always tried to provide what our viewers want on *The Meal of Fortune*. So by popular demand, we're going to…'

The screen froze then came back again.

'… do a little swap and get you to eat each other's dishes. We don't want to let our audience down do we? And if either of you leaves anything on your plate, you *both* die. You first, Marcus.'

The video buffered again. By the time it started up, they were accelerating across a car park towards the warehouse. All sound from the phone was completely drowned out now by their engine and the meaty roar of the firearms van overtaking them on the left. Somewhere behind them, an ambulance siren sounded too.

Henwell watched as Marcus Diesel picked up a fork and gingerly took a taste of Dermot's stir-fry salmon. He nodded with an appreciative smile then took a larger forkful. Next, the camera panned over to Dermot holding his fork over a plate containing a half-peeled carrot, two whole chicken fillets and an overdone fried egg, all swimming in a thick greasy sauce, presumably infused with poisonous chemicals.

'What's going on?' Anna swerved to avoid a pile of rubble ahead of them.

'He made them swap.' Henwell's voice was low and hoarse as

he finally managed to get the words out. He looked back at the screen where Dermot was still staring down at the plate of poisoned food. 'He let the Twitter poll decide.'

A figure all dressed in black stepped up behind Dermot and forced his face down towards the plate, a small black handgun with a silencer grinding into his temple. The camera panned around to catch Marcus Diesel's horrified reaction. But he just gave a little smile, followed up by a cheeky wink.

'Marcus knew.' It was the only explanation. That's why the chef had taken the first chemical, knowing it would win him the popular vote.

Anna stood on the brakes, skidding to a halt just a few yards from the warehouse entrance. Then she was out of the car and running.

'Wait!' Henwell pushed his door open and climbed out. 'There might be another…'

But she'd already ducked around two firearms officers and was sprinting for the door.

'ANNA!' He yelled again.

Then he was running too, trying not to think too much about the prospect of another bomb as he followed her towards the building.

Chapter 34

Anna lengthened her stride as she covered the last few yards to the warehouse, all set to kick the door in.

But it was already ajar. So she simply upped her pace and crashed on through, barely noticing as the door bounced back off the wall and caught her shoulder.

Behind her, she heard the thud of running feet and a voice calling for her to wait.

No way.

She'd seen it with her own eyes. The gun at Dermot's head, forcing him down towards the poisoned food. But there was still time. There had to be.

The corridor ended, with turnings to the left and right. Her eyes panned wildly from one side to the other.

'DERMOT!' She shouted out his name as she chose to go right.

'Wait.' The voice behind her was Henwell's.

'Check that way.' She wasn't waiting.

Marcus Diesel must have worked out it would be all about the Twitter poll.

Bastard, bastard, bastard.

Anna would make sure he regretted that. She reached a door on her left and kicked it open as more shouts from the firearms team filled the corridor behind her. They were the ones who were supposed to go in first, with their guns and body armour, making sure the building was clear. Not this time.

She stuck her head through the open door, but it was just an empty storeroom. The same scene greeted her behind the next door and the one after that.

Where the hell were they?

Other doors banged behind her as they were kicked in by Henwell and the firearms team. Anna moved on, booting another door open as she went.

Another empty storeroom.

Maybe they had the wrong place after all? But Simpson and the team in Leyton had already reported that they'd drawn a blank. This had to be right.

Another door. Another kick. Nothing.

Anna was fighting for breath now, her recent lack of gym time starting to tell. But she pushed on, even though she knew Dermot would already be coughing his guts up or lying dead on the floor with his insides all burned out. She forced the image from her mind. Angry with the terrorists for doing this. Angry with Marcus Diesel for the part he'd played. But far, far angrier with herself for letting it happen.

The image of Dermot writhing on the floor clawed at her mind again, so she kept on running and kicking out at doors until the corridor ended in a right turn.

And then she saw it. The narrowest slither of light escaping under a door up on the left.

'Here.' Anna called out, starting to move.

But the first two firearms officers had caught up and were already pushing past her.

'Let them go first.' Henwell was right up behind her now too.

The armed policemen reached the door and then stopped.

Actually STOPPED… Really?

They positioned themselves on either side of the door. The one on the left holding a hand up, fingers, counting silently down. Five four…

Sod that, Anna went on three. A quick kick sorting out the door and then she was through.

'STOP!'

The room far was bigger than the others. In the far corner she saw the mocked-up TV studio with its video wheel, brightly coloured podiums and cooking area. But the wheel was still and silent, and there was no sign of the man in the Anton Du Beurre mask or his helpful assistant with the gun. Just two figures crouched on the floor under the bright studio lights.

'DERMOT!' She crossed the room in a few quick strides.

One of the figures turned and looked up.

Marcus Diesel.

'Get away from him.' Anna didn't even bother trying to keep the anger from her voice.

The chef kept his eyes on her for a second then turned back to Dermot, who was doubled over as he vomited on the floor.

'We need the paramedics in here now.' Anna could hear the desperation in her voice and knew the tears wouldn't be far away.

Dermot vomited again then straightened, his face paler than any living human had a right to be. Behind she saw the two plates on the kitchen worktop.

Both were empty.

Marcus Diesel leaned in close to Dermot, saying something to him that Anna didn't catch. Then the chef patted the stricken man on the back; almost tenderly it seemed, before pushing himself up from the floor, abandoning Dermot to what was to come.

'You knew.' Anna was right up in the chef's face.

Marcus shrugged. 'What can I say? Clever, wasn't it?' A self-satisfied grin settled across his face.

Anna wiped it straight back off again with a right hook, stepping into the punch with enough power to put him on his fat arse. Then she knelt down next to Dermot, an arm around his shoulder as he puked his guts and what was left of his life up all over the floor.

Chapter 35

'What the bloody hell was that for?' The voice belonged to Marcus. 'You could have broken my jaw.'

Dermot bent over and retched again as the pain in his stomach got sharper. Bloody typical of the chef to be worrying about his face. He wasn't the one who'd just been poisoned.

'I still might.' Anna's voice came from right next to Dermot.

And just for a moment, he knew she was going to make everything all right. He tried to raise his head. Maybe he could try for a brave smile too? But no, even Anna couldn't make this go away.

He retched again, thinking about every last forkful he'd been forced to eat by the black-clad figure with the gun. He really hoped Molly hadn't been watching that.

A new sensation was building deep in his guts. Burning, stabbing then burning again as the poison got to work. He bent over once more, both hands on his stomach.

'How do you feel?' Anna's voice was still close.

'Not great.' The first words he'd managed since finishing the food.

'Why did you hit me?' The anger was rising in Marcus's voice.

Couldn't he just shut up for a moment? This wasn't about him.

'Because you knew.' Anna snarled at the chef. Then she was speaking to Dermot again, as she held him closer. 'You're going to be…' She trailed off. 'The paramedics are coming.'

The pain had another go, jabbing and stabbing at his guts then roaring up through his stomach to burn at his throat. All he wanted to do was to lie down and curl up on the floor. He didn't care, as long as the pain went away.

NO! Molly elbowed her way back into his head. Dermot tried to sit up straighter, determined not to give up that easily.

'Where are the paramedics?' Anna was shouting now.

'They're coming. Had to wait until it was safe.' Henwell's voice boomed over Anna's shoulder.

The man had a nerve showing up here. Dermot tried to raise his head to tell the policeman exactly what he thought of him.

But Marcus was talking again. 'I didn't know they'd swap the meals.'

'Yes, you did. You just said that you knew.' Anna snapped back.

Dermot was dimly aware of the chef climbing back to his feet. He looked up and saw a smile creeping across Marcus's face, despite the blood flowing freely from his nose.

And why not? He was the one who'd survived. Dermot felt another stab of burning pain.

'If you wouldn't mind moving back a bit please, Miss.'

Anna took her arm away and stood, someone in green kneeling in her place.

'What's he taken?' The paramedic's voice was calm and measured, for all the good that would do.

'Hydrochloric acid and…' Anna's voice caught for a second.

'Sodium hydroxide,' Marcus cut in. 'He's going to be fine.'

'You think so?' Anna looked like she was going to punch the chef all over again.

'Don't you get it?' Marcus switched to a bad imitation of a Belgian accent. '"*You don't need a degree in chemistry to know that on their own either will be just as deadly as any poison…*" That's what he said, remember?'

Exactly. And Dermot had just consumed a large quantity of them both.

'Well, I did do a chemistry degree.' Marcus sounded quite proud of the fact. 'If you mix them together, you get plain old salt and water. "*On their own*" either is deadly. Together they're harmless.'

Dermot looked up at the chef because actually, now that he came to think of it, he wasn't sure he was quite at death's door.

'He's right, you know.' The paramedic was nodding. 'But it would only work if you got the volumes just right.'

'I just tried to do the same amount of each.' Marcus didn't sound quite so sure of himself now.

The paramedic pulled out a torch and shone it into Dermot's mouth. 'I'd expect severe blistering on the tongue and all around the mouth if you'd ingested either chemical.' He turned the torch off and looked up at Marcus. 'It looks like you managed to get your measurements spot on.'

Dermot bent over and rested his head on the ground as the realisation hit home.

He was going to see Molly again.

And maybe he and Anna could still…

Because he wasn't going to die.

'That's why I took the acid.' Marcus was on a roll now. 'I was pretty sure you'd give me the sodium hydroxide if you got it.'

'So why's he being sick?' Anna didn't sound quite ready to accept it yet.

It was a fair question.

'I guess it might have been all that salt that you get when you combine them.' Marcus flashed another grin. 'And the chicken might not have been quite cooked through.'

Great, Marcus might not have poisoned him with the chemicals, but there was a good chance the chef had given him salmonella. 'It was disgusting, especially the egg. Who has an egg with chicken anyway? That's wrong on so many levels.'

The paramedic stood up and reached down to help Dermot to his feet. 'We'll still need to get you checked out properly. But you should be fine.'

Dermot stood slowly, shaking his head at the chef. 'You've actually managed to poison me without poisoning me.'

'Nothing like gratitude, is there?' Marcus tried to sound huffy, but he was far too pleased with himself to carry it off.

'You're right. I'm sorry. And thank you.' Dermot reached out and shook the chef's hand. Marcus may have been a five-star, copper-bottomed arsehole, but his quick thinking and knowledge of chemistry had just saved both their lives. 'I didn't know you had a chemistry degree.'

'I said I did a degree. I didn't say I got it. I got chucked out after the first year.'

Jesus.

'And I'm sorry I hit you.' Anna smiled at the chef. 'What you did was clever and brave.'

'It was nothing really.'

As if. Marcus would be dining out on this one forever.

But none of that mattered right now because Dermot was alive and Anna was hugging him again, not even seeming to care that he was covered in sick.

'You sure you're feeling OK?' She stepped back and looked him in the eye, her hands resting on his shoulders.

'Never better.' He gave her his best wounded-hero smile, then threw in a little wince to show how brave he was being.

'I'll come to the hospital with you.' She smiled back at him.

Perfect.

'Me too.' Henwell stepped up next to her. 'We'll need to question you once they've checked you over.'

Couldn't the great idiot question Marcus and leave him to Anna?

'Cool.' Anna turned and looked up at the policeman with a smile. 'We can compare notes afterwards.'

Hang on.

She kept on smiling up at Henwell.

Afterwards?

And it wasn't just any kind of smile either. It was THAT kind of smile.

And Henwell was smiling down at her too.

No way. No. No, no, no, no. NO! This could not be happening.

Dermot had nearly died, Marcus was going to be completely intolerable for the rest of his life and now Anna was flirting with the big galoot of a policeman. She couldn't be interested in him.

Could she?

Dermot doubled over as a fresh wave of hot sweats and stomach cramps swept in. This time when he threw up, he made sure he got it over Henwell's shoes and halfway up his trousers too.

That would show him.

Part Three

RVP

Another seven days later…

Chapter 36

Henwell slowed the car as he approached a bend, the high hedges on either side of the narrow lane making it impossible to see if anything was coming the other way.

Seven days they'd spent chasing shadows. Forensics hadn't turned up anything from the fake TV studio; there'd been nothing on the CCTV nearby and there was still no new intelligence from MI5.

But they would catch the terrorists. And it would be tonight.

RVP2411. Raymond Van Perrie, 24th November.

Henwell was certain the killers would carry on, despite their failure with Dermot Jack and Marcus Diesel. And he was equally sure that the incident with the chemicals had been a simple mistake. A case of the terrorists just not knowing their chemistry. Marcus or Dermot had been meant to die. But the terrorists were certain to have a big finale planned to make up for it.

That wasn't going to happen.

Raymond Van Perrie and his family had been whisked away in secret to enjoy a few days of hospitality in a Highlands safe house, courtesy of Police Scotland. And the Met had plenty of surveillance teams and a good chunk of its armed response units stationed around the Dutchman's north London home.

All week they'd watched and waited, knowing the terrorists might spring their trap early, just like with Dermot and Marcus. But there hadn't been a sniff.

The clock on the dashboard read 3pm, just hours of the day left. The attack would come soon. Right now, Henwell should have been enjoying the familiar surge of adrenalin as the operation reached its climax.

But no.

He slowed once more, recognising the blind bend where he'd nearly smashed into an oncoming tractor on his first journey to the safe house four days before.

Back then, the anger and frustration had been all shiny and new. He'd misjudged his speed, mind still very much on the meeting he'd just had with Simpson.

Off the case, or as good as. The DCI would be taking personal charge of the entire investigation. That had been the gist of it. It always had been his operation after all.

Henwell's team had identified the van, found out about the stolen ID and tracked down the pickpocket. But then they'd been meant to, hadn't they? Just another part of the terrorists' plan. And it was a false trail that had left Simpson seething in an empty warehouse in Leyton while Anna and Henwell had found the captives.

Served him right as far as Henwell was concerned. Simpson had jumped at the chance to take all the glory, before taking the time to think it through.

So the DCI was doubly determined to get the credit tonight. No doubt it would propel him another rung up the ladder. And meanwhile Henwell…?

He dabbed the brakes, realising the car had sped up as the anger took hold once more.

… Henwell was in charge of babysitting Marcus bloody Diesel and Dermot sodding Jack. Oh, and getting information out of them that might help when the case came to court.

'Your remit always was the celebrity angle.' Simpson hadn't even bothered to sound patronising as he'd put Henwell firmly in his place.

He took the car around another bend, catching a faint note of a now familiar smell. It had taken him three washes to get the whiff of Dermot's vomit out of his trousers. But some of it must have rubbed off on his car seat.

That about summed things up.

The only concession he'd managed to wring from the DCI was to be allowed to keep the team of uniforms and civilian support staff. With Roberts at the helm, they were busy taking the same meticulous approach that had helped them identify the pickpocket. Working outwards from each of the celebrity murder crime scenes, they'd checked the CCTV in ever-expanding circles, looking for any vehicles or individuals that appeared in more than one. Going far further out than the original investigation. It was a long shot, but it would be good to have some actual evidence linking the terrorists to the other crimes, once they'd caught them.

Henwell slowed the car to a stop at a crossroads, waiting for a few extra seconds to check he wasn't being followed, before accelerating on up the country lane. This would be his third visit to the safe house, an old farm tucked away in rural Essex. On both previous occasions, he'd failed to extract anything useful, the interviews taking place against a backdrop of cool hostility from two men, who'd made it clear that they blamed Henwell for their ordeal.

Difficult to argue with that one. He held himself responsible too. Henwell sighed as he slowed for another bend, eyes on his mirror again to recheck for any sign of a tail. This investigation had been his chance to get straight back out of celebrity crime into a proper job. But it looked like that wouldn't be happening anytime soon. But he'd just have to take the hit and live to fight another day. There wouldn't always be someone as ambitious as Simpson standing in his way. But then there wouldn't always be the chance to take down a bunch of terrorists either.

He slowed again for a sharp right turn, and with just a few hundred yards to go to the safe house, Henwell turned his mind properly to what awaited him.

Dermot and Marcus – boredom, frustration and resentment all much stronger than their fear now that the terrorists were about to be taken. Both of them ready to have a go at him for easy sport.

Lidstone, enthusiastic and eager to please as ever. Henwell was quite looking forward to seeing the lad actually.

And Prim.

With Roberts focusing on CCTV, Simpson had somewhat surprisingly offered the DS's continued services for safe house duties. Henwell wasn't sure what she'd done to be banished to the sidelines of the investigation. Maybe being witness to the DCI's impotent rage, as he'd tooled around in the wrong warehouse, had been enough. Watching her fighting to hide her simmering anger and sense of injustice had been about the only highlight of the visits for Henwell. But Prim was too professional to let it affect her job and had cast herself in the role of the safe house's mother hen, cajoling and haranguing Marcus, Dermot and Lidstone to make the whole thing work somehow.

Henwell still wasn't looking forward to it, except that… He turned into the driveway to see Anna's little red car already outside the house. She was leaning back against the door, deep in conversation on her phone. As ever she was dressed casually, a suede jacket over what he'd come to think of as her trademark jeans and T-shirt. Looking good without seeming to make any sort of effort.

He hadn't seen her since the night of the rescue, and they hadn't spoken in a couple of days either. Not since she'd broken the news that Felicity Diamond was the mole.

Ah…

That hadn't gone down well with Connor and the Met's senior brass. It was fair to say relations between the two services weren't at their best right now and MI5 had agreed to let the Met lead the operation, while it focused on getting its house in order.

That didn't mean Henwell and Anna couldn't keep channels of communication open. Still, he'd only half expected her to agree when he'd suggested she join him to interview Marcus and Dermot. His reasoning had been sound enough; they might find out something that would help in the hunt for Felicity Diamond.

Yeah right… And that was his only reason?

He waved as he brought his car to a halt next to hers, wondering whether she'd realised his invitation hadn't been 100 per cent motivated by professional considerations. But they wouldn't be working together for much longer. So why the hell not then? Maybe he could still salvage something good from this whole mess.

Anna cut the call and waved back, a smile lighting up her eyes.

Was she wearing a little more make-up than usual? And hadn't she done something different with her hair?

Suddenly, Henwell's relegation from the investigation and all of Simpson's game playing didn't seem to matter quite so much.

Chapter 37

Well, this was nice. The four of them, all sat around the wooden table. The air was so thick with tension that Anna thought you could probably have served it up with a spoon.

She looked across the farmhouse's huge kitchen to where DS Prim seemed to be running a full training course for DC Lidstone on how to make a cup of tea. It didn't look like there'd be any chance of a drink to calm things down any time soon.

Next to Anna on the bench seat sat Henwell, back against the wall. Probably the safest place for him, given the hostility radiating from across the table.

He turned to catch her eye, lingering for perhaps a second too long. And not for the first time she wondered why he'd really asked her to come along today.

Her eyes flicked back to the two men opposite her. Marcus Diesel slouched back in his chair, his relaxed posture entirely at odds with the angry glint in his eye. Dermot, on the other hand, was sitting forward, tension lurking behind his forced smile.

'So, is there is anything you can remember, anything at all?' Henwell was going through the motions, even though he must have realised it was all a waste of time. Dermot and Marcus had nothing for them.

Nothing that would help them catch the terrorists.

And nothing that would lead them to Felicity Diamond.

The little mole came sniffling and snuffling along the dark alleyways of Anna's brain once more. At first, there'd only been anger when Lawson had told her MI5 were letting the police take the reins. But soon enough, Anna had realised catching Felicity would be enough for her. The thought of looking into the girl's eyes as she tried to justify what she'd done had kept Anna going through the long nights of fractured sleep.

'No, there's nothing.' Dermot leaned back in his chair with a rueful shake of his head, at least trying to be civil.

Anna hadn't seen him since the night of the rescue, and couldn't help wondering how he was coping. The safe house might have kept him physically secure, but there was no way of telling what the long hours of enforced brooding had done for his mental wellbeing. Guilt gave her a sharp little prod in the ribs, suggesting that perhaps she could have made more of an effort to come and see him.

But then she had that treacherous little mole to catch. And there was far too much baggage between her and Dermot for Anna to be playing counsellor.

She watched as Henwell bent down and pulled a folder from his briefcase, slowly removing two large photos, stills taken from the video. The first showed the host in the Anton Du Beurre mask, the second the figure with the gun, all decked out in black. 'And there was nothing about these two?'

Again Dermot shook his head, at least trying to cooperate.

'Why does it matter?' Marcus Diesel leaned forward, giving the pictures a cursory scan. 'You're going to catch them later anyway. Oh no. Wait.' He aimed a nasty smile in Henwell's direction. 'It won't be you, will it. You're here with us because you screwed up.'

'Mr Diesel.' Henwell raised a hand.

'Lucky for Raymond Van Perrie, I'd say. He'll be safer with you off the case.' The chef shook his head, eyes still on the policeman.

The silence ticked on for three maybe four seconds before a clattering noise from over by the sink suggested that the tea-making might not be going to plan.

Anna caught Henwell's eye. They both knew they'd messed up. But Marcus Diesel seemed keen to lay the blame squarely at Henwell's door. Of course, he was forgetting that it had all been Anna's idea and that the policeman had saved Emilie's life.

'This isn't getting us anywhere.' Anna broke the silence, catching Dermot's eye with a little frown.

Help me out here.

'Look… We're sorry about what happened.' If Marcus was

winding him up, Henwell was hiding it well. 'But you're safe now. And tomorrow, we'll have the terrorists in custody and you can go home.'

'No thanks to you.' Marcus was still glaring across the table. 'You should be back directing traffic?'

'It doesn't really work like that.' Henwell held the chef's stare.

The sound of clinking mugs heralded the arrival of the long-promised tea. Hopefully that would calm things down a bit.

'Who wants sugar?' Lidstone stumbled as he reached the table, nearly sending the tray of mugs flying.

Henwell and Marcus were far too busy with their staring match to notice.

'Um, err… I'll just leave it here, shall I?' The big DC finally picked up on the tension and backed away.

'I understand that you're upset.' Henwell's voice was still level and calm. But then presumably he'd had far worse abuse in the interview room than anything Marcus Diesel could possibly dish out. He reached out and took a mug, placing it down in front of Anna before doing the same for the two men opposite.

'Thanks.' Marcus grudgingly picked up his tea and took a sip. He pulled a face and put the mug straight back on the table. 'Jeez, Danny. That's filthy. Hasn't Maddie taught him anything?'

'I've told you it's Madeleine, or DS… Oh, never mind.' Prim turned away with a dismissive shake of her head and started showing Lidstone how to do the washing-up.

Anna looked down at her own oily tea then decided against it; Marcus was probably right on that one. And with nothing new to be learned, there was little reason to stick around for more abuse. She turned to Henwell, who gave her a nod and a quick smile, clearly thinking the same. She smiled back for a second or two then turned away to find herself looking straight down the barrel of Dermot's stare. His friendly smile was gone, eyes boring deep into hers.

Jesus… Seriously?

Her heart didn't so much sink as throw itself off the nearest tall building. It was obvious what he was thinking. Dermot had caught the little smile she'd exchanged with Henwell, and clearly now he thought…

But there was no Anna and Henwell.

Yeah, OK… Maybe she'd thought about it a couple of times in the odd idle moment. But that was certainly none of Dermot's business. She felt a flare of anger. Couldn't he just let it go? She'd been pretty damned clear there could never be anything between the two of them.

So why, oh why hadn't she just toughed it out? Held his gaze and made it clear she didn't care what he thought.

But no.

Instead, she'd let her eyes slide away, her cheeks reddening like an embarrassed schoolgirl. Confirming to herself, as well as Dermot, that there was at least a hint of truth in his suspicions.

Chapter 38

She'd come, actually come. And just when Dermot was starting to worry she wouldn't; had almost given up on the whole idea in fact. That had to mean something, didn't it?

Anna had hurried across the gravel driveway with a broad smile spreading across her face before giving him a big hug.

There was no reason for her to be here today. This was just more routine questioning. She was here to see him; it was the only possible explanation. Dermot had breathed in the scent of her, feeling something close to happy for the first time in a week. Then she'd pulled away with another smile, her eyes on his.

And suddenly, all the dark thoughts of the past week had started to fade. The kidnap, the cell with the stinking bucket and the fake game show were soon far away as Dermot's hopes had moved smoothly up through the gears. Once he was out of here, they could meet up.

A drink, dinner even.

Chat about old times.

Maybe think about future ones.

But things had started to change once they were all sat round the kitchen table.

How could he help but notice the little looks and smiles between Anna and Henwell?

He'd tried to dismiss the idea at first.

No way.

It was his imagination, nothing else. Just like back in the warehouse – Anna smiling up at Henwell as Dermot had puked his guts up all over the floor. Some sort of hallucination brought on by his near poisoning. At least that's what he'd convinced himself on the way to the hospital that night.

But aside from Lidstone's filthy cup of tea, there'd been no poison today, no hallucination.

Henwell was flirting with her, clear as day. And Anna was

flirting right back. Seemed like the pair of them had spent those two long days Dermot and Marcus had been prisoners going all gooey-eyed over each other. No wonder it had taken them so long to come to the rescue.

He kept his eyes on her now, as she looked away, a little flush of colour lighting up her cheeks.

Guilty as charged.

But how could she?

He'd nearly died. Dermot breathed deeply, trying to control the sudden stab of jealousy. Then he dismissed the whole idea. Nothing was going to happen between Anna and Henwell. Even the thought of it was preposterous. She'd soon see the big policeman for the great lumbering idiot he was.

And Marcus had just gone and given her a helping hand, going at Henwell far harder than he had before. Hopefully, it would have reminded Anna that it had all been the policeman's fault. Now Dermot just needed a few minutes alone with her.

'Right. If you've got no more pointless questions, I need a wazz.' Marcus stood, giving Henwell another long stare before heading for the door.

Anna's eyes flicked back to the policeman. Another little glance.

Another smile.

'What was that all about?' She managed to tear her eyes away from Henwell and look at Dermot as the door shut behind the chef.

'Sorry, he just gets like that sometimes.' He shrugged with what he hoped was a disarming smile. 'Most of the time actually. He's got this condition. It's called being a prick. Sadly there's no cure.'

A ghost of a smile flitted back across her face.

'You try being stuck in here with him. At least when we were prisoners, we were drugged half the time.'

Anna's smile broadened and Dermot felt something inside him start to soar.

Henwell wasn't smiling as he started to pack up his briefcase.

'If you do think of anything else, please let us know.' He stood up and reached out a hand to Dermot. 'Once again, I'd like to extend the fullest apologies of the Metropolitan Police for the inconvenience.'

Inconvenience…? Surely he meant incompetence. The man had a cheek. But Dermot wasn't about to lose his cool now. Instead, he stood and leaned across to take Henwell's hand.

Magnanimous.

Understanding.

And most of all, forgiving.

They were all virtues that would look good in Anna's eyes.

'Yes, best be off.' She stood too, not troubling herself overly with Dermot's virtues, if she'd even noticed. She nodded towards the door. 'Let him calm down a bit.'

'Danny, DS Prim.' Henwell nodded over to the two officers. 'If they do remember anything, let us know.'

'We will. Bye, sir.' The big DC turned with a wave, a pair of ridiculously small yellow washing-up gloves on his hands.

Dermot followed them out into the hallway then along to the front door.

'Bye then.' Anna paused, offering a hand this time instead of another hug.

'Look, I just wanted to say…' Dermot knew he needed to get it out before she left. 'Last year, I never got the chance to thank you properly.'

She smiled. 'All in the past, and it's classified, remember.' She threw a glance at Henwell. 'Need-to-know basis.'

Ha! It looked like Dermot had stumbled on a little weakness in the big cop's oversized armour. He stole a glance at Henwell as a look of irritation crept across the policeman's face. Out of the loop and pissed right off at his kindergarten levels of security clearance. Maybe Dermot could make him a badge out of Lego to make up for it.

But when he looked back at Anna, she was still reaching out for a handshake.

There really wasn't going to be a hug.

'See you.' He took it and shook, deciding it was best to play it cool.

'After this is over.' She held his hand for a couple of seconds longer. 'We should meet up. Talk.'

There you go. Anna was asking him now. Dermot wanted to run up and down the hallway. Instead, he just smiled and tried to hold her gaze in a way she'd find meaningful. 'I'd like that.'

The long game… That's what he was playing here. Give Henwell enough time to show what a dick he really was and rule himself out of the running. Dermot was already heading back down the hallway when a memory pulled him up.

No, not one but two.

The first… That man, Lawson, outside the train station all those years ago with all his veiled threats, making it clear to a teenage Dermot what would happen if he tried to see Anna again.

The second… Last year in the park.

The same man and more or less the same threats, just not quite so veiled.

And twice Dermot had backed away.

Well, not this time.

Sod the long game. He turned and hurried back towards the front door as it started to swing shut.

Chapter 39

Anna closed the door behind her and followed Henwell towards their cars, shivering a little in the crisp chill of the November afternoon.

'We can meet up. Talk.' Really, she'd actually said that? Anna had regretted the words as soon as they'd come out. It had been to stop Dermot from saying anything else. But all she'd done was deal with the embarrassment of the immediate situation by kicking the problem further down the road.

But she'd make good on her promise to meet up with him. It wouldn't be fair to disappear again like last time. Then she would put it to bed once and for all.

Not until after Felicity had been caught though.

'OK, then. Fingers crossed for tonight.' Henwell reached his car and turned with a shrug as he dug in his pocket for his key.

'It'll all be fine.' She smiled and nodded.

A dark cloud passed across his eyes. Anna knew how frustrated he was at being sidelined from the operation.

'There is one consolation though.' He smiled and took a step towards her. 'Since we're both free, do you fancy going for a drink tonight?'

Oh, OK… Let's just process that one. She'd been pretty sure he was keen. But you could never be sure. Now at least she knew.

He held her gaze. 'I mean, I just thought. We can still get an early night.' Then he reddened. 'No, I didn't mean…'

Anna tried not to smile. He couldn't have made more of a balls up of it if he'd tried. The tough cop had just shown he had a softer side, which was quite attractive actually.

Now wasn't the right time though.

'Look, I'd love to. But let's just wait until all this is over.' She reached out and put a hand on his arm.

'OK.' He nodded slowly, his face lighting up as he realised she wasn't saying no. 'Definitely?'

'Definitely.' She smiled again, already looking forward to it.

They both turned quickly at the sound of the front door opening to see Dermot emerging with Lidstone behind.

Anna realised her hand was still on Henwell's arm and she quickly whipped it away.

Too quickly, which only made it all the more obvious.

'Err, sorry, boss. I couldn't stop him.' The big DC still had the washing-up gloves on.

'I think he is allowed in the garden on his own, Danny.' Henwell shook his head and smiled.

'Yes, OK. Sorry, sir.' Lidstone turned and almost ran back into the house.

'Anna, have you got a minute?' Dermot was already coming crunching across the gravel towards them.

'Catch up later?' She turned to Henwell with a little wave.

'Yep.' He nodded then turned towards his car.

Dermot stopped in front of her as the policeman pulled the door open before performing some sort of limbo act to contort his tall frame into the driver's seat.

'Anna, I, err…' Dermot's voice was every bit as hesitant as Henwell's had been. 'Look, I just wanted to say…' He paused again, looking at his feet.

Like buses, weren't they, men? Two at once and all that. But the destination of this second one was a place Anna had little desire to re-visit.

'I'd really like to see you again.' He raised his eyes, holding her gaze. 'I mean properly see you.'

Well that was straight to the point. Anna's mouth was desert dry as she struggled to find the words to let him down gently.

'We could just go for a drink like you said. See how it goes.'

No, no they couldn't. Best get this over with now. There was no sense in keeping him hanging. Anna swallowed, but the words wouldn't come because… Because somewhere, lurking in a treacherous corner of her mind, a small part of her did want to see him. Thankfully the rest of her brain swung into action, slamming a heavy door shut on that dark little corner, turning big keys and sliding heavy bolts across. Then she set off a high explosive charge, burying that little corner under tonnes and tonnes of rubble.

Get out of that.

'Listen…' Anna trailed off as she realised that she hadn't heard the sound of Henwell's engine. She turned to steal a glance towards at his car.

He was sitting with his phone out, making a terrible job of pretending to check his messages, while watching them out of the corner of his eye. He looked up with a wave, making out he'd only just noticed her watching.

Well, this wasn't at all awkward.

Henwell looked away again.

'Look, I just don't think…' She turned back to Dermot as the rest of the words finally came. 'There's been a lot of water under the bridge.' Not enough to sweep away all the baggage though. 'It's just not going to happen. I'm sorry.' She watched as his face crumpled in on itself. 'It just wouldn't work.' It couldn't, not in a million years.

'It's him, isn't it?' Dermot's face hardened as he nodded towards Henwell

'No.' The word was out just that little bit too fast, and Anna knew she wasn't fooling him. But that was ridiculous, this wasn't just because of Henwell. Nothing had happened between them. It was because she didn't want it.

'I heard you. "Catch up later." Date, is it?' There was an edge to his voice now.

'No, it's a live operation. We're waiting to find out if they've caught the people who tried to kill you.'

He just shook his head. 'The two of you seem to be getting on well.'

'We're working together. It kind of helps if you get on with your colleagues.' For God's sake. Why was she even bothering to explain herself?

'Don't think I didn't see you, making your big eyes at him.'

'I wasn't making big eyes at him.' This really was getting silly.

'I've just got quite big eyes.' She did actually and she'd make them at whomever she damn well liked.

Dermot's own eyes were dark and reasonably big as well. He rolled them skywards as he let out a big theatrical sigh.

'Oh piss off. What about you and little Emilie?' Hang on... Why was she even going there? She didn't care, OK?

'She's my as-sis-tant.' He emphasised each syllable as if Anna was some kind of idiot.

'And I'm sure she's been assisting you in lots of ways.' Stop it, stop it. STOP IT! Anna set off another explosive charge raining down more rubble on that dark little corner, just to be sure.

'Like you said, it kind of helps if you get on with the people you work with.' He held her gaze for a few more seconds, letting out another long sigh as he closed his eyes.

Why couldn't they at least try to part as something close to friends? Actually, just doing the parting bit would be a start. But fate and issues of national security had kept displaying an unhappy knack of throwing them back together.

'He's a complete idiot, can't you see that?' When Dermot opened his eyes they were flashing with anger. He stared at her for a couple of seconds more, before turning and stalking off back to the house without another word.

A little whimper came from under the rubble in her mind, but it was faint enough for her to ignore.

Dermot opened the door and took himself inside without a backward glance, but without slamming it either. He probably felt that this gave him some sort of moral victory. Well, it didn't, OK?

Tosser.

She turned and started towards her car.

'What was that about?' Henwell already had his window down.

'Oh, you know. Just Dermot being Dermot.'

'All OK, though?'

'Yes.' Because actually it was. Anna felt better already. And sod it. She stepped across to his car. 'I've changed my mind. Let's do tonight. Why don't we make it dinner?'

Chapter 40

Jesus...

Dermot stalked back up the hallway, his own scornful tones ringing harshly in his ears. How had he thought any of that would actually help? He'd managed to go from a situation where Anna was suggesting they meet up for a drink to a full breakdown in relations in just a few short minutes.

When exactly had he learned to be such an arsehole? Even Marcus wouldn't have behaved like such a tool. He headed back into the kitchen to find the chef sprawled in a chair, watching as Lidstone and Prim put the washing-up things away.

'Well, that told them.' Marcus grinned. 'I couldn't be doing with any more questions.'

'It's an investigation; they are supposed to ask...' Dermot stopped himself. Why was he even defending them? Anna certainly didn't deserve it. And as for Henwell?

'Come on, you think he's just as much of a dick as I do.'

Much, much more so, actually. Dermot slumped down opposite Marcus.

'Lovers' tiff, is it?' The chef nodded towards the front door.

'Please. I'm not in the mood.'

'Must have been a bad one. But plenty more fish in the sea. Young Belgian ones?'

'Just leave it, alright.'

'Oh come on. I've seen the way she looks at you.' Marcus glanced over at Lidstone and Prim, keen for an audience, but they were still busy with the plates and cutlery. So he turned back to Dermot. 'I'm just so bored. I can't sleep. There's nothing on TV. And Lidstone won't play cards anymore.'

Hardly surprising, given the huge amount of cash Marcus had taken off him over the past few evenings.

'And Maddie's not up for anything.'

'Apart from protecting you.' Prim threw the chef a filthy look.

'We don't need protecting now. The terrorists are off after RVP. We should all go out, hit the town to celebrate our last night together.'

'That won't be happening.' Prim had finished putting the dishes away and was walking towards them.

'You could come with us, let your hair down.'

'I couldn't think of anything worse.'

'Be like that.' Marcus sniffed. 'What about you, Danny? I bet you know how to get yourself some action.'

Lidstone reddened as he shook his head.

Marcus sighed, climbing slowly to his feet. 'As we're stuck here, I'm going to show you how to make a proper cup of tea. Who wants one?'

'OK.' Lidstone smiled eagerly.

Prim nodded, looking less sure.

'I'll pass thanks.' Dermot stood and headed for the door, suddenly keen to be on his own. And to somehow try to forget what a dick he'd just made of himself with Anna.

*

'What else?' Dermot pushed himself up from the bed and walked over to the window, the unfamiliar phone to his ear. Loaned to him by the police, it was bigger than the old one he'd lost when the terrorists had taken him and it felt uncomfortable in his hand.

'Just lots of offers for Marcus.' The distaste was apparent in Emilie's voice as she spoke the chef's name. She'd been manning the office single-handed during Dermot's week in the safe house.

'Anything interesting?' Marcus hadn't mentioned the sacking again, so Dermot guessed he was still the chef's agent, although right now he was finding it hard to care. He zoned out as Emilie rattled through a list of lucrative-sounding opportunities, thinking again about Anna and how badly he'd messed it up. He tuned back in just as Emilie finished.

'… and there's another packet-sauce offer, a saucepan promotion and a new range of BBQs.'

The endorsement offers for Marcus were hardly a surprise. The chef's clever little trick with the chemicals on the spoof *Meal of Fortune* show and the dramatic rescue had grabbed the headlines, refusing to let go in the face of war, famine and environmental disaster. *Love Island*, rumours of a steamy affair on *Strictly* and further exposés about a prominent seventies TV personality had barely got a look in. Wave after wave of outrage and sympathy for Marcus Diesel had played out across social media too. The celeb community showing their genuine and heartfelt support, just a handy click away from millions of followers. Marcus had even been mentioned in Parliament and received twelve marriage proposals, presumably from the kinds of women who wrote to jailed serial killers.

'Oh, there was one more. I wrote it down somewhere.' Papers rustled as Emilie scrabbled about.

But Dermot was still thinking about the look in Anna's eye as he'd turned away. There really was no coming back from that.

'Here it is, a toaster-and-kettle-set endorsement.'

'Really?' Suddenly Dermot was interested. It was the sort of deal usually reserved for those in the highest echelons of TV cheffery. Your Jamie Olivers, or your Ramsays – certainly Delia back in the day. Shelf space in all the big department stores and supermarkets, maybe even TV advertising spots? But even that could wait. 'I'll look at it when I'm back in the office. All OK for tonight?'

The evening was set to be a big one for Anton Du Beurre, co-hosting one of the year's leading celebrity bashes.

'I wish you could come.' Where Emilie's tone had been all business like before, she now sounded wistful, sad even. 'We both wanted you to be there. It's such an important night for him.'

'I know. But he'll be just fine.' The booking was proof, if it was needed, of the steep trajectory of the chef's rise to fame. But Dermot knew Anton would be able to pull it off. 'He's a pro.'

'We'll miss you all the same.' Emilie's voice was even quieter now.

An image of her beautiful face floated into his head. Maybe there could be something between them, once he'd got Anna out of his system. Or perhaps Emilie was the one to help him finally get over her.

He pushed the idea away as they said their goodbyes, but a small part of him was already looking forward to seeing her at the office on Monday. He went and lay back down on the bed, his mind turning back to Anna. But within minutes he'd drifted off to sleep.

*

It was dark when Dermot opened his eyes. He propped himself up on one arm, hand scrabbling around on the bedside table for his phone. Maybe it was already the next morning and it was all over.

But the time on the screen read 5pm.

He lay back again, head spinning; more tired after the hour's sleep than he'd been before. Perhaps he could drift off again?

But that wasn't going to happen; his dry mouth was crying out for water. He stretched as he stood then padded over to the door, hitting the light switch and closing his eyes against the glare. Then he headed out onto the landing, stopping to peer down into the dark hallway below.

That was odd. Why were all the lights off?

'Hello.' He headed down the stairs, then stopped as the floorboard on the bottom step creaked in protest. It was the only sound he'd heard since he'd woken.

'Lidstone? Prim?' He took another step forward. 'Marcus?'

There was no light from under the kitchen door, nothing from the sitting room either.

'Marrrwaagghhh.'

A hand clamped over his mouth, as a strong arm wrapped itself around his chest.

Dermot twisted his head, thrashing from side to side, as he fought to get the hand from his mouth so he could shout out.

But his attacker wasn't going to let that happen. Fear was meant to give you strength, wasn't it? But clearly his own sense of self preservation had been off sick the day that memo had gone round.

He felt himself lifted off the ground, propelled forward.

Again he tried to fight, this time throwing an elbow backwards and meeting flesh. But it didn't seem to have any effect.

This was supposed to be a safe house. The clue was in the name, wasn't it? But the terrorists had found them anyway, even though they were scheduled to be going after RVP today.

Where were Lidstone and Prim? And what about the other officers they'd been told were stationed nearby? Sodding Henwell… The policeman had let them down again.

Both of Dermot's feet were off the ground now as he was half carried, half pushed towards the front door. He tried again to squirm his way free, but it was no good. Instead he went for another swing of the elbow. This time he was rewarded with a muffled 'Ouuffff' as he connected with soft flesh.

He swung again harder.

Another grunt. But they were already halfway along the hall now, Dermot's feet slipping on the wooden floor.

He tried to shout through the hand over his mouth; surely one of the police officers would hear him? But then wouldn't the terrorists have dealt with them first? He felt a pang of fear as he thought about what they might have done to big clumsy Lidstone with his filthy tea and washing-up gloves.

They were near the end of the hall now. His attacker pushed him on towards the front door then out into the coldness of the late afternoon air. Dermot dug his heels in, gaining a bit more grip on the gravel as he swung his elbow and missed again. And now instead of being pushed forward, he was being turned around, which might give him his chance.

A head-butt.

A kick in the balls.

Go for the knee. Wasn't that what you were taught in self-defence?

Then run.

The hand stayed firmly over his mouth as he was spun round. And then he found himself looking straight into the gloating eyes of his attacker.

Horribly familiar eyes.

Chapter 41

'This is a great place.' Anna put her fork down and smiled across the table as she reached for her wine glass.

Henwell returned the smile, taking a sip from his own glass, pleased he'd chosen the informal little Italian over somewhere more showy. Anna's dinner suggestion had caught him on the hop and the decision on the restaurant had taken him almost as long as choosing what to wear. In the end, he felt he'd got it about right on both counts. The trattoria on Frith Street served good, simple food, with attentive but not overly fussy service. And he'd stuck to a familiar shirt and pair of jeans, after dismissing several options, including a jacket and tie. The poor girl would have felt like she was at some kind of interview or disciplinary procedure.

Anna had done nothing to explain her dramatic about-face outside the safe house. But it must have had something to do with her conversation with Dermot. Henwell wasn't complaining, of course. It seemed like she'd made a real effort too. Her hair looked newly washed and shiny, and there was a touch more make-up than she'd been wearing earlier as well as a hint of perfume. And if he thought she looked good in her work clothes…?

He'd had to remind himself of the need to breathe as she'd walked confidently through the door about five minutes after he'd arrived – tight black jeans with a grey top under a woollen jacket. Simple and understated, but then Anna did the rest by just being Anna.

They'd chatted away easily enough after making their choices from the menu. She seemed as keen as him to avoid the subject of work, so they'd stuck to things like books they'd read recently and films they wanted to see. Pretty much what Henwell assumed ordinary people talked about on a date.

By the time the mains had arrived, even more of the tension of the investigation had slipped away, as they chatted about travel and holidays. Coincidentally, they'd both been to northern Spain the year before, visiting San Sebastián within days of each other. Like him, she'd loved the tapas and the bars in the narrow streets of the old town. Anna's 'we' suggested she'd been part of a now-defunct couple at the time, but she hadn't shared any more details. Henwell had been happier disclosing his travelling companions – two old mates from his police college days. They'd rented bikes and cycled for a few days along the coast into France, eating and drinking too much by night to work off the calories with their few meagre hours in the saddle each day. Anna nodded along, eyes occasionally darting to her phone on the table. Checking to see if there was any news rather than a sign she was bored, he hoped. It was past eight o'clock now, and they were both keen to get an update on what was happening with the terrorists.

Their waiter bent in to clear the plates. 'Would you like to see the dessert menus?'

Anna shook her head. 'Just a coffee for me please, espresso.'

'Espresso's great for me too.' It felt like the evening was on the way to winding down, but Henwell was confident he'd done enough to earn himself a second date. And things would be even more relaxed once the operation was over.

The waiter moved away, and Anna stole another glance at her phone then looked back at Henwell, this time with an appraising smile. 'You never did tell me how you ended up on this celebrity crime squad.'

'It's a long story.' And not one he really wanted to tell. But at least she hadn't called it CRAPPIE.

'Coffees aren't here yet.' She gave him that smile again, and he wondered whether she'd perhaps heard the story already on the MI5 grapevine.

'I ran a team in the drug squad.' He was still deciding how to spin it. 'We got some big results, very big ones. But the view was I'd cut a few too many corners.'

'Whose view, Connor's?'

'Among others. He didn't seem to care we were taking drugs and criminals off the street. He was more worried that the force might be embarrassed. Bumped me down to DI and offered me this or white-collar fraud.'

'And you didn't fancy going after middle-class tax dodgers?'

He felt a ridiculous flush of pleasure as she smiled at his comically raised eyebrow.

'What sort of corners?' She leaned in, lowering her voice, definitely interested now.

It wasn't something he'd ever discussed outside the internal inquiry. But then Anna was clearly no stranger to bending the odd rule. She was the one who'd suggested using two civilians as bait. And she was staring at him intently, those brown eyes impossibly large.

'Just a bit of unauthorised surveillance on some of the gangs, tapping their burners. I guess it was a grey area, legal-wise.'

'And it worked?'

At least she was still smiling.

'Like a dream. Until someone let on to the brass, and they got all sweaty about unsafe convictions.'

'And were they? Unsafe?'

'No. We used the intelligence to build a rock-solid case each time.' He fought hard to contain the bitterness in his voice as he thought back over it again.

Anna sat back, eyes still on his. 'Do you regret it?'

'No. Not really. We put some serious criminals away. None of the convictions have been challenged.' And I wouldn't have met you. But of course, he left this last bit unsaid.

Their coffees arrived and they both used the opportunity to check their phones again.

'What's the story with you and MI5?' Henwell felt it was his turn to ask the questions now – find out more about the enigma that was Anna Preston.

She smiled. 'My father was in. I always wanted to be like him.'

'Retired now?' Henwell winced, knowing he'd got it wrong the moment the words were out.

'He died when I was at university.'

'I'm sorry.'

She gave a sad little smile. 'Retirement wouldn't have suited Dad. He wasn't really cut out to sit on the sidelines, telling anyone who'd listen that the Russians were still a threat. And he'd have got no satisfaction out of being right.'

Whatever she said, he could tell it still hurt.

'And your parents?' She turned the questions back to him, which had to be good.

'Nothing as exciting as MI5. Dad was police in Derbyshire, ended up as a desk sergeant and agony aunt to half the station. Mum was a teacher. Both retired now. Divide their time between gardening and bothering me about the lack of grandchildren.' He felt himself redden as she smiled. 'Not that I'm in any sort of hurry.' He took a sip of coffee, eyes on the cup. But when he looked up again, she was smiling. She'd done a lot of that tonight.

Then her eyes slipped to her phone again. 'Sorry. I've got to check.'

'Me too.' But there was no news. Whatever the terrorists had planned, they were leaving it late. Maybe he should call Simpson? But then he knew the DCI would give him pretty short shrift. 'Anything your end?'

Anna shook her head as she put her phone down. 'There will be though. Tonight's the night. Shall we get going?'

He waved for the bill, insisted on paying when the waiter returned. 'My treat. You'll just have to get it next time.'

'Maybe.'

Non-committal, but he was still confident he'd get that second date. But then he found himself thinking about Anna and Dermot Jack. What had there been between them? Was there still anything now? Both were questions he felt he couldn't ask without seeming like a bit of a nob. Not yet, at least.

His phone buzzed in his pocket as they stood. He tensed as he pulled it out. This might be it.

But it was only Roberts. The sergeant was probably just ringing for news. Henwell could call him back later. But then he changed his mind. Roberts wasn't everybody's cup of tea, but he'd worked hard and proved a lot of Henwell's first impressions wrong. He had as much right to ask for news as anyone else.

'Sir.' The sergeant cut in before Henwell could even say hello. 'The CCTV. We've got him. Same man within a mile of four of the crime scenes near the time of the murders. It can't be a coincidence.'

No, it couldn't. Henwell's eyes flicked to Anna, but she must have sensed something and was already moving around the table, crowding in next to him.

Roberts and the team really had done a good job. It wouldn't be enough for a conviction and they'd have to get more evidence to build a case. But Henwell was sure this would be the start of it.

'Texting you the pictures now.'

His phone pinged. Then again and again.

'You won't believe it.' Roberts' voice faded as Henwell moved the phone from his ear to scroll through the images. Then he turned it round so Anna could see.

'Hang on. That looks like…' She leaned in for a closer look.

The baseball cap made it hard to see straight away but when you looked for a second or two, there could be no mistake. And straight away Henwell's mind was flipping back on the original investigation. How he hadn't been barking up the wrong tree at all, just edging out along the wrong branch. The link had been there right in front of him.

And he'd missed it.

'We need to get back to the safe house now.' Anna was still staring at the picture.

He put the phone back to his ear. 'Great work, Sam, got to go. Call DCI Simpson, he needs to see this.' Then he cut the call, scrolling through to Prim's number and waiting as the phone rang, then went to voicemail.

Lidstone next.

Voicemail again.

Back to Prim.

Voicemail.

Come on!

And then he called the safe-house landline, listening as the phone just rang and rang.

Chapter 42

'He's not answering either.' Anna cut the call as Dermot's phone clicked through to voicemail. Then she redialled, feeling her heart start to hammer faster in her chest.

'Still nothing from Prim, Lidstone or the safe house.' Next to her, Henwell ended his own call. 'I'll get an armed response team out there.'

And when Anna looked into his eyes she saw the same fear she knew would be visible in her own. So she called Dermot's phone again, listening as it went to voicemail once more. She cut the call and sent him a text instead.

Call me NOW!!!

'Any news, sir?' Henwell was on the phone to Simpson, his voice low and urgent.

Anna knew that, like her, he'd be hoping that a vanload of unsuspecting terrorists had just driven up and fallen straight into the trap.

Proving all their new-found fears wrong.

But no. He gave her a quick shake of the head, before telling Simpson about the lack of response from safe house and asking for a firearms team before ringing off.

'There's an armed team on its way. Let's go. I'll get a car to come up from Charing Cross.'

Anna punched in Dermot's number again.

Voicemail.

Why wasn't he picking up? She tried to convince herself that there were plenty of innocent explanations. All she could hope was that he was still in a huff and was ignoring her calls. She thought again about the picture of the man in the baseball cap, still not quite believing it. But the evidence had been there in front of her eyes.

'Car in two minutes.' Henwell was heading for the door.

Anna followed, trying Dermot once more. Voicemail again.

Seriously, call me now. She bashed out another text message, hoping, hoping, hoping he was just sulking after their spat.

The terrorists had never deviated from their plans. But then they'd never had a reason to before, never had any unfinished business. She redialled again, hurrying to keep up with Henwell as he reached the door. Outside the lights of the approaching patrol car already painting the night blue.

ANSWER THE SODDING PHONE!

Her stomach fell away as she allowed his message to play out, listening to the voice of the man she'd had an argument with.

And then left to die.

Suddenly he was right there inside her head. That final look in his eye as he'd turned and crunched away across the gravel, bitter and angry but a little bit crushed too. And right then, Anna had been happy that she'd never have to see him again.

But not like this.

She shook her head as the hot prickle of tears started behind her eyes, turning away so Henwell wouldn't see.

'How did they know where the safe house was?' Henwell raised his arm towards the approaching police car as if hailing a cab.

Felicity.

Anna felt her anger flare then die. The treacherous little mole had been in the wind by the time they'd put Dermot and Marcus in the safe house. Maybe the police had a leak of their own? Or perhaps Anna or Henwell had led them there? But now wasn't the time to worry about that.

The patrol car sped up to them then braked sharply. Henwell opened the back door for her, before hopping into the front. That was about right wasn't it? In the back seat where she belonged; little more than a useless passenger now. Anna climbed in, trying Dermot's number and silently pleading for him to answer as the car pulled away.

But the call just rang and rang before clicking to voicemail once more.

Chapter 43

Dermot looked into the eyes of his attacker, trying to spot any hint of remorse.

But there was nothing.

Just that evil glint as the face broke out in a grin.

'I still can't believe what we've done.' He turned away from Marcus Diesel with a shake of the head and picked up the pace, weaving through the dawdling pedestrians on Oxford Street.

'What I've done, you mean. You'd still have been stuck in that safe house if it wasn't for me.'

'If you hadn't practically abducted me, you mean.'

'Look, I'm sorry, OK?' Marcus fell in next to him, doing his best to look contrite.

'No, you're not.' Dermot knew the chef had never given a damn about how anyone else felt.

A broad smile spread across the chef's face. 'Yeah, OK. You're right. But we're here now. And you've got to admit it was a good plan.'

Yes it was. Which was about the only reason why Dermot hadn't punched the chef's lights out. He just shook his head again and pressed on through the crowds, turning left into Argyll Street. There were bound to be consequences, but he'd worry about them after the night was over. In the meantime, there was work to be done.

*

'Don't get much call for pick-ups from that place.' The driver from the local taxi firm had turned to Marcus and Dermot with a toothy grin.

Not surprising really, from a safe house.

Marcus's escape plan had been to book a taxi to meet them at the top of the lane then drive the five miles to the little local station for the 5.30pm train back to London. But with the driver's ears on red alert for gossip, he'd sensibly kept quiet during the fifteen-minute cab ride. So it wasn't until they'd been sitting in the empty train carriage rattling their way towards Liverpool Street Station that the chef had revealed all. 'You know that cup of tea I made? Well, the doc had given me some sleeping pills, and I kind of hadn't use them all.'

'You drugged two police officers? Are you out of your mind?' Dermot hadn't wanted to believe it. There had to be so many laws against that sort of thing.

Marcus had just shrugged. 'They'll be OK. And we've got places to be.' That's when he'd pulled his phone out and brought up the details of tonight's big event on the screen. 'Look. It's the perfect opportunity to show everyone that I'm back in business.'

'You realise we're going to be in so much trouble. We could still go back.' They'd only gone a few stops. 'We'd be there before anyone misses us.'

'No way. I've just drugged two coppers. And just think of all the publicity.'

Marcus was right. He was the man of the hour after his little trick with the chemicals had gone viral. Making a surprise appearance at one of the year's biggest celebrity bashes was definitely going to grab even more attention. Dermot had already started to warm to the idea. They'd deal with the consequences another time.

The train had trundled its way into Liverpool Street a little after 6pm. They'd agreed to meet near the venue just before 8 o'clock, then grabbed separate taxis home to shower and get changed into their evening best. For once, Dermot had resisted the temptation to advise the chef to tone down his outfit. Tonight wasn't the time for him to be understated.

*

They headed on down Argyll Street, skirting around a couple of dawdlers eating pizza from the street cafés. The scent of salami and melted cheese soon had Dermot's stomach rumbling. But food was going to have to wait. He felt a smile spread across his face as they walked on. The kidnap, the boredom of the safe house and even the mess he'd made with Anna seemed a long way behind him now. They were about to steal tomorrow's headlines and break the internet all in one go. He turned and smiled at Marcus as they stepped around a knot of tourists. For once, the man had erred on the right side of taste – traditional black tie with not a check, polka dot or anything orange in sight, not that it would matter.

Ahead of them, the crowds were thick around the barriers cordoning off the red carpet in front of the London Palladium Theatre. Dermot put a restraining hand on Marcus's shoulder, stopping him about ten yards away. He knew well enough that the red carpet had a set of rules and timings all of its own. First up the wannabees, with the has-beens at the end and the really big celebs taking the prime slot in the middle. He watched the crowd push forward against the barrier as a volley of flashbulbs lit up the night. It seemed like it was peak A-lister time right now. He kept his hand on Marcus's shoulder as the chef tensed. But there was no sense in risking the opportunity by mixing it with the really big guns.

'Marcus?' A woman to their left was the first to notice him.

'It's Marcus Diesel.' The murmur spread through the crowd.

'Marcus.'

'Marcus.'

'Marcus.'

More and more heads started to turn. Then the chef's name was ringing out all around them. Dermot took his hand from the chef's shoulder, like a jockey loosening the reins and letting his thoroughbred run free. The crowds parted as Marcus strode forward, his name taken up now like a chant. He vaulted the barrier, landing perfectly on the red carpet with arms spread wide to accept the adulation. Dermot breathed again, a face plant would have ruined the effect somewhat.

Two security guards started to move in then stopped when

they saw who it was. More voices joined the rising chorus as photographers fought to get Marcus's attention for that one special shot. And in the crowd, phones were held high to get that killer social media pic.

Dermot made his way through the tightly packed mass of people to a small gap at the end of the barrier, manned by three more security guards. There he waited while Marcus progressed like a Roman general in his triumph.

But, of course the man himself was in no hurry, milking the crowd for every last drop of applause. Smiling and posing as he went, reaching out to shake hands and sign autographs.

Dermot smiled to himself. He'd definitely get the chef a new TV gig now. And not some poxy fish advert either.

Primetime even.

He reached for his pocket as he felt his phone vibrate.

Anna. The screen showed he had five missed calls and a couple of texts.

Ouch… Best not answer though, not being at the safe house and all.

Finally, Marcus ran out of carpet. He gave one last wave to the crowd then turned and sauntered over. 'He's with me.' The chef smiled at one of the beefy security guards who'd moved to block Dermot's way.

'Of course, Mr Diesel.' The man stepped back to let Dermot through.

'Did you see that?' Marcus grinned as they headed up the theatre steps and pushed through the doors.

Dermot nodded with a smile of his own. 'Come on, let's get a drink. I think we both deserve one.' With the red carpet appearance done, their night's work was all but finished. He led the way up a staircase, following the sign for the VIP bar. Their names weren't on the door, but that really wasn't going to be a problem.

And so it proved, the woman with the clipboard ushered them inside with a huge smile, her eyes on Marcus. The bar itself was wall to wall with celebs, agents and assorted hangers-on; all enjoying the last few drops of VIP champagne before heading off to watch the show. Dermot cast a nervous eye around. With Anton hosting, there was always a chance they might bump into him. And there was no way of telling how Marcus might react if he came face to face with the man who'd replaced him on *The Meal of Fortune*. But thankfully there was no sign of the Belgian. With the curtain call just minutes away, he'd be in his dressing room getting ready to go on.

Marcus headed into the bar, edging his way through the crowd towards a waiter with a tray of champagne. They'd only made it a few feet when a former *Dr Who* actor stepped up to clasp Marcus by his shoulders and shake his hand. Then an ex Bond girl, with an extravagant triple kiss, followed by a comedian who'd somehow managed to revive his career despite being caught with a sex worker in a Coventry hotel a couple of years back.

Dermot reached for his phone as he felt it buzz again, remembering he hadn't spoken to Molly that day.

Anna again.

No chance. She'd be livid if she found out they'd done a runner. So best not speak to her yet. Everyone would be a lot less touchy once the terrorists were under lock and key.

Marcus only made it a few more steps before he was stopped again.

A footballer turned TV presenter.

A newsreader who'd won *Strictly*.

Another former *Dr Who*.

Dermot's phone buzzed again. A text from Anna this time.

Call me NOW!!!

Looked like they'd been busted. And those capital letters suggested she was beyond mad.

Marcus shook hands with a quiz-show host, then a woman who presented *Antiques Roadshow*, a TV gardener and a third former *Dr Who* – what was it with these Time Lords? All had come to sympathise and congratulate. To fawn a little even. And to raise a glass while quietly thinking how jammy the chef had been. And how hard they'd kick him, next time he was down.

Marcus finally reached the waiter and hooked them both a

glass of champagne. Within seconds, he'd started to gather a crowd. A sixties pop star, a dame of the theatre and a former Director-General of the BBC. It was illustrious company for a lowly daytime TV chef. Especially one who'd been a serial winner of the TV's Most Annoying Man award, and was generally regarded as a complete arse.

Dermot took a slug of champagne, not even bothering to look when his phone buzzed again. Marcus's little group was swelling further – a former boxer, a reality show presenter and an *EastEnders* actress who looked like she'd forgotten to get fully dressed for the evening. Predictably, she was commanding the lion's share of the chef's attention.

The group started to disperse as the bell rang and the bar began to empty for the show.

'Did you see that? She was all over me.' Marcus bounded over. 'Said that I should try my hand at acting.'

Dermot thought not. Best for Marcus to stick to what he knew; there was enough cash to be made in TV cookery. But tonight wasn't the night to piss on the man's chips.

'I think I could be really good.' The chef grinned and threw back the last of his drink. 'And I got her number.'

Dermot snagged a couple more glasses of champagne from a passing waiter, ignoring his phone again. They'd done what they needed to, and sitting through a two hours of variety acts had little appeal.

'Thanks.' Marcus took the glass with a big grin. 'Have these then go to the pub?'

Exactly what Dermot had been thinking. 'I might even buy you dinner.' He pulled out his phone as it buzzed once more.

Urgent. Call now. PLEASE!!!

At least she'd asked nicely this time. Not that he was going to. But the phone rang again as he glugged down more champagne.

'Aren't you going to get that?' Marcus was right beside him, trying to get a look at who was calling.

A thought suddenly stuck him. Maybe Anna was ringing to tell him they'd captured the terrorists? Or even to apologise for her behaviour earlier? Maybe she was going to suggest they meet for that drink after all? Somehow Dermot doubted that. But whatever she wanted, it looked like Anna was going to carry on calling until she got through. And he was going to have to 'fess up to what they'd done at some point.

He thought about it for a second or so more before finally answering the call.

Chapter 44

'Dermot? Is that you?' Anna pressed the phone closer to her ear, as she saw Henwell's head snap round towards her from the front seat.

'Are you there?' She tried again. The call had definitely been answered this time.

No reply.

'DERMOT!'

'Yes, yes. I'm here. I –'

'Thank God.' Anna cut across him. 'Why didn't you answer?' She fought to keep her voice steady as the words tumbled out. 'Are you OK?' She put the phone on speaker as Henwell leaned in to listen.

'We're fine.'

Well, he certainly didn't sound scared. Anna felt herself start to relax. 'What's going on?'

'Look, it's not a great time.'

'Not a great time? I've been ringing for ages. Where are you?'

'At, err…' The pause was just a beat too long. 'We're at the safe house.'

'No you're not.' He was a terrible liar.

'Yes we are.' His voice rose with feigned indignation.

'Put Prim or Lidstone on then.'

'Can't right now.'

'Thought not. Where are you actually?'

Another pause, then a big sigh. 'In London, at the Palladium. There's a big event tonight. We thought it would be a good idea for Marcus to make a bit of a splash.'

'*I* thought, you mean.' The chef piped up in the background.

No surprise there. Dermot might have been an idiot, but he wasn't completely stupid. 'We can't get a response from the safe house. We thought the terrorists had found you.'

'Ah.'

'What do you mean, "Ah"?'

'What happened to my officers?' Henwell leaned even closer, the anger rising in his voice.

'They, umm… They were asleep.'

'Oh, for God's sake.'

Anna couldn't tell whether he was angrier with Dermot and Marcus for skipping out or with Lidstone and Prim for letting it happen. But there was relief in his voice as well. Like her, he'd feared the worst.

'We're coming to get you.' She nodded at Henwell, who told the driver to turn round and head for the theatre. 'We need to get you somewhere safe.'

'You said we were safe.'

'I need you to listen and stay calm.' She wondered how to break it to him.

'I am calm. Or I was until you said that.'

'We need to talk to you about Anton Du Beurre. We think he's the –'

'The target?' Dermot cut her off. 'You said it was RVP.'

'I know. Just listen –'

'Anton's the target and you didn't tell me?'

'LISTEN TO ME. Anton's not the target. OK?' She paused again, but there was no easy way to break it to him. 'We think he's one of the terrorists.'

Dermot's laugh was like a bark down the phone. 'He can't be.'

'We've got evidence.'

'Why would he be killing celebs?'

'We don't know, but he's part of this. Look, I know he's your client, your friend. But he tried to kill you. He's planning to kill RVP tonight. Is there anything you can tell us about him that might help?'

'That it's not him.'

'Please, you've got to listen to me.' Why couldn't he take it seriously?

'No, you listen to me. Anton can't be coming to kill RVP because he's here.'

She felt a chill run right through her. 'You're with him now?'

'No, I'm with Marcus. Not a good idea for them to mix. He thinks Anton stole his show.'

'He *did* steal my show.' The chef cut in again.

'But you're sure he's there?' Anna ploughed on, ignoring him.

'He's the host. He wouldn't miss it. It's his biggest-ever gig. It's The Royal…' Dermot trailed off.

'What? Hello.' Anna wasn't sure whether he was still on the line.

When he spoke again his voice had gone very quiet. 'I think you've got the wrong target…'

Then he told her who RVP really was.

Actually not 'who'… More like 'what'.

Chapter 45

'The Royal Variety Performance?' Anna repeated Dermot's words back, the tension in her voice revealing that she knew he was right.

The real RVP. Right here where he was standing. Of course it was. More celebs than you could shake any number of sticks at.

But Anton? A terrorist? Dermot was still struggling to take that bit in. The Belgian was just interested in being on TV and making oodles of cash from his cookware endorsements. A bit stroppy at times maybe, but then he was a chef.

But then… Something came back to Dermot from the night in the warehouse, almost taking the wind out of him like a punch in the guts.

That voice…

There was a reason the voice behind the mask had been so familiar.

Bastard.

It hadn't been an impersonation, more like Anton disguising his voice with a bad parody of his own accent. Dermot felt a cold certainly settle on him. It was all true.

He heard muffled talking on the other end of the line and then Anna was speaking to him again.

'OK, we'll be there in less than ten minutes. The protection team with the Royals at the theatre has been informed. Local station too and armed support's on the way.' The siren in the background threatened to drown her out.

'Why didn't you know?' Dermot stepped away from Marcus, lowering his voice. 'Why would they go after some washed-up Dutch footballer when they could hit a theatre full of celebs? Get a couple of Royals too.'

'All the other initials were individuals.' This was Henwell.

The idiot was still trying to cover for himself when everyone knew it was all his fault.

'There's nothing we can do about that now,' Anna cut in. 'But we'll sort it out. Don't worry.'

Easy for her to say. She wasn't the one in a packed theatre with a bunch of murdering terrorists and… Oh God. 'It's going to be another bomb, isn't it?'

'We don't know that yet.' But her voice betrayed her. 'They'll get the Royals out first then evacuate the whole place. Just get out of there. We've got this now.'

Too right. No way was he planning to stick around.

Across the bar, Marcus was still helping himself to the last of the champagne, walking back with another glass for Dermot.

'Hang on…' There was more muffled conversation and then Anna came back on. 'The Royals are out now. They're about to evacuate the whole place.'

'OK, we're leaving.' Dermot cut the call and started to move towards Marcus as the high-pitched wail of the fire alarm ripped through the air.

'It'll just be a false alarm.' The chef offered him one of the champagne glasses.

'No.' Dermot whipped both glasses from Marcus's hands and put them down on a table, then bundled him over to the door.

'Hey. I was drinking that.'

'We've got to go.' He ushered the chef towards the stairs as the first evacuees from the auditorium started to filter out; all harrumphing and grumbling their way down the stairs, assuming like Marcus, the alarm had gone off by accident. By the time they reached the first-floor landing, the crowds had swelled and the going was getting much slower.

'Sod this.' Marcus leaned close to Dermot's ear to be heard over the alarm. 'Let's go back and get more champagne.' The chef turned and started to push back through the crowd.

'No.' Dermot grabbed his arm. 'We've got to get out.'

'Bollocks.' The chef pulled away.

Dermot grabbed at him again, missing this time and catching an elderly woman on the shoulder.

'Sorry.' He held up a hand.

'Piss off.' She gave him a death stare as she shuffled by.

'Marcus. Come on.' He managed to get hold of the chef's arm this time. 'It's the terrorists. They're here. They've got a bomb.'

'WHAT?' The chef shook his head and pointed to his ears, clearly struggling to hear over the alarm as the surging crowd pushed them apart.

'I said it's Anton. He's the terrorist.' Dermot staggered back further as the crowd flowed past them, shouting to be heard. 'He's got a BOMB!' He pushed forward and grabbed Marcus again.

A blonde woman next to them snapped her head round, eyes widening as she let out a scream.

'Bomb.'

'Bomb?'

'BOMB!' The word started to bounce around the crowd, panic spreading in its wake.

'Anton?' It wasn't the bomb Marcus was worried about though. 'Tony fucking Butter, what sort of a name is that anyway? Waffle muncher stole my show.'

Dermot lost his hold on the chef's arm as the crowd pushed them apart again.

'*MY* SHOW!' Then Marcus dropped his shoulder and charged back up the stairs, sixteen stone of muscle and fat (mainly fat), giving the crowd something else to panic about.

'NO! WAIT!' Dermot shouted as loudly as he could.

But the chef was already too far away to hear him over the alarm and the panic of the frantic crowd.

Bollocks.

Dermot took one last look towards the exit and safety, cold fear rising up inside him.

Bollocks, bollocks, bollocks.

Then he turned and followed Marcus back up the stairs towards Anton De Beurre, the terrorists, their bombs and whatever else awaited them.

Chapter 46

The driver slowed the car, double-checking for pedestrians before accelerating across the next junction.

Henwell stared through the windscreen, eyes focused on the traffic ahead.

How had they got it so wrong? Raymond Van Perrie had always seemed like an unlikely choice for the terrorists' last hurrah. Just not quite famous enough compared with the victims.

Now they knew why.

Anna leaned forward impatiently, her head and shoulders between the front seats, perhaps thinking they'd have been there by now if she'd been driving. She was probably right.

Henwell grabbed for his phone as it buzzed in his pocket.

Simpson.

The DCI cut to the chase. 'How far out are you?'

'About five minutes.' Henwell looked across at the driver, who nodded. He just hoped the time they'd lost by heading for the safe house wasn't going to cost them.

'Armed response have got an ETA of about eleven minutes.' Simpson's voice sounded tense and hollow.

For good reason. That wasn't good.

Apart from the royal protection officers, it had been a case of light-touch policing at the theatre, mainly because a big chunk of the Met's resources was focused on the trap at RVP's north London house. Too far away to get the theatre in time.

'And you're sure it's him?' There was an edge in Simpson's voice, the sound of a forthcoming inquiry that would highlight the mistakes in his investigation; of a glowing career losing a little more of its shine.

'Yes, sir. We've got him on CCTV close to five of the murders.' Henwell had just had a text from Roberts letting him know that Anton Du Beurre had been caught on another camera, this time with someone who might have been an accomplice. 'It can't be a coincidence.'

'No. It can't.' Simpson sighed. Evidence produced by good hard police work like that was the kind the DCI valued most. He wasn't about to question it. 'Superintendent Jarvis is in charge at the theatre now that the royal protection team have left, but...'

The signal crackled and broke up as they made another turn.

'... did you get that, they're not responding.'

It looked like the terrorists had already taken the police officers on the ground out of the equation.

The signal broke up again as they slowed to a stop, the narrow street ahead completely blocked by traffic. The driver pulsed the siren, but the cars in front had no way of getting out of the way.

'You'll be first on the scene.' Simpson's voice was back. 'I don't suppose there's any point in telling you to wait until SCO19 arrive.' It was the closest the DCI would ever come to telling Henwell not to follow his precious rulebook and go in without armed back-up.

'No sir. No point at all.'

'Thought not. But be careful.'

'I will.' Because if it all went tits up, Simpson would still be the first to blame him.

The driver leaned on his horn and switched the siren to a more urgent, high-pitched tone. But the traffic didn't look like it was going to start moving any time soon.

'Can you turn around?' There was no mistaking the tension in Anna's voice.

'It's all backed up behind us.' The driver shook his head.

'Got to go, sir.' Henwell ended the call as he pushed his door open and scrambled out.

Because Anna was already out of the car and running ahead of him towards danger once again.

So much for being careful.

Chapter 47

'WAIT!' Dermot shouted again as he tried to pick his way through the crowd.

But Marcus wasn't waiting. The chef pushed towards the entrance to the auditorium.

A theatre usher stepped in front of him, arms waving frantically, his words lost beneath the wail of the alarm.

Marcus just barrelled on through, shoving the man back against the wall.

'Sorry.' Dermot did the chef's apologising for him as he sped on past and into the theatre proper.

Marcus was already halfway down to the stage, so Dermot took the steps three at a time, trying his best to close the gap. But the chef still had a good lead by the time he reached the bottom and ran to the stairs at the side of the stage.

Dermot's foot caught a step and he stumbled and nearly fell. By the time he looked up again, Marcus was up on the stage and disappearing behind the curtain. Dermot reached the bottom and ran up the short flight of steps to the stage. Tentatively, he pushed through the heavy curtain, then stopped; eyes searching around in the gloom. But there was really no way of knowing which way the chef had gone. He breathed in deeply, hands on hips as sanity finally started to do its thing.

What did Marcus actually think he could achieve? Stop a gang of terrorists single-handed? Dermot didn't think so. But if the chef wanted to get himself blown up, that was his lookout.

This was just madness. Protecting Marcus from all kinds of folly was par for the course for Dermot as his agent. But his responsibility didn't extent to getting himself killed. Nowhere near.

He took a step backwards, then another and started to turn.

Then he stopped again. There'd be no more money to be made from Anton now, while Marcus would be just about the hottest man on television. But not if the chef was dead.

But that still wasn't enough to make Dermot carry on. He reached out and grabbed the curtain, ready to pull it back and run up the auditorium steps and out to safety. Then he let go again and turned back.

Because this wasn't just about the money. Marcus might have been a prize bellend, but he was Dermot's prize bellend, so to speak. And it wasn't so long ago that the chef had saved both their lives. There was no way Dermot could just leave him.

He scanned around the back stage area again as his eyes became more accustomed to the dim light, trying to figure out which way Marcus had gone. But it was useless. He'd just have to take a punt. He was about to start heading left when a movement off to the right caught his eye. Marcus was running back towards him, arms waving frantically.

The man had come to his sense. Thank God.

'Come on.' Dermot started towards him. 'We need to get out of here.'

But the chef just shook his head and grabbed Dermot's arm. 'You've got to see this.'

'No.' He didn't have to see anything. 'We've got to go.'

'We can't.' Marcus turned and ran back the way he'd come.

Bloody hell! Dermot wavered again. But it really was too late to turn back now. He followed the chef through a door and down a short flight of stairs into a long corridor.

'Listen.' Marcus stopped.

All Dermot could hear was the alarm.

'Come here.' Marcus put his ear against the first door on the left.

Dermot did the same and could just about make out another noise competing faintly with the fire alarm. A bang and then a faint shout. He looked at the writing on the door, *Denny Sharpe*. It was a name he knew from somewhere.

'It's locked.' Marcus tried the handle and then hit the door with his shoulder. 'And this one too.' He reached out and pulled on door handle opposite.

The wail of the fire alarm finally stopped.

Jesus. Dermot let his forehead rest against the door, allowing himself to think that it might be all over.

That there were no terrorists.

No bomb.

And that they might just be OK.

But as the ringing in his ears died away, Dermot heard more banging. And more desperate shouts from behind all the doors up and down the corridor.

He tried the handle again, but it wouldn't budge. Suddenly he remembered where he'd heard the name Denny Sharpe. A stand-up made good, toning down his risqué act to make a nice living as a game-show host.

He ran to the next door. Locked again. More shouting and banging from the other side.

He hit the door with his shoulder, but it was far too sturdy. The chorus of banging and shouting rose again.

Louder.

Faster.

More fevered.

Where were the police, the theatre people?

Where was Anna?

This wasn't over at all.

He pulled out his mobile and hit her number.

Chapter 48

Anna ducked around a group of dawdling pedestrians and ran on along the pavement. The traffic on the road was still at a standstill, angry shouts and horns cutting through the cold night air.

'Excuse me.' She called ahead at the next group of people, but there was no response, so she stepped down into the gutter to squeeze past.

'Police. Out of the way.' Henwell's voice echoed behind her, followed by angry shouts, suggesting he was taking a more direct route through the knot of pedestrians.

They could still stop this. Anna had to believe that.

She pushed on, ducking past a cyclist who'd cut up on the pavement. And it was all down to Dermot that they still had a chance. If he hadn't been such an idiot and left the safe house, they'd never have known they had the wrong target. Well not until it was too late.

Her phone vibrated in her pocket as she veered left, cutting between two gridlocked cars and crossing the road to the clearer pavement on the other side. No time for calls now.

But then it might be important. She fished the phone out, reading the name on the screen, slowing just a little as she put it to her ear. 'Are you out?'

Henwell closed up behind her as she slowed a little more.

'Err, not exactly.' Dermot's voice was fast, frantic. 'It's the celebs, the performers... They're all locked in their dressing rooms.'

'I told you to get out.' Why couldn't he just do what he was told for once?

'If the bomb goes off... There's nobody here to help them.' The anger in his voice grew. 'Why aren't there any police here?'

'We can't get a response from them. We think the terrorists might have taken them out.'

'Jesus, Anna, you said you had this.'

Henwell was alongside her now, his phone to his ear too. 'They've cleared the audience.'

Of course they had, because that was part of the terrorists' plan. They hadn't killed anyone but celebrities yet, so why start now? They'd probably have set off the fire alarm themselves if the alert hadn't been raised. Just another distraction.

'It's the celebs…' She relayed what Dermot had just told her to Henwell, and then spoke back into her phone. 'We're about five minutes away. You've just got to get out.'

'No.' The anger in Dermot's voice was stronger, but there was determination there too. 'We have to help them.'

'Have you ever defused a bomb?' But even as she said it, the words felt wrong. Her brain had been churning away since he'd told her the performers were all locked in their dressing rooms. That just didn't figure. It would need a hell of a lot of explosives to kill them all. And security would have been tight with the Royals due to attend. There was no way they could have smuggled a big device in. 'Actually no, I don't think it's a bomb.

'OK, good.' He was starting to sound calmer.

She doubted he'd stay that way. 'More likely to be some kind of gas.'

'And that's supposed to make me feel better?'

No, but it made perfect sense. With a gas like sarin, they'd only need a small amount, easy enough to smuggle in. Her brain was working on fast forward. If they released it into the air-con system, the celebs would be sitting ducks in the dressing rooms. That's why the terrorists had locked them in. It had to be gas.

'Listen, Dermot.' She and Henwell parted to round a drunk staggering down the pavement towards them. 'I'm going to hang up now.' It was the very last thing she wanted to do with him still inside the theatre. 'I need to speak to our tech team, get the layout of the theatre. If all the doors are locked, it might be an electronic system they can override.'

The shouting and blaring of horns were getting louder. Up ahead she saw a crowd on the pavement and a van abandoned in the middle of the road.

Henwell still had his phone to his ear as they slowed to push through the crowd. 'Mobile units are struggling to get close to the theatre.'

And that's when she knew that similar vans would have been abandoned in other key roads leading to the theatre. Yet again it seemed like the terrorists had all the bases covered.

Anna edged clear of the crowd and started to run again, speaking into the phone once more. 'Please just get out.'

'We're not leaving.'

'Jesus, Dermot.' Why did he have to keep trying to play the hero? 'You've seen what he's capable of. You can't talk him out of this.'

'We're not planning on doing any talking.'

'Don't be an idiot. We'll get people there. People with breathing equipment, who know what they're doing. Just get out.'

Henwell was back alongside her, shaking his head. 'Fire brigade won't be able to get through all this either.'

So much for the cavalry.

'OK. Listen to me.' Anna took a breath, hating herself for what she was about to do. But Dermot was right. He and Marcus were there on the spot and might be their only chance of stopping this. 'There'll be a services room somewhere. Just find it and turn off the air-con. Smash the control unit if you have to. Then get the hell out. If you see Anton or the terrorists, run. We're only a few minutes away.'

'We're on it.'

'And just be careful.' But the line was already dead. Ahead a young couple stepped out of a bar directly into her path. But Anna wasn't stopping. She barrelled straight on between, nearly losing her phone as she sent them sprawling on the pavement.

No time to apologise.

She ducked between two cars and crossed the road again. Another right then a left, scrolling through her contacts until she found Sophie Harper's name.

'Sophie, it's Anna. The Palladium Theatre. I need a full floor plan.'

'Give me a second.' The tech team leader knew not to waste precious seconds asking why.

'And try to hack into their system. The celebs are locked in their dressing rooms. See if you can override it.'

'Sure thing.'

Anna knew Sophie would be typing furiously as she spoke.

'OK, emailing plans to you now.'

'Thanks, let me know if you have any luck with the locks.' Anna cut the call and ran on.

'About three more minutes.' Henwell lengthened his stride and moved ahead of her.

With the plans to the theatre and a bit of luck, they might be able to get to the terrorists while Dermot and Marcus were still hunting around for the air-con room.

But that was all they had left to rely on now.

Luck.

Chapter 49

This was what he'd wanted, wasn't it? A chance to show Anna that he was a hero? But now it was here Dermot wasn't quite so sure. Be very careful what you wished for.

He ran on down the corridor, the sounds of banging and shouting ringing in his ears. Marcus puffed along behind, riding shotgun; Tonto to Dermot's Lone Ranger. Or should that be the other way round? They wouldn't be here now if it wasn't for the chef.

The shouting and banging from the dressing rooms seemed to get louder and more desperate with every stride Dermot took. The names on the doors were printed large enough to read, even at full sprint.

Windblown – a talent-show-winning dance troupe.

Bang, bang.

Malkie Moy, then *David Smith* – the first a comedian and the second some kind of magician.

Bang, bang, bang.

Fem-Sync – hip-hop girl group.

Bang, bang, bang, bang, bang, bang.

Two more comedians and another magician as the corridor stretched on.

The Harmonists, a male voice choir. Not sounding in key right now.

Tom Randall – a talent-show-winning singer.

Lucy Evans – England footballer turned reality star.

Darren Casey – famous for being famous? Dermot wasn't sure.

All celebrity life was here. And it would all be extinguished in a puff of poisoned gas if they didn't find that air-con room. His lungs were bursting now, but he stretched his legs, forcing himself on. Marcus was just about managing to keep pace behind him. How long was this bloody corridor anyway?

Next up an escapologist; or not, given the trouble he was

having getting past a simple locked door. Then a fortune teller. Presumably one without the foresight to have stayed at home that night.

Another magician.

Boyband.

Dance group.

Marcus's footsteps were still pounding away just a couple of yards behind him.

Bang, bang, bang.

Another choir, another dance group, another comedian.

Shouting, screaming, yelling, crying.

A sword swallower. Surely he could have hacked his way out.

Anger, frustration and terror echoed through every door. And the celebs trapped in their dressing rooms didn't even know about the gas.

Up ahead, Dermot saw a glowing green sign for the stairs. Down was the obvious way. Weren't things like air-con always in the basement? He reached the door and pushed it open, waiting for Marcus to catch up. Then together they headed through, leaving the banging and the screaming behind.

After that, the rest was simple enough. Down two flights of stairs, left along the corridor and there it was, third door on the right with a handy sign.

Aircon and Utilities

Easy.

All they had to do was go in there, find the big red button marked air-con and turn it off. Dermot didn't really have a plan beyond that. Probably didn't need one.

Anton and the terrorists would be long gone; everything set to bring death at the flick of a remote switch.

He nodded at Marcus as he reached out for the handle. Then he pushed the door open and stepped inside.

The room was big and packed with all manner of serious-looking machines, all with banks and banks of controls, lights and buttons. The nerve centre of the whole theatre it seemed. Beyond the machines, he could see only dark shadows where more machines presumably lurked. How exactly were they supposed to find the right button to press among all that?

Dermot took another couple of steps, deciding where to start looking. Then he stopped dead as a figure emerged from the shadows behind one of the biggest control units.

Anton Du Beurre.

No mask this time, the real thing. Confirmation if it was needed.

Dermot felt himself flinch. The Belgian moved towards a big pipe coming down from the ceiling into the top one of the control panels. In one hand he was carrying a small cylinder.

The gas.

Dermot flinched some more.

The cylinder was small, less than a metre long. The kind you might use at a BBQ, if you weren't expecting too many guests and didn't plan on cooking them too much food. Would it really be enough to kill all the celebrities?

Anton looked up slowly, finally noticing he had company. But there was no sign of surprise on his face, just what looked like a genuine smile. Round his neck hung a mask. Not the bad version of his own face he'd worn on the spoof game show but a serious-looking gas mask. Clearly he believed the cylinder was plenty big enough to do the job.

'Well, well, well.' The Belgian smiled, playing it as he did on TV. The quiet, confident charm and twinkly little Poirot eyes. 'If it isn't Batman and Robin. Here to save the day.'

Dermot didn't know if that was an upgrade on the Lone Ranger and Tonto.

'I'm glad you could make it.' Anton really did seem pleased to see them. 'Now I can congratulate you personally on your survival.' He stopped for a little chuckle. 'Although given the situation that might be a little premature.' He knelt down and rested the gas cylinder on the floor, pulling some sort of hose out from his pocket.

'Stop right there.' Dermot started moving forward, quickly closing the distance to a few feet.

'Oh please, let's just dispense with the amateur heroics. It's all a bit late for that.' Anton's eyes moved down to the cylinder again. Then he reached out and secured the hose to the top.

'I said stop.' Dermot raised a hand.

'I'm afraid I can't do that. Tell me though, you don't seem surprised to see me here. Why is that?'

'You've been blown, Du Beurre.' Marcus stepped forward. 'The police and MI5 know it's you.'

'That is unfortunate. I had hoped to continue my career once this was done.'

'No chance.' Marcus took another step.

Dermot turned to the chef as he heard the anger rising in his voice. With two against one, they could take the Belgian. But they both needed to stay calm, do this together.

'You stole my show.' Sadly, staying calm didn't appear to be on Marcus's agenda.

'No. You lost it a long time ago. And I was so much better than you.'

'You think?' Marcus was clenching and unclenching his fists.

'The police are on their way.' Dermot's words were aimed as much at Marcus as they were at the Belgian.

Just stay calm.

'The ratings don't lie.' Anton gave a sly smile. 'We were even about to go primetime, weren't we, Dermot?'

'Primetime?' Marcus turned to him now, his face a mixture of hurt and betrayal. 'You got HIM onto primetime? With my show?'

'Wait! He's just trying to –'

But it was too late. Marcus lunged at the Belgian, arms windmilling around as he charged. Anton, in contrast, was the image of fluid efficiency. He stood up and neatly stepped aside in one motion. Then he grabbed a long spanner from the table next to him and swung it hard into Marcus's face.

Marcus stopped, looking puzzled as a gash opened up above his left eye.

Then the Belgian brought the spanner back down on the top

of his erstwhile attacker's head. Marcus wobbled a bit, looking even more confused, then crumpled to the floor, twitching a couple of times before lying still.

Anton shook his head as he turned back to Dermot. 'He really shouldn't have done that. Two against one you might have had me, even with this.' He held up the spanner.

Dermot looked down at Marcus's prone body as his own anger came. He took a step forward, then another.

'Ah. Ah. Ah.' Anton waved the spanner. 'Not a good idea.'

But Dermot didn't have a choice. He either needed to get to that gas cylinder, disarm Anton and get help for Marcus or delay the Belgian until the Police and MI5 got there. He edged forward, then jumped back as Anton swung at him.

'I told you, stay back.' It was as if a switch had been flicked inside Anton. So calm and in control seconds before, he snarled the words; his eyes were wide and spittle flew from his mouth.

Dermot skipped in again and then back as Anton swung once more.

'Why are you doing this?' A little chat might delay things long enough for Anna and the police to get there.

'You wouldn't understand.'

'Try me.'

'Ha!' Anton laughed. 'That's your plan, is it? Keep me talking until the police get here?' The switch seemed to have flicked back again and the Belgian was calm once more. 'It's not a very good one.' Anton swung the spanner again. 'I just need to connect the other end to that air-con system, turn the valve, and all those lovely celebs will be dead.'

Dermot wasn't going to let that happen. He ducked in again and back, just managing to avoid the spanner. But this time his foot caught on an uneven piece of floor and he was down. He rolled to the side, knowing Anton would be on him in a flash, spanner arcing down to smash his skull. But the Belgian stayed where he was, calmly bending down to place the spanner on the floor before fastening the free end of the hose to a nozzle on the air-con unit. He smiled as he stood again, holding the gas cylinder tightly to his chest. 'Handy this. It's really for introducing cleaning agents into the system, but just as good for poison gas. I just need to turn this valve now.' He let his hand rest on the top of the cylinder.

Dermot climbed quickly back to his feet, knowing he'd only get one more chance. 'I can get you help.' He edged forward. 'If you stop this now. I can say you weren't always like this.' He took another half step closer, careful not to let his eyes rest for too long on the gas cylinder. Just a couple more steps and he might be able to reach out and pull it from Anton's grasp.

'I think that's close enough, don't you?'

'OK, OK.' He raised his hands but didn't step back. 'But I mean it. I can help you.'

What was keeping Anna and the police? Probably Henwell insisting they fill in a risk assessment form before they did anything.

'You'd do that? For me? You really would?' Anton's eyes opened wide, a weak smile leaking over his face. 'After everything I've done?'

'Yes.' When he let his eyes flick down, he saw that Anton's hand was no longer on the valve. 'It's not your fault. You just need help.' Dermot edged forward again, the cylinder almost in reach now.

Then the Belgian's whole face changed. The snarl back on his lips, dark rage flashing in his eyes. 'You really did think I'd fall for your plan. I'm not that stupid.'

Oh yes he was. Because just as Anton's hand closed on the valve again, the door behind Dermot finally crashed open.

He spun round to see Anna, a gun held firmly in both hands and pointed straight at the Belgian chef.

'Drop it.'

Then he turned back and smiled at the Belgian. Not such a bad plan after all.

Chapter 50

Anna stepped into the room, keeping her eyes firmly on Anton Du Beurre. 'I said drop it.'

The Belgian stood very still. He was holding some kind of gas cylinder, Marcus Diesel lying prone on the floor behind him.

'Thought you'd never get here.' Dermot was trying his best to sound blasé. 'I kept him talking.'

'Well done.' She stepped in closer. He'd bought them some time, but this wasn't over yet. Best if he just kept quiet now and left it to her. She locked her eyes on the Belgian. 'Put it down.'

But the man just shook his head. 'And then you'll shoot me.' His hands gripped the cylinder tighter.

'No, but I will if you don't put it down and step away.' She tried to slow her breathing, ready to take the shot if she needed to.

'You know what I've got in here? It's a sarin derivative. The tiniest amount would be enough to kill them all. You too. Dermot as well.' Anton gave a shrug. 'A quarter of a turn would probably do it. I think I could manage that even if you did shoot me.'

'Anton, please.' Dermot raised his hands. 'You don't have to do this. We can help you.'

'Didn't you try that one already?' The Belgian's eyes flicked to Dermot then back to Anna.

'Leave this to me.' She raised the gun, aiming it directly at Anton's forehead. The Glock 26 pistol may have been a small weapon, but it was still powerful enough to take him down. A headshot was riskier, but it was her only chance of the clean kill that would stop him turning the valve.

Anton held her gaze.

Staring down the barrel… People used the phrase with good reason. So much scarier when the gun was pointed straight at your head. Anna knew that because she'd been there. She kept her eyes zeroed in on Anton's, ready to take the shot if she still had to.

The Belgian blinked once and then again, eyes flicking down to the gas cylinder. When they came back up to meet hers there was doubt there, fear too.

She had him.

'Anton, please look at me.' Dermot's voice was hoarse and broken. 'You don't have to kill anyone else.'

'You're not helping.' Seriously? Did he have to? Anna tried not to let the anger creep into her voice, eyes still on Anton. 'I've got this, OK.'

'You'd never have got here if it wasn't for me.'

'Really, we're doing this now?' She hissed the words, not daring to take her eyes off the Belgian. If he looked away for just a second, the spell might be broken. 'Put it down.'

And then, very slowly, Anton smiled. Actually smiled. 'You've both made the same mistake.' His hand tightened on the valve.

'DROP IT.' Her finger tightened on the trigger.

'You think I'm the threat.'

Yes, because he was.

'But I haven't killed anyone. Well, not yet.'

Yeah right. Eight dead celebs tended to suggest otherwise.

'Actually he's right, they were all on me.' Felicity Diamond stepped out from behind one of the big control units, the gun in her hand pointed at Dermot.

Anna felt herself reel, struggling to believe what she was seeing as her rage threatened to boil over. Not just a mole but a murderer too. Anna wanted to swing the gun round and shoot Felicity in her smug little face. But she knew she'd never make it. To try would be certain death for Dermot. And Anton would be free to turn on the gas.

'Your turn to drop it I think.' Felicity's face was a deathly white, her voice strange, as she somehow managed to speak without moving her lips.

But when Anna looked more closely, she realised that the hand holding the gun wasn't Felicity's at all. Both it and the voice belonged to the person standing behind her, one arm wrapped tightly around the young MI5 officer's neck

'I'm sorry.' This time Felicity's lips did move, her voice shaky and scared. 'I'm so sorry.'

'I said drop it.' The figure behind Felicity moved the gun to point at the girl's head.

Anna lowered her own gun slowly and let it fall to the floor.

Chapter 51

'Emilie?' Dermot heard the clatter of Anna's gun hitting the ground as the figure behind Felicity emerged from the shadows.

'Surprised?' The Belgian girl's smile was all innocence, just like the one she'd worn around the office. She pushed the gun against Felicity Diamond's head as her eyes swivelled back to Anna. 'Now kick it over here.'

Dermot watched as Anna kicked the gun and their only weapon skittered its way across the floor, coming to rest against the far wall. Things were starting to move way too fast for him now.

Anton? Yes, he could believe that at a stretch. But Emilie? She'd worked with him for six months. He'd taken her to lunch, shown her the ropes and pretended not to notice when she'd stood a little too close. She'd had a mega crush on him.

'Thank you, my dear.' Anton nodded at Emilie with a smile.

The bastard. He must have forced her to help him, even coercing her into doing all of the killing. Dermot tried to catch Emilie's eye. 'You don't have to do what he says. We know that none of this is your fault.'

'Dermot.' Anna tried to cut in.

He ignored her, stepping forward instead. He knew these people, she didn't. 'I can make sure you get help.'

'Isn't that what you just said to Anton?' Emilie's voice was cold and hollow, her eyes dead.

The poor girl was terrified.

Terrified and holding a gun, not a great combination.

'Emilie, please.' He stepped towards her. If he could persuade her to give up the gun, he was confident Anna and he would be more than a match for Anton.

Another step.

'Dermot!' Behind him, Anna's voice was little more than a hiss.

He raised a hand to quieten her again, eyes still on Emilie. 'I know you're not a bad person.'

Felicity Diamond squirmed, shaking her head madly.

'Stop it.' Emilie barked the words into her captive's ear, grinding the gun into her temple harder.

'DERMOT!' Anna's voice was louder now, more insistent.

He turned to catch her eye with a frown. Why couldn't she leave it to him?

'Please don't hurt her.' He looked back at Emilie again, standing his ground, but not risking another step for now. 'We know he made you do it.' His voice faded away as a sudden realisation came. 'The chemicals. That was you, wasn't it? You didn't want me to die. Look, I know how you feel about me…'

Her laughter cut him off. 'Then you're an even bigger fool than I thought. You were supposed to think I was head over heels in love with you.' She rolled her eyes. 'Far easier to get all the info I needed on all those old clients. And you didn't suspect a thing.'

'But the chemicals?' She'd saved him, hadn't she?

Emilie's face darkened. 'That was Anton. He actually liked you for some reason. Wanted to give you a fighting chance.'

'But can't you see? He's manipulating you.' He risked another half step forward, little more than eight feet away now.

'No, Dermot, he isn't.' This time the voice was Anna's. 'It's been her all along. Isn't that right, Emilie?'

'Yes.' It was Anton who replied. 'It was her. She killed them all.'

'Only because you were too weak.' Emilie spat the words, her eyes bulging wide. 'We were supposed to do this together.'

'And we will.' Anton held up the gas cylinder, his eyes shining as he looked over at Emilie. 'I won't let you down again. I promise.'

So that was it. Anton was utterly besotted with her. And she'd used that to manipulate *him*.

'Now get back, both of you.' Emilie waved the gun towards Dermot and Anna. 'Up against the wall.'

Anna caught his eye with a nod and together they stepped backwards.

'Do it now.' Emilie's gaze was back on Anton, her voice in-istent.

'But why?' None of it was making any sense to Dermot. 'Why re you doing this?'

'You really think I'll fall for that one, buying you time as I xplain my diabolical scheme?' Emilie sighed as she moved the un to point at his chest. 'This isn't the movies.'

He kept his eyes locked on hers, too afraid to look at the gun. If I'm going to die, I'd like to know why.'

'You'll still be dead, so what does it matter?'

'It matters to me.'

'Not to me, it doesn't.' Next to him, Anna let out a long sigh. She's just a psycho. It'll be the same old self-serving crap.'

What was she doing? They had to keep Emilie talking until nore help arrived. It was their only chance.

'Seriously, nobody cares.' Anna shook her head with another igh.

No… Dermot cared.

Something flashed in Emilie's eyes then. It looked like she ared too.

And suddenly he realised that Anna was playing the same game s him after all, just more subtly and with lots more skill. But hen she had been to spy school, where presumably they taught ou this kind of stuff, so you didn't have to busk it if the time ver came.

'You want me to tell you?' Emilie's hand was shaking as she noved the gun back to point at Felicity's head.

'Not really, no.' Anna shook her head again dismissively.

Oh… Maybe Anna wasn't playing the game after all.

'Well, I'm going to tell you, OK?'

'For God's sake.' Anna turned to Anton. 'If you're going to do t, just do it.'

'No. STOP.' Emilie was shouting now. 'LET ME TELL YOU.' She was pressing the gun into Felicity's temple. 'And if ou don't listen, I'll blow her brains out.'

'OK. OK.' Anna held up her hands.

Dermot let out a long slow breath. Anna had pushed Emilie right up to the edge, delaying her even further. And distracting her too, he realised now. Because in the shadows behind the Belgian girl, a tall figure was slowly emerging from the darkness.

Chapter 52

Henwell took another slow step forward as he listened to the rise and fall of the voices from the other side of the room.

The decision to split up – Anna's decision – looked like being one of the better ones they'd made since all of this had begun. His own decision not to sign out a gun that morning seemed less good.

But with armed response still minutes away they couldn't afford to wait. So they'd agreed Anna would take the main door while he worked his way to a second entrance round the back. It looked like the plans Sophie Harper had sent to Anna's phone might just be what made the difference.

He took another step, bringing him to the end of an aisle of storage shelves and into the shadow of one of the big control units. Now he had a full view of the room for the first time, full pictures to go with the sound.

'You have no idea, do you?' Emilie held the gun to Felicity Diamond's head, her voice shaking with poorly suppressed rage.

Henwell hadn't wanted to believe it when he'd first heard her voice. He'd rescued her, carried her out of a building as it exploded behind them. But he knew now that he was no hero. They'd never been in any danger, the whole thing staged to put her beyond suspicion. He took another careful step forward. Ahead of him, Emilie was in the middle of the room. An easy target. But there was a hell of a lot of ground for him to cover.

'The French, the Dutch. They hate Belgians.' Emilie's voice rose higher as she lost a little more control. 'They always have.'

Anton Du Beurre was perhaps ten feet off to her right, a gas cylinder in his hands. Beyond the two Belgians, Dermot and Anna stood with their backs to the wall. Both of them had seen him, although Anna was doing a far better job of hiding it than Dermot, who kept looking his way. Henwell took another couple of careful steps, trying to up the pace. There was no telling how long he had.

'And you British are no better.' Emilie's words were like poison. 'You always joke that there are no famous Belgians, except Tin Tin and Poirot. And they're not even real.'

'What about Jean-Claude Van Damme?' Dermot chimed in, clearly trying to do his best to keep the conversation going.

Good man.

'That's an easy one.' Emilie didn't sound impressed.

'Rubens?' Anna's cultural references were clearly a bit more highbrow than Dermot's.

'Yes, OK. Go on then, some more.'

'Err… What about…' Dermot trailed off.

'Audrey Hepburn.' This was Anna again.

'Yes!' The Belgian girl sounded impressed. 'Not many people know that.'

Henwell took another step forward. Hoping they could keep the game going a bit longer. But he knew stealth would only get him so far. At some point, he'd have to go hard and fast. But who to take down first, Emilie or Anton? She had the gun, but he had the gas – an almost impossible choice.

'Any more, Dermot?' Emilie was toying with him.

'Yeah, umm… That cyclist. Eddy Merckx?'

She nodded.

'Kevin De Bruyne.'

'Everyone knows footballers, they don't count.'

'The Smurfs.'

Emilie snorted. 'I bet Anton told you that one.'

'OK then, Van Gogh?' Dermot was beginning to sound a little cocky.

'No. NO! He's Dutch.' The anger was back in Emilie's voice. 'You see, you don't know any others. Because nobody ever gives us a chance.'

'What about him?' Anna was pointing at Anton. 'He got the chance.'

'On daytime TV?' Emilie gave a dismissive snort. 'That's not famous.'

'About to go primetime though.' Anton sounded more than a little hurt. 'Tell her, Dermot.'

'He's right.' Dermot nodded, his gaze flitting dangerously towards Henwell.

'That doesn't count, it was all part of our plan.' Emilie shook her head.

'This was never about destabilising the economy, was it?' Anna was shaking her head in disbelief. 'You're just killing off celebs to give more Belgians the chance to be famous.'

'Of course.' Emilie made it sound like the most natural thing in the world. 'But we needed help. Money, logistical support, a few other things. Our backers were keen we did as much harm to your economy as we could.'

Henwell took another step. Out in the open now, he decided to go for Emilie first, try to get the gun.

'But how…?' Dermot shook his head. 'How did you manage to do all this? He's a chef. You were just my assistant.'

'That's what you think.' Emilie there was something else in Emilie's tone now. It sounded like pride. 'We were both VSSE, the Belgian secret service. Until we got, how should I put it, a higher calling.'

'I didn't even know Belgium had a secret service?' Dermot shrugged.

'That just shows how good we are.' The pride in Emilie's voice grew stronger. Then her tone hardened again. 'And that's another thing people don't know about us Belgians. Our secret service is actually the second oldest in the world, after the Vatican.'

It was unclear whether she was hacked off at the lack of recognition of Belgium's snooping pedigree or the fact the Pope had got there first. Henwell took another cautious step forward.

'But why Britain?' Anna sounded genuinely puzzled. 'There must be plenty of celebrities in France or the Netherlands?'

'Because of what you did. You kicked us out.'

Henwell was close enough to see the confusion spreading across Anna and Dermot's faces.

'You don't even know about that, do you?' Emilie nudged

Felicity forward, the gun still pressed against her head as the pair moved away from Henwell. 'Over a quarter of a million Belgians came to Britain as refugees during World War I.'

Henwell paused, weighing up his options. With the prospect of a long history lesson, he might be able to wait it out for the armed response team. But they wouldn't know what they were dealing with. If they came in blind, there was a good chance Anton would have time to turn the gas on. He had to end this now.

And fast.

'There were Belgian schools, churches, shops. Whole towns.' The pride was back in Emilie's voice. 'They worked hard, helped the war effort.' Emilie pushed Felicity another step forward.

Henwell changed his mind again. With Emilie moving even further away, he'd have to go for Anton. Anna and Felicity should be able to tackle the Belgian girl. And maybe Dermot could help too?

'When it was over, your government sent them all back. And it broke my great-grandfather's heart. His name…' She paused, clearly for effect. 'Was Thibaut Lemaire.'

Dermot and Anna looked back blankly.

'You see, you've never heard of him.'

Neither had Henwell. He took another careful step.

'He was a music hall star, a variety performer. He tap-danced, sang funny songs, told jokes.'

Sounded awful, probably deserved to be sent home.

'He was one of the biggest music hall stars during the war.' There was now a faraway tone to Emilie's voice. 'He could have gone into films, made it in Hollywood even. He had far more talent than that clown Charlie Chapman.'

Henwell had covered about a third of the gap. Soon he'd have to abandon stealth and just go for it.

'But he was sent back with all the rest.' She shook her head. 'We don't share your love of variety-based entertainment in Belgium. He finished his career playing to half-empty halls in places like Antwerp and Bruges. Liège. Ghent even.' For some eason this last place seemed to inspire particular disdain from Emilie. 'And it killed him.'

'You can't blame Britain for that?' Anna kept her eyes on Emilie, managing to avoid looking at Henwell.

'YES, I CAN.' The Belgian shouted the words as she stepped forward once more, taking her further away. 'But at least now others might get the chance he never had.'

Henwell was in two minds again now – go for Anton or gamble on getting to Emilie, who was clearly the more dangerous of he two. He just needed to get a couple of steps closer. Then he'd make his mind up.

But that decision became largely academic as a floorboard creaked under his foot and Emilie spun around and fired her gun. Pain bloomed in Henwell's shoulder and he felt himself falling to he ground.

Chapter 53

Anna was moving before the sound of the gunshot had finished echoing around the room, her eyes on Henwell as he dropped to his knees.

One step, two steps, three; she was halfway across the gap to Emilie, who was still facing away from her.

Another shot rang out, but Felicity was now fighting for the gun and the bullet buried itself harmlessly into the control panel behind Henwell. He stayed on his knees for a second or so more and then slumped sideways onto the floor.

But there was no time to worry about him now. Felicity had managed to drag Emilie to the ground. The two of them were still fighting for the gun as they rolled away from Anna.

'Dermot. The gas!' She kept on running towards the fight in front of her, eyes flicking to Anton as she went.

The Belgian seemed frozen, his face clouded with concern as he looked over at the fight.

'Just do it!' Emilie was on top of Felicity, trying to break her grip on the gun, as she yelled at Anton.

Her shout seemed to snap the chef out of his trance. But it was too late; Dermot was already moving. He flew across the gap and crashed into Anton. Something halfway between a rugby tackle and a shoulder charge. Unconventional but effective. The gas cylinder bounced out of the Belgian's hands as he fell backwards with Dermot on top of him.

For a second or so everything seemed to stand still. Anna watched the cylinder hit the floor. It bounced once, twice, and then started to roll. When it came to a stop, the hose was still attached. But she was sure that Anton hadn't managed to turn the valve.

'Keep him away from the gas.' She was going to have to trust Dermot while she helped sort out Emilie.

The Belgian girl was trying to twist Felicity round to get her into a chokehold. But Felicity used the momentum against her opponent, rolling her over again. Felicity had excelled in all her self-defence courses, but it was clear that Emilie was well trained too. She brought an elbow up into Felicity's face, sending her head snapping backwards. Then Emilie wrestled her arm free and brought the gun round to point at Anna.

Six feet away, maybe a little more. Anna knew there was no way he was going to make it so she dived to the side instead, even thought she knew it was probably too late.

But Felicity reared up again, blood streaming from her nose as she grabbed at Emilie's arm. Anna heard the bang and felt the rush of the bullet as it cleared her shoulder.

Just.

She was nearly on them now. Emilie tried to aim the gun again, but Felicity had a firm hold and was pulling it away. So Emilie changed tack, pushing with Felicity rather than fighting it. With all the resistance gone, the barrel swivelled round to point at young MI5 officer.

'NO!' Anna surged forward, but the sound of the gunshot was already in her ears. She crashed into Emilie and the two of them rolled across the room. But as she fought to get on top, she realised the Belgian still had hold of the gun.

They rolled again.

Over the other side of the room Dermot had got himself between Anton and the gas cylinder, kicking out to keep the Belgian at bay.

Good work.

Another roll.

Now she saw Felicity on her knees, her top and trousers already stained red. And behind her Henwell, a trail of blood on the floor as he crawled slowly towards the gun over by the far wall.

But Anna knew he'd never make it in time. This was all on her now. She grabbed Emilie's gun as they rolled for a final time, banging it hard on the floor.

Once.

Twice.

Three times.

'Bitch.' Emilie cried out as she lost her grip and the gun slid away across the room.

Anna pushed her off and sprang to her feet in one easy movement, steadying herself and getting low as Emilie jumped up too.

Anna edged round, eyes focused on Emilie's, trying to keep herself between the Belgian girl and the fight between Anton and Dermot. She feinted once then went with a sweeping kick designed to take Emilie's legs from under her. But Emilie anticipated and jumped back. Anna moved forward, knowing she had to stay on the front foot and keep Emilie away from the gas cylinder. And with the gun removed from the equation, Anna was confident she'd have the edge.

She feinted again, pretending to go for another high kick with her left leg, ready to move in and finish it with a punch to the side of Emilie's head, but her opponent spun away. Then she kicked out at Anna, seemingly out of nowhere, catching her full in the chest. Anna staggered backwards, just about managing to stay on her feet. But she wasn't quite so confident anymore. Especially after Emilie smiled a nasty little smile and slipped an evil-looking little knife from her belt.

Chapter 54

Dermot ducked away as Anton came at him again. Then he stepped to the side to keep himself between the Belgian and the gas cylinder. He was breathing harder and knew he was moving more slowly than when the fight had started. But Anton was tiring too, his breath coming in ragged gasps.

The next time the chef came at him, Dermot didn't duck away, hitting out with his right hand instead, catching Anton flush on the jaw with perhaps the best punch he'd thrown in his entire life.

The Belgian staggered and fell backwards, landing on his arse as a look of surprise spread across his face.

What now? Attack while Anton was down and try to put him out of the game, or play safe and guard the cylinder?

He decided to play it safe, taking a step back and steadying himself for the next attack as the chef climbed to his feet again.

'Just turn it on.' Across the room Emilie was starting to sound more desperate as she faced off with Anna, the pair of them circling round and round. Then a sudden kick from the Belgian girl sent Anna staggering backwards.

'Give it up.' Anton closed in again, blocking Dermot's view of the other fight. But the Belgian was moving more warily after the punch.

All Dermot had to do was keep him away from the gas until the armed response team came crashing in. How hard could that be? He craned his neck to get a view of what was going on behind Anton. Anna had managed to stay on her feet and was blocking the Belgian girl's path again.

Just play for time. That's what they both had to do now. Then he saw the knife glinting in Emilie's hand and realised that simply holding Anton off was no longer an option.

Anna needed his help.

He watched as she pushed Emilie back with a kick to the ribs. But she wouldn't be able to avoid the knife for much longer.

Across the room, Henwell was crawling slowly towards the far corner and Anna's gun. He'd been shot, fair enough. But couldn't he have got a bloody move on? The man still wasn't pulling his weight if you asked Dermot. Felicity Diamond was slumped in a heap and Marcus hadn't moved. Both looked like they needed urgent attention. Dermot would have to take Anton out and disconnect the gas cylinder. Then maybe he could help them all.

The Belgian moved in closer.

'Just do it.' Emilie shouted again, as she dodged another kick from Anna.

Anton tensed, looking like he was getting ready to make another charge. Then he stopped, his eyes darting off to the left. Dermot followed his gaze. The spanner the Belgian had used to take down Marcus was on the floor about three yards away. Whoever got their hands on it first would have the advantage.

Anton looked back at him and for a second their eyes locked. Dermot moved first, going for the spanner. Anton followed, fully committing.

Sucker.

As Anton charged on Dermot pulled up, then turned and scooped up the gas cylinder, hoping he'd bought himself enough time. He flicked the release button to remove the valve connecting the tube to the air-con pipe. But wouldn't budge.

Come on!

He pushed again and tried to turn it. But the valve was stuck fast. He twisted harder, still nothing. It must have been damaged when Anton dropped it.

The Belgian had the spanner now. He raised it over his head, roaring as he charged.

Dermot pushed again.

Nothing.

He gave up on the valve, trying instead to yank the far end of the hose out of the connection to the air-con unit. But it didn't want to give.

Anton was nearly on him now, shaping to bring the spanner down onto Dermot's head.

Across the room, Emilie had put Anna on the floor with a kick to the knee and was moving in with the knife.

Come on!

Dermot pulled the cylinder as hard as he could, stumbling backwards as the hose finally jerked free.

Then Anton was right there, the spanner arcing down.

Instinctively Dermot held the cylinder up to protect himself.

CLAANNNNG. The sound of metal on metal crashed around the room. Anton roared in pain as all the force of the blow vibrated back up his arms. But he kept hold of the spanner.

Anna had rolled away from Emilie's attack and was trying to get to her feet. But there was something wrong with her right leg and she shouted out in pain as it collapsed under her.

Dermot raised the cylinder to block the next blow. Again Anton yelled out as the spanner pranged back off the metal. But the strength of the blow knocked Dermot to the floor. The Belgian stepped in closer, madness in his eyes as he took a breath and a second or so to compose himself for the final blow.

Dermot stole a last desperate glance across at Anna, who was trying to stand again. But her knee gave out as Emilie closed in with the knife. She needed help now.

Henwell was still dragging himself across the floor, even more slowly than before.

'You really should have stayed out of this.' Anton lifted the spanner back over his head, sweat streaming down his face.

Dermot scrambled backwards in a last desperate effort to get away. Then he called out Anna's name and rolled the gas cylinder towards her as hard as he could.

Chapter 55

'ANNA!' Dermot's cry for help rang out across the room.

Couldn't he see she was a bit busy right now?

Emilie stepped in closer as the pain in Anna's knee sang out.

He'd just have to…

But something at the back of her brain was processing what she'd heard. Not a plea, or a cry for help.

A warning.

Then she heard another noise and her eyes flicked towards the gas cylinder skidding across the floor towards her. She reached out, managing to get her fingers on it before it slid on by.

Emilie was right above her now, her eyes glinting as brightly as the knife she was swinging down towards Anna's chest.

Two things flashed up in Anna's brain as she tried to get proper grip on the cylinder.

With the gas disconnected, the celebs were safe.

And she now had a weapon.

So she swung it as hard as she could at Emilie's knee.

A third thing occurred to Anna as she heard the crunch of metal on bone and the Belgian girl's roar of pain and fury.

If she had a weapon, it meant Dermot didn't. She risked look over as Anton swung the spanner downwards.

At the last second, Dermot rolled aside, and the weapon cracked into the floor inches from his head. But there was no more time to watch. Emilie was up on one knee, the other leg bent and useless like Anna's. But the Belgian girl still had hold of the knife.

She raised it high above her head and stabbed downwards.

Anna blocked with her free hand, trying not to lose her grip on the cylinder with the other.

'You can't stop us.' Emilie was on top of Anna now. Both hands on the knife as, inch by inch, she forced it down towards Anna's throat, the madness burning like a fever in her eyes.

Anna pushed back, feeling the touch of cold metal on her skin as Emilie leaned in closer.

And closer…

And closer…

Rage distorting the Belgian girl's beautiful face.

And closer…

Until she was low enough for Anna to swing the gas cylinder into the side of her head, distorting those beautiful looks even more. Then Emilie fell sideways, out cold before she even hit the floor.

'Emilieeeee.' The girl's name was a howl of pain from deep inside Anton. He raised the spanner again, bringing it down hard.

Anna heard the crack of bone as Dermot got an arm up to block the blow. She tried to stand, but her knee gave out again. So she started to crawl instead, even though there was no way she was ever going to get there in time.

Anton howled out Emilie's name once more as he raised the spanner for the killing blow.

Chapter 56

Everything seemed to slow right down as Dermot took a final desperate glance around the room.

Anton holding the spanner high above his head.

Anna, eyes wide as she yelled his name and tried to crawl to him.

Emilie slumped on her side, blood seeping from the wound on the side of her heard.

Marcus lying still, probably dead by now.

And Henwell still crawling towards the bloody gun. He'd never make it, even if they were all here until next weekend.

Dermot raised his one good arm, the other shattered and lying uselessly by his side. But there was no pain.

Not yet.

Probably never would be now.

Things started to move at normal speed again.

Anton's back arched further as he prepared to bring the spanner down one last time, his cry of animal rage filling the room.

Anna was still crawling, closer now.

Henwell still getting nowhere.

Was this how it was going to end for Dermot? Bludgeoned to death by a fake TV chef, behind the scenes at one of the UK's premier celebrity events? It was certainly a novel way to go.

But at least all the celebs were safe.

Anna too.

He looked across at her, still giving it her all to get to him, even though she must've known she'd never make it.

All those might-have-beens came flooding back.

He looked up at Anton, the spanner held high over his head. The bastard was really milking it now.

Just get on with it.

Oddly Dermot felt calm now, a sense of peace started to descend on him.

Oh no it bloody didn't.

No way.

He didn't want to die, not like this at least.

In fact, not at all.

He tensed, trying to hold his arm up as firmly as he could as Anton did some more bellowing and started to bring the spanner down. But the rage on the Belgian's face was morphing into something else, something close to bewilderment. He strained as he tried to bring the spanner down to open up Dermot's skull. The weapon though seemed intent on defying gravity.

Anton strained again, his face a deep crimson, sweat flowing freely. Then the spanner flew upwards out of his grasp, almost as if a giant magnet on the ceiling had pulled it away.

The Belgian started to turn, just as the spanner came back down onto the top of his head. Then his eyes lost focus and he slumped sideways to the floor.

And there stood Marcus Diesel, breathing hard and grinning down at Dermot even though the blood was still pumping from his own head wound. 'I told him didn't I…?' Marcus took a deep breath. 'Told him it was… It was my fucking show.' Then the chef's eyes rolled backwards and he fell to the floor next to Anton.

That's when the pain in Dermot's arm finally kicked in. But Anna was with him now, soft words washing over him as she cradled his head in her hands.

'We did it.' She smiled down at him, tears on her cheeks. 'We did it.'

He started to smile back, but his eyes were already closing.

Epilogue

Two weeks later…

A Few Loose Ends

It was a little after 3.30pm, the last of the afternoon light fading fast. Anna checked she was still OK for time then clicked to play the video on her screen, leaning forward to plug in her headphones as it loaded up.

The grainy footage started to roll, the intro music drowning out the buzz of the office. Then the famous old Pathé News logo appeared, followed by the titles.

New Belgian Star Takes Music Hall Stage.

And there he was – Thibaut Lemaire, the man who'd unwittingly started it all more than a century before. He smiled broadly as he danced his way through a song. Despite the jaunty tune, it seemed to be imploring the brave British Tommies to do a variety of highly unsavoury things to the 'filthy Hun' with their bayonets.

Anna let the film run for a few more seconds then hit stop. Despite Emilie Pieters' claims, it looked like her great-grandfather had been little more than an average talent at best. Lemaire hadn't been entirely forgotten in his home country though, with a small museum dedicated to his life in his hometown of Florenville near the French border. The curator, a friendly enough woman, had been only too happy to help. Then again, it was unlikely that she was overburdened with enquiries, or visitors for that matter.

Anna had contacted her, posing as a researcher for a new TV documentary about wartime entertainers. The information the woman had provided included copies of Lemaire's letters. Written mainly to a sister in Antwerp, they told of Lemaire's bitterness over his forced return to Belgium after the war. The poison and vitriol against the British had increased with each passing year. It was a hatred that had dripped its way down the generations, finally finding an outlet in Emilie.

The Belgian secret service had reluctantly revealed that she had indeed been one of theirs. A promising recruit and junior officer by all accounts, until her increasingly erratic behaviour had led to warnings, disciplinary action and then dismissal. This contradicted Emilie's own claim of a 'higher calling', of course. But whichever way you looked at it, the Belgian secret service had trained up a psychopath and then cut her loose. Otherwise, details were sparse. It wasn't every day an agent went rogue and launched a terrorist attack on a friendly nation. So no surprise perhaps that the Belgians were playing it tight-lipped.

The little information they'd provided on Anton Du Beurre, not his real name of course, suggested that, unlike Emilie, he'd been a model agent. His superiors had been both surprised and disappointed when he'd resigned. But they'd never linked it to Emilie's dismissal, and nobody had thought to ask questions about his unlikely reinvention of himself as a TV chef in the UK.

A couple of clicks and Anna had opened up the file she'd been compiling on the Belgian pair. At the top, a picture of Emilie, taken at HMP Bronzefield, the high security women's prison where she was awaiting trial. She'd scowled at the camera, her face still bruised and swollen around the fractured cheekbone. A line of stitches ran across her forehead, further evidence of Anna's work with the gas cylinder.

Predictably, neither Emilie nor Anton was cooperating with the police investigation. Both were lawyered up, alternating between requests to be sent back to Belgium for trial, and threats to plead insanity.

Emilie could probably have pulled that off, on account of being batshit crazy. Not Anton though. He'd just been obsessed with the Belgian girl. If mindlessly following your dick counted as insanity, the mental health wards would have been overflowing with men.

But all that was for the police and the courts. Anna had agreed to hand her dossier over to them by the weekend. The Met would focus on the prosecution while MI5 concentrated on tracking down the mysterious 'backers' that Emilie had alluded to. Anna could only hope that the police investigation would start to move with a little more pace now that Henwell was back on active duty. Emilie's bullet had made a mess of his shoulder, but the doctors said he'd been lucky and should get something close to full mobility back.

Felicity Diamond had been luckier still. She'd technically died as Anna held her hand in the ambulance on the way to hospital. Eight hours of complex stomach surgery had followed and she'd remained on the critical list for a further six days. But now, a week further on, she was sitting up and hungry for updates on the case as well as banana ice cream.

Anna hadn't yet admitted to Felicity that they'd written her off as a traitor. Some deep digging on Emilie's laptop by the tech team had revealed that the Belgians had been the source of the suspicious payments.

Maybe she could have a word with Lawson about keeping it among the few people who'd been aware of Felicity's suspected treachery? Not least because Anna knew she would've been dead if it hadn't been for the girl's bravery. Dermot too probably, as well as Henwell, Marcus Diesel and dozens of celebrities.

Felicity had spent the ten days following her kidnap locked in a windowless room, listening through the wall to Emilie and Anton's daily debates on the pros and cons of keeping her alive or killing her. She wasn't clear why the Belgians had taken her to the theatre. The current theory was that they'd planned to pin the whole thing on her so Anton could carry on with his TV career.

Anna stretched and checked the clock on her screen. She still had time to kill, so opened up the BBC website and clicked on the live link to the Met press conference that was about to start. With the terrorist threat eliminated, MI5 had retreated into the shadows. That was what they did. DAC Connor and Marcus Diesel were showing no such coyness. The police had a tarnished reputation to repair and the chef probably had a new cookbook on the way.

The camera panned around the conference room at New Scotland Yard, lingering on the assembled journalists, before turning to the faces at the top table. Marcus Diesel first, looking relaxed if a little unseasonal in a lime-green jacket and orange Hawaiian shirt.

The media had eagerly eaten up the tale of how Marcus had become a double hero. Not content with his quick thinking on the fake game show, he'd then gone on to almost single-handedly thwart the terrorist attack at the theatre and save all the celebs. At least that was how the story was being spun.

Fair dues, Marcus had undoubtedly played his part. And the Met had been happy to ride the extra wave of positive publicity the chef's involvement brought to the successful prevention of the terrorist conspiracy. Nobody seemed keen to dwell on quite how close it had all come to complete disaster.

Next, the camera panned to Henwell, looking confident and relaxed in a dark suit and crisp white shirt, showing no signs of his injury. Then Connor, decked out in his full dress uniform between the two other men, ready to take as much of the credit as he could.

And then… Anna waited for the camera to move on, but it returned to Marcus.

No Dermot? Anna felt a little pinch of irritation on his behalf. Surely he deserved to be up there as much as any of them.

More so, probably.

But then wouldn't this be how he wanted it? Orchestrating things from behind the scenes as he tried to wring out every last ounce of publicity for his client.

Well, good luck to him. It was the least he deserved. Anna's guilt hadn't been confined to her suspicions about Felicity. She'd only seen Dermot once since that night at the theatre, dropping by his room at the hospital to check how his broken arm was doing after surgery.

And to thank him for saving her life.

Their conversation had petered out into an uncomfortable silence, neither of them quite able to say what they wanted. Anna had left quickly, bending down to give him a stiff hug, still not sure at that point whether they'd ever see each other again.

On screen, the camera lingered on Marcus until the press officer called the room to order and Connor kicked off with his introductory remarks.

'It makes me very proud…'

What, to grab all the credit? Suddenly Anna couldn't be both-red with it. She shut her computer down and reached for her ag. If she left now she'd have time to walk it, rather than othering with the Tube.

*

ast question please.' The press officer smiled as she prepared to ring proceedings to an end, pointing to a smartly dressed blonde oman at the front who had her hand raised.

'Jenny Harlow, *Daily Mail*.'

She was one of the few real crime hacks in a room crammed ith showbiz writers and gossip columnists. Henwell stiffened, nticipating a question more challenging than most they'd nswered over the past hour.

'Does the success of this investigation vindicate the decision to vest valuable police resources in the celebrity crime squad?'

He smiled to himself. The journalist had been one of his most ocal critics in the early days. But now she was lobbing him one hit out of the park.

'Well, Jenny, I think –'

But Connor raised a hand to cut him off. 'I'm sure I speak for l Londoners when I say that DI Henwell and his team have roved both dedicated and tenacious in solving these vile and ffensive crimes. Celebrities from all areas of the entertainment usiness can rest assured that they're safe. My decision to invest sources in this area has more than paid off.'

Henwell smiled to himself again. If Connor wanted the lime-ght, he was welcome to it.

'Thank you, ladies and gentlemen.' A barrage of further ques-ons rose up from the gathered journalists, but the press officer eld up her hands as she stood and led the way from the room.

'A word if I may, Detective Inspector.' Connor turned to him ith a suspiciously genuine smile as they headed through the oorway into the smaller room next door.

'Of course, sir.' Henwell checked his watch. A 'word' with th DAC could take anything up to an hour and he'd need to ge moving soon.

Connor beckoned him over to one side as a second doo behind them opened and Dermot Jack strolled in, his left arm i a sling. He gave Henwell a nod before heading over to Marcu and patting him on the back with his good arm.

'In light of recent circumstances, I've decided to restore you t the rank of DCI. Pay and benefits too.'

OK… Good but hardly unexpected.

'And I think we can probably find you something more suite to your talents.'

Henwell looked for a trace of any agenda in Connor's smil but there was nothing.

'We've got a DCI vacancy coming up in homicide.'

Heading up one of London's major investigation teams with shot at promotion to detective superintendent. It was a highl sought after role and would put him on the same footing a Simpson.

'Thank you, sir. I'll certainly think about it.'

'Think about it? I thought you'd have jumped at the chance i your position. You're not considering staying with CRAPPIE Connor's eyes were wide open.

'CAPPE, sir, I think you'll find.' He'd almost certainly take th job, but Henwell was still a little torn. Celeb crime might hav been a backwater, but it was starting to feel like a backwater he' made his own.

'You can't move him.' Dermot stepped up next to Henwel cutting in on the tail end of the conversation. 'It would be a P disaster. They think he's a hero.'

'You too, by all accounts, Mr Jack.' Connor turned his smil up a notch or two as he changed the subject. 'You should hav been with us for the press conference.'

Dermot shook his head. 'Some of us prefer to avoid that so of thing.'

Henwell stifled a smirk. Dermot had sussed the DAC in les

than ten seconds. He was almost starting to like the guy.

'Well, gentlemen, busy day. Must be off.' The DAC moved to reassert his importance by being the first to leave.

Henwell turned to Dermot as Connor stalked off. 'Listen, err…' Suddenly he felt awkward. 'I'd like to say thanks again. If it wasn't for you –'

'And me.' Marcus sounded indignant.

'Yes, and you.' Henwell tried to keep the weariness from his voice. They'd just spent the best part of an hour hearing about the chef's bravery, mainly from the man himself. 'There'll be a commendation for you both, I would think. And we can forget about you drugging two of my officers too.'

'Oh.' The smile faded from the chef's face. 'You know about that.'

'Yes. But then if you hadn't done it, we'd never have known we had the wrong target.' Henwell stretched out a hand.

'Exactly.' Marcus was smiling again as he shook it.

'And thank you again.' Henwell turned and offered his hand to Dermot. Maybe they should keep in touch, arrange to go to the pub and share stories from their different worlds. But right now he had far more important places to be.

*

Jesus… For a moment Dermot had actually thought Henwell was going to suggest they go for a pint.

OK, he might have developed a grudging respect for the big copper over the past few days, but the idea of the two of them sharing stories down the pub was a step too far.

'Come on.' Dermot guided Marcus towards the door. 'We've got the photo shoot in half an hour.' He led the way down the corridor towards the car park.

'Do I have to?' The chef let out a sigh as they stepped outside.

'What's wrong?' Anything that made Marcus want to avoid publicity had to be serious. Maybe it was to the with the bang on head he'd received from Anton?

'It all just feels too much.'

'This is what you wanted, isn't it?' He put his good arm round the chef's shoulder. With Anton now in jail, Marcus was set to become Dermot's biggest-earning client once again. He really needed the chef to bring out his A-game.

'All I want is the show back.'

'I'm working on that.' He hadn't told Marcus about the contract offer he'd received from *The Meal of Fortune's* producers that morning because they'd lowballed the fee.

Dermot knew it.

And they knew that he knew too, especially with the show going primetime.

He was determined to hold out for as much as he could get and didn't want Marcus rushing to sign.

'The shoot won't take long and it's good publicity.'

Heat Magazine was putting Marcus on the front cover, backed-up by a six page story covering his heroic exploits.

Dermot led the chef across to where their car was waiting, the engine already idling. But suddenly the thought of twenty minutes in a confined space with Marcus was too much for him. It would only be further badgering about the show, interspersed with more about how brave the man had been.

'Tell you what, why don't you go on ahead. I'll call the production company again and chase up the contract. I'll see you there.'

'OK, but don't abandon me.' Marcus headed for the car and then turned. 'We're still going for a drink afterwards, right?'

'Sure.' Dermot watched as the security barrier lifted and the car nudged out into the heavy traffic on the Embankment. He looked around for a cab then decided to walk it, not bothered about the cold and gathering darkness of the December afternoon. And with the London traffic as bad as ever, he'd probably still get to Covent Garden before Marcus. It would give him a chance try to clear his head too. He cut across the car park and out onto the road, feeling the pain in his arm as the pills started to wear off.

In the end, it had taken two operations to deal with the injuries

Anton had inflicted with the spanner. But the doctors were confident there'd be no lasting damage. The same though couldn't be said for his pride. Dermot still wasn't quite ready to believe how badly Anton had duped him. Or what a fool Emilie had made of him.

But then who were the fools now?

He stopped and took a couple of deep breaths. Hadn't he promised himself enough times over the past weeks that he wasn't going to dwell too much on what had happened with the Belgians?

Or with Anna.

It really was time for him to move on. There could never be anything between them, even if she had been interested. Their lives and the worlds they occupied were just too different. She could have made a little bit more of an effort though. One quick hospital visit didn't cut it as far as Dermot was concerned. But then that was something else they clearly differed on. And all the more reason to put her behind him.

He started walking again, heading around a corner then stopping once more as he noticed one of his shoelaces had come undone. Tying them up wasn't easy with one arm in a sling. He bent down, remembering how Molly had laughed at him the first time he'd asked her to do them for him. Thinking about his daughter brought a smile. Thoroughly overexcited about Christmas but far too grown-up at nine years old to admit it. Dermot was planning to take her away for a few days in the school holidays but hadn't decided where yet. He managed to tie the laces first time, the idea of the holiday with his daughter finally chasing Anna from his mind.

So why, when he looked up, was she right there? Walking towards him down the pavement, lit up by the street light above her head.

He blinked, shaking his head to chase the image from his mind.

But no, it was definitely Anna – skinny jeans and a long coat over a plain white T-shirt. A smile lighting up her face, big eyes opening impossibly wide.

Hope welled inside him. Of course… She'd have known he would be at the press conference and had decided to come to see him after all.

The possibilities he'd worked so hard to dismiss just seconds before were suddenly spinning back around in his head.

Anna waved, her smile widening. He raised his good hand and smiled back, the possibilities starting to firm up that little bit more.

And that's when she stopped, the smile slipping away as she looked down and saw him crouching there in the shadows. Her gaze slid past him…

… to the person she'd been smiling at all along.

The man she'd really come to meet.

Dermot knew exactly who he'd see when he turned around.

Long legs eating up the distance.

Big flat feet echoing on the pavement.

A wide smile across his smug, newly reinstated DCI face.

The lucky, lucky bastard.

Acknowledgements

gain many thanks to the members of my writers' group, whose nput and support helped shape this book. All fantastic writers nd wonderful people.

There aren't a whole lot of folks to thank for their time in ffort in helping me do research because I generally prefer naking things up. You can get a good enough knowledge of how ne police work by watch TV cop shows. But I have to give a hout out to the BBC's *Spooks.* It's a great source of knowledge bout how a fictional MI5 might go about its business.

Gratitude does have to go though to John Le Carré obviously. 'he man is immense. And sorry for spoofing your title.

And as ever, thanks to my wonderful family, Megan, Dylan nd Annabel for the support that helped me get this done.

A last word

Tinker Tailor Soldier Chef is a lock-down book, not exclusivel written during the lock downs of 2020 and 2021 but finished, re written and re-shaped during that difficult time.

A part of me felt a little guilty to be working on something s frivolous while all the world seemed to be going to hell. But helped keep me going and hopefully it will raise a smile, mayb even a laugh or two among readers. And I think that's quit important right now.

If you've enjoyed reading *Tinker Tailor Solder Chef*, please te everyone you've ever met about it. And please do drop b Amazon or wherever you buy your books and leave a nic review. These are really important for authors, especially inde pendent ones without the backing of big publishing companie Even if you haven't enjoyed it please leave a review. Feedback always good and if you're too mean, I'll just get my legion c followers (six and counting) to troll you.

Also check out the first in the series, *The Meal of Fortune,* featu ing Anna and Dermot, faced with another set of barely plausib circumstances involving Russian gangsters, loan sharks, dancin bears and the Eurovision Song Contest.

Game of Scones

Anna and Dermot may return in *Game of Scones,* a pacey, twisty comedy thriller, involving political intrigue and hi-tech skulduggery with murder, mayhem and possibly a Cornish Cream Tea or two thrown in. But this will depend on how many people buy this book and whether they give me some nice reviews. Go on…

Printed in Great Britain
by Amazon

23451927R00189